AN ECHO OF MURDER

ANNE PERRY

AN ECHO OF MURDER

A William Monk Novel

BALLANTINE BOOKS ● NEW YORK

Copyright © 2017 by Anne Perry

All rights reserved.

Published in the United States by Ballantine Books, an imprint of Random House, a division of Penguin Random House LLC, New York.

BALLANTINE and the HOUSE colophon are registered trademarks of Penguin Random House LLC.

Originally published in the United Kingdom by Headline Publishing Group, London.

Hardback ISBN 978-0-425-28501-5
Ebook ISBN 978-0-425-28502-2

Printed in the United States of America on acid-free paper

randomhousebooks.com

246897531

FIRST U.S. EDITION

Book design by Karin Batten

To Ken Sherman, for years of friendship and good counsel

AN ECHO OF MURDER

1

"It's a bad one, sir." The policeman shook his head as he stepped back on the wharf, allowing Commander Monk of the Thames River Police to reach the top of the stone stairs leading up from the water. Monk moved onto the dock itself. Hooper had made fast the two-oar police boat the pair had come in and was close behind him.

To the south, the Pool of London was already busy. Huge cranes lifted loads of bales from ships' holds and swung them ponderously over to the docks. The water was congested with boats at anchor, waiting their turn; barges loading; ferries going back and forth from one side of the river to the other. Black masts were a tangle of lines against the backdrop of the city and its smoke.

"What's unusually bad?" Monk asked. "Who is he?"

"He's one o' them Hungarians."

"Hungarians?" Monk's curiosity was piqued.

"Yes, sir. Got a few of them around 'ere. Not thousands, like, but enough."

The policeman led them past stacks of timber into a storage bay, then opened the door into one of the warehouses.

Monk followed, and Hooper after him.

Inside was just like any other warehouse—packed with timber, un-opened boxes and bales of goods—except that no one was working.

The policeman observed Monk's glance. "Sent 'em home. Only make it more muddled," he added. "Best they don't see any of it."

"Was it one of them who found him?" Monk asked.

"No, sir. Didn't know 'e was even there. Thought 'e were at 'ome, where 'e should 'a been at that hour."

Monk was beside him now, keeping step across the floor and to the stairs that led up to the offices.

"So who did?"

"A Mr. Dob— something. I can't say them names right."

"Lead the way," Monk directed. "I suppose you've called the police surgeon?"

"Oh, yes, sir. And I didn't touch a thing, believe me!"

Monk felt a chill of premonition, but he made no reply.

At the top of the stairs he followed a short passage, then came to a door. There were low voices murmuring inside. The policeman knocked once, then opened it and stood back for Monk to go in.

The room was fairly large for an office, and the light was good. Monk had seen death before. It was a large part of his job. But this was more violent than usual, and the raw smell of blood filled the air. It seemed to be over everything, as if the poor man had staggered and fallen against the chairs, the table and even the walls. Now he lay on his back on the floor, and an army rifle with its fixed bayonet was stick-ing up from his chest like a broken mast, crooked and looking as if it would fall awry at any moment.

Monk blinked.

The middle-aged man kneeling on the floor beside the body turned and looked up at him. "Commander Monk. Thought they'd send for you," he said drily. "Not a job any man'd keep, if he could push it off on someone else. Place opens onto the water, so I suppose it's yours."

"Good morning, Dr. Hyde," Monk said bleakly. He had known and respected the police surgeon for some time. "What can you tell me, other than that?"

"Dead about two hours, I would say. Not entirely a medical opinion. Could be longer, except that the warehouse itself was closed until six, and he hasn't been here all night, so he must have come since then. No way in here except up these stairs."

"But at least an hour and a half?" Monk pressed him. It was a tight time period, and that should help.

"Still warm," Hyde answered. "And the first workers got here about an hour ago. Your friend here"—he gestured to the policeman—"will tell you that none of the men on the warehouse floor came up here. So if it was them, then they're all in on it, lying their heads off. You could try them, of course." He looked back at the corpse. "Looks plain enough. Bayonet through the chest. Bled to death in a few minutes."

Monk looked around the blood-spattered room.

"I didn't say immediately!" Hyde snapped. "And there are cuts on his hands and arms. In fact all the fingers on his right hand are broken."

"A fight?" Monk was hopeful. This man was big, heavy. Whoever fought with him should have a few good bruises as well, possibly more than that.

"Not much of one." Hyde pulled his face into an expression of disgust. "One man armed with a fixed bayonet, and the other apparently with nothing."

"But his fist was damaged," Monk argued. "So at least he got in one pretty good blow."

"You don't listen, man! I said his fingers were broken. All of them, and it looks intentional. Not evenly, as they more likely would be if he hit something. Dislocated and broken, like deliberate mutilation."

Monk said nothing. It was conscious brutality, not the result of hot temper, more like calculated torture.

Hyde grunted and looked back again at the corpse. "I'll give you the rifle and bayonet when I've taken it out of him, at the morgue. There is more to the wound than just this. There's blood on all those candles

over there"—he gestured to several tables and ledges—"and those
torn-up bits of paper. But none on his hands. I suppose you noticed
that?"

Monk had not. But he had noticed that the man's mouth was badly
disfigured, and covered with blood.

"Is that more than just bruising?" he asked. "A punch in the mouth,
against his own teeth?"

Hyde bent closer, and was silent for several moments. "No," he said
at last. He swallowed. "It looks like he's knocked—or pulled—most of
his teeth out. Poor fellow."

"Who is he?" Monk asked.

The other man in the room came forward. He was of average height
and ordinary build. In fact, there was nothing unusual about him until
he spoke. His voice was penetrating, even when quietly used, and his
eyes were an extraordinarily clear and piercing blue. He looked at Monk
in a way that might have been deferential. "His name was Imrus Fodor,
sir. I knew him only slightly, but we Hungarians are not so many here in
this part of London that we are strangers to each other." He spoke English with barely any accent.

"Thank you." Monk looked at the man steadily. "How do you come
to be here, Mr. . . . ?"

"Dobokai, sir, Antal Dobokai. I am a pharmacist. I have a small
shop on Mercer Street. I came to deliver a potion to poor . . . Fodor. For
his feet." He held up a brown paper bag.

"Do you normally make your own deliveries?" Monk asked curi-
ously. "And at this hour of the morning?"

"If I am not busy, yes. It is a small service. It pays in loyalty, and I do
not dislike the walk, especially at this time of the year." Dobokai's eyes
did not waver for an instant. There was such an intensity of emotion in
him that Monk found it hard to look away. But if he had set out to perform a small kindness, and come in to find this bloody carnage, it was
hardly surprising that he was emotionally raw. Any sane man would be.

"I'm sorry you had to discover this." Monk meant it. If he found it
shocking himself, what must this ordinary domestic chemist feel, when
it had happened to a man he knew? But better to ask the questions now,

while the memory was part of his immediate experience, than have to revisit it later. "Can you tell me what happened from the time you left your own premises?"

Dobokai blinked; his concentration was obvious, and intense. He managed to continue while Hyde's assistants came in and put the body on a stretcher. They maneuvered around so as not to bump into anything, and carried the body out. Hyde followed immediately after them, leaving Monk alone with Dobokai and the policeman. Monk knew the young man would be making a plan of the building, and finding every possible way anyone could have come in or gone out.

"I woke early," Dobokai said quietly. "At about six I decided to collect some of the medicines that needed delivering today. I put Fodor's potion in a bag." He opened another bag and showed Monk several screws of white powder.

"And then . . . ?" Monk prompted.

"I know that Mrs. Stanley rises early too. Can't sleep, poor woman. I delivered her opium at about half-past six—"

"Where does she live?" Monk interrupted.

"On Tarling Street, right near the crossroads."

"And then?"

"I took Mr. Dawkins his laudanum. He lives a little farther down, on Martha Street," Dobokai replied. "Then I stopped at the Hungarian café on the corner of the High Street and had a cup of coffee and a pastry. I knew they wouldn't be open for business here until eight o'clock, which is when I arrived."

Monk turned to the policeman. "Did any of the men get here early?"

"No, sir, I asked them. According to what they say, they all came at the same time: eight o'clock exactly. The dead man was very strict. Bit of a martinet about time. Dock any man who was late."

Dobokai interrupted. "But he very rarely kept them late, and if he did, he paid well for it."

"And all the men came here together?" Monk pressed.

"Yes, sir, that's what they said—all of them," the policeman agreed. "Looks like he was killed before anyone got here. Agrees with what the doc said. Sorry, sir, the police surgeon," he amended.

"But you came up here, Mr. Dobokai?" Monk reaffirmed. "Just after eight. Were the workers all here?"

"Yes. I . . . I went up to give him the potion, and I found . . . this." His eyes flickered around the room, then back at Monk. He had a naturally sallow complexion, but now he looked ill.

"Did you happen to notice the men working downstairs when you passed them? Was there anyone you knew?" It was perhaps a foolish question, but sometimes people recalled more than they expected to, even trivia that seemed of no importance.

"Yes, sir," Dobokai replied, a little color returning to his face. "There were seven men. I know them by sight, but that's all."

Monk was surprised at the exact number. "Whereabouts? Can you draw a sketch for the constable?"

"Two were on the big bench just inside the door," Dobokai answered without hesitation. "One standing in the middle of the floor. And four along the bench at the back. They had tools out. Three wood saws, and the last one had a pair of pliers in his . . . left hand."

"You are unusually observant. Thank you."

"Not a day I'll forget," Dobokai said quietly. "Poor Fodor. Before you ask me, I have no idea who would have done this to him. He seemed a very ordinary sort of man to me. Lived alone. His wife's dead. Worked hard to build his business up, and he was doing well. I think . . . I think you've got a lunatic here. The place is . . ." He turned around slowly, looking at the blood, the broken candles, their wicks scarlet as if they had been dipped in the dead man's wounds. There must have been sixteen or seventeen of them, all different shapes and sizes. "What sane man could do this?" he asked helplessly. "I will help you to solve this. I know them. I will translate for you, for those whose English is not good. Anything—"

"Thank you," Monk said, cutting him off. "If I need your help, I shall ask you, and be grateful for it." He understood Dobokai's fear, his need to feel that he was doing something, not just standing by. "First we shall speak to the men. I'll have someone go through Fodor's business accounts—monies due, owed, and so on. That may tell us something."

Dobokai looked at him skeptically. "This is how you settle overdue debts in England? I have been here in your country for many years, Commander. Before I was in London, I was in Yorkshire. Good steel-making country. Good people. This is not business, not English business."

Monk looked into Dobokai's remarkable, clear blue eyes, and realized his error. He had underestimated this man. "No, of course it isn't," he agreed. "We have to go through the motions, just to exclude the possibility. But you are right. This is hatred, a terrible, uncontrolled passion to destroy. Yet I don't want to frighten people if I can avoid it. And we must find out all we can. Looking into his business is as good a way to start as any other. It will allow us to ask questions."

"I see. I see," Dobokai said quickly. "A way in. Of course. I should have understood. Yes. You cannot tell people there is a monster loose; they will panic. I shall tell no one how . . . what a horror this is. You will ask people what they have seen, and bit by bit you will work it out." He looked around the room again. "Such hatred," he whispered, not to Monk but to himself.

Monk had the powerful feeling that Dobokai was realizing something that he had never seen before, not fully, not like this. In due course, perhaps he, Monk, would find out what it was.

"Thank you, Mr. Dobokai," he said more gently. "We'll stay here a little longer, speak to the workers, the neighbors, and see if anybody has noticed anything different. In case we need you, leave your exact address with Mr. Hooper, outside, and let us know if you think of anything further."

"Yes," Dobokai agreed. "Yes, of course." Now he was unsurprisingly quite relieved to excuse himself and leave the awful room, escorted by the constable.

Monk looked around again, alone now. Everything he saw—the splashes of blood, the blood-daubed candles, two of them a dark purple, close to blue, the torn-up paper, which looked like it might be a letter of some kind—all of it spoke of rage, absolutely out of control, almost beyond sanity. What sane man did this to another?

But where had such extreme feeling come from, that no one had seen it? Or perhaps they had? If he looked in the right place, surely he would find something to tell him that Fodor himself had been aware of it. And there would be others who could help, colleagues of Fodor, friends. Such hatred did not spring into being without a deep foundation.

Hooper came back from questioning the employees and searching the building for traces of entry or exit. He and Monk had worked together for some time now, two or three years at least. Hooper was a big man, soft-spoken, but there was a depth of both intelligence and emotion beneath his controlled manner; Monk had seen it in his extraordinary loyalty. When everyone else had considered Monk guilty of error, and worse, Hooper had risked his own life to save him, not to mention his career to defend him.

"Sir?" Hooper asked.

"Oh . . . yes." Monk swung round to face him. "Learn anything?"

"Nothing that looks useful," Hooper replied ruefully. "No one broke in. Can't climb up from the water anyway. Back entrance locked and bolted from the inside."

"So we're starting with the entire community to pick from," Monk concluded.

"Dobokai . . ."

"Right. That is, if he was really mixing ointment for the dead man's feet. Have to check it." He looked around the room. "You'd think someone who hated this violently would be pretty clear the moment we saw him. Probably baying at the moon, with blood on his teeth. But he can't be. He'll probably look like anyone else . . . most of the time."

Hooper shrugged. It was true. Obvious eccentrics were sometimes the sanest people of all—and repressed, obedient followers, when they finally snapped, could have unimaginable monsters inside them.

"Have to see what we can find out about Imrus Fodor, poor devil," Monk said. "I suppose most of his neighbors and customers will speak English?"

———

FODOR'S HOUSE WAS PLEASANT, ordinary on the outside, like all those along the street, but inside unusually comfortable, and definitely full of character. They had found his door keys in his office at the warehouse, so breaking in was unnecessary. They stood in the hall and looked around.

"Not English," Hooper said, but there was interest in his voice, even a degree of respect.

Monk looked at the paintings on the walls. Several of them were of horsemen in dress he had never seen before. One was of a city he did not recognize. It had old-fashioned outlines, foreign to England, but was very beautiful, like a creation of the imagination rather than a replica of history. He also noticed a beautiful, gentle painting of a mother and child, surrounded in gold.

"He wasn't a poor man," Hooper observed, looking now at the furniture. "That hall table would fetch a good price. And the mirror above it too. Good glass, and the carving is perfect."

Monk started through the other rooms, touching very little but gathering a strong impression of the dead man's taste, and very considerable expenditure on his home. Fodor knew quality and style, and clearly had the means to indulge them. And yet there was no extravagance and no sense of making an effort to impress. Nothing was new. Interesting. Had he brought everything with him from Hungary? Or were his possessions acquired from something uglier? Obtained via blackmail? Fodor's death showed the kind of hatred that spoke of someone over whom he had power. Was it the power to hurt, to rob, to destroy? Why now? That was always the question with any violent crime—why now?

"We have to look very carefully into his last few days," Monk said. "Last week or two. What happened that a man who lived in a house like this suddenly got attacked as he was, with such hatred?"

But a careful search of the rest of the house turned up nothing that seemed to tell of an unusual event. There was no diary, nothing marked on the calendar on the kitchen wall, no notes, letters or invitations.

"Start next door," Monk said, peering up and down the street. "Looks well kept, as if there's somebody there a lot of the time."

Hooper smiled. "Yes, sir. I saw the curtains twitch."

"Right. I'll go this way," Monk said. "You go that." He pointed in the other direction. "See you at the station."

Hooper gave a half salute, and walked away.

They asked the neighbors all sorts of seemingly ordinary questions, trying to find anything unusual, or, at the very least, what they thought or felt about Imrus Fodor.

"Nice enough man," Mrs. Harris said, one door down to the right. She was about fifty, perhaps a year or two older than the victim. "Not that I knew him, of course. Hungarian, he was." She added that as if it were an explanation.

"Did he speak good English?" Monk asked.

"Ah . . . well, yes, I suppose so. But for all that, he wasn't like us. Couldn't be, could he?"

Sometimes Monk chose to be obstructive, to see how an interviewee changed what they said when they were off guard with annoyance. He decided to use this strategy now.

"I don't know," he replied. "I don't think I've ever even known a Hungarian. What are they like?" He kept his expression polite with some difficulty.

"Like?" she said stiffly. "I don't know what you mean."

"You said he was not like us," he reminded her.

"Well, he wasn't English, was he!" she snapped.

"I believe not."

"You ever met an Englishman called Fodor?" She raised her eyebrows.

"No. Was he rude to you? Untidy? Disrespectful? Unclean? Noisy? Did you ever see him the worse for drink? Did he have women coming and going in the house?"

She looked taken aback. "Well . . . no. Except Mrs. Durridge, of course. She came and cleaned for him, and might have cooked, for all I know."

He got little more from Mrs. Harris, or the next people he spoke to. But the man behind the counter at the corner tobacconist's was more forthright.

"Not enough work around here for us, never mind all the foreigners coming in," he said darkly. "Not that he was bad," he added. "Took on a few workers, 'e did, but mostly 'is own, like. More foreigners. But what do you expect? Foreign newspapers they've got too. Print them right 'ere. That pharmacist fellow, Dobokai, 'as something to do with that. Not any idea what they're saying about us. Can't read a word of it. Could be anything."

"Perhaps it's news from Hungary?" Monk suggested.

The man grunted. "They're different, that's all. And now look what's 'appened! Got himself murdered. Don't want that kind of thing 'ere."

"We don't need any more," Monk agreed. "We've got enough of our own violence without help."

The man looked at him narrowly. "What's it to you, then?"

"Police," Monk replied. "Want to find out who did this to him, and get them put away as soon as possible."

"Right. You do that!"

"Need your help. I don't know the area here," Monk replied.

"Where do you live, then? You foreign too?"

"Other side of the river," Monk replied. "Just about straight across from here. Up from the Greenwich Stairs a bit."

"Well, what do you want to know?"

Monk surprised himself. "What do you know about Antal Dobokai?"

"Interesting fellow . . ." The tobacconist gave it some consideration. "Quiet. But, underneath it, thinking all the time. Educated. But in Hungary, o' course, where 'e comes from. Does sums in 'is 'ead faster than most of us can on paper, an' always right. Was an architect once, so rumor 'as it. Harder to find work over 'ere. We got our own. But seems 'e's doing all right. Why? You think 'e done it?" There was both skepticism and amusement in his face.

"No," Monk replied. "Looks as if he's the one man who couldn't have, so far."

"Why's that, then?"

"Time. Can't be in two places at once."

"Bad thing. You're police: Was it as bad as talk 'as it?'"

"Pretty ugly. Someone hated him, or was out of his mind in some way or other. Is there strong feeling in the community? Rivalries? Feuds?"

The man looked slightly surprised. "They're different, I suppose, them Hungarians, but civil enough, if you're civil to them. Don't bother me. Of course, there's always them that don't like anyone who's different, dresses different, acts different, like. Stick-in-the-mud, like. Like old Sallis around the corner. 'Good enough for my father, and 'is father before 'im, good enough for me,' 'e'll say. Like change is an insult."

"Did you know Fodor?"

"Some. Nice enough. Always got a good word or two. Never walks right by you, like some. But then, they're all different, like we are."

We, and them. Monk noticed it over and over. He stayed a little longer, then moved on a block or so and asked a greengrocer, then a cobbler. It was late afternoon and he had learned nothing unexpected when he met up with Hooper again.

"Not much help," Hooper said, shaking his head. "Known locally, especially among the other Hungarians. Quite a few of them in the area. All come to the same place. Reckon I'd do the same if I had to live in some other country. Not like I would! Why'd they come here? Ones I spoke to were doing well enough. Why not stay at home, where you're just like anyone else?"

"Did you ask them?"

Hooper smiled ruefully. "Got enough people asking that, like they'd no right to be here. Got nothing useful, sir. Everyone says what you'd expect them to. He was all right, but still a foreigner." He shook his head. "This was someone who knew him well and hated him, or is a madman."

Monk had reluctantly reached the same conclusion.

"Or someone who hated newcomers," Hooper added. "Felt a bit of that. Some people find change threatening."

"Then they should go and live out in the countryside," Monk said tartly. "The city's changing all the time. That's what's both good and bad about it. I heard the same, but it's just grumbling, as some people grumble about the weather."

"Somebody hated the poor devil," Hooper said as they began to walk. The sun was lowering in the sky, pavements already partially in shadow. "Perhaps we should get Dobokai to help us? He might pick up inflections we don't. He knows the people and he speaks the language. Most of them seem to have pretty fair English, but they still speak to each other in Hungarian. We might be missing something."

"I think I'm missing everything," Monk said with a touch of bitterness. "It's not a random lunatic. There was hatred in that room—deep, irrational, personal hatred. Whoever it was drove a bayonet through his heart, extinguished candles in his blood, broke his teeth and his right hand. And they hacked off his lips. We've got something terrible here, Hooper, whether it's English or Hungarian or something we haven't looked at yet. Wonder what the candles mean. Nobody lights seventeen candles just to see by. Did you notice two of them were dark, a purplish-blue color? Does that mean something? Or was it just what he had? There's no panic yet, but if we don't solve this murder, there will be. Word will spread, and no doubt get worse in the telling."

"Yes, sir, I know," Hooper said quietly, keeping in step with Monk so exactly that he did not need to raise his voice. "You'll be putting more men on it tomorrow?" It was barely a question.

"Yes, all we can spare."

MONK ARRIVED HOME LATE, although it was still light. No lamps were lit yet in the street as he walked up the hill from the ferry. As he turned onto Paradise Place and looked back, the sun was making a polished shield of the still water of the river, marked here and there by the black hulls of moored ships whose masts barely moved against the backdrop of the sky above the city. The air was still warm. There was no wind to rustle the heavy leaves of the trees in Southwark Park. Violence seemed a distant nightmare.

He walked the last few steps and opened his door.

Hester heard him and came into the hall from the kitchen. She was not a traditionally beautiful woman, perhaps a little too thin, and certainly there was far too much courage in her face, and too much intelligence for her demeanor to be comfortable to most men. There had been a time, long ago, when he had found it aggressive. Now it was what he loved in her the most.

He went straight to her and hugged her, surprising her with the fierceness of his grip.

After a moment she pulled away, concern in her eyes.

He could tell straightaway that she had not heard of the murder in Shadwell.

"You didn't go to the clinic today?" he asked.

The shadow in her eyes was immediate. The clinic was in Portpool Lane, to the north of the river. She had founded it several years ago, to take in and treat women off the streets who were ill or injured. It was her final role as a nurse, a career that had begun with Florence Nightingale, and the Crimean War. Now others ran the clinic, but she still took part.

"Sorry," he said. "I meant you haven't been out, or you would have seen the headlines in the evening papers. We had a pretty terrible murder in Shadwell, just along from the Wapping Station."

"On the river?" She turned and led the way back to the kitchen. The kettle would be on the hob, as it always was at this time of evening.

"Just off it, but practically on the Shadwell New Basin. Regular police were glad to get rid of it. The victim works with boats. Hungarian. There's a bit of a community there. Just a few hundred, at the most."

Hester pulled the kettle onto the hottest part of the stove, which was stoked and lit only for water and cooking. It was more than warm enough in the house, so it wasn't needed for heating. The only thing Monk could think about was hot, fresh tea. Hester had no need to ask.

"Cold beef and bubble and squeak for dinner?" she asked. "And I've got apple pie."

It was exactly what he wanted, especially the pie.

2

Mᴏɴᴋ ʙᴇɢᴀɴ ᴀɢᴀɪɴ ᴇᴀʀʟʏ the next morning by going to see Dr. Hyde at his office next to the morgue.

"Can't tell you anything helpful," Hyde said immediately. "You must have made your own estimate already, and there's nothing to add. Death was due to loss of blood. Happens when you stick a bayonet through the heart. Very messy, very melodramatic, but a quick way to go."

"Hardly a merciful way," Monk said sourly. "You're not telling me there was no hatred in it?"

"Far from it." Hyde gave him a sharp look. "Rage! Takes a lot of strength to skewer a man like that. On the battlefield you would charge so you'd get up that impetus. Whoever did this was in a fury—either that, or was terrified. And since he held the bayonet, and presumably took it with him, and there was no sign of poor Fodor having had any-thing with which to defend himself, rage looks far more likely. Could be vengeance, but if it was, whatever Fodor did must have been damned appalling."

"So you can't tell me anything more useful than either the murderer had an intense hatred, born from something that ought to stand out in someone's past, or else there's a raving madman who has so far been invisible; come out of nowhere, and seems to have gone back there again?"

Hyde raised his eyebrows as if mildly surprised. "I didn't create the situation, Monk. If you wanted a peaceful and predictable job you should have been a bookkeeper or a greengrocer." He moved over to his desk, which was littered with papers. "I can tell you that the killer seems to have taken the victim totally by surprise. Man never had a chance. He was big, in good health, and he made no attempt to defend himself."

"So he wasn't afraid?" Monk deduced. "He didn't think he had any reason to be."

"Looks like it. If it was an old quarrel, it was one-sided. You'd better learn a lot more about Fodor. I don't think this one is going to unravel itself for you with just a tweak here or there. Now, if you want a cup of tea, the kettle's on the shelf, and you know where the burner is. Otherwise get out of here and leave me to get started on the day. Accident down on the Surrey Docks. I've got two more bodies to look at."

"Thank you," Monk replied with a faint smile. "I've put three more men on it. I'd better go and see how they're doing."

"Fairly decent lot, the Hungarians," Hyde added. "Not the dregs, by any means. Some of them could be political fugitives. You could look into that. They had a rough time from the Austrians, always the underdogs. But I believe they've got a lot more latitude in the last few years."

Monk had been intending to do exactly as Hyde suggested, but he thanked him anyway, and left the morgue. It was always cold in there, even in the summer, and the smells of lye and carbolic made him think of the even worse things they concealed.

He walked back to Shadwell—it was not far—and he saw Hooper when he reached the dock itself.

"Morning, sir." Hooper looked grim. "I've asked along the streets. Everybody I've spoken to so far is pretty jumpy. Some of these Hungarians have been here several years, and speak English quite comfortably, but most still have trouble with it. It's easy to misunderstand little things. That fellow Dobokai is willing to help, and so far he seems to be the one person whose whereabouts mean he couldn't have killed Fodor."

Monk would rather not have used Dobokai, but it seemed he had no choice. He told Hooper what the police surgeon had said.

Hooper stared across the open water of the dock, the sunlight on his face. In the distance rang the shouts of men working and the clank of chains as loads were made fast, ready to lift.

"Looks like a big job, sir. We're outsiders to them, for all they live here in our city. They'll be polite, but won't let us in, if you know what I mean."

"We need to find out all we can about the last month or two of Fodor's life. Hatred like that doesn't come out of nowhere—unless we really are looking for a lunatic . . ."

"I've got a couple of men asking whether any strangers have cropped up lately," Hooper replied. "Most people around here can be accounted for. Business, work here, buying or selling something, relations. People are badly upset by this killing. More it sinks in, the worse it gets. Every-one knows about it now."

"Then we'd better get started," Monk agreed. "We'll dig into Fodor's past. What do we know about him so far?"

Hooper's expression was blank. "Honest in business, well-mannered, good employer, doesn't have any debts, sober, agreeable, quiet and clean, generous . . ." He stopped.

"I take your point," Monk agreed. "No reason on earth to wish him dead. Therefore his associates are all innocent and we should indeed look for a random lunatic from outside the community. It's going to be hard work."

"Yes, sir. In a way, you can't blame them. When you're in a strange country that looks after its own, you've got to look after your own as well."

Monk did not bother to reply.

They found Antal Dobokai on the pavement outside one of the cafés run by a Hungarian family. There were pastries on display in the window, and a rich, spicy aroma drifted out through the door. Dobokai seemed almost to have been expecting them.

"Good morning," he said with only partially concealed satisfaction. "Have you discovered anything of help?"

"Not a great deal," Monk admitted. There was no point in pretending: it would appear weak if he lied. "Either it was a random killing, which in the circumstances looks unlikely, or else there is an old enmity of great depth, of which most people were unaware."

Dobokai appeared to be thinking; there was a discernible hesitation before he answered. "Or there is another possibility," he said slowly, picking his words as if his familiarity with the language had suddenly deserted him. "That poor Fodor was the focus of a dislike that exists in some people for those who are different."

"London is packed with people who are different," Monk pointed out. "Especially in the dockside areas. Just about every nationality in the world is here, and many of them look a lot more different than you do. I couldn't tell you were not English, until you spoke."

A brief smile crossed Dobokai's face, and vanished. "Then you are not as good a detective as your position suggests," he said frankly.

Hooper looked away, and Monk had a fair idea he was smiling.

As if to rob his words of offense, Dobokai continued, "Our women wear their clothes a little differently, if I may say it, with more . . . flair. And we have different bones, just a bit." He touched his own slightly more prominent cheekbones. "Wider," he added. "We try to learn your ways, but we will not abandon who we are."

"If that were so," Monk said more gently, "then why Fodor? Why not anyone? There must be some reason behind it, some chance that made whoever it was choose him. And choose yesterday. That may be our only opportunity of finding the murderer. We would be grateful for your help, Mr. Dobokai."

"Of course," Dobokai agreed, nodding slowly. "You are right. However repulsive, or difficult to equate with sanity, there is always a reason. I will help you find it, before . . . before people forget what they have seen or heard and the trail goes cold." He gave a brief smile, there and then gone. But the remarkable blue eyes were bright.

"What do you know of Fodor yourself, Mr. Dobokai?" Monk asked. "Do you know where he came from in Hungary, and when?"

"Yes, of course. Do you wish me to spell it for you? Our spelling is . . . unlike yours."

"I would be obliged," Monk answered. "In fact, perhaps you would tell me some of what you know of most of the members of the community who have come here in the last few years."

"Fodor has been here for twenty years or more," Dobokai told him. "But of course I will tell you of those who have come recently."

They went to Monk's office in the Wapping Station. It was quite a long morning's work, but Dobokai gave them a list of all the main families in the community, with their occupations and the approximate dates of their arrival. In most cases, he could also give the town or the area in Hungary from which they had come.

"You are surprised?" Dobokai said with a twist of his mouth. "If you were obliged to begin your life over again in a strange country, one with no ties to your own, and not speaking your language, would you not seek out men who could advise you, help you find a place to live, at least some kind of work to pay your rent, to eat? Would you not ask where to buy the food you like? Where to get decent secondhand furniture? Where to rent rooms; who was honest; where, now and then, to hear news from home?"

When they had finished discussing the fifty or so families that made up the core of the Shadwell Hungarians, Monk and Hooper went with Dobokai, at his suggestion, to eat lunch at a small Hungarian restaurant.

The menu was not large, but on Dobokai's advice, Monk chose a stew with both pork and beef, unusually spiced with bay leaf, garlic and several flavorings he could not distinguish. Dobokai explained to him, with some pride, that Hungarians often mixed meats, and were expert with dozens of spices.

For dessert they were offered Dobos torte, a layered sponge cake with chocolate buttercream inside and a thin slice of caramel on top. Telling himself that he was being polite, Monk accepted a second helping.

Dobokai took them to meet Ferenc Ember, the immigrant doctor who treated the medical ills of most of the community. As they went into his surgery, and waited the half hour or so necessary while he saw his patients, Monk imagined the misery of being ill in an unfamiliar place and trying to explain your symptoms to someone who was impatient with your stumbling attempts to find the words to describe intimacies few people discussed at all, let alone with strangers. Pain, fear or simple embarrassment made many people tongue-tied. To have someone familiar to speak for you would be a godsend.

Ember was quite a young man, no more than in his late thirties, but he looked tired. His fair-skinned face had little color, and he kept nervously pushing his hair off his brow.

"Antal!" he said with relief when he saw that Dobokai was with Monk and Hooper. "What can I do for you?"

Dobokai introduced them, then spoke quietly to Ember in Hungarian. Monk had no idea what he was saying. There was not a single familiar word in his speech, nothing of Latin or Germanic root.

Ember offered his hand. "I will do what I can to help, but I'm afraid it will be very little. I cannot tell you anyone's illnesses—that is confidential . . ." He regarded Monk anxiously. "You have the same here, yes?"

"You might be able to narrow the possibilities a little," Monk suggested.

"I'll . . . I'll try," Ember promised. "I don't know that . . ."

Dobokai shook his head. He ignored Monk completely and began asking Ember questions about chronic illnesses that seemed to be totally irrelevant. He moved to asking about some of the children in the area and what Ember might need in order to treat them successfully.

Hooper shifted position impatiently.

Monk agreed. This was wasting time and had little more to offer than Dobokai had already provided in his knowledge of the community. Monk drew a breath to break the rambling discussion, but Dobokai held up his hand to stop him. It was an arrogant gesture, and Monk felt his temper rise. Ember answered in Hungarian, and Monk sat back, but he could not tolerate it much longer. It was a display of Dobokai's importance in his own circle, and so far of no use at all.

As if sensing a greater tension, Ember stopped, turning to Monk.

"Mr. Monk will want to know," Dobokai assured him. He too looked at Monk. "Dr. Ember is telling me of a very nasty incident a couple of weeks ago. A teenage woman, Eva Galambos, was accosted by a young man. She was not badly hurt, but she was very frightened. Her brothers paid the young man a visit, and advised him that he might come to a great deal of harm if he did that again. The matter became worse. Relations have gone downhill. It is not unusual, but others have taken it up and now more people are involved. It reminds them of other matters, older quarrels. You know what I mean?"

"Yes," Hooper agreed quickly. He looked at Ember. "I imagine you know who among your people has been injured."

"It happens," Ember said, nodding. "We are strangers here—guests, if you like. It is better we don't make trouble. We are not going to win. But it is a small thing. Just young ones being . . . unwise. Young men fight. It happens. What happened to Fodor was quite different. That comes from old wounds. Very deep."

"Do you know of such wounds?" Monk asked, expecting no more of an answer than he could read in the man's eyes.

"I see only bits and pieces," Ember replied. "I do not put them together necessarily. I do not want a story I cannot help or heal. These people will not trust me, and I can do nothing, no good. I must consider all."

"Does the number seventeen mean anything to you?" Monk asked. "Perhaps to do with a ritual of some sort?"

Ember looked blank. "No. Why?"

"There were seventeen candles in the room where Mr. Fodor's body was found."

Ember shook his head.

Dobokai made a little sound in his throat, as if he were choking. When Monk turned to look at him, his face was pale.

"Seventeen!" Dobokai gasped, forcing the word out of his mouth.

His hands were clenched in front of him. "Are you saying there were seventeen candles?"

"Yes. You saw them."

"I . . ." Dobokai took a deep breath. "I didn't count."

"What does seventeen mean?" Monk asked more sharply.

"There is . . . or I heard there is . . . a secret society, and 'seventeen' is their . . . watchword, password, whatever you like. I know very little about them, and I don't want to know. But they are believers in the occult. Were any of the candles different colors?" His blue eyes were brilliant, almost luminous.

"Yes," Monk answered slowly, recalling what he had seen. "Two were dark, I think a blue or violet color. Why?"

"Purple," Dobokai said, as if the very word were laden with meaning. "Purple for power, to use it over people . . . dark power. I don't know anything more, and I don't want to find out. As soon as I knew even that, I stopped. There are things it is better not to know." He started to shake his head.

"Hungarian or English?" Monk asked urgently.

"I don't know," Dobokai answered. "Perhaps it is everywhere."

"Did you hear of this secret society in England, or before you came here?"

"Here, in London. But from a Hungarian. But . . . maybe this is a perversion of it." He shook his head. "And before you ask me, the man I learned that much from has left London, and I have no idea where he has gone."

"Thank you. Please let me know if you think of anything more."

"I want to do everything I can to help you," Dobokai assured Monk, looking not at him but straight ahead. "These are my people. I need you to understand them, as much as you can. It is a terrible thing that happened to Fodor. Forget what I said about seventeen, please! One of us is a devil—or one of your own devils is loose here. Perhaps it is some deranged creature who feels he has suffered an injustice at the hands of one of us and is determined to take his revenge."

Monk considered those possibilities for several moments without replying. Finally, he simply acknowledged Dobokai's help again, and repeated his thanks to Ember.

"What do you think about this 'seventeen' business?" Hooper asked as he and Monk turned to walk away.

Monk was shaken. He hated secret societies of any sort. They gave people a power they almost always abused. Even Dobokai, who had otherwise appeared very steady, seemed to be frightened by the thought.

"There might be something in it, or possibly it's just a coincidence. Let's stay with the usual greed, jealousy and revenge for the moment."

OVER THE NEXT TWO days, as he spoke to most of the families in the community, both Hungarian and English, Monk began to form a much clearer picture of their relationships with each other. They felt a natural closeness to those who shared their roots and memories and, above all, understood the complicated nature of the hope for a new life in a new country. Under the superficialities, London was still so different from the places they had left. They had lost the certainties they once had, the shared familiarity of environment and histories, without always realizing the good in their new lives, along with the bad.

It was Dobokai who drew out all this information for him, whether it was intentional or not. He had an odd way of questioning people. It took Monk all of the two days they spent together to understand his method. It was very indirect, often seeming pointless.

"How are you today?" he asked one middle-aged man, Lorand Gazda, sitting on a riverside bench, gazing shortsightedly at the water.

Gazda shook his head. He had a long nose and a halo of graying hair. "Good of you to ask," he said slowly.

"Hard times," Dobokai commiserated. He turned to Monk. "Lorand used to be a wealthy man, but he lost his lands in the revolution of 'forty-eight. Backed the fighters for freedom." He put his hand briefly on the man's shoulder. "Like a lot of people. Got more freedoms from Austria now, but it's been too long in coming for some."

Monk had enough history to be aware that most of Europe had

risen in rebellion against oppression of one sort or another. In some places the attempt had come close to succeeding. For a brief moment it had seemed to be the beginning of a golden age. Then the old order had crushed the uprisings, one after another. Paris, Rome, Berlin, Budapest, Vienna—all had entered a new oppression, worse than before. Only England seemed to have remained unscathed, a haven for so many fugitives. But he knew that only from the history books, and word of mouth. It was back in the time he could not remember. And circumstances had taught him that he himself had been in California during the height of the civil unrest, in the gold rush of '49.

But that did not matter now. He had not had to leave the place of his youth. It was still there, he simply could not remember it.

Dobokai was still commiserating with Gazda, pointlessly, it seemed.

"Still, you like to go down and watch the river," he said conversationally.

Gazda's eyes lit up. "It's a good river," he agreed. "A great port." He spoke straight back to Dobokai, as if Monk were beyond the periphery of his sight. Perhaps he was.

"Shadwell Dock," Dobokai said as he nodded.

The muscles in Gazda's face tightened.

Monk started to pay attention.

"I expect you were very upset about poor Fodor's death," Dobokai went on, a note of sympathy in his voice.

Gazda winced and turned away, staring into the distance, although how far he could see was questionable. Monk doubted that as an actual witness he would be any use, even if he had been on the dock at the time.

Dobokai lowered his voice even more. "We have to do something about it, Lorand. We can't let such a terrible thing happen again. What do you think?"

Monk stirred impatiently. Dobokai was frightening the man for no reason. This was an isolated incidence of hatred. Nothing like this had happened before and there was no reason to think it would ever be repeated. He was about to interrupt when Gazda did instead.

"He was a good man, Fodor was. Had his faults, of course. Everyone does. But he was generous and he never spoke ill of anyone else. We're not taking people's jobs, Dobokai. You've got to make them see that. We're just taking care of ourselves, like everybody. We've got a right to do that. Englishmen have gone all over the world, where they had no business. Can't they make room for us here?" He shivered, although he was sitting in the sun. "I don't understand it. Why Fodor? And why so . . . so savage? Are they barbarians?"

Dobokai glanced momentarily at Monk, then back at the older man.

"We must help the police catch whoever it was, Lorand," he said gently. "They don't want him to get away with it any more than we do."

"Don't they? Why should they care? Fodor wasn't one of them!"

"Because they're civilized people," Dobokai answered with conviction. "This will make news everywhere. Do you think they want other people to believe that's the kind of country this is? That this happens to people who come here? Pride, Lorand! Pride. Would you want people to think we Hungarians are like that?"

Gazda stiffened. "You show me who I can tell, and I'll tell them."

"You tell what you can to Mr. Monk here. He's a policeman. Too important to wear a uniform anymore. Talk to him."

Monk relaxed. Perhaps he had misunderstood Dobokai. He was a far better judge of human nature than Monk had given him credit for.

Monk stayed with Lorand Gazda for well over an hour and learned a great deal about the community. He heard who had lent money and who had borrowed it, and what the interest had been. He struggled to write down names he could barely spell, and had to wait for instruction. There were love affairs, some illicit, some in which three people were involved. He heard of kindnesses and petty revenges, marking in his notes those he considered worthy of looking at more closely. They probably meant nothing, but it was somewhere to begin. Gazda answered all his questions, Dobokai translating where it was needed, the odd memory, a concept for which the man did not know the words in English.

At last Monk rose to his feet and thanked him.

"You'll find him, won't you?" Gazda said eagerly. "You'll stop whoever did this?"

Monk drew in his breath to warn that it would not be easy, but he
would do his best. Then he looked at Gazda's weary face, and felt the
fear in him. He had been a stranger in a strange land that did not really
want him for far too many years. He was clinging to his pride with a
desperate hold.

"Yes, Mr. Gazda," he said, making a rash promise he only hoped to
keep. There was no certainty. "I hope it will be soon, but however hard
it is, we won't give up. You belong here, and he doesn't."

Dobokai did not say anything, but after they had excused themselves and left Lorand Gazda, he gave Monk the addresses of the families he thought it most profitable to speak with. By the time Monk
checked in at the Wapping Police Station before going home, he had a
better knowledge of the Hungarian community at Shadwell than he
had of the neighborhood across the river, where he had lived for years.
But he still could not like Dobokai—there was something about the
man that made him unforgettable, a kind of restlessness, a hunger. He
was annoyed with himself for it. It was unfair. It was the very prejudice
that he despised in others. He, of all people, should know better than
that.

He thought about it again on the ferry across to the south bank, as
he sat in the stern and watched the light on the water, soft, feeling the
air cool a little. There were gulls circling above. The skyline of the city
was so familiar he could have recognized a single crane out of place, a
ship larger than usual, taller masts against the sky.

And yet not so long ago it had been new to him. When he woke up
in the hospital, everything was new, strange, even his own face in the
looking glass. He'd had to learn friend from enemy, and there were so
few of the former, and too many, well earned, of the latter.

But at least he spoke the language, and the patterns of his profession were woven deeper than conscious knowledge.

Yet for how many years had he been afraid of the unknown, always
expecting the worst? How many times had he been caught by surprise
by his own ignorance of what everyone else seemed to know? He should

understand these people and their suspicions of unjust judgment, disliked simply because they looked and sounded different. Of course they stayed together! Who wouldn't? The constant wariness was exhausting. You couldn't know how much until you had to learn everything anew; take nothing for granted; never assume; think, watch, listen all the time.

Dobokai did not know that of him. No one did except Hester, and, more recently, Hooper. He'd had to tell Hooper or lie to him. And he cared too much what Hooper thought of him to do that, which surprised him. From everything he had learned of himself during the past, he had not cared what anyone thought of him. Runcorn, once a friend, then an enemy, and now a deeper friend again, had told him as much.

Could he keep his promise to Lorand Gazda, and, by implication, to Dobokai?

Why Fodor? Why now? Hooper had spent the day learning all he could about him, and it amounted to very little. If anyone knew ill of him, they were not willing even to hint of it. Loyalty? Fear? Blindness, willful or otherwise? Or was there really nothing to know? Was he simply a victim of opportunity?

And the seventeen candles? Was there really a secret society, or was that Dobokai's superstitious imagination? Where did one begin to look for such a group? Even the idea of it made him uncomfortable. His inquiries would have to be discreet. He would ask the Metropolitan Police, privately.

That was something else to have one of his men do: contact all the police stations along the banks of the river and see if there had been any similar crimes. Not likely, or they would have come forward. The evening papers had been full of Fodor's murder, demanding that the police do their job and find the monster. More than one had suggested it was some Hungarian vendetta, and sooner or later all London would be at risk.

THE NEXT MORNING MONK visited one of the men Dobokai had suggested as bearing a possible grudge against Fodor over an old business deal. His name was Roger Haldane, and he was as English as Monk himself. Dobokai had suggested him, obliquely, as a suspect, a man who found himself surrounded by foreigners and his familiar neighborhood subtly but completely changed.

Haldane's house was on James Street, near the Baptist chapel. The door was opened by a maid, who was probably about sixteen, and as handsome as you might find in the best houses in Mayfair. She politely informed Monk that Mr. Haldane was out already, but if he cared to wait, she would ask if Mrs. Haldane would see him.

He accepted the invitation and a few minutes later he was sitting in the small, tidy parlor, with its one bookshelf and one very fine photograph of a young man, perhaps about twenty years old, when Adel Haldane came into the room.

He rose to his feet.

"Good morning, Mrs. Haldane. My name is Commander Monk. I am head of the Thames River Police. It is very kind of you to speak to me without notice like this."

She was a handsome woman with thick, fair hair and high cheekbones. Her pale skin was completely unblemished, although she was well past forty, probably closer to fifty.

"I assume you have come about the murder of poor Mr. Fodor." Her speech was almost unaccented, but there was just sufficiently different a rhythm in it for him to guess that she was part of the Hungarian community, at least before she married an Englishman.

"I am sorry to trouble you, but you may have knowledge or observations that could help us."

A shadow crossed her face. "Have you no idea who did this?" she said quietly. "Do you think it is one of our 'neighbors' who hates us so much? Why? We have done nothing so different from anyone else. We do not break the law, we pay our rents and taxes. We don't steal from anyone! What is wrong with being different? We don't even look different, like Chinese, or lascars, or Africans. London is built out of people from everywhere." She stopped abruptly, as if she had said too much. "Poor Imrus was not perfect, but he was not a bad man." Now there was

a catch in her voice, and Monk thought it was out of real grief, not simply shock or fear. She was mourning one of her own people, perhaps a
friend, not thinking of damage to herself. He liked her for it.

"Fear does not need to have a good reason, Mrs. Haldane. A bad
one, or a stupid one, works just as well. Was he good at his trade, his
business?"

"Yes, yes. Do you think it was envy? Someone who thought they
would lose custom to him?" She realized suddenly that they were still
standing. "Please . . . sit down, Mr. . . . Mr. Monk."

He sat down, partly to be more comfortable, but also to let her know
that he did not intend this simply to be a few questions and answers.
Maybe from her he would get a sense of what Fodor's life had been like.
He had to have been far more than just the victim of an atrocity. There
had been hate in the crime—deep, uncontrollable passion—but so far
Monk had learned only cold facts.

"Tell me about Fodor," he said to her.

She sat down slowly in the chair opposite him. She was not simply
giving herself time to frame an answer; she was unconsciously graceful,
out of habit smoothing her skirts. She sat upright, her back straight, her
poise perfect. For an instant he had a half-forgotten memory of a gov-
erness with a ruler, poking the back of a young girl who slouched in her
chair. Then it was gone.

"He was a man with charm," she began tentatively. "I think he was
not aware of it. He could be very funny. Have you noticed how people
like someone who makes them laugh? And he appreciated craft—a well-
made clock, or a vase of good color, or proportions. And good food. He
would eat everything on his plate, and compliment the cook." She hesitated, and Monk thought she was remembering specific instances, not
generalities.

"Yes," he agreed, recalling times when he himself had appreciated a
loveliness of some sort only because Hester's pleasure in it had stirred
his own awareness of it. Even Oliver Rathbone's love of the sophisti-
cated beauty of old coins and knowledge of who had used them had
awoken his own. Richness could be added to anything, in the most

ordinary-seeming moments. "To take pleasure in what is good is the greatest compliment to it," he added.

She smiled at him, gratitude in her face, and then suddenly tears. She ignored them. It took a certain grace to be able to do so.

"He was well-known in our community," she went on. "If someone wished to injure us, killing him would be a way to begin. But why would they? What harm are we doing? The English come to our restaurants and like our food. They like our music. I thought . . . I thought they even liked most of us."

"It is only one person who has done this," Monk pointed out. "And it might be personal to Fodor, not because he was Hungarian at all." He searched for something more concrete. "He seems to have been success-ful at his business, a man in his late forties, and yet he was not married. Do you know why that was? Was he courting someone? Perhaps some-one English?"

She stared at him. Was it his imagination, or was she paler?

"He was married . . . once," she said quietly. "His wife died in Hun-gary. Over twenty years ago, before they were able to leave. I knew her as a child, long before they were married. We . . . we were friends. Leav-ing was . . . very difficult."

He tried to imagine it. Had she died of an illness? Violence? An ac-cident?

"I'm sorry," he said quietly, and he meant it. He could not imagine being driven out of anywhere. Even leaving home on his first adventure as a young man, the waking up in a strange bed, the ache where home and those he had loved would have been—all part of what he had lost, wrapped in the hidden memories, the roots that did not exist.

"He did not marry again?" he asked.

For a moment an expression crossed Adel Haldane's face that he could not read, but it was definitely an emotion rather than a thought, or even a memory. Had she too lost someone she loved romantically, or parted from them when she left Hungary?

"Could it be an old enmity?" he asked. "A debt from the past?"

"I am not sure," she admitted. "If so, I think it would be one he did not understand, or did not remember." A faint smile touched her mouth.

"Some people speak of the past as if it is always with them, like an unseen garment. Others seem to want to let go of it, as if never looking back. Imrus was one of the latter," she went on. "That irritated some, but most were helped by that way of thinking. 'No one can change the past,' he used to say. 'But the future is different. Everything you do changes that, one way or another.'" She forced a whole smile now, brave and completely hollow. He saw her grief through it. "I liked that about him," she said huskily.

Before Monk could continue, they were interrupted by the noise of footsteps outside in the hall. Then a moment later the door opened and a large, burly man came into the room. His fairish hair was receding a little, making his brow more pronounced, and the summer sun had caught his cheeks. He was not handsome, but he had presence, and the lines in his face suggested a general affability. He glanced at Adel, then concentrated on Monk, waiting for him to explain himself, and his presence in the house.

Monk rose to his feet, but he did not offer his hand. This was a formal visit, not one of friendship.

"Mr. Haldane. My name is Monk, Commander of the Thames River Police. Mrs. Haldane has been giving me a little history and background on the Hungarian community in Shadwell. I am most obliged to her."

Haldane took a deep breath. "Is that a polite way of saying she was talking about her people?" His expression was ambivalent, something between anger and acceptance. "About Fodor?" he added.

"About the circumstances of his death," Monk amended slightly. The tension in Haldane was subtle, too faint to guess if it was pity or anger. "But mostly the difficulties faced by people adjusting to a new place, new and different customs."

"You think his murder was something to do with his being Hungarian?" Haldane asked. He pursed his lips. "Possible. They're mostly decent people, but in some ways different. Can't ever forget that." He seemed to relax a little, then waved his hand to indicate the chair Monk had risen from, and sat down next to his wife. She did not move, either away from him or toward him. Her eyes were on Monk.

"Just small differences," Haldane went on. "It's mostly the food you notice, and the smell." There was a shadow of distaste in his face, there and then gone again. "Not bad, just different. And of course they always favor each other. But then, I suppose we favor our own as well. It's natural."

"Have there been incidents of unpleasantness?" Monk asked, making it seem as casual as he could.

Haldane hesitated.

Monk wondered if he was trying to recall or, more likely, weighing exactly what to repeat.

"A few," he said at last. "People forget, often, that, at least to some, they don't belong here."

Don't belong here. Half the people in London did not "belong" here. They had begun somewhere else. That was one of the good things about London.

Monk forced himself back to the issue. "We all prefer certain people to others," he said smoothly. "But this attack was very violent indeed, brutal, filled with hatred, not mere distaste . . ." He stopped, seeing the distress in Adel's face. Her skin was drained of color, her eyes fixed on his, her mouth twisted in hurt. He had momentarily forgotten that she knew Fodor, and liked him.

"I'm sorry," he said with very real regret.

He saw the expression on Haldane's face change from confusion to anger.

"We have nothing to tell you," he said abruptly. "My wife and I get along perfectly well with the Hungarians, but there are others who don't. In the past some have been unpleasant about it, but never anything like this. You should look at work, property, businesses. See whose jobs Fodor took, or whose workmen he poached, what contracts were lost. If I knew, I'd tell you, but I don't. Of course there's tension, quarrels. There are in any community. I'd be a fool to deny it, and you'd be a fool not to see it for yourself. But we don't wear our quarrels on our sleeves. I don't know who did this. For everyone's sake, I'd tell you if I did. Now please go." There was deep emotion in his voice. He made a movement toward his wife as if he was going to touch her, gently, even put his arm around her, then he changed his mind and withdrew it sharply. Instead he rose and took a step toward Monk.

Deliberately, Monk refused to back away. He stood and looked directly at Adel.

"I apologize for reminding you of the violence, Mrs. Haldane," he said gravely.

He turned back to Haldane, studying the man's face, seeing in it mixed and powerful emotions. Were they in response to the horror that Monk had named, or some deeper conflict of his own? He was a minority in this part of the city, in the streets he frequented.

"There were seventeen candles," he said suddenly. "Do you know what that means?"

Haldane's face turned white, and for a moment he seemed speechless.

Monk waited, feeling that he had hit a nerve, hoping he had.

"No," Haldane said eventually. "Does it mean . . . something?"

"Apparently there is a society . . ." Monk explained.

Haldane relaxed, his heavy shoulders seemed to ease, as if the muscles let go of the tension. "Really? You mean Fodor belonged to it, and broke one of their rules, or something? That's . . . horrible."

"You haven't heard of it?" Monk asked the question without expecting an answer. Everything was in the emotions behind the words. The mention of the society, far from upsetting Haldane, had somehow brought him relief.

Adel's expression he could not read.

He thanked them again and excused himself, then turned and went out of the room, across the hallway and out the door into the street, aware that there was something he had not understood, or even that he had missed entirely.

MONK SPENT THE REST of the day, with the help of Antal Dobokai and a street map of the area, seeing who might have noticed anything unusual. Dobokai was roundabout in his questioning, always asking something else first, seeking people's opinions on issues: What did they think? What did they want? Were they comfortable? Were the local services good? Did the milkman deliver close to them, did the grocer's boy, did the chimney sweep come around regularly? Monk grew impatient and found it hard to restrain himself from interrupting.

But by late afternoon, as the sun was low and his feet ached from walking on hot pavement, he realized that he had established the whereabouts at the time of the murder of all the people he had met. He knew their homes, their occupations and, from most of them, what they thought and felt about living in London in general, and of Fodor in particular.

The woman they saw last, in her own home, was perhaps fifty years old, still handsome, marred only by the stoop of her shoulders and the very evident fear in her eyes. She spoke only the most broken English, and she told her story to Dobokai in her own language, leaving him to translate.

It seemed she had gone into a grocery shop to buy herself half a dozen eggs and some baking supplies: flour, sugar, eggs, and ground almonds, holding up a group of other customers. She had been unable to find the English word for another flavoring she wanted and mistakenly chose a word with an entirely different and rather vulgar meaning. From the other customers' laughter and cruelty, she had realized her mistake, with considerable embarrassment. She had tried to apologize and explain what she had meant, but they would not allow her to.

One of the women had suggested that she used the word because she was a prostitute, or, more accurately, a whore. She did not understand how, but the whole ugly incident had escalated until all four of the other women had convinced each other that she was seducing their husbands and many other men in the area, with practices a decent woman would not defile herself to repeat.

Subsequently she had not dared to go out shopping. Men she did not know had followed her, making lewd offers and suggestions. One woman had actually attacked her in the street, and she had been assaulted twice by men who believed she was a whore but had refused them her favors.

Dobokai was very gentle with her as she recounted her story, the tears running down her face, but once they had left her house he turned to Monk, his bright blue eyes blazing.

"You see?" he said quietly, his voice rasping with emotion. "That is the truth that people are ashamed to admit. There is your hatred, the violence you saw against poor Fodor's body."

Monk looked at him without immediately replying. He had seen violence before, and long-held-in hatred. He knew that certain men had hated him, and in some ways not without reason. The very nature of feeling impotent against someone who is hurting you, depriving you of what you long for and—perhaps worst of all—in some way belittling you, begets a fury that overwhelms all other reason, even your own physical survival. It can feel as if your very identity is threatened by their victory. He had seen it more than once, but most recently in McNab, the customs officer who had lately become his enemy. He could even understand it.

"Thank you, Mr. Dobokai," he said quietly. "I understand it is hatred we are looking for. The question is, is it from someone he knew well, caused by an injury, real or imagined? Or is it some rage at Fodor for being an immigrant here, identifiably different?"

Dobokai was silent for so long that Monk concluded he was not going to reply, since he had half turned away.

"Yes," he said suddenly. "Have you considered looking further into . . . 'seventeen'? I will listen carefully. And discreetly, of course. But I will hear things that you do not." He saw Monk's expression. "I know these people. You don't. But, above all, you don't speak their language. Even those of us who speak English quite well still use our own tongue when we are in our homes, or among ourselves. Wouldn't you? If you were in a strange country where everyone else knows the rules, the little unspoken ones, so small nobody thinks of them? Not a boulder you fall over—a piece of grit in the eye." His smile was very slight, just a twitch of the lips.

Monk knew exactly what he meant, but he argued all the same.

"You seem very comfortable with English, Mr. Dobokai."

Dobokai instantly argued back, although he could not keep the satisfaction from his face at the compliment.

"I have been here longer than they have," he replied. "Here in England, not in London. I told you I spent some time in the north." His blue eyes were very bright and still. "I hear the north in your voice too, now and then."

Monk suddenly felt very vulnerable, as if this odd man whom he increasingly disliked had stripped him of a layer of covering, even concealment. He had tried to weed out all the Northumbrian from his voice, long ago. He had a sudden, needle-fine memory of not wanting to be thought provincial, unsophisticated compared with southerners, Londoners. Was that how the Hungarians felt? Newcomers, judged as foolish because there were too many strange things they did not understand.

He could not let Dobokai catch him in a prevarication. It was a weakness.

"Very perceptive of you." He smiled back slightly. "I grew up in the north, with tough, quiet men of the sea." He knew at least that much was true, although it was something he'd discovered, not remembered.

Dobokai stood motionless, then he said good night briefly and walked away, leaving Monk to go along the riverbank, toward Wapping and the shortest ferry home across the darkening river.

SCUFF WAS BUSY TIDYING the shelves in the four rooms that Crow rented in order to run his clinic. It was certainly not a hospital, but it served as such to hundreds of the poor along this part of the Thames bank. Crow had begun as an apprentice, as Scuff was now. But his skill was extraordinary. To Scuff, at eighteen, Crow seemed the finest man alive, apart from Monk.

Monk had found Scuff, an orphan mudlark, along the tidal edges of the river, surviving by salvaging and selling bits of coal, brass screws and fixtures washed up and left. He, and scores of other children, lived in such a way. Monk was new to his appointment as Commander of the River Police and, in Scuff's eyes, sufficiently ignorant of the facts of life, especially on the water, to be a danger to himself and all those he was supposed to protect. For the price of an occasional ham sandwich and cup of really hot tea, and because he liked Monk, Scuff had undertaken to educate him before he made a mistake from which he could not be rescued.

Of course, Monk imagined he was teaching Scuff, and Scuff was too diplomatic to explain to him otherwise. They had become friends. As Monk learned more of life on the river, which he did rapidly, the relationship had grown deeper, and the balance of it had changed. Scuff had begun to learn about life also.

In some dangerous exploits Scuff had been badly frightened, and for safety's sake, Monk had taken him to his home in Paradise Place. There, Scuff had slept in a bed, a real one, with sheets, in a room all to himself. At the time, warmth, safety, good food cooked specially for him, had seemed the most important thing to happen to him. Looking back now, its importance diminished. What really mattered, what had changed Scuff's life, though it appeared then as an uncomfortable inconvenience, was that he had met Monk's wife, Hester.

To begin with, Scuff found it awkward. Monk he knew and almost understood, as much as one could understand a policeman and an adult who presumably had never had to beg for his survival one meal at a time, and to sleep wherever he could find a dry place sheltered from the wind. But Hester was different altogether. She was a woman, perhaps a lady. She had probably never even seen the muddy tidal stretches of the river, let alone slept in a cardboard box!

She did not have any children of her own, and Scuff, who claimed to be eleven, was far too old to need a mother! If there really was a God above, as some people seemed to think, please let Him stop her from treating him like a child. It would be embarrassing beyond imagination.

But Scuff need not have worried, as Hester treated him like an ordinary person. She was even polite to him! But she was very quick to tell Scuff if he was not polite back. At first he was horrified, then he realized he rather liked it. She was treating him like an equal. As if he was a real person, not just a stray nuisance she needed to be kind to.

He stayed more and more often.

She had wanted Scuff to go to school, learn to read and write and do sums. It had been awful, at first, like being put in a kind of prison. Gradually he had discovered, after he had caught up, that he was quite good at that sort of thing.

It was when he realized he wanted to practice medicine like Hester, not be a policeman like Monk, that he kept to it with all his will, actually getting up early and staying up late, studying his books. If Monk was disappointed at his choice, he hid it very well. Scuff hated to disappoint him, even worse to hurt his feelings, but medicine was what he wanted. Not just to be like Hester, but because its art, its passion, its rewards filled his mind with such intensity there was no room left to want anything else. Medicine was his career now. Hester had been a nurse with the army during the Crimean War. She had even been out on the battlefield herself, after the fighting was over. She wasn't a doctor, but she was as good as many of them, better.

"How are you coming on?"

Scuff turned and saw the lanky figure of Crow in the corridor behind him. Crow had dark eyes and black hair. The term "crow" was dialect for a doctor, but it suited him perfectly quite apart from his occupation. Except that no bird of any sort had a huge, white-toothed grin like Crow when he saw something funny, or exciting, or someone he really liked, such as Hester.

Crow had wanted to be a doctor for a long time, but something had interrupted his study before he had taken the exams. He had practiced without qualifications, and without charging people, for years. He worked among the poor, even the destitute, taking gifts in kind, when they could be spared, and nothing at all when that was the circumstance.

At Hester's urging, he had finally taken his exams, and was now officially a doctor. He had made a terrible fuss at the time, afraid of failure, of all past misjudgments rising up again, but he had passed, his skill undeniable. He was more than grateful now, and therefore this was an excellent place for Scuff to begin an apprenticeship.

Scuff had his school learning, but nothing that would allow him to go to a proper university. He would follow in Crow's footsteps, the hard way. He too would learn, not from reading about patients in books or from professors, but by helping real people in trouble.

"Well?" Crow demanded.

Scuff brought his attention back to the present, recited a list of the supplies that were low. They had money now: not a lot, but enough to get the things they needed, at least in small quantities. One could never foretell what was going to be required.

"Good." Crow seemed pleased. It must have been better than he expected, because the lightning grin was back. "Money coming tomorrow, I think," he added. He was prevented from saying anything further by a noise at the outside door, and a moment later the sound of feet on the wood floor.

Crow went immediately, and less than a minute later he called out loudly for Scuff.

Scuff put down his pencil and paper and went to the other room. As soon as he was inside he saw Crow, bent almost double as he staggered to help a man who had all but collapsed sideways. The man was ashen-faced and could hardly stand. His left arm hung uselessly at his side and there was blood on the sleeve of his shirt, near the bend of his elbow. It had dribbled all the way down to the cuff, now stiff with old, dried stains.

Scuff shot forward and took some of the man's weight. He tried not to touch the elbow, but it was impossible not to brush it as they eased him onto the low table at one side of the room.

"Just lie still," Crow said to him. Scuff could see from his eyes that he was already aware the man was in a very bad way.

He knew what would be next: they must examine the man and see what the damage was, and—if indeed it had happened some time ago— the extent of any infection that had set in.

"What's your name?" Crow asked the man.

"Tibor . . ." the man said hoarsely.

Crow reached out and Scuff put the small, very sharp scissors in his hand. Crow carefully cut the cloth away, talking to Tibor all the time, telling him what he was doing. He found it easier to work in silence, but he knew that the sound of a voice was comforting. It was clear that he knew exactly what he was doing. Scuff had learned with surprise, and only afterward, that sometimes Crow was only hoping and keeping faith with his determination.

When the wound was laid bare even Scuff could see that it was several days old. The skin was unhealed, the gashes clear where several knife strokes had gone deep. They could not have caught an artery, or he would have bled to death, but from the pallor of his skin, the livid puffiness below the wound and the lifeless hand, Scuff knew instantly what Crow feared—gangrene. In fact, he could already smell it.

"When did this happen?" Crow asked Tibor.

The patient stared at him as if he had no idea what he meant.

Crow tried again. "How long ago?" he asked, indicating the wound without touching it.

Tibor looked young, no more than thirty. His would have been a handsome, sensitive face were he not clearly terrified. He must have some idea that his condition was serious, and that perhaps it was already too late to save him. Scuff had seen people terribly ill before, and known they would die soon. It was part of the practice of medicine. Some of these people were old. Some were children. Crow had told him that when it ceased to upset him, it was time to get out of medicine and look for something safe and easy to do. Something where it did not matter whether he succeeded or not.

"Yesterday?" Crow asked. "Day before?"

Tibor shook his head, not more than an inch or two, but it was denial. "Day . . ."

"Several days ago?" Crow guessed. "Night? It happened at night?"

Tibor nodded.

Crow held up his fingers. One? Two? Three? Four?

Tibor nodded at four. His eyes never left Crow's.

Crow went on with his careful examination. When he had finished inspecting the wound, he looked more closely at the arm. He did not look at Scuff; there was no need to. The flesh was already dying. Even Scuff could see that.

"Tibor," Crow said quietly. "What kind of a name is that? You're not English, are you?" It was not really a question. "Where do you come from?"

"Budapest," Tibor said huskily, but he pronounced it with a familiarity no Englishman would have had.

"Do you speak English?"

"Little . . . little bit."

"Can you tell me what happened to your arm?"

Tibor struggled, and tried to mime some kind of blow, but the gesture was weak. With the use of only one hand, he could not express enough.

Crow looked up at Scuff. "I need to know what happened," he said in little above a whisper, and speaking rapidly, as if he did not want Tibor to understand. "If it's as bad as it looks, the only way to save him is to take the arm off at the elbow, or even at the shoulder, if this has gone too far. But I have to know if there's anything in there: a bullet or the tip of a knife, or whatever caused this. I daren't use ether on him—he's too weak. I can't just go exploring. That, on top of taking it off, could be enough to kill him."

Scuff nodded. He did not want to understand. He could imagine what the poor man was going to feel. But he knew they had no choice. Gangrene was a death of the flesh. It did not heal. All the doctor could do was hope to save the life of the patient by seeing that it did not spread to the rest of the body. But without a language in common, Crow could not even get permission for that. And without permission, if he died, it would be a crime. That did not even take into account the horror of the patient who saw his arm being cut off, and did not understand the necessity.

"I'll find someone who speaks Hungarian," Scuff promised. "There are loads of them around Shadwell. I'll run."

"Good. Get anyone who can help. Don't waste time trying to find someone who knows him. Go . . . We've got to do this tonight."

Scuff obeyed without saying anything more. He went out the door into the side bend in the street. The early-evening air was cool off the river. He knew the feel of the incoming tide, the smell of it: fish, salt, estuary mud. It was different from the ebb. He had lived on the river all his life, and he understood it as a stranger never could. Hester had taught him some of its history, and he knew that too, even if it was not out of books.

The longest street in London. His street. The roadways and alleys were incidental, subject to change. The Thames was the great highway.

He walked quickly, ideas flitting through his mind. Where should he look for someone who could help, and would agree to? The light was fading. He saw the changes in it on the wind rippling over the water. He could read a clock, but it was still instinctive to turn to the sky, especially on a clear evening like this.

People would be out walking, on their way home. Many shops would be closed. The open ones would be run by locals. Would they even know what a Hungarian was? It would be quicker to start in Shadwell itself than to stop here and there and waste time trying to explain.

Where would people go at sundown? Home. Or to the tavern! Men there would have time to speak to a stranger. He was not a child anymore to go almost unnoticed. He was taller than Hester. In another few years he would be as tall as Monk. Already he looked older than he was, except that he had no need to shave more than once every few days.

He knew where the taverns were; everybody did. They were the sort of landmarks people used.

The nearest he knew from the Shadwell Dock was the Saracen's Head, toward Cable Street. He stopped, hesitating at the door, then went inside. It was early in the evening and there were few people there. He felt very self-conscious, now that it came to the moment to ask. Crow would not have cared. He would have thought only of the sick man and his need. Hester certainly would not have doubted herself. She had faced army generals, in uniform, without backing down. If she was scared, no one guessed it.

He walked over to the bar.

"Yes, sir?" the landlord said, then took a closer look at him, doubting his ability to pay for a drink.

"Good evening, sir," Scuff said with as much dignity as he could. He was mimicking Monk's accent, or perhaps it was Hester's. She was a Londoner, as he was, even if she was a lady. "I'm on an errand for a doctor. He has a very badly injured patient who speaks little English. Do you know of anyone who could turn Hungarian into English for us, and the other way too?"

The landlord frowned. "Injured, eh? Like 'e bin in a bad fight?"

Scuff remembered with a chill the murder there had been just a couple of days ago. The victim of that had been Hungarian. He drew in his breath and let it out. His mind raced.

"Not really. More like an accident. Just the one arm, nothing on the rest of him," he replied. "He can't even tell us who did it to him, or if he fell, or what happened. At least not so we can understand. All I need is someone who can help us speak to him . . ."

"Dunno," the landlord replied. He looked around the room at the half-dozen or so men there. "Any one o' you know someone as can speak 'Ungarian?" he said loudly. "Got a doctor's lad 'ere as wants to know. Need 'elp ter make 'im understand what to do for 'isself, like?"

He was regarded in silence.

It annoyed him.

"Come on! The place is crawling with bleedin' 'Ungarians! One of you must be able to speak English."

More silence.

"Lot o' bleedin' heathens, you are," the landlord said, slamming an empty tankard down on the bar. "Well, you could try the feller what lives over on Pinchin Street, just the other side o' the railway line. 'E's English as you or me, but I 'eard someone say as 'e speaks all kinds o' foreign. 'E's a doctor, or 'e was. Maybe 'e'll 'elp yer. You all bein' doctors, like."

"Thank you. Do you know his name? Or what number on Pinchin Street he lives?" Scuff was desperate. Time was short. Crow had said he had to operate tonight, or it would be too late. "Please!" he added. "He's going to die if we don't help him! I don't know about Hungarians, but that's not what we do."

"No . . . I don't . . ." the landlord began.

"Fitz . . . something," one of the men at the farthest table said. "I think it's about number fourteen, or thereabouts."

"Thank you," Scuff said, almost over his shoulder, as he went back to the door and out into the street again.

He half walked, half ran along Cable Street to the place where he could cross over the railway line, go just a few yards, then turn left into Pinchin Street. He prayed a few words to the God Hester had taught him just a little about. He was supposed to love people. If He did, perhaps He could make this doctor be at home! If he wasn't, Scuff had no idea where to begin looking for him. Maybe he had a landlord who would know? What good to anybody was a doctor you couldn't find? Out healing somebody else—the answer was obvious. People did die, whatever they believed in. Scuff knew that. Hester had to as well. He should ask her sometime.

Fourteen? Where was number fourteen?

Twelve. That must be next door. He stopped at the door, panting for breath. He did not have to run very often now. He reached for the knocker and banged it loudly, more than he'd intended. But nothing happened. He tried again, this time meaning it as loudly as he could.

The door opened and a large man stood just inside with his table napkin stuck in the top of his shirt. The anger drained out of his face as he saw Scuff's expression.

"What is it, lad?" he said with alarm.

"Is the doctor in?" Scuff asked, still breathing hard. "He's English, but they said at the tavern that he speaks Hungarian. We need his help. This man's going to die if we don't operate on him tonight, but he doesn't understand anything we say." He drew in a deep breath. "He only speaks Hungarian. Please?"

"You must mean Fitz. I'll get him for you, lad. Just wait there." He closed the door, in what was perhaps a habitual precaution.

Scuff stood on the step, shifting his weight from one foot to the other for what seemed like an age, but was probably no more than two or three minutes. Then the door opened and a different man stood there. He was a little over average height, fair-haired and clean-shaven, but his face was pale and there was a kind of hollowness about his eyes.

"You were looking for me?" he asked quietly. He might understand Hungarian, but he was most definitely English, and a gentleman, his voice with the same inflections as Hester's.

Scuff gulped. "You the doctor what speaks Hungarian?" In his tension he forgot the grammar he had been taught. "'Cos if you are, we need you to help us, or this man's going to die. He's got a bad wound in the elbow and gangrene's setting in. We got to operate tonight, but he doesn't understand a word we say. Please . . ."

The man shook his head, a grief in his face that was overwhelming. "I'm not up to that. It's a hard operation and . . . and not many come through it." He shook his head. "I'm sorry . . ."

"I don't want you to operate!" Scuff all but shouted at him. "We can do that! We just need you to speak to him. We got to tell him what we're going to do, and that it's his only chance. Please . . . You—" He stopped. Shouting at this man would not help. There was enough pain in his face already. "Please, Mister . . . Doctor . . ."

"Herbert Fitzherbert," the man replied. "But people call me Fitz. Do you need any instruments? I still keep them . . ."

"No," Scuff said. "No, thank you, sir. We got everything that'll do any good. Please just come wi' me?"

The man stepped out and closed the front door behind him. "Then lead the way."

"You can speak Hungarian, is that right?" Scuff asked without breaking stride as he hurried toward the railway line.

"Yes, really quite well."

"But you sound English, just like Hester . . ."

Fitz caught Scuff by the arm, pulling him to a stop. For a man so pale, his grip was remarkably strong. "Did you say Hester? No, no, I'm sorry." He let go again.

"Yeah. Why?"

Fitz shook his head. "Nothing. I knew a Hester once. Long time ago, in the Crimea . . ."

Scuff momentarily forgot the urgency. "Hester was a nurse in the Crimea. She's sort of . . . like my ma. Not really, but 'like' . . ."

"Hester Latterly?" Fitz's voice shook.

"Yeah, before she married Commander Monk."

"Commander? In the navy?"

Scuff gave a bleak smile. "No, Thames River Police. We gotta go, sir. The man's in a very bad way. We gotta get back through Shadwell, just into Wapping."

"Yes, of course," Fitz agreed immediately, beginning to walk rapidly again. "Are you studying medicine yourself?"

"Yes. Crow is the real doctor, but I'm learning from him," Scuff said, quickening his own pace.

"So this . . . Did you say 'Crow'?"

"Yes. He's a proper doctor. Got all his qualifications now," Scuff assured him.

"Too late to change now," Fitz said ruefully. "Although I don't doubt you. Hester . . . my Hester . . . would never let you study with someone who wasn't worthy."

They were across the railway now, into Wells Street, then left to St. George Street down toward the river. They would take the cutting through Gravel Lane going upriver. The streetlamps were lit, but they were few and far between here. There was no point in trying to read Fitz's face.

They must hurry. The patient was everything, his own hunger or curiosity nothing. Hester had taught him that even before Crow had reinforced it. The doctor must take care of himself in order to do his job, nothing more—at least until the crisis was past. Crow had few big rules, dozens of small ones. Clearly the big ones were unquestionable.

They went the rest of the way to the rooms where Crow lived and ran his clinic, and where most of the time now Scuff lived as well. He went home to Paradise Place only once or twice a week.

He opened the clinic with his own key, Fitz on his heels. He led the way straight to the room where Tibor lay, restlessly, moving now and then as if trying to ease himself. His arm was covered with clean, damp cloths, and even from the doorway Scuff could smell the sharpness of camphorated wine with ammonia.

Crow looked up as Scuff closed the door, and his dark face filled with relief. He only glanced at Scuff, then looked at Fitz. "You speak Hungarian?" He asked the only thing that mattered at the moment. There was no time for courtesies.

"Learned it on the way back from the Crimea," Fitz replied. He came close to the table and regarded the patient for several moments in silence. "I am a doctor myself," he explained simply. He lifted the damp cloths and examined the arm without touching the flesh.

Scuff, standing beside him, could see that it was dying. He had seen gangrene only once before, but the grayness and the faint odor of rot, almost masked by the camphorated wine, were things he would not forget.

"It'll have to come off, if you're going to have any chance of saving him," Fitz said quietly. "Do you want me to tell him that?"

"Yes," Crow answered. "His name is Tibor."

Fitz leaned forward a little and put his hand on the man's good arm, gently increasing the pressure until Tibor opened his eyes. They were haggard, and filled with fear.

"Tibor," Fitz said quietly but very clearly. Then he spoke in a language unlike any that Scuff had heard before. And he'd heard many on the docks as he grew up: French, Spanish in particular, and some German. This was totally unfamiliar.

He looked at Crow quickly. He seemed to know that this was right. Was it? Could they save this man? Or would they only be subjecting him to horrific pain, for no reason? Scuff could not imagine having a limb cut off a living body—on purpose! Would it not be better to let him die quietly, and whole?

He could not read Crow's face. Did he know what he was doing? Or was he only guessing, wearing a mask of certainty underneath which he was as blind and afraid as Scuff? He had not questioned this before. The patient must always believe in you. They would not fight to live unless they trusted you, and believed there was a chance. That was one of the first things Scuff had learned.

Suddenly he realized that he must take the fear out of his own face as well. Tibor might look at him and see it. He forced the faintest of smiles.

Fitz turned to Crow. "He understands," he told him. "He knows it is his only chance. We'll go ahead."

"Thank you," Crow acknowledged. "I have everything ready." He gestured toward the table in the corner. Whatever was on it—saws, knives, forceps, needles and silk thread—was hidden by a white cloth. Tibor did not need to see it unless he had to.

Scuff opened his mouth to say that Tibor had said nothing in reply to Fitz, then he realized that the patient had moved his head—a slight nod. Perhaps the sound he had made had been "yes" in his own tongue.

Crow was hesitating.

"Do you know much of the use of ether?" he said to Fitz.

"Enough to know it is pretty risky when a man's as advanced as this. I heard they made use of chloroform in America in their Civil War just over. Still had a lot of bad results. I'd advise . . ." He stopped. "I'd advise you to think hard before making a decision," he finished. "But quickly," he added with a wry smile.

"No time," Crow replied. He looked very steadily at Fitz. "Thank you for coming," he added with intense feeling. "I need you both." He included Scuff in his glance, then moved over toward the table at the side, ready to begin.

Fitz drew in his breath to reply. He looked at Scuff, seeming almost panicky.

Scuff smiled back at him. "Thank you," he said. He knew Fitz had had no intention of staying and helping beyond being a translator, but Crow was not giving him time to argue.

"Scuff!" Crow said sharply. "I have everything ready. I shall need each item as I ask for it. Be ready to pass them when I say. Keep the linen ready, split roller. Have it steeped in the hot camphorated wine now on the stove. I shall need several pledgets at least. Sprinkle them with camphor. You know where it is. I may need compresses in hot wine to cover him up to the shoulder. And bandages to cover the whole area too. Once we begin, it must be as quick as possible. With the tying of the ligatures, under a minute would be good."

Scuff was astounded. Under one minute!

"Yes . . . yes, sir!" He went straight to the stove, checked the wine steaming in a large iron pan, then laid out the other materials Crow had asked for.

He returned to find Crow and Fitz standing on either side of the table, Crow with the blade in his hand.

Fitz was holding Tibor's right hand in a hard, strong grip, and talking to him in his own language.

Crow took a deep breath, held it an instant, then let it out slowly. He gripped the blade and cut open the shoulder, which was already white as if there were no blood in it. The arm below, leading to the elbow and the site of the original injury, was already a bruised-looking blue, as if it were dead.

Tibor gasped and closed his eyes. What agony he felt Scuff could only guess.

Crow continued cutting, and the bone came away, leaving flesh behind that scarcely bled. He tied the arteries immediately with the thread Scuff passed to him. He did it with extreme care, leaving out the nerves accompanying them.

The flaps of flesh left were brownish in color, and looked to Scuff to be unnaturally dry. The disease was already in the armpit.

Very carefully Crow brought the flaps of skin across the wound, toward each other, almost meeting but not quite.

"Linen," he said, without looking at Scuff.

Scuff passed him the split roller of linen, which had been freshly steeped in the very warm camphorated wine. As Crow placed it on the wound, Scuff then passed him the pledgets of lint, sprinkled with camphor, and then the long compression bandage, also dipped in hot wine. Last, he passed the supporting bandage to swathe and hold the whole lot over the place where the arm had been.

It was done, for the time being. It seemed as if the clock on the mantelshelf above the stove had barely moved.

Scuff looked at Fitz, who was still holding Tibor's other hand in both his own, and speaking to him softly, although Tibor's eyes were closed and the skin on his face and neck was so pale it seemed he must be dead. Perhaps the shock of pain had stopped his heart?

"There's still a pulse," Fitz said quietly. "But it's thready, irregular and very faint."

Crow nodded and looked across at the clock.

"Very good," Fitz told him. "Twenty-five seconds, apart from the ligatures. Can't be too hasty with them, or you'd miss something. Pay for it later."

"Is twenty-five seconds good?" Crow asked him.

"I've seen seventeen, in the hospital in Scutari. But this man's got a better chance here. It's clean." He did not add any more, but Scuff saw the sweat break out on his face, beading his brow and upper lip, although the room was no more than comfortably warm. To Scuff his expression was unreadable, but he knew pain when he saw it so naked in anyone, the horror of some memories his mind could see, crowding him from the past, wounding indelibly.

"Scuff," Crow said quietly.

Scuff did not hear him, except as if he had spoken in the distance, and from another room.

"Scuff!"

"Yes, sir?"

"Chicken soup. It's on the cooking stove in the kitchen. Bring a small bowlful for Tibor. And then fetch a little of the best claret we have."

"Yes, sir . . ."

"Now!" Crow stared at him more closely, as if to make sure he was all right.

Scuff moved with alacrity. He had not seen an operation like this before, but he had seen Crow set broken bones, and stitch up badly bleeding wounds. He knew that the shock suffered was often the thing that killed. Crow had warned him of it often enough. Too many operations that seemed to have gone well still resulted in death.

In the kitchen he found the soup, tasted it on the end of a long wooden spoon and found it delicious. He filled the bottom of one of the earthenware bowls and took it, with a spoon, back to the room where Tibor was now lying, ashen, propped up in one of the two beds. They very seldom kept people for any duration of time, but occasionally it was necessary. Some treatments required days of supervision. Sometimes people got worse after treatment. He had seen a few die, even after everything they could do.

He looked at Crow.

"Feed it to him," Crow instructed. "Just a tiny bit at a time. Shallow spoonful. Don't force it."

Scuff met his eyes, hoping he would relent, but Crow only nodded again.

Scuff walked to the edge of the bed. He looked at Tibor's face: his eyes were sunken with shock. He looked bewildered.

Scuff smiled at him. "This is chicken soup," he said. "No bones, just a little barley broth. It tastes really good." He knew that Tibor probably did not understand, but he could hear the tone of voice and know that he was being cared for.

Scuff half filled the spoon and carried it slowly to Tibor's mouth.

"Try it," he told him.

Tibor obeyed. It took him a moment to swallow, but he did not regurgitate it.

Scuff offered a second spoonful, and then a third, and a fourth. Crow had told him over and over how important it was that a sick or injured person did not become more ill just from the lack of liquid in their body. Nothing worked without liquids.

Crow poured a little of the claret into a glass and Scuff then tried with that also, but Tibor was exhausted.

"I'll watch him," Crow said, just above a whisper. "Scuff, get some sleep. I'll come for you in a few hours, or if I need help." He turned to Fitz and held out his hand. "Thank you. I'd like you to stay until morning, but I can't reasonably ask you. You must have your own patients to see tomorrow. But I'm grateful you came."

Fitz smiled. The gas lamps were bright enough for a surgeon to see what he was doing in the middle of the room, but toward the sides they cast shadows sideways that highlighted the lines in Fitz's face, around his eyes and mouth, and threw into relief the pain within him.

"Thank you," he answered. "But I think that when he regains consciousness he will not remember all that has happened, and he may be very frightened. Of course the pain will be less than an amputation from a shattered bone, or from having part of the arm blown off, because the gangrene had already killed so much of it. But you took it back to the living flesh, and that will hurt badly for a long time. I should stay to explain to him the necessity of removing the arm and, now that it is gone, of doing all he is advised in order to regain his strength. He is very weak. We still have a long way to go."

Crow understood. "But your other patients . . . ?" he asked.

Fitz's face tightened and his eyes were bleak. "I don't practice anymore, not in the way I used to. I only help here and there."

Crow was clearly taken aback. He studied Fitz for several moments. Scuff watched both men. He knew that Crow was perplexed. To him the practice of medicine was a holy calling, and to be allowed to follow it was what he had aspired to for most of his life. For Fitz it was clearly different. There was no way to tell what had called him in the first place, or what had happened since, only that now he was exhausted, as much in his mind and will as in his body.

"Then I would be very grateful for you to stay," Crow replied. "There's a place for you to sleep. We have two beds. Scuff goes home sometimes, but more often he stays here. We work early and late. There is no point in his taking a ferry ride back and forth simply to sleep in a different bed. I'll stay up with Tibor and watch him; sleep in the chair, perhaps. You can have my bed. We haven't got an extra room to spare, but Scuff's quiet enough."

"Thank you," Fitz said, accepting. "Call me if he wakens and you need me."

Scuff led the way, rather self-consciously, to the small room off the side of the clinic floor, which he shared with Crow when he slept there. Of course, in the days before he met Monk, he had slept wherever he could find a little shelter, and there was loneliness, but never such a thing as privacy. At Monk's house he had his own room. That, and a bath, were the greatest luxuries imaginable. Along with hot food, of course, as much as he wanted.

But this doctor, with his fair, sensitive face and his way of speaking like Hester, like a gentleman, was something quite different. What was he used to?

Fitz took his boots off, then his jacket and trousers. He did not seem to be self-conscious at all.

"You all right here?" Scuff asked, then bit his lip with annoyance at himself. What was he going to do if Fitz said he was not all right? It was a stupid thing to have said.

"Didn't Hester tell you what it was like to sleep on the battlefield?" Fitz asked with a slight smile. "This is clean, dry and quiet. It's heaven."

Scuff looked around the bare room with its scrubbed wood floor and mismatched furniture. Fitz was right. But it was friendship and learning that made it really valuable. How easy it was to get used to comfort. He had almost forgotten what it was like to be cold most of the time, and wet far too often. Of course, Fitz didn't know that Scuff had lived on the riverbank for more than half his life—well, almost more. He could not really remember his first five years.

"I know what it's like to sleep outside," he said impulsively. He did not want this friend of Hester's to think he was soft. "They only took me in when I was eleven." Actually he didn't know how old he was, but eleven was a good enough guess.

"Where were you before that?" Fitz asked, swinging his feet up and lying back on the bed, his arms linked behind his head.

"Riverbank," Scuff replied, taking his own boots and trousers off, then lying under the blanket in the same position.

Fitz did not turn to look at him. "You must be pretty good at looking after yourself."

"Yeah," Scuff agreed. "Mr. Monk was new to the river then. I taught him about it . . . a bit."

Fitz smiled, as if the thought was pleasing to him. "And he made you go to school, I imagine?"

"Yeah. I hated it at first, but then it wasn't so bad."

"So you're working up from the ranks, as it were." That was an observation, not a question. Fitz was staring at the ceiling. "Sometimes it's the best way. You'll have to learn the theory, but reality is the best teacher. Just don't ever get to the point where you think you know it all."

"Did you really know Hester out there, in the war?"

"Yes." Fitz's voice was far away. When Scuff looked at him, Fitz was staring at the line where the wall met the ceiling. The lamp was turned low, so he could not have seen much, but he was concentrating as if he could see lots of things, and there was a great sadness in the lines of his face.

"Did she do doctoring too?" Scuff could not help asking. When would he ever meet anyone else who could tell him?

"Oh, yes. Not in the hospitals. The doctors wouldn't have let that happen. But out on the fields there were hundreds of wounded sometimes, lying all over the ground, so you had to pick your way between them. See who you could possibly save. No time to ask anyone's permission. Please God you never see anything like a battlefield. It's the most terrible sight on earth. The only things worse are the sound of men in agony, and the smell. Blood . . . and death. Death has its own smell." He abruptly stopped talking.

Scuff wanted to say something, but he couldn't think what that would be. He wasn't sure that Fitz was even talking to him. Perhaps he was just remembering. He lay still for a while, but Fitz did not say anything more. His eyes were still open, but he was silent.

Scuff found himself blinking. His eyes stung, as if there were dust in them. He turned over to be a bit more comfortable, and the next moment he was asleep.

HE WOKE UP WITH a start to find it daylight already. He could see faintly blue sky beyond the window. Fitz was half propped up on the other bed. His eyes were closed, but his body was tensed and tears were running down his face, gray-white in the early light.

Scuff had no idea what to do. He could see the man's distress as clearly as if he had been sobbing openly, and yet it appeared that he was still asleep and this was the result of some appalling dream. Scuff was a bystander, observing what was acutely private. Yet he was also the passerby who should stop and help. Which was worse, to intrude or to pretend not to have seen, because you had no idea what to do?

Was it a present agony that caused such grief? Or was it something haunting him from the past, even the past as many years ago as the war, and a thousand miles away in that peninsula that stretched off Russia down into the Black Sea? Hester had shown it to Scuff on the map, and traced the route she had gone, by sea, to reach the port of Sebastopol.

Fitz groaned as though a physical pain racked him, and Scuff saw that his hand, lying beside him, was clenched until the knuckles were pale.

Scuff got up and reached for his trousers. He was just pulling them on when Fitz let out a gasp, and then a long moan of despair. It was so filled with pain that Scuff could not let it be. He went over and put his hand on Fitz's. It was as hard as bone, as if his fingers had no flesh at all.

"Dr. Fitz!" he said very clearly.

Fitz opened his eyes. For a moment he could not seem to focus, then slowly he looked at Scuff and the life returned. He blinked several times.

Scuff scrambled for something to say.

"Would you like a cup of tea, sir? I'm just going to see if Crow's all right, an' how poor Tibor is doing. I daresay he'll need more of that wine heating up, if he has to . . ."

Fitz blinked. "Yes . . . Yes, of course. Tibor . . . the dressings. Yes, I'd like a cup of tea. Make it strong, if you please." He looked up and down at Scuff, as if trying to place him. Was he looking for a soldier's uniform? Had his nightmare taken him back to the war?

"I'll get it for you, sir," Scuff said. "And I'll tell you how Tibor is doing. I expect Crow will need a bit of a break."

"Yes . . ." Fitz blinked. "Yes, of course he will." He pushed the fair hair off his brow and seemed to be collecting his wits.

"There's water over there." Scuff pointed to the big ewer and the basin in the corner. Then he went out of the room and into the big clinic space, where Crow sat looking haggard. His hair had fallen over his brow, black as the bird for which he was named.

"Cup o' tea, sir?" Scuff offered.

Crow nodded. "And pull the cheap wine over onto the heat. We'll need to change the dressings." He straightened up a bit, moving stiffly. "How's Fitz?"

Scuff kept his back to Crow and walked over to the stove. "All right, I think. I'll get us all a pot of tea."

"Good."

Ten minutes later Fitz came into the main room. He was very pale, but composed. He had not shaved, because he had no razor with him, but he was washed and dressed, his hair combed. He spoke calmly and accepted a cup of hot tea from Scuff, then consulted with Crow as to what to do next for the patient.

They began by taking off the dressings, carefully unwinding the bandages and lifting them away. Scuff could see that they were stained with a yellowish serum, but there was little leakage of blood, and the flesh had not the odor of death. Tibor himself had his face turned away. He was not ready yet to look at the wound and see that his arm was no longer there. That time would come.

Fitz talked to him gently all the time Crow was working.

"Scuff!"

"Yes, sir?"

"I need a potion for Tibor," Crow directed. "Get out for me the best claret again, cinchona bark, and Hoffman's Anodyne Liquor. I'll come and mix it in the right proportions. But you make a note, for future use. When it's ready, I'll go and catch a little sleep." He blinked as he said it, as though he had grit in his eyes. "Give him a small spoonful every fifteen minutes. You can see the clock. Watch it. If there is any change in him, other than slightly for the better, then you must come and waken me immediately."

"Yes, sir. What do I do if he won't take it?"

"I'll wait with you for the first one—"

"I'll stay," Fitz interrupted. "We'll manage. You must go and sleep." He gave a very slight smile. "We may need you later . . ."

Crow was too exhausted to do anything but agree.

IT WAS A LONG day. Crow slept quite a lot of it. Scuff did exactly as he had been told, and all the time Tibor was awake, Fitz talked to him in Hungarian. It seemed to encourage him greatly. He accepted a spoonful of the liquor every fifteen minutes, except once when he was sleeping so deeply that, after checking his pulse and his breathing, Fitz told Scuff not to bother.

Early in the afternoon Crow came back, washed and shaved and wearing a clean shirt. It was pretty thoroughly worn and patched in places, but he looked much better.

Before he did anything for himself, he looked carefully at Tibor and told Scuff to prepare more camphorated wine, mixed with bark.

Scuff knew the proportions because he had done it before, for other deep wounds. Next he made a good broth and seasoned it with cinnamon and cloves. When Tibor had taken that, he gave him a glass of the better claret.

"Now we must wash him," Crow went on. "Make him more comfortable. I'll prepare etherized vinegar. You get the flannel we have and put it in the lower oven to be thoroughly warmed. We will need it so that at no time is he chilled. You know how to do that."

"Yes, sir."

As the afternoon moved into evening, Crow gave the patient an enema made with a decoction of cinchona, strongly camphorated, while Scuff changed the bed to make him clean and comfortable for the night.

By dark, Tibor seemed to be resting quite well. Fitz went out and bought food for the night and the following day. When he returned Crow told Scuff that he should go home to Paradise Place for the night, and return by nine o'clock the next morning.

"Thank you, sir," Scuff said, accepting with profound gratitude. He would have stayed if Crow had asked him, but right now he wanted to escape the confines of these rooms, the sight of pain he could not help, the shock of seeing the dead flesh of a limb cut off a living man, and knowing what Tibor's distress would be when he realized fully what had happened to him.

CHAPTER

4

HESTER WAS WORKING QUIETLY in the kitchen in their home at Paradise Place. She had spent some of the day at the clinic in Portpool Lane, which she had started several years ago. The huge, rambling building had been a profitable brothel, which Monk and Sir Oliver Rathbone, their lawyer friend, had acquired almost by chance. Of course there had been a good deal of skill on Rathbone's part as well. They had turned the place into a free clinic for women in trouble, homeless and ill. It was run on charitable donations, and Hester had enlisted the aid of a number of women well placed in Society, and of generous disposition, to elicit the funds. Others actually worked there in person.

The bookkeeping was done by a highly talented, scruffy, eccentric and disreputable man named Squeaky Robinson. It was he who had owned and run the place as a brothel before. Rathbone had allowed him to stay there because his skills were superb and his knowledge of every nefarious art of the street comprehensive. Their trust in him had proved well-placed. Hester had to admit, ruefully, that she had even become fond of him. He was outwardly uncertain of temper, but actually he was extraordinarily loyal. He spoke of respectability as if it were some unmentionable disease, and torture would not have forced him to admit that he treasured it more than any other benefit that running the affairs of the clinic would have brought him. It was even more important to him than the original reward of a home, food and legitimate employment.

Hester herself was not as necessary there as she had been in earlier days. She seldom had to spend nights there now, and some days wasn't needed at all.

She missed Scuff, but it gave her great pleasure that he wanted to practice medicine so intensely that he was prepared to sacrifice even the pretense of independence. She stood at the stove preparing a dinner of lightly cooked vegetables to have with sausages. She had no idea when Monk would be home. This brutal murder in Shadwell was drawing him out early in the morning and keeping him out after dusk, which was a long day in summer. He was exhausted, but any strong leads were eluding him.

Portpool Lane was nearer to the center of London, a long way from Shadwell, or any of the docks. Hester had little idea of the Hungarian community. But she knew prejudice. It was universal. It might be based on race, religion, social class or education, or a dozen other things. It seemed always to stem from a fear of the different, the belief that somehow it threatened one's own safety. The cause could be anything from speech you did not understand—the thought that people were talking about you, laughing at you, planning your downfall somehow—to threats to your job or changes to your familiar neighborhood. Men seemed to fear that the strangers would take their women.

The worst fear of all was that people of another faith would make you question your own belief in your place and value in the world, the old certainties you had grown up with that kept the darkness inside imprisoned where it could not spread and consume you with doubt, until you no longer knew who you were.

Hester was thinking on this while she chopped mint and parsley to put in the potatoes. They were old ones to be mashed; it was a little too early for the small, sweet-tasting new ones. She heard a light footstep outside the back door and the next moment Scuff came in.

She was delighted to see him, but she could not miss the pallor of his face, or the deep smudges of weariness around his eyes. She knew better than to comment on it. He hated fussing. It made him feel as if she thought he was still a child, unable to look after himself. He had let her know that, more than once. He was approximately eighteen, a young man. She had known many soldiers no older than that.

"Hungry?" she asked as casually as she could.

"Yes. I . . . I think so," he replied.

She noticed that he smelled faintly of carbolic and there was a small stain of blood on one of his shirtsleeves. She looked at him more closely.

"It was an operation," he said, taking one of the hard-backed kitchen chairs and sitting astride it, looking at her over the back, his arms folded. "Crow took off a man's arm at the shoulder. It was gangrened. I think he might live."

"And you helped?" She wanted to keep calm, but she remembered with a sudden shock of horror the first time she had encountered gangrene. It was the smell of carbolic that brought it back, strong enough to mask the sharp, sour-sweet odor of dead flesh attached to a living person.

"Yes." He was watching her.

"How did he get so bad?"

"I don't know. He was too ill to say much. And he's Hungarian." He waited to see her reaction to that.

"From the community at Shadwell?" she asked.

"Don't know. The thing is . . . he hardly speaks any English at all." His face was very pale. She noticed how blue his eyes were.

She waited.

"Crow said to me that we had, at the very least, to tell him that we had to take his arm off, if he had any chance to live. And it would be better for him if there was someone who could speak to him properly while we did it . . ."

"So you found someone from the Hungarian community?"

"Yes. But he is actually English. He speaks like you . . ." He stopped, waiting to see her reaction. It seemed the natural thing to do.

"What is it?" she asked. "There's something else. Has it to do with the murder in Shadwell?"

"Not that I know of. But the man I found is a doctor too, a real military doctor, from the Crimea. He knows you."

"Knows me?" The room seemed to fade to a small, bright spot where the lowering sun came in through the window, onto Scuff's head. How young his cheek was, barely showing soft, fine hairs where his fair beard was hardly worth shaving, and the tiredness of his eyes, hollowed around with pity and exhaustion. "Are you sure?" she asked, then immediately knew how pointless that was. She had known most of the many doctors in the Crimea, those who survived and those who were lost.

"Yes." Scuff was still watching her. "He said his name was Herbert Fitzherbert. That's not just any kind of a name . . . You do know him!"

He must have seen the shock in her face, flooding around her like an incoming wave that knocks you off balance and sucks you under.

"Yes, I did . . . but he was lost at Inkerman. I saw him myself. There were so many dead, but some were beyond recognition." She stopped. She did not want the memories of overwhelming death, broken bodies of men and horses, blood and flies everywhere. Friends and strangers. A line of Byron came to her, very much unbidden, of Waterloo: "in one red burial blent." She certainly did not want Scuff ever to imagine what it had been like.

"He said to call him Fitz. He talks like you. He's a bit taller than I am, fair hair and a face that's . . . full of thought. He doesn't smile much, but I think he sees a kind of amusement in things that other people don't. I can't really describe him . . ."

She had a flash of memory of Fitz in uniform, looking out of place among the dashing red-coated soldiers with sabers at their sides, early in the war, before the battle at Balaclava and the slaughter there. Before the killing winters when men froze to death. He looked like a man playing at soldiers, to please his friends. He could see the joke of it that they could not. But it was wistful, even then. The joke was not funny, only dismal, and eventually tragic.

"Yes, that's Fitz," she answered, refocusing her vision to the present. "We thought he'd been killed."

"Well, he wasn't," Scuff said. "He said he'd come back across Europe. Spent some time in Hungary; that's how he spoke their language. He seemed to speak it easily. As if he could think in Hungarian."

The memory almost overwhelmed her: even in the exhaustion of that day, her grief at Fitz's death had been sharper than all the rest. She did not want Scuff to know that.

"You have to, if you're going to speak it well," she agreed. She wanted to know what had happened to Fitz, how he was, if he was safe—well, all kinds of things. But the recollection of that day returned to her as if it had been only weeks ago. It was all clear again.

She had been helping the stretcher-bearers find anyone still living, and perhaps savable. She had turned the men over, gently, trying not to tear open wounds already terrible. She had not even recognized him when she removed the body half covering him and seen his face. He was motionless, eyes closed, drenched in blood. She touched him, and he was cold. It was only when she wiped his face that she knew him, and a wave of grief came over her, so intense that for moments she could not move.

It was the orderly who broke the nightmare, and made it real. She could hear his voice now. "You can't 'elp that one, miss. 'E's gone. God rest 'im. But there's one more 'ere we can mebbe save."

And she had gone, rising to her feet and staggering after the orderly, hardly knowing what she was doing. Somewhere there was a man they might save. They must be quick. Concentrate on the moment. There would be time for grieving afterward.

And she had grieved, along with everyone else. She recalled the long nights on duty out in the open when she had been so cold that her hands were numb and her bones ached. They had made ridiculous jokes and laughed too hard, because their world was all touched with absurdity and desperation. In her mind she relived one evening after a battle, sharing the last of the water out of a leather flask and a couple of stale army biscuits. Fitz had raised the flask and given some elaborate toast, as if it were the best brandy, and smiled at her. She had amused him with something that sounded funny at the time. They had laughed, until he had turned away, tears in his eyes. She had said nothing. It was a friendship that defied words. All the things that could not be said were understood anyway.

None of it could be shared with anyone else. She had buried it in her mind, along with most of the other things about the Crimean War that had to be left behind. She had a new life, with gifts beyond price.

She looked up at Scuff, searched his face and saw that he was struggling to say something also, or perhaps uncertain whether to say it or not.

"Is he all right?" she asked. "I really thought he was . . . dead." Bland words, but what else was there to say?

"I don't think so," he answered almost under his breath. "I don't know. He helped us, and he was good. His hands were . . . good hands, delicate . . . if you know what I mean. I think he could take forceps and pick up a single hair. Or stitch so beautifully it wouldn't matter if it showed . . ." He stopped, unsatisfied with what he had said.

"That's Fitz," she agreed. "Did he sew up the wound?"

"No . . . Crow did that. He did it all. Fitz said he doesn't do much medicine anymore. Hester . . ."

She waited. She could feel the beating of her heart as if it were a dull knocking inside her, impatient.

"When I saw him this morning, when I woke up . . . Crow had sat up with Tibor all night . . . until five. Then Fitz and I took over."

"When you woke up, what?"

"I don't know if Fitz was awake or asleep, and dreaming. But there were tears on his face. I think something hurt him too much."

"I think you're right," she replied. "It happens . . ." She had seen it in the Crimea, and since. There are things you can't share, except with those others who were part of it. The people at home don't want to know. They can't take it away from you; they can only feel useless. There are not words created to describe the horror of some things. And why would you want to burden them with it anyway? They cannot help, and they cannot carry it for you. The only ones who need to know are the authorities who by their ignorance create it. And they refuse to believe. Emotionally, they cannot afford to. Their guilt would disable them.

She fell back on the truths she knew from long familiarity. "You need to eat," she told him. "I imagine you still have . . . Tibor, did you say? . . . You still have him at Crow's clinic?"

"Yes. I'm going back tomorrow morning. Fitz is staying there to help tonight."

"Of course. I'd have been surprised if you'd told me he left."

"You liked him, didn't you?"

"Yes. I liked a lot of people. In times and places like that, you find the best in people . . . and sometimes the worst, though not often. Even if you aren't hungry, you should eat. If you don't, you'll only wake up in the night and want something then."

He smiled. He had known that was exactly what she would say. And the vegetables did smell very good. If she put sausages with that—and he knew they would be in the oven still hot—it would be really good.

"Yes," he agreed. He tried to make it sound like a concession to her, but the look on her face said she did not believe it for a moment.

It was not long afterward that Monk came home, also too tired to do anything but eat and then sit back in silence. He asked how Scuff's day had been, but was willing to accept a simple answer.

After Scuff had gone to bed, Monk woke up a little.

"Anything further on the Hungarian murder?" Hester asked him. She did not need to elaborate. They had discussed the murder in Shadwell either obliquely or directly every day. The newspapers were speaking of it less now than they had five days ago, but the demands for answers from the police became more shrill with each new edition.

"No," he replied. "We've got endless documentation of where everyone was at the time it must have happened. But people lie for all sorts of reasons, and plenty of accounts are simply errors about the time. People defend the ones they love. Because they don't know they're innocent, they just can't believe they could be guilty, so they think they know. I might do the same. They're just decent people like anyone else, only a little more afraid because they're strangers here, even those who've been in London for years."

She knew he was thinking of himself as well. He very seldom spoke of it anymore, but he had no memory and therefore very little idea where he had spent most of his life. He had deduced it from what other people said. He understood the sense of having lost roots more than perhaps any other policeman in London could.

But she also knew he would not want to discuss it.

"You said the murder was very savage . . ." she began.

"Yes. It wasn't a robbery. Nothing was taken. And the violence used was far beyond what was necessary to kill him. And other things: the broken fingers, the candles dipped in blood, the torn letter—all done after he was dead."

She shivered. "Is that part of some ritual? Something Hungarians would know but we don't? Something from their history, maybe, that would give it meaning?"

"Not that anyone will tell me."

She watched him as he stood up and walked over to the window. It was dark, and time to draw the curtains. There was a tiredness in him she had not seen for some time. She should have been looking more closely. The failure after several days to find a good lead was depressing at any time, but it seemed—not from what he said but from what he had not said—that these people, torn up from their roots and trying to build new lives with so little to start from, mirrored the feeling he had had himself not so very long ago.

She watched him draw the curtain across, shutting out the night, and she longed to comfort him. But she knew the fact that she had seen his vulnerability would hurt him all the more.

"Is this Dobokai any use?" she asked as casually as she could.

"Yes," he answered after he had turned around to face her and begun returning to his seat. "But I can't afford to trust him. I'm double-checking everything. If I read him correctly, he thinks the answer could lie with an Englishman called Haldane, who's married to a Hungarian. A rather handsome woman."

"Does Fodor's murder have anything to do with him being Hungarian?"

"I really don't know. They're different in culture and in beliefs. And there's the assumption that they favor their own."

"Don't they? If I were settling in a new country, with almost nothing, I'd favor my own too," she pointed out.

"Yes, I've noticed," he said with only an edge of sarcasm.

Then she saw he was smiling.

"Well, they aren't exactly my own at the clinic . . ." she started. "Except that they are other women . . ."

He laughed. It had a raw edge, but it was still laughter.

She did not say anything more. She would leave it a little while, and then talk of something else. She longed to be able to go over and put her arms around him, but that would seem too much like pity just then. Even Scuff would have resented it. You give that kind of comfort to children and animals. Not to men, however much they actually want it. She would eventually, but she would choose the time.

"Scuff did very well today," she said in a little while. "He assisted with an amputation."

"Really?" Monk sat more upright.

"Yes. An arm. Gangrene. He's learning such a lot. I was afraid at first that Crow was taking him on out of kindness, but not now."

"How did a man come to get gangrene bad enough to lose an arm?" Monk asked.

"I don't know. He is Hungarian, and Scuff can't tell us. At least not yet. But if he knows anything, he'll come and tell you. As long as it's not a confidence from his patient. If—"

"I know," he said across her. "You're proud of him, aren't you."

It was not a question, it was an observation, but she answered anyway. "Yes, I am. Enormously."

"But that's not why you told me. Another Hungarian . . . What sort of accident was it?"

"I don't know." Now she understood what he meant. "But I'll ask Scuff to find out. The thing is, Scuff told me that an old friend of mine, a colleague at the hospital in Scutari, a man I thought was dead, is helping Crow . . ." Hester leaned forward in her chair, eager to explain all about Fitz and to share the extraordinary news that he was now living in Shadwell.

IN THE MORNING SHE offered to go to see Crow, and particularly to take him fresh supplies of some of the things she knew he would need. She had seen enough amputations to know how closely they needed care in the first few days. Crow would have little time for going out at all. And she had never asked him whether any of his patients had ever been able to pay him. She was quite aware that not many would have been, and it never made a difference to the care he gave. She would give him at least half of the supplies without telling him the price.

She put off thinking what she would do if Fitz was still at the clinic—if indeed it really was he. It sounded so like him—and the name was so distinctive—it was hard to imagine how it could be anyone else.

The war had ended fourteen years ago. Had he really been wandering around somewhere in Europe for much of that time? Her life had changed so dramatically in the same years. She had returned from Sebastopol determined to revolutionize nursing in England. She had learned so much. She knew all Miss Nightingale's principles of fresh air and cleanliness. Like her, Hester had little patience with regulations whose misguidedness cost lives, and untold pain that was too often completely unnecessary.

And, also like Florence Nightingale, much of her effort had been ignored or contradicted. Finally she had made herself unemployable because she argued, and at times lost her temper.

Her personal grief perhaps had something to do with it. She had arrived back in England and gone straight to her family home. She knew her eldest brother, James, had been killed in the Crimea; that he had died bravely and unnecessarily, like so many. What she had not known until she returned was that her father had invested money in one of the most vile confidence tricks imaginable. When he had lost it all, and the friends he had counseled had lost their money too, he felt that there was no honorable course open to him but to take his own life.

Charles, the younger brother, had been unable to prevent it, or to save their mother from dying of distress.

Hester had not been there to help. In his own agony, Charles had blamed her for being absent when she was so desperately needed. Her strength of will might have saved them all.

She had not spoken to Charles for years now. She could think of nothing useful to say. How could she explain her experience in the Crimea to him, the dedication to nursing, the call to go and do whatever she could, rather than stay at home and marry suitably? They had never seen the world in the same light. And all the grief or regret would change nothing. She did not want to quarrel with him. He had been there through all the pain, and done what he could. It helped nothing to go over it again.

She hoped he was happy. Hester could not recall if she had ever tried to tell him how happy she herself was. He would hardly approve of Monk. Another quarrel she did not want. Probably Charles would deplore her more-or-less adoption of a mudlark off the Thames banks.

If this really was Fitz, how could she tell him she had truly believed him among the dead in that wretched battle that had killed so many? It was nearly sixteen years ago, but she could remember snatches of it quite vividly. The noise of gunfire, the shouting, the screaming of men and animals terribly wounded. Three times she had stopped searching for men, in order to put a horse out of its agony. She hated doing it. Even now the memory made her feel sick.

Fitz had been doing the same while the last few shots of the battle went on, rescuing whomever he could. This was no time to wait for the last retreat. She could see his face in her mind's eye, haggard from weariness and the endless, pointless destruction. People with whom you had shared a biscuit or a can of coffee for breakfast now lay mangled on the ground. Sometimes they were still alive. She could not always tell the scarlet of blood from the scarlet of a tunic. Which was the reason for the color, of course, just as with the red gun decks on the warships of Nelson's day.

Her memories were rambling, avoiding recalling the moment when she had found him—his body. But what did the past matter now . . . if Fitz was actually alive?

She reached Crow's clinic and went in. There was a woman cleaning the floors, her long-handled mop in her hands and a large bucket of water on the floor. It smelled like carbolic. Perhaps she was paying her debt to Crow in the only way she could.

"Good morning," Hester said with a smile.

The woman smiled back but did not speak, just quietly resumed her work.

Hester found Crow in the main room, and standing beside him was a man a little less tall, fair-haired and clean-shaven. His face was very pale, and his eyes were tired; only his smile was exactly as she had remembered it.

"Hello, Hester," he said. His voice was instantly familiar, as if the last time they had spoken had been only days ago.

"Hello, Fitz," she answered, her mouth dry. "Scuff told me you had been here helping."

"Ah, Scuff. Fine boy. He's going to be a good doctor one day. He knows how to learn."

Hester put the basket down and looked at Crow. "I've brought you a few extra supplies. I thought there would be things you might run short of."

Crow's expression was touched with humor. "Of course. You've seen more amputations than I ever will. Thank you."

"How is he this morning?" she asked.

"Good manners, or professional opinion?" Crow's eyebrows rose.

"You want my professional opinion?" She did not want to intrude. Fitz was well experienced, although perhaps not in caring for men with all the time in the world, and a good chance they might live. At least the patient would not be infected with cholera or dysentery here. Those, and starvation rations, or the cold, had been responsible for more deaths than enemy gunfire.

She looked at Crow, meeting his eyes. Was he waiting to show off his success? Or was he concerned that not all was well? A moment's consideration convinced her it was the latter.

"Yes. Of course."

She followed him into the room where the patient sat slightly propped up on the pillows of a wooden bed. Scuff was by his side and he looked up the moment he heard them come in. He was clearly relieved to see Hester.

"He's a bit feverish," he said to Crow. "Came on just ten minutes ago." He knew enough to be exact.

Crow strode over and looked earnestly at Tibor for several seconds, then touched his brow. He turned to Fitz.

Fitz joined him, regarded Tibor carefully, then also touched his face.

"I think we need to look at the wound again. Something is not well."

"Can I help?" Hester offered.

"Yes, please." Both men spoke together.

Hester went to the sink, washed her hands and told Scuff to make sure the camphorated wine was hot but not simmering. He had done it before, and did not need further instructions.

The patient was now distinctly feverish, beginning to toss and turn a little in his bed. It was necessary to restrain him to prevent unnecessary pain or further injury when they removed the bandages. This Fitz did.

Crow unwound the bandages. As soon as they were off, it was obvious that the wound was bleeding again—fresh, bright red blood. Instinctively, he looked at Hester. He had not dealt with a gangrenous limb amputation before. He knew she had. He would assume Fitz had too, but he had only just met him. Hester was the one who had long stood by him and finally had persuaded him that, in spite of his past troubles and sometime failures, he was a good doctor and could get his formal qualifications.

Hester looked at the wound. She too knew what Fitz had done in the past, but not what had happened in the intervening years. He was an intensely familiar stranger. They had been as close as two people can be who have faced death and fought it side by side, and dealt with both victory and defeat. But that was years ago. She had no idea what had happened to him since then, except that the mark of it was imprinted deeply in the pain of his face, the uncertainty in his eyes.

"We must clean out the wound," she said calmly. "And find which vessel is still bleeding, and stitch it. He seems to be recovering, but he is very weak." She looked up at Crow. "Are his organs working?"

"Yes," Crow replied without hesitation. "I gave him an enema of cinchona, camphorated. He evacuated several stools overnight. And he had no pain or difficulty in passing urine. He seemed to be doing well."

"He is," Hester assured him. "But we must find the source of this bleeding. There is a vessel that has broken its ligature somewhere." She looked across at Fitz.

He was smiling at her, but there was pain in whatever memory it was that stirred in his mind.

"Do you wish me to tell Tibor?" he asked. "Or are you asking me if I agree? Didn't Scuff tell you? I haven't dealt with this sort of thing for years."

"The wounds are the same," she answered. "And the bodies. If medicine has changed, it isn't much. The American Civil War has taught us a bit, so I have read. But for most of us, in war or not, it's much the same as it has been since the Napoleonic Wars. That's longer than I've been alive—just!"

"But you're—" Fitz began, then stopped himself abruptly. "Yes— that's longer ago than I wish to think of."

She wished to know what had happened to him. Perhaps she wanted to explain that she had thought he was dead.

Or maybe she did not want to tell him after all. What was there to say? Friends in war were not always friends in peacetime afterward.

She turned instead to Scuff, who was standing a little behind her, waiting.

"I'm going to look for the vein and see if I can tie it, but I must be quick. He will not survive a long painful ordeal. Mix me *colophonia*"— she watched his eyes to be certain he understood—"with powder of bark. And when I have it, prepare the draft of stomachic you gave him yesterday evening. Bring me also a small amount of good wine and, separately, in a spoon, a gram and a half of opium. Be absolutely exact."

Scuff nodded and went to obey.

"Now we must find the bleed and tie it," she said, looking first at Crow, then at Fitz.

Fitz hesitated.

Crow offered him the forceps.

Fitz waited another moment, then stretched out his hand.

Perhaps Crow did not notice it, but Hester did. There was a very slight tremor, even before he touched the metal. He hesitated, then withdrew his hand.

Hester knew she had not imagined it.

"I'll do it," she said quietly. "You've been up all night." That was irrelevant, and she knew it. In the Crimea many of them worked all day and all night, and all the next day, with only catnaps now and then. There was so much to ask him, and to explain. But there was no time yet, and she did not want it to sound like excuses. Memories were muddled, exhaustion blurred times and events and left only emotion— grief—and now guilt as well. She should have had them take him anyway, even across someone's back, not leave him there with all the other dead.

"It would be good if you could talk to him," she said. "I don't know that he can hear. Let him know what we are doing, and that he is recovering and it will be all right. I can't do that—not in Hungarian anyway."

Fitz was not looking at her. "I will," he agreed, and immediately began speaking to Tibor in a soft voice. She had no idea what he was saying, but she saw Tibor turn his head slightly toward him.

She opened the flap of skin covering the wound and very delicately began to explore to see where the blood was coming from.

It did not take her long to find the bleed. It was in a small vessel, thank heaven, not a minor artery. She told Scuff to get her the needle, already threaded. One more swab to see clearly, and then she tied it off.

She left it for Crow to swab the wound again, then close the skin over it. With Scuff's help, he rebandaged it with some lint soaked in *colophonia* and bark.

She looked at her own hand. It was perfectly steady, but her stomach felt anything but. What she had done took her memory straight back to the battlefield, when she'd had to do such things because there was no surgeon, and no time to waste. There was no risk to measure. If she did nothing, the man would die. All around was chaos, the living and the dying side by side. Some cried out; others lay silently. There was still smoke in the air, and the smell of horse sweat, gunpowder and blood. She did not want to remember it, any of it, and yet she felt like a traitor in deliberately choosing to forget.

Someone was talking to her. It was Scuff.

She turned to him.

"Cup o' tea?" he offered. "Or would you rather some wine? I can find some of the decent stuff that doesn't smell of camphor."

"Tea, thank you." He was inches taller than she was now, and still growing. She looked up at him very slightly and smiled. He could not even imagine what was in her mind. Please heaven, he never would.

Fitz was still talking to the patient, calling him by name. There was a little color in Tibor's face and he seemed to be out of the worst of his distress.

Five minutes later the three of them were sitting at the table reserved for eating. It was warm near the stove, but they all seemed chilled and no one wished to move away.

"I think he'll rest better tonight," Crow said to no one in particular.

Hester sipped her tea. It was very hot indeed and far too strong and sweet, but she knew it was intended to be medicinal. Scuff knew she usually drank it far differently from this. It made her smile.

"Have you something for Tibor to eat?" she asked.

"Good broth," Crow replied. "We quite often get paid in bones, and we always keep barley."

Fitz was silent. There was a strange, pensive look in his face, without the touch of humor she remembered as nearly always being there. Now it flashed only occasionally, and was gone almost as soon as it came. What had happened to him in the years of crossing Europe? Had he belonged anywhere, even for a while?

"Hester?" It was Crow's voice recalling her to the present, his face filled with concern.

"I'm sorry. I was just . . . thinking Scuff had better stay here with you tonight, just to watch Tibor—"

"I'll stay," Fitz cut in. Then he looked at Crow questioningly.

"Thank you." Crow accepted without hesitation.

Hester saw the play of emotions across Scuff's face: relief, disappointment, doubt as to the reason he was allowed to leave. Was he less useful?

Crow understood. "We'll need you tomorrow," he told him. "Don't know when that fever could begin again. He's improving, but it's a long way to go yet. And we'll need more supplies. I'll give you some money. We'll need more cinchona bark, and a lot more camphor—we're going through it rapidly. And more bones, with some meat on them, to make broth. And bread. We've little enough for ourselves to eat. Can you carry all that?"

Scuff gave him a withering look. But his reply was civil enough.

They were all weary. Hester bade them good night, and she and Scuff took their leave and walked together as far as the ferry across to their own side of the river.

It was almost dark, and the air had a softness to it, even though it was damp with the breath of salt, and a dozen other things she barely noticed anymore: the fish, the tar, the estuary mud when the tide was low enough to expose the shingle.

Neither of them spoke, but it was the silence of comfort, not of unease.

They were standing at the dockside waiting for the ferry crossing toward them when Scuff spoke.

"Was he a really good surgeon?" he said at last.

"Yes." He had been one of the best. "Not just his skill," Hester went on. "But he never gave up. He told me once that he got over his fear of being shot or killed himself by concentrating on the wounded, and trying to think of new ways to help the shock of injury. That was what killed a lot of people . . ."

Scuff understood. "You mean body shock, not surprise."

"Yes. He was always steady, even when we were fired on, which happened occasionally, not very often. He always sounded as if he wasn't afraid, and he knew what was going to happen. A lot of people survived because of him."

Scuff thought for a few moments.

The ferry was still far away, not making much headway against the current's sideways pull.

"I'm not sure I would like that kind of responsibility," he said finally. "What if I'm wrong? Then nobody'll believe me again."

"If they were badly wounded, you wouldn't get the same people again. Just survive this moment, save this patient, or if you can't, at least ease his pain. Above all, ease his fear. Don't let him die alone, if you can help it." Memory swamped her as she spoke those words.

Images crowded her mind. She remembered a wooden cart piled high with bodies, horses straining to pull it up a stony road on a hill. Three times they had got stuck. One body had fallen off, and they had taken minutes to get him on again. The wind had cut like ice, and her feet kept slipping.

They had reached the hospital at last, most of the wounded still alive. They had carried them in as gently as they could, to the overcrowded wards. Was it even worth the fight? The odor of human waste caused by cholera and typhoid was heavy in the air. In the end, disease had killed more than sword or gunfire.

She did not want to remember it. Even the fellowship did not make up for the loss. They had laughed at ridiculous things together, not really funny, just absurd. They had cared for each other; it was the only sanity left to them.

What had happened to all those women she had truly believed she would never forget? And yet she had forgotten. They were tied to a past she did not ever willingly recall. Living now meant burying that and locking the door on it, like a cellar one would never enter again. Place a piece of furniture across to hide it.

Was that a betrayal? Or was going back to it a betrayal of the life and the gifts of the present?

Scuff was standing beside her. She knew he was watching her face. He had his own memories of cold and hunger, and loneliness. She put out her hand and took his. She felt his fingers close over hers. His hands were bigger than hers now, but they weres still smooth-skinned, always clean: the hands of a doctor.

OVER THE NEXT TWO days Hester went to see Crow and Tibor several times. Crow spent most of his time there, and, more often than not, Fitz was there also. Tibor had one more episode that put him on the edge of death. The fever returned, and in his twisting and turning on the bed he must have torn something loose. He began to bleed badly again.

Crow was taking a rare sleep, and as if by long instinct, Fitz tore off the bandage and dressings, now soaked in blood. Hester had ammonia and many cloths and bandages ready.

Fitz put his hands into the wound, talking all the time, whether Tibor could hear him or not. Even Hester found the sound of his voice soothing as she struggled to keep the wound clear enough for him to see what he was doing. She felt with him, as if her fingers were exploring the open wound looking for the abscess that might be the cause of this infection.

He looked up at her briefly, then bent his head again. He moved his hands very slightly, delicately. His face reflected total concentration.

"Got it," he said after what seemed an age but was actually perhaps two seconds. It was a large abscess discharging a considerable amount of purulent matter, mixed with a black substance.

She watched, holding her breath. She saw Fitz's fingers dig deeper, under the pectoral muscle. He glanced up and met Hester's eyes, certainty in his.

"I've got it. A fistula. Big one. If we clean it out, I think we'll find the orifice of the artery that's still bleeding. Scuff?"

"Yes, sir!" Scuff was there at his elbow.

"Thread me one of the curved needles. I'll need it to reach in here and put a ligature on it. I'll need a sponge to clean it out, then pledgets of soft linen. Sprinkle them with camphor and bark powder. You know how to do it. Have them ready. Then I want a new dressing, and a cordial draft, if he can take it. It's going to be a long night . . . if he survives this."

Scuff disappeared to do as he was instructed.

Hester watched and assisted as she could, but it looked as if it might well be useless. Tibor's face was almost bloodless and he was scarcely breathing. She took his pulse, but it was fluttering and hard to find.

Fitz finished the last bandage.

"Stimulants," he said to Scuff. "Want a little cordial ready if he should stir enough to take it."

Scuff obeyed. When he came back a few seconds later, Fitz applied the warm etherized cloths to Tibor's body.

Several times Hester drew in breath to say it was pointless, but she knew Fitz would decide that for himself.

Scuff watched from a few feet away. She wondered how she would comfort him when Tibor finally died. He might feel like a child inside, confused and defeated by the failure, but he would not appreciate being treated like one.

And what about Fitz? He had done all anyone could, and more than most would have tried, but that would be of no comfort to him. Would he see it as his own failure? Would it add to the devastation inside him?

They kept working at the very gentle friction, adding a little warmth, for ten minutes with no apparent good.

No one spoke.

Hester glanced across at Scuff. His face was tense and pale. She knew he had to learn all these things, including that, even after doing everything you could, people might still die. You felt cold and guilty, but there was no time for self-indulgence. It would be at the cost of your attention to the next person, whose pain was also real and who needed you now.

She turned to Tibor. Should she tell Fitz to stop?

Tibor's eyes opened and he took a deep breath. He was frightened, but he was very definitely awake.

"Cordial," Hester said to Scuff.

He poured it carefully, grinning like a child at Christmas.

Very gently Hester lifted Tibor up enough for him to sip the cordial, and a few moments later a faint color returned to his cheeks.

Fitz nodded, his eyes calm, as if he had known all the time that it would work. Then the laughter was there, at himself. He took a glass of good claret from Scuff and knocked it back as if it were whisky. But when he put the glass down his hand was shaking, just a tremor, but enough for Hester to see it.

5

MONK WAS FAR TOO proud of Scuff to let him know just how much. He was aware of how hard it would be for him, both intellectually and emotionally, to succeed in such a challenging profession. Scuff had had the strictest of all early upbringings, surviving on his own from, as far as Monk could tell, about the age of six. The punishment for failure was death. Only God knew how many children died from the cold, or of hunger that robbed them of the strength to overcome even mild illnesses.

But that was a far cry from the rigors of learning facts about the human body and how it reacted to disease, injury and medicine.

Yet Monk was also, after the initial response, glad that Scuff had not wanted to follow him into the River Police. The questions there would be entirely different. It was hard enough to watch any of his men be attacked, hurt or, on rare occasions, killed. Could he do it in the case of the closest thing he had to a child? Would he have overcompensated and made it more difficult for Scuff than for any other new recruit?

Monk was a brilliant detective; he could acknowledge that without immodesty. His skill in leading men, disciplining them, inspiring their loyalty, was a much more questionable matter. In his early days he had been unmanageable, until not even his many successes were enough to keep him from being dismissed. Looking back now, after having to lead men himself, he thought they had been very patient with him, more than he was prepared to be with anyone else.

A young man with Monk's brilliance and Hester's instinct and courage would be superb. But Scuff was not theirs by birth. He would have to survive with his own gifts, and all the encouragement they could give him.

He asked Scuff about the progress of the Hungarian patient whose arm had been amputated, but only out of his care for Scuff and Hester. His mind was more deeply absorbed in the growing difficulty of solving the murder of Imrus Fodor. Now, a little more than a week after his death, Monk had a welter of knowledge about the whole community. It meant he could exclude many people as suspects, which was better than nothing, but he still had little idea even of why Fodor had been killed, let alone by whom.

Monk was at his desk at the River Police Station in Wapping. The air was cool and clear this early, the light slanting across the floor through the open doorway, reflected from the ripples as the high tide reached just beyond the dock edge.

Hooper was in early too.

"No one admits to knowing anything about a ritual with candles and blood," Hooper said, as he knocked and stepped into Monk's office. "Or broken fingers," he added. "Other than the obvious. He touched something he shouldn't have. Speared through the chest could mean anything. It missed the heart. Bad anatomy, or bad aim?" His smile had a bleak humor to it. There was something unreadable in Hooper, a well of deep thought Monk did not understand, but he trusted his own judgment of character. He also respected others' privacy.

Hooper was one of the very few people to whom Monk had confessed his own lack of any past he could recall, good or bad. He had been forced to when he feared there was a grudge held against him that would endanger his men. He did not want to lie to Hooper, but he also could not afford to.

Monk had told him about the coach accident fourteen years earlier, in 1856, just after the Crimean War. It had wiped out all his memory of the past. He had rebuilt a career, a life, but the unknown still haunted him. Even then, he had been forced to admit all this to Hooper by circumstance. It had not been a willing confidence.

Hooper had never mentioned it again.

"I hate relying on Dobokai for so much," Monk said with feeling. "But it would take me twice as long without him."

"Haven't caught him in a lie," Hooper said. "And I've tried. I've cross-checked everything I can." He looked down at the papers in front of him, then up again at Monk. There was anxiety in his face, and distaste. "Do you think this violence is against the Hungarians, sir? Are they really threatening anybody? You might avoid them, not use their shops or cafés, not let them into your clubs or taverns. But this is . . . rage! Fury right out of control. You don't just go and skewer somebody through the heart like that, break his fingers and dip candles in his blood, unless you hate him so much you've . . . lost your mind."

"I know," Monk agreed. "I've been looking for something so . . . visceral . . . it started a hate like that. Whatever it is, nobody is speaking of it."

"A secret society?" Hooper suggested. "Something that began in Hungary, before they even came here?"

"Possible," Monk agreed. "But what started it again here, now? Are they all lying to us? Or is it something only a few of them know about? I've got the dates each of them arrived, or at least what they say."

"They don't all come from the same part of Hungary," Hooper pointed out. "Or they say they don't."

"A much worse thought than some secret society troubles me." Monk spoke very quietly. "What if the person who did this is one of us and the root of it is some hatred of strangers, immigrants?"

"Why the Hungarians?" Hooper asked, frowning a little. "They're pretty law-abiding. They don't look all that unlike anyone else. There aren't even that many of them, not like thousands! I can't find them cornering any markets, and I've looked. They aren't taking other people's houses, or jobs. Well . . . not many. Bound to be a few. And why now?"

"Always back to that," Monk agreed. "Why now? What happened to make it erupt all of a sudden? We should look for anything that changed. Who died recently? Who lost a child, or a wife?"

"Or a husband?"

"No woman would have the strength to drive a bayonet into a man's chest like that. The man was over six feet tall, and heavy. By the way, do we know where it came from yet?"

"Yes, sir. There's a bit of a museum over on Cable Street. Just a few things from a military collection. One of their bayonets is missing. Didn't notice it at first because they're not in any sort of order. Anyone could have taken it. Rifle's missing the firing pin. Couldn't shoot anyone with it, so they didn't bother to report it. Full of apologies." He gave a twisted smile. "I notice you didn't say that a woman wouldn't have had the *will* to use it."

"I'd rather face an angry man any day than a woman whose child I'd hurt," Monk replied with feeling.

Hooper looked at him. "Or anyone she loved," he added very steadily, without blinking.

Monk was reminded with a sudden sharpness how much Hooper knew about him, about the time he had nearly died in the river when somebody in a boat had mowed him down, almost drowning him and the ferryman. The bruising had lasted many days, and he was lucky not to have had bones broken. Anger and violence can come very quickly, far too easily.

"If we can find what started this, we'll have him," he said. "Back to Dobokai. I hate asking that officious little—" He stopped, stood up and walked around his desk to the wide space on the floor. "I'm being unfair. I dislike him because I'm certain in my own mind that he's using this case to climb to some sort of office among his own people. But they need someone to speak for them, and he would be good at it. He's certainly the most fluent in both languages, and he always seems to be listening, asking people what they want."

"What do you want me to do?" Hooper asked. "I was going to look into the contradictions in all these statements. So far all I've found is mistakes that anyone might make, and the sort of lies people tell so as not to look foolish, or a bit greedy or too quick to criticize. Some are protecting their families, or hiding a bit of flirting, or drinking too much. I'd be more worried if they all matched exactly."

Monk thought for a moment.

"Go with your instinct," he said at last. "If we uncover any real dishonesty, it would be worth looking into. Maybe it started off as a reaction against their community that got out of hand."

"Do you think that's what it was?" Hooper tried to keep his face expressionless. "One of us hating Fodor in particular, or immigrants in general, enough to do that to one of them?"

"No, I don't," Monk said after a moment's thought. "I think it's personal. But I've asked in case I'm wrong."

MONK SPENT THE EARLY part of the day visiting Adel Haldane again, to ask if she could tell him anything further about Fodor. Both she and her husband had known him when he first arrived in England, some twenty years ago. Monk could not believe, however, that at the root of the murder was a hatred dating back so far and lying dormant all this time.

"Did you know him in Hungary?" he asked her. They were sitting, outwardly relaxed, in her comfortable parlor. It was decorated mostly in the English style, to suit her husband, but with a few ornaments that had a different character, and two very lovely pictures of a city he took to be Hungarian. Certainly, from the architecture, it was not English. In pride of place alone on the mantelshelf was a photograph of a young man, high-cheekboned, pensive, almost beautiful in his unmarked teenage vigor. He bore a considerable resemblance to Adel.

She saw Monk looking at it.

"My son," she said quietly, a catch in her voice. What was her emotion? Pride? Love? Looking at her again, Monk was certain it was mixed with some kind of pain.

"He is very like you," he observed. The remark could hardly have been original; others must have seen it too and said the same.

This time she smiled. "Yes, he is. That was two years ago. He is away studying now. He wants to be an architect. It is a long course."

"But a fine profession. You must miss him."

She blinked quickly. "I do. But it is right for him to go. I cannot keep him at home . . . all the time."

Was that what he could see in her face, a mother missing her only child?

She turned back quickly to his unanswered question. "No, I did not know poor Fodor in Hungary. I met him the first time here, in Shadwell. We all liked him. He was funny, and quite often kind. He was a great one for making the best of things; even in the early days when he found it hard to speak English, he got used to English ways . . . and to the different weather. It is not as hot here, or as cold, but there is so much more rain, and the fog coming up off the river. We used to laugh about it, make silly jokes, so as not to let it get us down. That seems like a . . . a long time ago." She stopped abruptly, tears in her eyes.

"I'm sorry to disturb you, Mrs. Haldane, but we are not finding out very much. We still have no idea what made this very violent crime happen. It was not a sudden quarrel arisen. Fodor did not defend himself."

"You know that?"

"Yes. When a man defends himself it leaves bruises, cuts and scrapes. There were none. He was not expecting the attack."

Her face was suddenly very white.

"Mrs. Haldane?" He leaned forward, closer to her. "You've remembered something?"

"Agoston," she said quietly. "Agoston Bartos. He got here only three years ago. His English is very bad. He is finding it difficult. But something happened to him. You will need someone to translate for you, but I'm sure Antal Dobokai will do that. He is very good. Very helpful."

"Do you know what happened to Agoston?"

"Some kind of . . . attack. I don't know more. You should get him to tell you."

"How did you learn about this incident, Mrs. Haldane? Did someone tell you? Agoston himself, perhaps?"

"No! I saw his injuries when I was in a café and he was there also. It happens . . . sometimes."

"But you're telling me of this one time . . ."

"It was worse than most. And I think poor Agoston did nothing whatsoever to cause it."

"Does the number seventeen mean anything to you, Mrs. Haldane?"

"I remember you asked before. No . . . No," she repeated more firmly. "Nothing I can think of."

Monk knew that there was no point in pressing her, at least not now. But he would remember it.

He thanked her again, and left.

Outside in the street the air was warm, and the breeze smelled of tar and horse manure. He could hear children playing hopscotch on the pavement, and laughing. He walked briskly, asking one or two people he passed if they knew where Dobokai was. Each of them nodded and pointed him onward.

He found Dobokai outside the tobacconist's, talking earnestly to the owner. He was recognizable at a considerable distance. He had a peculiar stance, stiff, as if he were adjusting his weight to balance something, although he was of quite average build. Perhaps it was the angle at which he held his head, as if he were always listening.

Monk was only a couple of yards from him when he finally turned, and Monk saw that he and the tobacconist had been poring over a news sheet printed in what looked like Hungarian, and that Dobokai appeared to be angry. He seemed deliberately to compose himself.

"Ah! Good morning, Commander. Were you looking for me?"

It annoyed Monk to be so easily read, and it flickered across his mind to say it was the tobacconist he had come to see. He thrust the impulse aside as childish.

"If you can spare the time, Mrs. Haldane has told me of an event that might be relevant, but the man who can tell me the details apparently has very little English. I cannot afford to have misunderstandings."

"Ah!" Dobokai's interest quickened immediately. "I shall be happy to be of any service I can. Not much English, you said? Never mind. If Mrs. Haldane says it may be of importance, then we must see. A very good woman, Mrs. Haldane. Puts up with her husband's quick temper with great patience. I suppose she knows how very much he cares. Who are we going to see?" He smiled and nodded to the tobacconist, leaving the newspaper with him, and started to walk along the pavement, so that Monk had to catch up with him.

They needed to make a few inquiries in order to find Agoston Bartos, but it took no longer than half an hour. He was having lunch at a café, sitting in the corner by himself. Monk's first impression was of a shy young man with a thick head of hair and a charming face. He smiled as soon as he recognized Dobokai, and spoke to him in Hungarian.

Dobokai replied, and then introduced Monk. This took sufficiently long that Monk assumed it included his title, and therefore that he was a policeman.

Bartos immediately looked alarmed. A distinct shadow of fear crossed his face.

"You have no need to worry," Monk said, smiling at him, then giving Dobokai a swift glance of irritation. "I am only looking for information, something you may have seen or heard." He waited while Dobokai translated what he had said.

Bartos spoke to Dobokai hurriedly, clearly still worried. He seemed to be denying something. There was fear in his eyes, and he shook his head vehemently.

Dobokai said something to him, then turned to Monk. "I have asked him to tell me the whole story. He will tell me, and I will translate for you. If I am slow, it is because I want to get it exact. May I order luncheon for us while we do this? I remember you liked the Hungarian food we ate before."

"Thank you," Monk said, accepting. He was happy if they all ate; it might put Agoston Bartos more at his ease. It would look to others as if they were having a conversation rather than Bartos being questioned.

Dobokai got to his feet, walked over to the counter and ordered for everyone. Within a very short while the proprietor reappeared with bread, which was crusty on the outside and clearly just out of the oven. He also brought a carafe. It was unlabeled, but the moment Monk tasted the wine he knew it was good. It was rich, soft but not too sweet.

The stew that came a few moments later was excellent. He asked what it was, and received an answer that named spices and herbs he was unfamiliar with, but he wrote them down, thinking Hester would be interested, and thanked the waitress.

Dobokai began to question Bartos again, and then repeated the story to Monk.

"He went into one of the local hardware stores—ironmonger, I think you call them," he began. "English, not one of ours."

Monk nodded. He was listening to Dobokai, but watching Bartos's face. It was already flushed. The events clearly still embarrassed him.

"He went to the counter," Dobokai related. "There was a nice-looking young woman there. He asked if she would help him. He wanted various nails and screws, and a certain type of screwdriver and a pair of pliers. They struck up a conversation. She asked him what he was build-ing, presumably to be sure of giving him the right tools."

Monk watched Bartos's increasing discomfort. When he spoke again, his voice was urgent.

"There was a box on the shelves behind her," Dobokai continued. "It was very high. The ladder was awkward. Agoston went around the counter to hold it steady for her."

"She spoke Hungarian?" Monk interrupted.

"No, no." Dobokai shook his head. "Only a few words. That is why it was necessary for them to explain with gestures. For him to see two or three boxes of screws in order to choose the right ones. Then, as she was climbing down, he offered his hand to steady her."

Monk was beginning to understand. Bartos was a handsome young man, and his shyness at not speaking the language lent him an additional charm.

"Go on," Dobokai instructed.

Bartos took up the story again, but he was clearly distressed. His face was flushed.

"Go on!" Dobokai repeated. "Tell us. It could be important."

Monk drew in his breath to tell Dobokai to be patient, but Dobokai held up his hand in a gesture of silence, and spoke again to the young man.

After several long sentences, delivered with severe embarrassment, Bartos stopped and Dobokai translated. His usually rather sallow face was flushed with color and his blue eyes were almost luminous.

"One of the boxes of nails was knocked off the counter when she lost her balance a bit. They both bent down to pick them up and put them back in the box. At that moment the shop owner, the girl's father, came in and instantly misunderstood the scene. He cried out in accusation, and the next moment his son, the girl's brother, came bursting in also. He accused Agoston of intending to steal the screws. The girl protested, and the father slapped her. Agoston tried to stop him and both men set upon him, calling him names that he did not understand, but I do, and will not repeat them. They impugned the girl's virtue and called him a thief."

Dobokai reached across the table, grasped Bartos's hand and turned it over, revealing his wrist. Monk could see two jagged scars, healing well because they were very neatly stitched.

Bartos's face was flushed scarlet. "Not steal," he said desperately. "Not like—"

"Of course not!" Dobokai snapped. "Mr. Monk is not after you, he is after the man who attacked you!" He realized he was speaking in English, and repeated it in Hungarian, more gently.

"Please ask him if he had been in the shop before, or seen the young woman anywhere else," Monk said to Dobokai.

Dobokai repeated the question.

"No!" Bartos shook his head. "Never. I just buy." He held up his finger and thumb to indicate the length, then made a twisting motion with his hand.

Monk would be able to verify it, and he would do so, but now he wanted to know more about the incident. "And you left?"

Dobokai translated.

"Yes, he did. He was bleeding quite badly. You see? Your people are very polite, very civilized, but there are a few also who are not. Someone like that may have quarreled with Fodor. It is not we Hungarians who always have the suspicious minds and the quick temper. Agoston has no one to fight for him, or else maybe this would have got much worse. When it is family, especially if it is women, people do not forgive. Pride, you know?" His eyes flared with anger. "You touch my woman, she likes you better than me, I'll destroy you!"

"When was this, exactly?" Monk asked. He could make a guess from the healing of the wounds, but he would see how close that came to the truth.

Dobokai turned to Bartos.

"Two days before Fodor was killed," he said, translating the answer. "The hate is just below the surface. Stories get around, and they grow different and worse every time they are told again."

Monk turned to Bartos, but still spoke to Dobokai. "Ask him who stitched up his wounds. It's very professional. He's fortunate. It could have bled badly, and got infected."

The answer was what Monk expected.

"Dr. Fitzherbert," Dobokai told him.

"Thank you. Now the name and address of the shop where this happened."

Bartos shook his head, his eyes bright with fear.

Dobokai spoke to him quickly, before Monk could intervene. Monk did not understand his words, but their meaning was perfectly clear. He was insisting that Bartos tell him, giving him no excuse.

"You must," he finished, translating for Monk's benefit. "For the sake of the community. We cannot be treated like that and let people get away with it. Next time it could be a lot worse. No Dr. Fitzherbert there in time to stop the bleeding."

Bartos looked at Monk, then back at Dobokai.

"Wells Street," he said huskily.

Monk thanked him. When they had finished the excellent stew, and a little of the wine, he thanked them both again, paid his part of the bill, over the protests of the proprietor, and left.

He would ask Fitzherbert about the wound, and to confirm the date. But first he would go to the ironmonger and see what they had to say there.

It did not take him long to find it; the street was short and the shop front proclaimed its business. He walked in and immediately saw the long counter with its shelves up to the ceiling piled with boxes of screws, nails and other small metal fittings. The girl behind the counter was pretty, and no more than twenty at a guess. She smiled at him.

"Afternoon, sir. What can I get you?"

He noticed the name on the door. "Miss Bland?"

She looked puzzled. "Yes, sir?"

He introduced himself and explained that he was looking to confirm a story he had been told. He mentioned Agoston Bartos and the screws spilling to the floor.

"He didn't mean no harm, sir," she said instantly, the color flooding up her fair skin. "Me pa took it all wrong. I've . . ." She stopped.

Monk looked beyond her and saw the door to the back of the store open and a broad-chested man with graying hair come out. He walked up to the counter. "All right, Ruby," he said grimly. "I can take care of the gentleman. You go get some o' the paperwork done. Now, what can I get you, sir?" He looked hard at Monk, his eyes challenging. "Go on, Ruby!" he repeated without turning toward her.

She obeyed, her feet quick and light along the wooden floor.

"Sir?" Bland asked again.

"I'd like you to tell me about the incident almost two weeks ago when a young man came in here to purchase screws, and ended up going out so badly gashed in the wrist that he had to have it stitched by a surgeon."

Bland's eyebrows shot up but his look did not warm. "Ruby tell you that?"

"No. But she confirmed that it happened."

"Young girls get their heads turned by any foreigner with a smooth face and smarmy manner. I won't have them coming in here and making eyes at her." The color was rising in his face too, not from embarrassment but from deep anger.

"He came in here for a box of screws and she climbed up the ladder to fetch them," Monk replied. "What more happened that warranted you attacking him enough to draw blood? Were you trying to slash his wrists?" He was startled at the rage in his voice. It did not stop him from going on. "He came here to our country seeking a new start, and suddenly the simple act of asking to purchase screws turns into a life-threatening assault by one of our tradesmen? Is that what we've become?"

Bland's face was scarlet. He leaned over the counter, toward Monk, his eyes blazing.

"We got a whole bunch o' them foreigners settling here, till our own place is not ours anymore! We're decent people! Now look at us! The newspapers are writing about us like we're lunatics. Who sticks a bayonet in a man's chest and dips candles in blood all around the room? We never 'ad that before they came."

"Rubbish!" Monk snapped. "There's been crime in London since before Julius Caesar landed."

"Remember that, do you?" Bland said right back.

"Did this young man assault you?" Monk went on, ignoring the comment. "I don't see your wounds. I've seen his, and I'll find the surgeon who stitched them up."

"You going to take his word over mine? He didn't even speak English! Is that what we've come to?" There was thwarted fury in Bland now. He knew he was losing.

"I'll take the evidence," Monk said coldly. "I've seen where you cut his wrist, and I'll ask the surgeon how bad that was."

"You can't prove I did it!" Bland defied him.

"Yes, I can. I'll find the weapon you did it with. And if I'm very lucky, I might find you had an old rifle and bayonet too . . ."

Bland's face went gray. "God in heaven! You don't think I did that?

I don't like them strangers coming here an' changing everything what was perfectly good the way we 'ad it. And I may 'ave lost my temper when I came in 'ere and seen my daughter making eyes at him like a fool! But I didn't kill that other poor soul, with all them candles and blood, an' God knows what, I swear."

Monk believed him. And he was not pleased with himself for having lost his temper and deliberately frightened the man.

"I'll see what the surgeon says," he replied. "You've got a very nasty temper. And I'll remind you that attacking a Hungarian is attempted murder, just as much as attacking an Englishman."

Bland swore under his breath, but carefully and not loud enough for Monk to hear him properly.

Monk left then. He would have Hooper check on Bland's whereabouts on the night Fodor was killed.

HE WENT BACK TO Wapping, not so very far, then along to Crow's clinic. If Scuff was there, he would tell him where Fitzherbert lived, or Crow might know.

As it turned out, Fitz himself was there. He had clearly just finished changing some dressings and was washing his hands. He looked tired, but quite composed. Monk wondered if he had been up half the night. From what little Scuff had said, Fitz seemed to be willing to work long hours, unpaid. Monk wondered if it was his sense of duty, even dedication, or if perhaps he liked the company. Monk might have imagined it, but there was an air of loneliness about the man, as if he had been too long a stranger wherever he went.

Or was he seeing in Fitzherbert an echo of the man he himself used to be? Was this how he had looked to others, before he at last belonged?

Monk introduced himself.

"Good afternoon, Commander." Fitz put down the towel and walked over toward him. "If you came to see Scuff, I'm afraid he's out getting us more supplies. Tibor is our main patient, but there are others. We seem to run out of some things quite quickly."

Monk smiled slightly. This man had worked with Hester on the battlefield and in the military hospitals. He must have experienced all the things she so carefully would not—or could not—speak of. Even after all these years, that time was still too dark, too filled with an indelible sense of loss. He could see it in Fitz's eyes also: too much pain, too much death.

"Actually, it is you I would like to speak with. I was talking to a young man, Agoston Bartos, who had a jagged cut in his wrist. It had very clearly been stitched by a surgeon. He said it was you. Is that correct? He speaks little English, and I needed Dobokai to translate for me. I'm relying on his accuracy."

"He'd be accurate," Fitz replied, a shadow crossing his face. "He has the most remarkable eye for detail I've ever encountered."

Monk felt compelled to ask. "But you don't like him? Why?"

Fitz looked straight at him. He had a curious face, not quite handsome, and yet the sensitivity in it, and the intelligence in his eyes, the fleeting humor, made him enormously likable.

"I don't know," he admitted. "A totally unfair judgment. He makes me uncomfortable. I think he is ambitious to become leader of the community and, God knows, they need one. He seems to know everyone, and makes a point of asking about whatever they care for most, usually family. He always knows their names, and what they're interested in. Above all, he asks their opinions. It flatters them. It makes them think he cares. Perhaps he does."

Monk realized that he had summed up Dobokai very well—why some people liked him so much, and precisely why it was that Monk did not like him.

"What about Bartos's arm?" he asked. "You stitched that? What did he tell you about it?"

Fitz smiled with dry amusement. "You're checking what Dobokai translated for you?"

"Yes . . ."

"You underestimate him. He's far too fly to make such a mistake as that. Bartos went to the ironmonger, who's a hot-tempered fellow with a very pretty daughter. Sometimes I wonder if she's really his. She's as unlike him as could be—"

"How long have you been here?" Monk interrupted. "You seem to know these people very well."

"A few months, maybe half a year As a doctor you get to know people pretty well. I simply help them, advise them, stitch up the odd wound. Officially I don't practice anymore . . ." His voice trailed off, as if he had begun a sentence he had not planned ahead. As if he did not wish to discuss his skills or their use with the police.

"Agoston Bartos and the ironmonger . . . ?" Monk prompted.

"Oh . . . yes." Fitz seemed to bring himself back to the present with something of an effort. "It was a very nasty gash. Lucky he didn't catch an artery, or it would have been far worse. Difficult to stop the bleeding if he had. This was just messy, and painful. I daresay it frightened both of them. I actually hope it frightened Bland. He's a nasty piece of work if he's angered. And that doesn't seem to be too difficult where his family is concerned. I stitched Bartos up, and checked the day after to make sure he was healing. Healthy young man. No problem. Wound was clean, and he took care of it."

"Thank you. I thought they were telling the truth, but better to check."

Fitz frowned. "Are you wondering if Bland was responsible for butchering Fodor, poor devil?"

"Is it possible? Could Fodor have had an eye for Miss Bland?"

"Not impossible, but damned unlikely," Fitz replied. "But I surmise whatever it was, it will look unlikely until it is proved to have happened. If it were likely, we'd all know it by now. Sorry, but I won't be any help."

"But you know some of the Hungarian community," Monk persisted. "Is Bland typical? Dobokai keeps telling me there's some very ugly feeling against them, because they're strangers, a little different. Is he right? Or is he exaggerating it, to draw attention away from my suspecting one of them?"

"Or to make a political point," Fitz added. "I don't know. It seems a pretty filthy thing to use such an appalling killing as a building block in a political game, but people do. And there have been a few incidents, scuffles that came to very little. A few pieces of writing on walls, windows broken, that sort of thing. But you must know that."

"Yes. I wondered if as a doctor you had a better insight, even if you couldn't give me names or details. Any women . . . assaulted?"

Fitz bit his lip. "Yes, but not seriously. It happens everywhere. Find me a village in England, any village, they'll have their public nuisances, women who flirt too much, men who can't hold their drink, young men spoiling for a fight. Any excuse is good enough. The fact that the Hungarians are a little different certainly is. Get really different, like Indians, Africans, and they will stick to their own. Less of a threat. Lascars are all over the ports; here they come and go again. Nobody cares because you can predict them."

"You're observant."

"I'm a doctor. Survive by helping where I can," Fitz said a trifle ruefully.

Monk wanted to ask him why he had not come home to England as soon as he was healed from whatever injuries had kept him away after the war. But he knew from the expression on Fitz's face, the angles of his body, which were just a little stiff, that he would be intruding on a private grief. He was Hester's friend. They had seen terrible things together in a past Monk could only guess at. Perhaps they had helped each other survive it? She had not told him. It would be a grim piece of insensitivity for Monk to ask him about it now. And it was none of his concern.

Except one small thing.

"Did you know any of these people when they were in Hungary? You clearly spent some time there or you could not possibly speak the language so well."

"Good God! No!" Fitz looked amazed. "Don't you think I would have told you?"

"Yes," Monk agreed. "Yes, I'm sure you would have. Thanks for your help. Oh . . . how is Tibor? Do you think he's well enough to remember who attacked him?"

"Recovering, but he still has a long way to go. I'm not sure he'll ever have a clear picture of his attacker in his mind." Now Fitz was smiling again. "She was a very good nurse, you know. Hester . . ."

"Yes," Monk agreed, feeling suddenly excluded where it mattered to him astonishingly deeply. This man had seen her at her very finest, had endured terrible hardships beside her, won battles and lost some together with her. And Monk had never even seen such horrors, except once briefly, when he had been in America with Hester and been overwhelmed by actually witnessing the first Battle of Bull Run. The violence was shattering, unlike anything the imagination could create.

"Yes, I know," he said, not that he did. He meant that he believed, but he could not let Herbert Fitzherbert know that. "Thank you," he said again. Then, with a nod, he walked outside to the street.

HE WAS AT HIS desk at the Wapping Street Station a couple of mornings later when Hooper came into his office. His face was white.

"What is it?" Monk asked, his chest suddenly tight.

"Another one," Hooper said hoarsely. "Like Fodor." He took a deep breath. "Stabbed through the chest with a blade from a pair of shears. Not all that unlike a bayonet. Not just that—his fingers were broken, and his teeth. And there were candles, all round the place. Seventeen of them." He drew in his breath. "All dipped in blood."

"Hungarian?"

"Yes."

6

M ONK WAS STUNNED. FOR an instant he refused to believe it. Then he saw the gravity in Hooper's face and knew it was true. He rose to his feet slowly. He felt stiff. He should have expected it. If Fodor's death *was* the crime of hate that Antal Dobokai thought it was, then of course whoever the killer was would strike again. Hatred did not stop, only the perpetrator stopped, when he or she was forced to.

"Where is it?" he asked.

"Garth Street. That's just up from the Bell Wharf Stairs, between the High Street and Lower Shadwell Street, right on the water."

"Is that where they found him?" Monk asked.

"Yes, sir, in his own back kitchen," Hooper replied. "He's a widower. Been here about five years. Wife died soon after they got here. She was ill, and the journey was too much for her."

"Who is it?" Monk asked, keeping up with him as they went out the door onto the dock.

Hooper turned right, facing up the river toward Shadwell. "Lorand Gazda," he said. His voice dropped a little. "We interviewed him before, about Fodor. He said then that he did not know him very well. Couldn't help as to who might have had a quarrel with him. I believed him. I think he was both shocked and grieved. But then, any decent man would be."

Monk kept pace with him. This crime scene was farther from the water, but only by a matter of yards. Did he want the regular Metropolitan Police to take over the case? He was not certain. It would be a relief to share the burden with them, and certainly to have the extra manpower. But then it would be handing over a River Police case, not merely unsolved but without even a decent groundwork on which to build. They'd been working on it for ten days, and had nothing to show for it, except for having weeded out a number of people because they were probably elsewhere. For all that he had done to find out, there was no explanation for the seventeen candles.

Was it simply a matter of pride on Monk's part that he wanted to keep the case? There was no room for such arrogance. If this really was a crime of hatred against immigrants, then there were no grounds on which to hope it would stop.

Monk and Hooper walked the rest of the distance in silence. They turned at the High Street, down a dogleg a few yards long. Monk could not read the street sign; the better part of it was broken. Bell something. Then a right turn and they were in Garth Street, which was narrow, just a block from the river and the Bell Wharf Stairs, leading down onto the water. He could hear the tide surge against the stones and smell the damp in the air.

The mortuary wagon was drawn up at one of the houses, horses waiting idly. There was no one else around. Curtains seemed to be drawn, as if the people there were pretending this crime had not happened. The street was comprised of small, quiet, gray houses, with doors opening straight onto the narrow pavements. Some of the front steps were painted white; all were scrubbed clean.

Monk felt a twinge of pity for the residents. Poverty was an ever-present ghost. They must struggle to hang on to what was decent: regular work, enough food, a good reputation among their neighbors, no debt collectors calling.

They stopped at the door where two constables were standing outside, one of whom was River Police.

"Morning, sir." He straightened up and met Monk's eyes as if glad to see him.

"Morning, Stillman." Monk remembered his name at the last minute. He was new, very young.

Stillman and the regular constable stood aside and Monk went in, Hooper right behind him. There was no need to ask the way. All the internal doors were open and at the far end of the narrow hall the sitting-room door stood wide. Monk could hear the murmur of voices.

He was still unprepared for what he saw when he went into the back kitchen. The police surgeon, Dr. Hyde, was kneeling on the floor beside the body, which lay on its back, soaked in blood. From the chest there protruded the handle of half a pair of shears. Judging from the part he could see, Monk estimated there would be ten or twelve inches of blade sunk into the body.

But the horror that made his stomach lurch was the array of candles along the various surfaces of benches and shelves, all of them dipped in and smeared with blood. Without meaning to, he counted them. Exactly as in Fodor's room, there were seventeen.

A picture of a cathedral hung at a crazy angle on the wall, its glass shattered. Other ornaments were broken, but carelessly, as if in a destructive rage. A plaster figurine of the Virgin Mary lay shattered on the floor.

Monk looked at Hyde, then at Gazda's right hand. A glance was enough to know that these fingers were broken also—not just at the joints. They lay at such angles that they could not have been merely disfigured with blood and fearful swelling. Gazda's mouth also dripped blood from broken teeth.

It was a moment before Monk could get his breath, and control the nausea that welled up inside him.

"Morning, Monk," Hyde said grimly. "Body's exactly like the first. Even in a position pretty much identical. So is everything else the same, as far as I can see."

Monk looked around again, slowly. It was as if he had been hurled violently back into the past. Even the smell of blood in his nose and the taste of it in his throat were the same.

"I suppose it has to be the same man," he said slowly, stopping to clear his throat.

"God in heaven, I hope so!" Hyde rose to his feet and swayed a little. He looked older than when Monk had last seen him, and grayer. "I refuse to believe there are two such lunatics around in this area. As far as I can recall, even the damn candles are the same, seventeen of them, including two dark ones."

"It wasn't really a question." Monk forced his voice to be clear. "Is there anything you can tell me that adds to what we had before?"

"No. Except that your man seems to have a very precise pattern. There's nothing haphazard about this. This victim has no defensive wounds either; unless, of course, the injuries to his hands hide them."

"Was that . . . the finger-breaking, and so on . . . done after death, or before?"

"Just after, both times. Swelling would have happened if it had been before death. And so would bruising."

"A fight?"

"No. He bled to death, like the first one. Not instantly, but within minutes. When I get a better look I can tell you if the fingers were dislocated, like the first. At a guess, I would say they were. There's a terrible lot of hate here, Monk." Hyde shook his head. "Hard to believe they were totally random victims. They must have something in common."

"Was he killed here?" Monk asked. "Or is it possible he was killed somewhere else and then brought here?"

"No, it damned well isn't possible!" Hyde was clearly angry at such a stupid suggestion.

Monk looked around at the room. "Then he was visited here by someone he trusted, and he was attacked here," he said. "The room is staged. There's no sign of a fight. Nothing upset, scraped, scratched, broken, except the ornaments and the picture. The other decorations are fine. There are no marks on him except from the blow with the half shear, and his hands and mouth. He wasn't expecting anything from whoever it was. It wasn't a quarrel that got out of hand, or he would have defended himself—at least one punch, blow, something. He fell where it happened. He must have been standing about . . . here." Monk moved a couple of steps forward.

Hyde grunted his agreement.

"How big would his assailant have to be to drive that thing through Gazda's chest? How strong? What height and weight?"

Hyde pursed his lips and considered it.

Monk lifted his right arm and made the gesture of a violent stab downward.

"Not as tall as you," Hyde replied. "And with all his weight behind it, if he had any skill, not particularly strong." He stopped, seeming to go deeper into thought.

"What?" Monk demanded.

"More skill than the first time," Hyde replied. "Assuming Fodor was the first time. Either that or he was luckier this time. Haven't got the blade out yet. It might be sharper. Old bayonets tend to be rusty, less sharp. That would make a difference." He shrugged. "Now move out of my way and let me get this poor devil to the morgue so I can see if he can tell me anything when I look at him more closely. You can have the weapon when I've finished with it. Of course, if you could find the other half of it, it would probably help you."

"Thank you, Doctor," Monk said with only slight sarcasm. "I had realized it was half of a pair. One shear is no use, unless you have stabbing someone in mind." He stared around the room, trying to make any useful observation. It seemed so much the home of an ordinary man, Monk could see him here as if he were still alive. The chair was a little worn where he had sat by the fire. There were two well-used pipes in a jar on the mantel and, on an ornamental table, a metal box, which when he opened it proved to be well insulated and half filled with tobacco. There was a hand-embroidered tapestry on one wall, faded by sunlight, clearly old. He assumed the language of the inscription was Hungarian.

He looked at the shards of pottery from the figurine littering the floor. It was not broken as if it had been dropped. It had been deliberately smashed to pieces, and trodden on, ground under a heel.

In his mind, this room smelled not only of blood but of hatred . . . and something else . . . Fear?

He and Hooper studied it, and then the rest of the house, making notes all the way. Hooper also made a drawing of the back kitchen, including where Gazda had lain, and where they estimated he had stood before he fell. It changed nothing.

By midday Monk and Hooper left Garth Street and separately began to question all the people who had known Gazda, then compared their notes with what they knew of Fodor.

Monk had no wish to enlist Dobokai's help, but he knew it would save him time, errors, and the possibility of alienating the community even more.

As it turned out, Dobokai happened upon him, obviously with intent. Monk was at the corner of Cable Street, going toward where the majority of Hungarian émigrés lived, and Dobokai came out of the tobacconist's shop as he passed.

He looked very badly shaken. "Is it true?" he demanded, standing in front of Monk and so preventing him from going any farther forward. His face was pasty white, his dark hair slick at the front as if wet. "It is, isn't it? There has been another . . . murder!" It was more a challenge than a question.

"Yes," Monk admitted. He needed Dobokai's help. And much as the man discomfited him, he was the only person connected with Fodor who had a certain account of where he had been at the time of Fodor's death. That, for Monk, gave him no choice but to trust him. "How do you know that, Mr. Dobokai?"

Dobokai's black eyebrows rose. "Dr. Hyde is the police surgeon. He was at poor Gazda's house early, with police, and the mortuary wagon.

No one would say anything. What else would I assume? And forgive me, Commander, but you look as if you have seen something very terrible. Was it the same? The same man as before?"

"Yes. It seems inescapable . . ."

"What are you doing about it?" Oddly, there was no blame in his voice. It sounded more like a question of concern. "You need more men, Commander. You must still deal with all that goes on along the river—or would go on, were you not to continue your patrols. I have been here long enough to know that." His face took on a certain satisfaction. "The Pool of London is the busiest port in the world. You need the regular police to help you, perhaps under your orders? I will do all I can . . . but we are already afraid. It will only get worse."

"I know that, Mr. Dobokai."

"Of course, of course you do," Dobokai agreed, falling in step with Monk as he moved forward. "I have been doing all I can to reassure people that you are in control—but it is not easy. They are very frightened. This hatred is . . ." He shook his head minutely, almost as if he were too stiff to move without pain. "It is like a poison in the air. I know both victims so far have been men, but the women are very afraid. Who is going to be next? Their husbands? Their sons? I assure them that it will not be so . . . but I may be lying." He shrugged now, a hopeless gesture.

Monk was sorry for him. Likable or not, the man was doing what he could for his community. It was petty to allow a personal aversion to intrude into his feelings.

"I want to get more men, Mr. Dobokai," he said. "I intend to ask the Commissioner of Police to give us at least six more. As you say, it is no longer the isolated instance we hoped. Can you recommend anyone else who can translate for us?"

"Yes, yes. Of course. I agree, it is far better you have someone in addition to me. Many of our people speak English, but haltingly. We pick the words we know, and they are not always exactly what we mean. It is not a lie . . . it is a lack of the right words."

"I understand," Monk said. "And fear, for you are in a country that is still strange to you. You are afraid of being misunderstood, blamed because you are different. It can happen to lots of people, for lots of reasons." He struggled through his memory, such as it was, and through things he had seen over recent years. The different were frequently singled out for abuse or challenge, or as the butt of jokes too often cruel.

Dobokai was watching him, seemingly unaware of anyone else.

"Some animals will kick to death the ones that are different," he said very quietly. "A different color, a slightly different shape. Slower, perhaps. There is something primal in us that fears anything unlike."

They were walking in shadow now and the air seemed colder. Maybe it was no more than the turning of the tide, but it chilled Monk.

"I know," Monk said a trifle sharply. "I would like to think we are better than the animals, but perhaps some of us are not. I will do all I can, Mr. Dobokai. But until we catch whoever this is, I would be grateful for your assistance in translation and, even more than that, for helping to keep people as calm as possible. To keep up your comparison to the herd, I daresay you will also notice that the hunting animal frightens the herd to scatter it, and pick out the weak ones."

Dobokai winced, as if Monk had struck him.

"Yes," he said hoarsely. "You are right, Commander. This is very terrible, but you are right. Now if you excuse me, I must go. I have many people to . . . to tell comfortable lies to. Oh. You might try Mrs. Haldane to translate for you. She is very good at English. Her husband is English, you know? She has been here more than twenty years, and has a degree of intelligence and a feel for words." Then he turned and walked away so rapidly that in a few minutes he was around the next corner and out of sight.

MONK WORKED ON THROUGHOUT the afternoon. Hyde would tell him all there was to know, medically. Hooper was questioning people about anything at all that might be a common link between Gazda and Fodor. Other men were going up and down the streets of the neighborhood, checking and cross-checking where everyone had been, looking for possibilities, seeing whom they could rule out. They knew the questions to ask that would catch even the smallest evasions.

Hooper had two of the men from the regular police checking all the tailors and dressmakers, all the ironmongers and hardware stores in the area to find the source of the shears. They were also to check the candlemakers and ship chandlers along the waterfront for unusual purchases of shears of any sort, or large quantities of candles, especially colored ones. Everyone had candles, of course, for ordinary household use, but in these days of gas lamps, the number at each of the crime scenes was a remarkable amount, and colored ones were exceptional.

Monk himself went to see an antiques shop owner for whom he had once done a favor. He found him in his chaotic shop on Commercial Road East, about a mile from the Wapping Police Station, and farther from the river.

"Afternoon, Mr. Drury," he said as the bell on the door announced his arrival. He closed the door behind him and switched the hanging sign from "Open" to "Closed." "Sorry to take up your time, but I need a little advice."

The old man looked irritated, until he picked up his spectacles and put them on; then he recognized Monk. He was standing at his desk, a habit Monk remembered from some time ago. "I suppose I owe you," Drury said. "I should be glad enough to pay the debt. You looking for something stolen?"

"No. I need knowledge, of the esoteric sort I know you delight in," Monk replied, walking toward the back of the shop, careful not to knock anything over. All kinds of clocks, crystalware, figurines were balanced on top of carved boxes and piles of books.

Drury looked relieved. "Then come into the back. Haven't got a kettle, but I've got some excellent brandy. Too good to sell."

Monk smiled and followed the old man.

Drury poured two glasses, real brandy snifters with big balloon bowls and short stems, so the spirit could breathe. He handed one to Monk, then gestured to one of the two easy chairs and sat in the other.

"So what have you got?" he asked.

"Seventeen," Monk replied. "To be specific, seventeen candles in a room with a body speared through the chest—twice now."

Drury's eyebrows rose. "Really? That Hungarian business? So you have another?"

"Yes. Just today."

"Seventeen candles again?" Drury said with interest.

"Yes. Fifteen white ones and two dark bluish-purple."

"Burning?" Drury asked.

"No."

"Had they been lit?" Drury leaned forward a bit, his face tense. "All burned the same length of time? It matters. Did they go out or were they snuffed? And two were purple, you say?"

Monk struggled to remember. "They were . . . some were burned right down, others halfway. One or two not at all. Why? What does it mean?"

Drury thought for several moments. "I wonder if your man was interrupted," he said at last. "Either that or he didn't know what he was doing."

"What was he intending to do?" Monk felt as if he had grasped something and it had slid out of his hands. "Why two purple ones? Aren't they hard to find? Why exactly the same both times?"

"Don't know about the number seventeen. But candles are used in what some people intend to be magic. Purple represents power—for good or evil. But the candles must all be new, and you cannot put them out before they have burned their whole way."

"But what was he doing? The ritual must mean something to him, or why would he take the trouble? And the expense!"

"Could be anything, depending on what kind of ritual he thinks he's following," Drury answered. "Most candle magic is good, involving all kinds of benefits: health, peace, healing, that type of thing. Not bloody murder!"

"But the purple you said was for power?"

"Yes. But it could be merely efficacy, the strength to be effective."

Drury thought for a few more moments. "Could it be that the victims lit the candles? And they were nothing to do with the murder?"

"Both of them?" Monk kept the disbelief from his voice with difficulty.

"Maybe they have something in common that you don't know about." Drury pursed his lips. "Apart from a damned dangerous enemy!"

Monk stayed and they talked a little further. Monk finished the brandy and thanked Drury, then walked out into the evening, his thoughts not much clearer than when he had gone in.

He took the ferry home as the sun was disappearing into a bank of cloud, staining it temporarily scarlet. He felt as if he had barely begun, as far as the murder of Lorand Gazda was concerned. He had obtained considerable help from the Metropolitan Police. The Commissioner was acutely aware of the rise in public feeling. The newspapers were full of lurid accounts of the blood and the ritualistic aspects of both crimes. No one actually blamed the Hungarians for this, but it was implied in some news stories that somehow they had brought a barbaric and semi-superstitious nature with them from their own country. The candle ritual had been made the most of, and no journalist had missed the chance to exercise his imagination, and his prejudices.

Denials were pointless. Every new mention of it would only serve to remind people. One particular newspaper vehemently denied all the prejudices recounted in the other papers, and in doing so repeated every detail. Monk was furious, but the damage was done.

Now he sat in the stern of the ferry, too tired to think usefully, but the number seventeen went around and around in his head. Seventeen what? Had it any meaning, or was it a diversion, a chance? The dark masts of a score of ships gently tossed, drawing circles on the fading colors across the sky as the light dimmed, the brightness bleeding away. By the time he reached Greenwich, at the far side, the violet shadows were already darkening the east. All he wanted was to be home, and to forget it all. He even hoped Scuff would still be at Crow's clinic. He did not want to raise the energy to be interested in his day, although he would have made the effort. Hester would be gentle enough, would read his mood and stay a silent companion. She would say all she meant merely with a touch.

IN THE MORNING HE found Hooper already at the Wapping Station, kettle on the hob of the wood-burning stove that served all purposes. Its heat was unnecessary at this time of the year, but tea was always welcome, and sometimes a toasting fork and the upper grill made even several-days-old bread very palatable.

"Morning, sir," Hooper said, reading Monk's expression with a quick eye. "We should have half a dozen more men today. Do you suspect the ironmonger? We can see if poor Gazda ever took any interest in the daughter. I believe he was forty-three, so not so likely. But not sure that Bland sees very straight anyway. Could have imagined anything."

"Need to rule him out, at least," Monk agreed. "Did you feel the same sense of rage in this one as in the first?"

Hooper was silent for several moments. Monk actually wondered if he was going to answer.

"It was exactly the same," Hooper said finally. "It's so much the same; is this man following a ritual of some sort? Do the blood and the candles mean something specific?"

Monk shook his head. "I've asked a contact of mine. He says the purple candles are for power. But all the ritual is wrong. Candles should have been new, and burned all the way to the end. He has no idea what the number seventeen means."

"Could it be a Hungarian group? Something they brought with them from the old country?" Hooper asked.

"Then why wait until now? Seems more like vengeance for some new offense. I think we should take a look at the Hungarians who have come here more recently. I think I'll go back to Adel Haldane. She's very fluent in English. Dobokai suggested I should use her as a translator. The more I think of it, the better the idea seems to be. I might learn a lot from watching her as well. She would catch inflections, the use of ambiguous words or phrases."

"And tell you?" Hooper said doubtfully.

"Probably not, but if I'm not quick enough to catch the fact that she knows, I don't deserve to be in this job. See if the men from the regular police have found out anything about the shears. At least see who we can rule out."

Hooper gave a twisted smile, with humor in his eyes.

"Yes, sir."

A DEL HALDANE WAS TORN between her strong desire to help end the fear and misery in the community and her anxiety that her husband might not approve of her putting herself forward so obviously to help the police.

"I know I am asking a lot of you, Mrs. Haldane." Monk smiled very slightly. "But I don't speak your language, and you do speak mine, very well. I need someone who can help me understand the finer shadings of what people are telling me. Understanding the simpler things is too clumsy a tool to find whoever is doing this."

"You think it is one of us? A Hungarian?" A shadow of both anger and fear crossed her face.

"I don't know who it is," he replied quietly. "But I do know that two men have been killed in a violent and terrible way, and they were both immigrants from Hungary. If anybody knows of something that links them, some knowledge and experience, something in common, it is likely that someone could know who did these murders. Everyone will be questioned. For the native English I don't need a translator, I can send any one of my men—"

She stopped him. "I see. Yes. If I can help you understand us better and know that we are peaceful and hardworking people, wishing to be friends with the English, but not to have torn away from us the few memories and habits of our homeland, then I will do so. Of course I will."

"Thank you," he said, accepting.

It was a long task, finding people, asking them where they were when Gazda was killed, and who could substantiate what they said. Having Adel with him made it both easier and better in many ways. When people saw her they tended to be far more relaxed, and did not look for excuses as to why they were too busy to stop and talk. She was naturally skilled at putting people at ease.

Monk did not understand what she said, but it was clearly a greeting to begin with, then a question as to their health, well-being, how their work was going, and usually some question concerning family members. There was always a word of commiseration over difficulties, ending with the shock of another violent death among them.

It took the rest of the day, but not only was he able to make notes and cross-reference them to exclude a large majority of the Hungarians in the Shadwell area, but he also, because he had gone in her company, established a degree of trust. No one expected Adel to solve their problems or protect them, as many of them did with Dobokai, but they liked her. They were comfortable with her, and talked of peaceful familiarities: children, food, household things, even ever-present irrelevancies like the weather.

Monk remembered Hester telling him that when women speak to each other of trivial things, that is merely a vehicle. What they are saying beneath the surface is about interest, trust, understanding.

That was what Adel Haldane was doing now, and he was interested to watch her. Surely a great deal of what she was doing exercised the same arts as those of the best detectives? She was looking at the expressions of faces, listening to tones in a voice, sensing tensions, evasions, noting the things that were explained too carefully and the things that were not explained at all.

Adel was a pretty woman, good-humored and with a dry wit. Yet he detected, in moments when she thought he was listening to the witness, a deep sadness. She was well aware of the loss now of two lives, as well as the underlying courage needed always to make a home in a new place where everything required thought. Even so simple a thing as the traffic flowing on the opposite side of the street could be forgotten in the heat of an emotion.

He insisted they stop and take luncheon, and then, later in the afternoon, tea also.

"The candles, Mrs. Haldane," he said quietly, watching her face as they sat over tea. "There were seventeen candles at both murders," he continued carefully. "Two each time were purple, the rest white. Think carefully; are you absolutely sure you know nothing of the number seventeen or its significance?"

She was quiet for so long that he was about to ask again when at last she spoke. Her voice was forced, even though she smiled. "None that I can think of. A coincidence . . ."

"I've investigated many cases, Mrs. Haldane. I can't remember candles at a death scene ever before, unless they were the only means of light. None of these was lit, and they were put in many different places, wherever there was room for them: on mantelshelves, bookshelves, tables, even two on a flower stand. On both occasions, seventeen of them."

Her face was now so pale he was afraid she was going to collapse. But he did not stop. She knew something, and he had to learn what it was.

"Mrs. Haldane? What does seventeen signify?" he insisted. "A secret organization? A religious brotherhood? Political? Something criminal?"

"No!" she said quickly. She kept blinking, as if that would hide the fear in her eyes. "It's . . . it's a secret organization. I don't know what they do." She looked up at him. "No women allowed. I've just heard the word . . . the number . . . that's all. I don't know anything, I swear."

He said nothing.

She was breathing deeply, her chest heaving. "You're sure there were seventeen?"

"Yes, absolutely. Both times."

"Around Gazda? You're sure?"

"Yes, Mrs. Haldane. What does seventeen signify? What is its meaning?"

She shook her head, and something like relief slowly filled her face.

"I have no idea. I'm sorry." Now at last she smiled. "Thank you for the tea. The cake was excellent."

He knew he was going to get no more, at least for the moment. He paid the bill, and walked with her back to her house.

They were met at the door by Roger Haldane. He stood on the mat just within the frame of the doorway, a larger man than Monk had remembered, broad of shoulders and chest. But it was his face that commanded attention. His mouth was wide, turned down at the ends, his eyes dark-lashed but too shadowed to tell the color.

"Where have you been?" He looked at his wife as if Monk were not there.

She did not seem disconcerted, and certainly not alarmed. She smiled at him. "I was helping Commander Monk," she replied calmly. "As you know, he doesn't speak any Hungarian . . ."

Haldane's heavy eyebrows rose. "I thought Dobokai was doing that? How many does he need?" He still did not look at Monk, as if he were incidental to the issue.

She gave a graceful little shrug, pulling up the fabric of her pale summer dress. Haldane was watching every movement, every flicker across his wife's face.

"He is doing it for one of the other policemen," she said. "The investigation's a lot bigger now there's been another killing."

Haldane was still blocking the doorway. His eyes widened very slightly.

Monk tried to read the emotion in him, and could not. He knew of no reason why Haldane should hate any of the Hungarians, but the possibilities were numerous and easy to believe. How had his life been disrupted by a wife of courage and charm, who must have loyalties to her own people? Now that there were more of them, did he feel displaced, surrounded by foreigners?

Of course, the house was his; all money and other material possessions were his. A married woman owned nothing except what she earned for herself, if her husband allowed her to work. And even that was a very recent reform, hard fought for.

And yet in an indefinable way, Adel seemed emotionally to be the more powerful. She had charm, a certain warmth and sensuality that even Monk was aware of.

"I am very grateful to Mrs. Haldane for her help," he said, interrupting the exchange between them, both the words and the unspoken emotional tension. "Perhaps you can help me a little also, sir? Every person excluded narrows the places in which we have to look."

Haldane moved a little to meet his eyes. "I have no idea who did this."

"No, I imagine not, or you would have said so." That was not the truth. Monk was concerned that Adel Haldane knew something, even if it had occurred to her only as she spoke to him that afternoon. The number seventeen clearly had some significance. Was that because in some way Haldane himself could be involved? He was a man of intense emotions. There was, in him, a suppressed anger under the more obvious fear that everyone felt.

"Where were you the night before last, Mr. Haldane?" he asked. "And perhaps you might be able to rule out someone else, if you know for certain where they were."

Haldane took a deep breath and his knotted shoulders relaxed. He seemed smaller, calmer. A shadow of a smile softened his face.

"Of course," he agreed. "I had a drink at the pub in the evening. I can give you a list of everyone else I can remember seeing there. I came home with Willy Nathan. He lives opposite. He'll tell you the same. Don't know exactly what time, but it doesn't matter. We were together. My wife was waiting up for me." He shot her a comfortable, satisfied glance. "I was home all night. Had breakfast at home, before going to my business. By which time, I believe, poor Gazda was long dead."

Adel looked at Monk and she too seemed easier, the darkness gone from her eyes.

"That's true," she said. "I was here."

Monk felt a sinking inside him. Perhaps he was foolish even to have considered Haldane. The man had no witness for the time Fodor was killed. But Monk knew of no reason for him to have done it either. He was no further forward than he had been when he'd stood in Fodor's room and seen the blood-soaked body, exactly like Gazda's, and the seventeen blood-crowned candles. Everything was exactly the same— exactly!

And Dobokai could account for himself during every moment of the time Fodor was killed. Monk had checked it twice.

"Thank you," he said quietly, and turned to go home.

7

Tɪʙᴏʀ Hᴀᴠᴀѕ ʀᴇᴄᴏᴠᴇʀᴇᴅ, ʙᴜᴛ slowly. He had another feverish episode and, in his tossing and turning, tore open the wound. There was a second small vessel bleeding.

Crow was asleep after a long day with two sick children who had reached a crisis point. He had saved them, but the hours and the emotional exhaustion of alternating hope and despair had finally overtaken him.

Scuff watched as Fitz opened the wound yet again, quietly talking to Tibor all the time. Tibor lay as still as he could, his breathing irregular, clearly making an effort not to react to the pain and, even more than that, to the fear.

Scuff tried to stand still, but he found himself clenching and unclenching his hands and tightening the muscles in his left shoulder. He was whole. He could move without pain. He had both his hands. He had never before thought to be so intensely grateful for that.

He passed the instruments and medicines to Fitz as he asked for them. He had to pay close attention because Fitz did not alter his voice when he was speaking to Scuff rather than to Tibor, nor did he turn aside to face him.

Scuff got the next instrument ready. He knew what Fitz would have to do. He had already threaded the needle. All the possible medications were laid out—the camphorated wine, the bark powder, more lint soaked in wine, more clean bandages. He had also prepared soup, and the best claret they could afford. He would have liked to try a little of that himself, just to see what it was like, but it had to be kept for the patients who needed it.

Fitz worked quickly, talking to Tibor, his voice steady. Tibor managed not to move, except once when the pain reached deep inside him.

"Sorry," Fitz said in Hungarian, smiling faintly. "But it's good that you feel it. Means the nerves are alive. You're doing well." He turned to Scuff. "Pass me the lint, will you? Thank you." He rubbed the stitched vessel clean and dropped the bloody swab into the dish.

Scuff watched as he bandaged the wound up again, still talking. "Look at that, Scuff." He indicated where the flesh was pink and beginning to knit together. "Looks good." He repeated the words in Hungarian, smiling so Tibor would see. "Get ready with the big bandage, camphorated wine, then the outer one. Thank you."

When Fitz was finished they gave Tibor a sip of claret, then left him for a little while.

They sat together in the kitchen with a good, thick soup, and several slices of bread.

At first Scuff thought he was not hungry. The last thing he could have eaten was meat, and this was made with beef broth, albeit thick with potatoes and other vegetables.

"You must eat," Fitz told him. "We need you as a doctor, not another patient."

Scuff looked at him but said nothing. He felt as if his throat closed up at the very idea of eating flesh.

"Hester would tell you the same," Fitz went on, taking another spoonful of soup himself, and then biting into the bread.

"She never had to tell me to eat," Scuff answered truthfully. "I was always ready to eat anything that wasn't nailed down. That's what she said."

Fitz looked him up and down. "How tall are you? You must be close to six foot. You'll finish growing soon and fill out a bit."

"I expect."

Fitz took another spoonful of the broth, and his eyes, looking at Scuff over the top of his spoon, were bright with amusement. Then suddenly the humor died and something replaced it that Scuff could not name. Sadness, fear, a kind of joy as well.

"You need your own health to be a good doctor," he said when he had swallowed his mouthful. His slender fingers played with the bread on the plate beside him. "Sometimes you'll have to work all day and all night. You'll have to stay awake when you are so tired your eyes burn."

Scuff frowned. It sounded as if Fitz was being very dramatic.

"Perhaps not," Fitz corrected himself. "That's in battle. But you never know when a battle will come." He shook his head quickly. "There's really nothing else quite like a battle. Even a train wreck, a ship going down. And I've seen those too." He stopped abruptly.

"Have you?"

"Yes. You don't want to see a battle. Please God you won't have to. But you might see a plague, even here. You know to keep the rules . . ." His voice trailed off again. He seemed to be remembering something that was sharper to his inner eye than the quiet room around them, with its plain walls, scrubbed board floor and the stove always lit. Here they always had hot tea to revive people, heat for blankets if someone was in shock, and hot water to clean knives, scissors, needles. The Crimea was fourteen years ago. Doctors had learned a lot since then. Scuff knew these things from Hester, and she knew them from Florence Nightingale, and careful, forward-thinking doctors since then.

Did Fitz know all the same rules? Scuff knew what they were here in England, and much had come from the American Civil War, but was it the same in Europe, in Hungary where Fitz had been? Fitz had seen the real thing, battle day after day, dozens of men, even hundreds, maimed and killed.

He shook his head abruptly, trying to get rid of the pictures in his imagination, but they would not go.

"How . . . ?" he began.

Fitz was staring into the distance, his soup forgotten. Scuff wondered what he could see. He knew from Fitz's white knuckles gripping his spoon that it hurt him.

Suddenly Fitz was back again. "What?" he asked, puzzled.

"How do you even know what to do first?" Scuff said.

"The wounded get brought to you," Fitz replied. "No soldier is allowed to leave the field to carry a wounded man to the doctors. Special stretcher-bearers are sent out. When they bring the wounded in you deal with them as they come. A foot soldier or a general, they all bleed the same. Do what you can. Keep going. Think, then act. Immediately. Stop the bleeding. See if they can breathe. Do what you can. Move to the next one. All day, all night, if need be. Be careful with the water. There usually isn't much of it."

Fitz was holding his spoon so tightly, close to the rim of the dish, that it juddered against the china, but he did not seem to hear it.

"Fitz . . ." Scuff began.

Fitz was absolutely unaware of him. His eyes were fixed on something in his mind, and there was sweat on his brow and on his upper lip. In spite of the heat from the stove, he was shivering.

Scuff had no idea what to do.

"Fitz," he said urgently. "Fitz!"

Fitz did not hear him. He was staring at something miles away, perhaps long in the past, and it was so horrifying that he was lost in it. The sweat was pouring down his face and his whole body was trembling.

Scuff stood up and went around the table to him. It would be like waking a man out of a nightmare. Scuff knew about nightmares. He had had them for months after he was kidnapped by Jericho Phillips and imprisoned under the floorboards of his riverboat, unable to move, hearing every footstep and waiting to be dragged out, fearing the hideous things that had happened to the other boys.

And he had awoken terrified more than once, after dreaming that

Monk or Hester had been taken, or killed. He had even crept into their bedroom to make certain they were there. He had never told anyone that! You didn't go into other people's bedrooms, especially a woman's. But he had to know that she was there.

"Fitz!" he said again, more loudly.

Fitz took no notice of him. He was still on the battlefield, trying to do the impossible, and save everyone.

Scuff put his hand on Fitz's shoulder. Then he leaped away as Fitz rose and swung around, almost knocking him off his feet. His eyes were blazing and he lifted his hand as if to strike.

Scuff stumbled backward and tripped, staggering into the wall, knocking his elbow hard.

Fitz blinked and very slowly his eyes cleared. He saw Scuff, regaining his balance and, without thinking, holding his elbow where the pain shot through it.

"What . . . what is it?" Fitz asked, puzzled.

Scuff was breathing hard. He was frightened. He was not sure if he was scared *of* Fitz or *for* him.

"I gave you a start," he replied, choosing his words carefully. His mouth was dry and he was shaking also. "I think maybe you were half-asleep . . . or something. Sorry . . ."

They stood some feet apart, looking at each other.

Fitz spoke first. "I'm sorry. It happens to me sometimes. I start to remember . . . things. I forget where I am."

"Bad things . . ." Scuff said.

Fitz blinked. There were tears in his eyes. "Yes . . . very bad."

"I'll get you a cup of tea." It was the only practical thing Scuff could think to do. He would make it strong, and put lots of sugar in it. He waited for Fitz to accept, although he meant to do it anyway, as soon as Fitz sat down again.

Seconds ticked by.

Then Fitz seemed to shrink, to cave within himself, and he sat down.

"Sorry," he said, almost inaudibly.

Scuff let out his breath. "I'll make the tea."

When it was made he brought it over, already poured into two mugs. He had added enough milk to make it sufficiently cool to drink. The last thing he wanted was Fitz scalded.

They sat opposite each other in silence for several minutes, sipping the tea. At last Fitz spoke. His voice was very quiet, but still had the beautiful diction he never seemed to lose.

"I'm sorry. Sometimes the past just comes back so sharply I can't ignore it. I don't know whether I'm here in Crow's clinic in Shadwell, remembering the Crimea—Balaclava, Sebastopol, the Alma; blood, pain and broken bodies everywhere. Or if I am on a long night duty after a battle, and fell asleep and dreamed I was here." He stopped and took a little more of the tea. "Only Hester seems real, in both places." He smiled very slightly, and the look in his eyes was distant with memory.

Scuff did not want to lose him again. "She was good, wasn't she? She never says anything about it."

"She wouldn't want to upset you." Fitz sipped his tea again. "Besides, like most people who've really done something, she wouldn't boast about any of it. It would be . . . indescribably . . . vulgar. How could you boast about having skills that included someone else's agony, even death? There's nothing glorious about having your body hacked to pieces, seeing your own guts spill out and trying to hold yourself together with your hands. There's nothing you share with strangers or with those you love of watching people die, seeing terror and pain you can't do anything to help." He gave a deep sigh. "And it's a lie to tell people how brave someone was, how they spent their last strength trying to save someone else."

"A lie?" Scuff asked.

Fitz stared at the wall, or something beyond it. "Yes, deeper than words. Half the truth is the worst lie, sometimes. That kind of thing shouldn't be spoken of, except to those who already understand it. Nothing strangers should see, even in their imaginations. It's intimate, terrible . . . and final. One should not speak of it in trivialities, to serve some other purpose. It's not like dying in bed, at your right time. There's decency in that. These were young men, with all their lives ahead of them . . ."

Scuff thought he knew what Fitz meant, but it would be absurd to say so. He sat with the mug in his hands.

Fitz smiled at him bleakly. "But you're right, Hester was good. One of the best. She always did everything with a whole heart. She was so terribly angry at stupidity, she had no energy left to be frightened, even of generals. Every man is much the same under his uniform. When you're reduced to nakedness, illness, fear, needing a nurse to help you in distress and total incontinence, the only difference is between those who do it with courage and those who don't. He stopped for several moments, choked by memory.

Scuff did not interrupt him, but he watched closely to see that Fitz did not slip back into his previous state.

"Remind me sometime," Fitz said suddenly. "I'll tell you some of the things she did." His voice caught momentarily, emotion all but choking him.

"I will," Scuff agreed. "You should eat some of the bread."

"How like Hester you are!" Fitz smiled. "She was always telling us to eat, even when the food was barely good enough to give the rats! Always practical. I don't know what marvelous dreams went on in her head. She could recite poetry, if she wanted to. But she was always dogmatic about eating and sleeping. 'Sick men don't want your pity,' she'd say. 'They want your help. For that you have to be as strong as you can, and as full of energy and sense!'" He took several mouthfuls of tea. "And yet in the long nights waiting, watching the sick and the dying, she could be the gentlest woman I ever knew."

Scuff saw the emotion raw in Fitz's face, and understood it far better than he wanted to. He liked Fitz. He admired him intensely. But no one could have the part of Hester that belonged to Monk.

He tried to think of something different to say, something not connected with the past.

"It seems we have learned a few things from the American Civil War," he said, altering his tone to try to sound hopeful.

Fitz looked up. "Have we? The news I heard, it was just as bloody, violent and senseless as anything we've ever done. Which is damning it completely, I know, and I'm sorry."

"I meant in medicine," Scuff explained. "At least with the use of opium, which seems to be better than some things."

"Better for pain," Fitz agreed. "But we've known that from others, like the twelfth-century Jewish physician Maimonides. We just periodically forget. But you are right. From the little I heard, they have caught the ideas of open air and sanitation."

They were interrupted by Crow staggering out of the bedroom. He was blinking a little, his black hair tangled and half across his face.

Scuff got to his feet. "Kettle's hot. Would you like some tea? Tibor is asleep, quite peacefully."

Crow forced a smile. "Yes, I would. And yes, I know. I peeked in at him myself."

"You don't look as if you can even see where you are going," Fitz said, sympathy softening the edge of his voice. "Have something to eat. Bread and cheese?" He indicated the table.

Scuff put the kettle on again and brought him tea. Crow still looked weary. He moved slowly and there were dark smudges around his eyes. Scuff was suddenly painfully sorry for him. He had worked so hard to set up this clinic.

None of them knew if Fitz had been born to money, and a degree of privilege. His language and diction suggested it. He had certainly been to a good school, because he had a proper degree in medicine. He could never have been a senior army surgeon if he had not, whatever had happened to him since.

Scuff had no idea how Crow had grown up, only tiny glimpses of things, an isolated memory here or there, a reference to his youth that brought laughter, but the kind that was blended with hurt. Nothing that he had now had come to him easily.

He knew poverty and the diseases of the poor. But he had hardly any of Fitz's surgical skill. He was still very much learning as he went. It was the biggest achievement of his life that he had finally qualified as a doctor, rather than just giving help where he could to those who could not afford to pay him for it, except occasionally with a little food or un-needed clothes.

Now his only pupil was listening to Fitz and learning the things Crow could not teach him. Scuff owed him more than friendship. When Fitz was gone, he must think of something to say—or better, to do—that would let Crow know he understood the debt he owed him. And that more than that, he knew Crow would be there long after Fitz had returned to . . . wherever he belonged. If he belonged anywhere.

Much later that day, Fitz took his turn at sleeping and Scuff went with Crow to visit one or two patients who were ill at home. None of them was far enough away to necessitate more than a walk, or a short ride on an omnibus. Crow and Scuff took with them a satchel of various medicines, mostly powders in small, carefully labeled twists of paper. They were light and easy to carry. They would accept whatever pay-ment was offered. Crow very seldom asked for more. The people who could afford more had long taken themselves to a more regular physi-cian.

"You learning from Fitz?" Crow asked conversationally.

"Yes," Scuff answered instantly. "But of course most of it is things we won't have to use. I hope not anyhow. I wouldn't like to be an army surgeon. Not that there's any chance, but I'm glad of it. It's hard enough trying to help people that are sick 'cos of not eating right, or not having clean water or dry clothes and such."

"Rich people get sick too," Crow pointed out.

"Last longer," Scuff said drily. "Poor ones die first time round . . . a lot."

"The ones that survive to grow up are pretty tough," Crow argued. "Look at you."

"An' you!" Scuff countered, then instantly wondered if he should not have. "Sorry . . ."

"Don't be," Crow replied with one of his wide smiles, which showed just about all his teeth.

"I reckon it was bad, 'cos you never talk about it." This time Scuff was honest.

"It was," Crow agreed.

"Maybe we all get some bad times." They were crossing a busy road and Scuff was looking around for traffic, rather than at Crow's face.

Crow did not answer.

In fact it was not until they had seen two more patients, and were turning back in the general direction of Shadwell Docks, that he spoke on the subject again.

"It's not secret," he remarked. "At least not from you."

Scuff was still thinking of the sick woman they had visited. "What's not?"

"My father was a right bastard. He beat my mother, often." Crow was looking ahead of him, his face set hard at the memory. "I didn't know how bad it was until I was about twelve. She hid it from me. Protecting me . . ."

Scuff wanted to say something, but there wasn't anything that matched the misery or the anger he felt.

Crow kept on walking, still looking straight ahead, and his voice was thick with emotion. "Then he beat her so bad one day, she died. I think she was . . . ready to go. She couldn't escape any other way."

Scuff felt numb. He tried to imagine it, and he couldn't, even though he had seen women beaten, seen dead people.

"I took a chair and broke it over his head, before I knew she was gone already, too far to save anymore," Crow said. "I should have done it sooner. I . . . I wasn't strong enough . . ."

"Did you hurt him bad, I mean really bad?" Scuff asked hopefully.

"Yes. He never stood up straight again. But I ran. I knew if he caught me he'd kill me too."

"Where'd you go?"

"Onto the streets," Crow replied. "Down here. Near the river. I found someone to take me in, no questions."

"Good."

Crow gave a strangled little laugh. "Taught me a lot of tricks to make money in ways that the law doesn't allow. Not so much about honest trade, but I could read and write, so I learned for myself."

"Medicine?"

"Learned that practically, like you're doing. First with animals, then with people. Found a good man who loved horses. He helped a few people too, now and then." Now at last he turned to look at Scuff, needing to know what he thought and, perhaps even more, what he felt.

"Not as lucky as me, then," Scuff said casually.

THEY SPENT THE NEXT day working with patients they had known for some time. One mother with a sickly child was profoundly relieved to see them. Crow looked at the child carefully and pronounced her doing well. The mother's shining eyes and wide smile of relief were the only reward there could be. Every scrap of money she had went to getting good food for the child, and saving for a pair of shoes.

The next patient was an old man. He was fading rapidly, and he knew it. "Place is changing anyway," he said sourly. "Foreigners everywhere. Try to pretend they're like us, just 'cos their skin's the same color, but underneath they're as different as any one o' them. 'Ave you smelled the stuff they eat? Some o' them don't even bother to learn English." He glared at Crow.

A shadow passed across Crow's face, but he did not respond.

Scuff was not so tactful. He was very aware of how hard it was for Monk to find out anything deeper than a few surface facts that excluded much else about the Hungarian murders. There was nothing to single out anyone as guilty.

"Lots of people about like that," he said almost casually. "But I really hope it isn't one of us that's killing them . . ."

The old man glared at him. "O' course it isn't! It's a heathen way to kill anyone! Barbarians, they are. We don't do things like that, boy! Stabbed with a dagger through the heart, candles an' blood all over the place. That's foreign. 'Ow old are you that you don't know that?" He glared at Scuff with myopic eyes.

"I know the victims were both Hungarian," Scuff said innocently. "But they're Christian just like we are. Or say we are."

"You saying we aren't?" the old man challenged. "We're Christian, all right. It's them Catholics that aren't. You read your history books, boy. Owe their loyalty to Rome, they do, not to England and the Queen."

"Some of us—yes. Christian is how you act, not where you come from."

Crow touched him gently.

The old man snarled. "Well, that first one got 'isself 'round the women more than any Christian man ought. And that I know for sure. Seen 'im meself with more than one woman who ought to know better. Laughing and making fun, they were. Loose women among them 'Ungarians. Teaching our women bad ways . . . Who's surprised it ended in murder, eh? I'm not! Killed that foreign whoremonger! I say, good for 'im! Wouldn't tell you who he was if I knew."

Scuff took Crow's warning, and made no reply, even though there was one ready on his tongue. They did not speak of it again, but it stayed in Scuff's mind.

They took all day catching up with those they had not been able to see because of the events at the clinic, which of course included new cases, as well as accidents and emergencies.

Scuff watched and listened, learning all he could about the practical aspects of medicine, and learning also from Crow's manner. Quite often all he gave was advice and, perhaps more important still, comfort.

"Many things can't be healed," he said as they sat together at lunch, by chance at a Hungarian café. They watched the people and, although they did not understand the conversation around them, they heard the sharp edge to the voices, and knew that the Hungarians were afraid. The place was busier than usual.

"Standing with their own," Crow remarked. "Don't blame them. Fear is what is wrong with lots of people."

Scuff knew what he meant. He wasn't only talking about the people gathered here to get familiar food and feel comfortable speaking their own language, not even trying English. He meant also some of the patients they had seen. Constant anxiety produced all kinds of other pains: headaches, stomach upsets and of course short tempers, sleeplessness and stupid accidents that would not normally happen.

Scuff stirred his soup, which was very good. He liked the Hungarian food. The unfamiliar flavors were sharp and pleasing. They were spices he did not know, warm and aromatic.

"I wish we could do something. I don't understand what people here are saying, but I do when it's patients."

"You can't," Crow said bleakly. "Patients speak to us in confidence. And anyway, it's almost always about their health . . . or their private griefs."

"And gossip," Scuff added. "And families. If we really thought about it, we ought to find something." He shook his head and stared at Crow. "I know people are saying it's someone"—he gestured with an extended arm—"out there! But it isn't, is it? It's someone who lives here, probably English or Hungarian. Everybody's suspicious of anyone they don't know well. Even sometimes people they do. They are frightened and looking for a way out, someone to blame, so they can stop wondering all the time."

"I know. We do some of the worst things we ever do when we are afraid," Crow said unhappily. "But we have made a promise not to repeat what we hear in people's homes. That's why they let us in, and trust us."

"I know."

They sat silently for a while before Scuff spoke again.

"Isn't it also our job to find out who did this, if we can? And before they do it to anyone else?"

Crow's hand stopped halfway to his mouth with a forkful of food. He stared at Scuff, his eyes wide.

"You think he's going to stop?" Scuff asked him. "Why? If he hates the Hungarians, there's still plenty of them left."

Crow put the food down and sat unmoving for several moments. "Yes, I suppose we have to protect them . . . if we can. But what if we do say something, and we're wrong, because we know only half the story?"

Scuff shrugged. "I expect whatever we come up with will be less than half, maybe only one bit in dozens, but it could matter. Sometimes it's one little thing that ties all the rest together. Like if someone's ill. Say they get a fever, their eyes hurt, they get a terrible headache and a sick stomach . . ."

"Could be lots of things," Crow answered. "That's what I mean."

"And then they get a rash of a lot o' little spots . . ." Scuff finished with a smile.

"All right . . . measles. Yes, I see what you mean." He pushed back a lock of hair from his face. "We'll watch. We get around enough."

Scuff finished his soup and the last of the bread before he spoke again.

"I thought of something else . . ."

"Yes?" Crow asked suspiciously.

"It's all right for you to call me 'Scuff,' but I think I'd like to have a proper name, like you, or Fitz. Like I'd be a doctor one day . . ." He felt embarrassed saying it, but he was beginning to feel it quite deeply. Who would ever send for a doctor called Scuff? And since Tibor Havas, and watching both Crow and Fitz, especially Fitz, he was determined to be a real doctor, a good one, who could alleviate pain and fear, and most times make people better.

"I didn't know you had one," Crow admitted, a sudden sympathy in his face. "I apologize."

"I don't have one." Now Scuff felt awkward. He looked down at his hands. "But when Hester took me to church, they asked me what my name was, and she said William. I . . . I never asked her if I could keep it. But if I get to be someone . . . Monk's called William, but I could be Will." He looked up at Crow, uncertain of what he would see in his face.

It was the utmost seriousness.

"Right, Will. That is who you'll be from now on. I'll try to remember. And I'll tell Fitz."

"Thank you. But it's all right to call me Scuff when we haven't got a patient in."

"Good. Because I'll forget." Crow gave one of his wide smiles. "Will. I like it."

Scuff felt the heat burn up his face, but it was with pleasure. It gave him something very big to live up to.

IT WAS WELL AFTER midnight and one of those nights when, even though it was past the height of summer and the days were shortening again, it was warmer than usual and the clear sky was hazy with a spread of stars. The lamps were lit along the main streets, but away from them, on a narrow side street lined with houses, there was no artificial light to wash out the dazzle of the Milky Way sweeping across the arch of the heavens.

Scuff walked slowly, because the peace of being alone was like a soft blanket around him after the constant necessity of talk all day. He had gone quite a long way on the last call and was still at least a mile from Crow's clinic when he heard footsteps behind him. He turned, in case it was someone who needed him.

At first he could not see anyone at all, then he made out a dim figure, moving slowly. He seemed to stagger a bit. Someone who had drunk a great deal too much?

He would just have to sleep it off. Scuff turned away and continued toward the clinic. He was near Cable Street again where there were regular lamps every thirty or forty feet. He could not hear the footsteps anymore. Maybe the man had fallen? He really should go back and see. He might be hurt, or ill! It was irresponsible to ignore him.

A little nervously, he swung around to look, but with his back against the wall of a house so he was not outlined against the light.

Within a minute or two the man wandered toward him, and past him, as if he had not even seen that there was anyone there. His face was vacant, eyes fixed on something only he could see. Whatever it was must have been terrible, because his mouth was open in a silent scream. His chest and hands were covered with blood and it drenched his thighs as if it had streamed over him. It was Fitz. There was no mistaking his features, or even the torn remnants of his jacket and the once-white shirt with its faint pin-wide stripes.

For a long instant Scuff was paralyzed.

Then he drew in his breath. "Oh God!"

He had to go after him, whatever had happened. He had never thought of Fitz as a killer. Why would he? He had seen Fitz operate to save a man's life! A young Hungarian man. He had seen the pity in his face and heard over and over the gentleness in his voice as he talked Tibor through the horror and the pain of having his arm removed, cutting through the still-living flesh to take away the gangrenous dead.

Scuff pushed himself away from the wall and moved swiftly after Fitz. He caught up with him in a dozen strides and took his right arm. Fitz was right-handed; Scuff remembered that from watching him work.

Fitz stiffened and swung around, eyes blazing, focused at last.

"Fitz!" Scuff yelled. "It's me! It's Scuff! Are you all right?"

"All right?" Fitz said, as if the question made no sense.

"Yes. Are you all right?" Scuff repeated. "You're covered in blood. Are you hurt?"

Fitz looked at himself as if he was quite unaware of it. He raised his eyebrows. "Not surprising, I suppose," he said. His voice was strained, as if he was exhausted.

Scuff's mind raced. Where did Fitz think he was? Was he here in London at all? Or was he somewhere in the Crimea, on the edge of a battlefield, trying to judge whom he could help, and who was past anything but a prayer for his soul?

What should Scuff say to him? Was he dangerous to anyone? Did he have a weapon of any sort, even a scalpel? He wasn't carrying a case. His hands were empty.

"Fitz," Scuff said firmly. "Who's hurt? Whose blood is all over you?"

Fitz stared at him, then looked down again at his own blood-soaked chest and legs. He seemed completely lost.

"No idea. You don't ask men's names, Scuff. You just deal with the bleeding. If you can save their lives, they'll tell you who they are. It doesn't matter. Stop the bleeding. Always! Just stop the blood . . ."

"But you're not hurt?" Scuff persisted.

"No, of course not. Doctors don't get hurt. We're here to . . ." He stopped. His face creased with agony and he doubled over as if he could no longer stand. "Jesus, it hurts!"

Scuff was terrified. He was not competent to stop bleeding, especially here in the street, in the dark.

"Show me!" he said, his voice catching in his throat. "Please!"

Fitz grasped his thigh, the one place where there was actually no blood.

It took all Scuff's strength to remove Fitz's hands.

"It's not bleeding," he said desperately. He could hear the panic in his own voice. "Where is the wound? I can't help if you don't tell me."

Fitz straightened up slowly. "Don't worry," he said, suddenly calm. "We'll get it stopped. Just . . . let me see it."

Scuff realized that in Fitz's mind he was somewhere else. The blood was not his. The pain was one remembered, perhaps from when he had been left for dead on the field after that terrible battle.

"We need to find shelter," Scuff tried again. "Come with me. Please."

"Oh. Oh, yes . . ." Fitz shook himself and started to move forward again.

Scuff stayed close beside him, knowing they could cross Cable Street and get into some of the smaller streets or alleys on the far side, where the blood would be less obvious. Without the glow from the gas lamps, Fitz's clothes would merely seem dark.

They were almost there when a voice cried out for them to stop.

Fitz turned around before Scuff could stop him.

Antal Dobokai was coming toward them with two men beside him. Scuff knew him by sight. Dobokai was transfixed by the sight of the blood on Fitz. He stood motionless, his eyes wide and his face filled with horror. Both of the men who were with him stopped also. Then one lurched forward as if to grab Fitz by the arm.

Scuff blocked him. Hard. It had been a long time since he had had to fight physically to survive. Then he had been thin and underweight. His only chance to win had been speed, and to strike in an unexpected place. He caught the man in the solar plexus and sent him staggering backward to crash into the wall of the nearest house. Then he turned to face Dobokai, taking him to be the natural leader.

What could he say? Fitz was standing on the pavement as if he had no idea there was anything wrong. Scuff did not know where Fitz had been, or with whom, or whose blood it was.

Dobokai was advancing on him, his face set, angry.

"He's a doctor!" Scuff said harshly. "You stop someone else bleeding, and you get blood on yourself! What use is a doctor if he's scared of blood? I'm taking him home to get cleaned up."

They stopped moving toward him, but did not step aside to allow either Fitz or Scuff to pass.

"Whose blood is that?" Dobokai asked, his voice shaking.

"Whose blood?" Fitz looked down at himself, then back up at Dobokai.

"You're covered in it. Soaked." Dobokai moved his head jerkily. In the lamplight his blue eyes looked almost luminous. "Whose is it? Who's dead this time?"

"Nobody's dead." Fitz seemed to be coming back to the present. "Not my field of skill. Did a bit in Hungary. There was no one else this time."

"Hungary?" Dobokai demanded. "What's Hungary got to do with it? When were you in Hungary?"

"Years ago," Fitz said, clearly puzzled. "What's that to do with it? It's the same everywhere."

"What's the same, Fitz?" Scuff demanded, catching his arm and holding it hard.

"Birth," Fitz replied. "Childbirth. Sometimes it's messy. But they're both all right. Got the midwife at last. Bit of bleeding, but that's mostly afterbirth. Got to get it out or it can poison the mother. God, I'm tired." He looked at Scuff. "Can't we go home? I'm so tired I could sleep on the pavement."

"As soon as Mr. Dobokai lets us past," Scuff said, praying silently that Fitz was telling the truth. "Please . . ." He seemed to be saying "please" all the time tonight, but he dared not be angry. He had no idea if Fitz was being honest. Was there a new mother with her baby in her arms somewhere near here? Or another skewered corpse with broken fingers and blood-soaked candles?

Fitz looked ready to slide to the ground.

"You're supposed to be looking after these people," Scuff said angrily to Dobokai. "Not attacking a doctor who treats them for nothing, and actually speaks their language. What's wrong with you?"

Slowly Dobokai stepped aside, motioning for the other men to do the same.

"Thank you," Scuff said solemnly. He took Fitz by the arm and half dragged him toward his rooms. It was less dangerous now to go to Fitz's rooms, and lock the doors. Scuff had already determined not to leave him alone tonight anyway.

As soon as they got there, Scuff used Fitz's key to get in, and crept up the stairs as quietly as possible. He did not want to disturb any of the other lodgers, least of all the landlady. If Fitz was thrown out of here it might be difficult to find him another place. He could end up sleeping at the clinic, and there was no room for him there. They needed the space for patients who could not be sent home.

Once inside, Scuff locked the door, then turned to look at Fitz, who stood in the dark, close to the center of the room.

Scuff went over to the gas bracket on the wall and turned up the flame.

In the sudden burst of light Fitz looked down at himself and seemed for the first time to notice the blood soaking him.

"Oh dear," he said wryly. "Rather a lot. Looks worse than it is. Blood can frighten people. It's mostly afterbirth. Mess." He shook his head.

"But she's all right?" Scuff asked. "Are you sure?"

A flicker of irritation crossed Fitz's face. "Of course I'm sure. Do you think I would have left her if I weren't? Husband's there with her, and one of her aunts who's had children of her own. Got a bit difficult at one point, but a stitch or two and she's fine. Beautiful baby." Now he really smiled. "A girl. All perfect. Fingers, toes, everything. Even hair." His smile was far away. "Like pale yellow silk. Never seen anything so totally innocent in my life. She looked straight at me."

Now Scuff believed him. He had seen a newborn baby once. He had forgotten until now how it had looked at him.

"You should wash and go to bed," he said in a matter-of-fact tone. "Throw that shirt away. You'll never get that clean. Maybe the trousers too."

"Only have one other pair. I'll have to clean them . . ."

"I'll get you more," Scuff said rashly. "Can't keep those. You'll scare people. They'll think someone bled to death in your arms. Just take them off, wash and go to bed."

Fitz hesitated.

"Come on!" Scuff said crisply, holding his hand out to take the blood-soaked clothes.

This time Fitz obeyed. Perhaps he could see sense in what Scuff had said. Anything for the welfare of patients seemed to cut through the other things in his mind.

Scuff took the trousers and shirt and Fitz's key, and got rid of the garments in a large bin of rubbish about a hundred yards along the street. He walked back in the soft night, still warm even though some of the stars had clouded over a bit.

He let himself into Fitz's house again, crept up the stairs in his stocking feet, carrying his boots, and very quietly unlocked the door to Fitz's bedroom.

Fitz was asleep, his breathing silent and—judging from the rise and fall of his chest—quite even.

Scuff hesitated. Should he leave him? Was it all right for him to go back to the clinic and get some sleep, in his own bed there? Crow would be relieved to see him, and there would be lots of jobs to do. If he was unlucky, Crow would make him write up all the notes that weren't done yet. He really disliked that. It was true that he learned a lot, but there were so many long words that had to be exactly right. A mistake could hurt someone, even kill them. A medicine with a similar name could actually be quite different. A wrong dosage could be fatal. Fractions, weights, decimal points had to be exact, checked three times.

Actually that was what frightened him: numbers.

Suddenly Fitz moved. All the ease vanished from him and his body was rigid, then he began to shake, muttering something unintelligible, his voice sharp with panic.

Scuff ran over to him and clasped his arm, shaking him, but gently—just enough to wake him.

Fitz cried out as if the touch had scalded him.

"Fitz!" Scuff said urgently. "Wake up! It's just a dream . . ."

But Fitz was somewhere Scuff could not reach him. His whole body was juddering now, and he gasped as if he could barely get his breath. His skin was covered in sweat, his face wet with it, muscles looked tight and hard.

In his mind he was somewhere completely different. A battlefield in the Crimea, corpses of men he knew all around him. Some had been alive and well only hours before, maybe moments ago, others in agony, bleeding to death in front of him, and he couldn't help them. Or he was in one of the hospitals, every breath drawing in the stench of disease, people suffering hideously, and again he could do far too little to help them.

Or was it nothing like that at all? Would Scuff hear in the morning that there had been another murder? That another Hungarian had been stabbed through the chest, his fingers broken, candles snuffed out in his blood? Seventeen? Why seventeen?

Please God, no!

Would it be dangerous to force Fitz awake now, drag him out of the nightmare? Could it damage his mind? Or would he even imagine Scuff was a Russian soldier and attack him? Fitz was not very muscular, but he was lean, and Scuff already knew he was strong.

Now Fitz was weeping uncontrollably. Great sobs racked his body; he could hardly draw in his breath. He was suffocating!

"Fitz!" Scuff shouted at him.

It did no good. He might as well have whispered.

Dare he touch him? Fitz might be unnaturally strong, even enduring pain like this. And he was clearly in agony.

Scuff swung his arm back and then hit Fitz as hard as he could across the front of his chest, where it would do no harm. He yelled at him again. "Fitz!"

Fitz seemed to collapse, then the next moment he was weeping quietly, deep, gentle sobs.

Without thinking about it, Scuff put his arms around him and held him gently until at last the sobs stopped and Fitz seemed to have fallen back into a quieter sleep.

Scuff laid him back on the bed and covered him with the blankets. He was soaked with sweat, but it was almost as if a fever had broken.

Scuff stayed the rest of the night, and in the morning, when Fitz woke up, neither of them spoke of what had happened. Scuff made a stiff cup of tea for each of them, and toasted a little stale bread. Then he said goodbye, quite cheerfully, without making any reference to last night. He wondered if Fitz had actually forgotten.

The first thing he did was go back to the street where he had found Fitz. There was a café at the far end, just around the corner. They served chocolate, coffee, the sort of thing people like to have at that time in the morning. Tea and toast you could do easily enough at home.

He stopped outside the door. He realized his heart was beating like a hammer. Perhaps he was too early? It seemed no one had discovered anything yet.

But it was about eight o'clock. He knew that from the angle of the shadows. He pushed the door open and went inside. The place was full. People were talking cheerfully, as they used to do. The murders, two now, had pretty well silenced laughter.

Two men were sitting opposite each other. One raised his cup of chocolate as if in a toast. The other lifted his own cup and touched sides. They said something in Hungarian.

Scuff was staring at them.

As if aware of his scrutiny, one of them turned to look at him.

"Something good?" Scuff said awkwardly. He felt foolish.

"Yes, yes," the man replied in English. "Mrs. Dorati had her baby last night. A girl! Beautiful! Pavel was in early this morning, smiling so wide he could hardly speak. Said she is the most beautiful thing in the world. Here! Have some chocolate with us! Celebrate."

"Yes," Scuff agreed. His knees were so weak with relief that he needed to sit down anyway. "Yes—I will. Thank you."

CHAPTER

8

THE MURDER OF LORAND Gazda had added to the panic in the area,
and of course it had given Monk a few new avenues of investigation.
Some people could now be excluded as suspects because they could
prove that they had been elsewhere at the time of either one murder or
the other. But narrowing the field was far from good enough for Monk.

Examination of the bayonet and the shears had proved nothing.
The bayonet was old and blunt, and there were no clues as to who had
stolen it from the museum. Half of a pair of shears could have been
relegated to the rubbish heap, and anyone could have taken it from
there.

In spite of all the work the extra men from the regular police had
done, no one had observed either weapon being removed, or seen anyone with them. They yielded no trace of threads or other evidence as to
who had used them.

There was much in the newspapers, talk of panic, even police inefficiency—or worse, corruption. And every issue of newspapers, morning and evening, carried word of civil unrest in one area or another. To the south of the river there were outbreaks of violence in Deptford, Bermondsey and Camberwell. To the north there were smaller fights in Stepney, reports of crowds getting rough on Parsons Green and later in Blackwall. Some of these were exaggerated, but questions in Parliament and the calls for police resignations were increasing.

Hester could think of nothing to say to Monk that would be of any practical help.

Emotional help was a far more elusive and delicate thing. One clumsy word, a false note of encouragement that sounded either patronizing or uninformed, and it would wipe out anything good she might have said.

Every evening Monk came home pale with exhaustion and, more recently, without any new ideas of how to narrow down the still far too large field of possibilities.

"If I knew what started it . . ." he said on the fourth evening after Gazda's death. "Why does anyone hate so passionately that they'll kill like this?" He stared at her across the dinner table. It seemed strangely quiet without Scuff's company, much less enjoyable without his unquenchable appetite.

"Are you sure this is hatred against the Hungarians in general?" she asked. "It feels personal. That much cruelty is very intimate."

"No, I'm not sure," he answered. "But Dobokai is. I don't like the man but everything he's said so far has proven true. Certainly the Hungarians feel as if someone's against them. Why? You've traveled more than I have." He was searching her face, her eyes. "You've seen war close-up. Why does a whole nation suddenly become 'the enemy'? We're not at war with Hungary, and, as far as I know, we never have been. One of the few nations we haven't fought, and haven't invaded or settled, and they haven't invaded us." He looked puzzled, and worried, as if not to understand were his failing.

She must think of an answer that made sense. She could see his belief in himself was wavering.

"Fear," she said with only the barest hesitation. "You don't have to know what the threat really is, just what it could be."

"And what are a couple of hundred Hungarians going to do in a city like London? It's the biggest city in the world, and the heart of an empire that stretches around the globe."

"It doesn't have to make sense. People don't think of the rest of the world. We just live in our own villages within London. And Shadwell is changing. There are Hungarian shops where there used to be English ones. Somebody has lost their job."

His dark eyebrows rose. "So you stick a stake through their hearts, and dip candles in their blood?"

"Candles," she said quickly.

"Yes. I told you . . ."

"Maybe . . . maybe it's religious. The Hungarians are Catholic, aren't they?"

"Yes."

"William, the Catholic world is still very large, very powerful. When I was in Shadwell yesterday I heard someone mention that . . . and religious freedom, the right to be Protestant, if you want to be. It may be foolish, but fear of losing your religion and being governed by a foreign power, from Rome, is very real."

"A real danger?" he said disbelievingly. "Not now . . ."

"No! Not a real danger. It was at the time of Queen Elizabeth and the Spanish Armada. If the storm hadn't sunk them, we could have gone back to Catholicism. But nearly three hundred years ago, it was. And in Europe people still fight religious wars, Catholics against Protestants."

"And in Ireland," he added. "But this is Shadwell Dock. Nobody's threatening anyone's freedom."

"You asked me what makes people lash out so horribly, William. I think it's fear, and fear doesn't have to be rational. It's fear of ideas, things that aren't the way you're used to. Everyone you don't understand, because their language is different, their food, but above all their religion. The Catholic Church used to be the biggest power in Europe.

They excommunicated people who defied their rules, and suddenly those people became invisible, voiceless, homeless, exiled from the community. No baptisms, no marriages, no proper burials and, most of all, no confession or absolution for sins."

"When?" he demanded.

"All England under interdict in the reign of King John." Then she remembered that he had no memory of his youth, probably of half the things he had learned at school. Perhaps not even of school itself! "It doesn't matter now," she said quickly. "But religious fear seems very deep. It's much more recent that the Inquisition burned people at the stake for falling away from the Catholic faith—in Spain! And I don't know where else. Fear doesn't bring out the best in us, in or outside the law."

He looked downward. "I did ask you. I just wasn't prepared for that answer. But then, I wasn't prepared for blades through the heart and candles dipped in blood either."

"It might be nothing to do with religion of any sort," Hester said, trying to bring the discussion back to reason, likelihood, away from terror.

Monk smiled, as if he read her thoughts. "Don't tell me it's something ordinary," he said gently. "The very best you could say is that it's some kind of a madman, whatever his reason."

"I know. Perhaps I shouldn't have raised it. It was just the candles. It probably isn't anything to do with religion at all."

"It might be a secret society," he said reluctantly, doubt in his voice.

"You'll find out, if it matters." She stood up slowly. "For now, I'm going up to bed, and I'm more happy than I can say that I will be there with you, and my whole world will be no larger than that one bedroom." She meant it: the world beyond, even just that bit of it across the river at Shadwell, was too big and too dark to think of. She held out her hand, and he stood up and took it, gently, but still almost too tight for her to knock away—if she had wished to.

———

THE NEXT MORNING WAS one of those late-summer days when the sun shone so clearly there were no dark places anywhere, no alleys where the light did not reach, or where the wind had a cold edge.

Despite her talk with Monk the night before, it was not the Hungarians or even the new murder that was on Hester's mind; it was Fitz and the memory of seeing him that last time in the Crimea, dead, as she was sure, and having to leave him there. The little space they had on wagons had to be used for the living, those they might still save.

She had deliberately forced it from her mind so often, the memory had dimmed. She was trying to forget, and she had nearly succeeded. There was so much else in her life now: work in the clinic, work helping in cases, Scuff, other friendships, such as with Oliver Rathbone and, above all, Monk.

Now Fitz returned to her mind, with the guilt of leaving him, and the knowledge that he had not been dead. All the suffering, physical and emotional, that he had endured since then was, at least in part, her fault. The guilt was overwhelming. He might despise her for it, but she could not lie to him anymore, even if just by remaining silent. It was still deception, and it was for her own convenience.

FIRST SHE WENT ACROSS the river to the north bank, back to her own clinic in Portpool Lane, where Claudine, who was there most of the time, told her that all was well. Squeaky Robinson even forgot to pretend he was angry on seeing Hester. He was busy teaching Worm to read. Worm was an urchin from the riverbank, whom Scuff had rescued. He had no idea how old he was. Counting beyond ten was a skill that still lay ahead of Worm. But a good guess might place him at about seven or eight, though he claimed to be older.

Hester stayed only long enough to ascertain that all was indeed well. Then she traveled by omnibus the short distance to the docks. She had formulated in her mind a dozen times what she would say to Fitz, and it never sounded right. She sat in the omnibus with her shoulders tight, her hands clenched in her lap.

She reached Crow's rooms in Shadwell just before lunchtime, bringing some fresh ham sandwiches with her that she had bought from a peddler along the High Street. The running patterers—men who told the latest news in constant singsong free verse—were still going on about hideous murders, intertwined with gossip and current political comment.

Scuff was delighted to see Hester and immediately put on the kettle. He gave her the latest report on Tibor Havas, which was excellent. He would be able to go home very soon, possibly even today. Tibor was also quite well enough to eat three of the ham sandwiches, and join them around the table. He smiled at everyone, and had learned enough English to say "thank you," which he did quite a number of times, and to try other, longer sentences.

Fitz was not there, and now that Hester had made up her mind to tell him the truth, she could not leave it another day. He might not come again, and if he did not, she would have to go to his lodgings and find him. When something must be done, better to do it as soon as possible. Get it over with. Face the consequences.

Early in the afternoon Scuff called a hansom and rode home with Tibor, promising to see him settled, provided with fresh medicine, and with full instructions for his landlady, who was very willing to look after him. One of them would call by regularly to make sure his progress continued.

Hester was still at Crow's clinic later when Fitz arrived, and she had barely had time to greet him, trying to be natural and yet having to force herself to meet his eyes, when two men came in. They were supporting a third between them. His face was gray with pain and shock, his body twisted at an angle, as if he was desperately struggling to be free. There was a huge bandage around his shoulder, chest and left arm.

They looked immediately at Fitz, perhaps supposing Hester to be a house servant of some sort.

"Is Dr. Crow in? Please! This is . . ." It seemed the man could think of no words powerful enough to describe his need.

Fitz's decision was instant: it required no thought at all. He stood up and went forward, taking a great deal of the injured man's weight as he eased him toward the other room and the bed that only a few hours ago had been occupied by Tibor Havas. There were no sheets on it now, but the mattress was clean. He laid the man down on his right side, being careful not to allow the bandaged arm to touch anything but a pillow.

Both the companions stared at him in consternation. The elder spoke.

"When will the doctor be back? He's in a terrible state . . . can't swallow a thing! Not at all." He was a big man with gray in his hair, but he looked as lost as a child.

"Fitz is a doctor," Hester told him gently. "You were right to bring your friend here. He had a wound a few days ago, and you thought it was healing? Right?"

"Yes. You know about it?"

"No. I live on the other side of the river. But I was a nurse in the Crimea. I've seen this before."

"Is he going to die?" the younger man asked, his voice trembling a little. He looked no more than thirty.

"If it is tetanus, which is what it looks like, then I've seen it cured," she answered. "But it is not easy."

The men who had brought the patient in should not have to witness it. Their distress was unnecessary, and would only get in the way. There was no time to attend to them as well, or to explain.

She turned to Fitz. "I don't know what supplies you have after the last case. Shall I write out a list and ask these men if they will get what they can?" she suggested.

Fitz hesitated only a moment. His smile was slow and there was great sweetness in it. "I'll need you to stay and help, if that's what it is. Like . . . like the past." He turned to the men. "Wait a while. You did the right thing bringing him here. But I need to be sure. Hester, come with me. He's in a bad way."

The men looked at each other, then back at Fitz. They had no strength for trying to take the man any farther. They were frightened and desperate. It was the elder of the two who spoke.

"Is it catching? Can we go back to our families, or . . . or do we . . . ?"

"No, it's not catching from one person to another," Fitz said with assurance. "Unless you've got any cuts on you, and you handled whatever wounded him?"

They looked at each other, heads shaking. "No. That happened on an old cart that broke and ran down the hill. Should we destroy the cart?"

"Is it rusty?"

"Yes . . ."

"Then either be very careful of it or, if it's badly damaged, yes, burn it. Just don't let it cut you."

Hester checked with Fitz, largely as a courtesy, then wrote a list of medicines that the two men could obtain quite easily. She gave it to one of them, hoping that he had, or could find, the necessary money.

Then she went into the other room to help Fitz. He was already standing over the man, talking to him quietly. He had taken off his jacket and rolled up the sleeves of his shirt. Now he glanced at her, across the pain-racked body of the man lying so awkwardly.

She walked over to the table and helped him take off the bandages to expose the wound. She caught her breath as she saw it. It was a long time since she had seen such a mangled mass of flesh. She had grown used to dealing with women of the street who had been beaten or even stabbed, or who were riddled with disease, or weakened by hunger. But this violent destruction of a healthy man took her back to the horrors of war, as if she had been physically hurled through the years. She was a young woman again, far from here, spending every day in a desperate fellowship of skill, pity, exhaustion and dedication, even to the point of death.

Something had torn away the man's skin and most of the right scapula, and a portion of the trapezius muscle and the infraspinatus and supraspinatus muscles. She could not imagine the pain, or the shock to the body.

The division of the strangulated ligaments and the excision of the flaps of flesh had already been done by whatever doctor had first attended the man, probably immediately after the event. The loose, broken pieces of bone had been removed as well, and the wound dressed with a split roller, like the ones they had used on Tibor's wound.

She glanced up at Fitz and saw the anxiety in his eyes. It took her back to the days they had worked together, easily, knowing what to do, dealing with one patient after another, hundreds of men shattered and in agony, more than they could possibly deal with. They were a small, vivid part of a nightmare that consumed everything and everybody they knew. They kept going, borrowing strength from each other.

She looked down again. The injury must have happened a few days ago, because the wound had begun to heal around its edges when this new attack had seized it. She had seen it before—tetanus. It would spread outward from the wound until it affected the whole body. In a few hours he would be in a state of severe muscle spasm from the neck and back all the way down his spine, locked in an uncontrollable agony. He would be thrown back on his shoulders, his jaw totally locked. Swallowing would be impossible. It would not be long after that before he began to sink, and death would become inevitable.

"We haven't long," Fitz said to her very quietly.

She knew what he meant: no indecision, no weighing one treatment against another. A slow decision, however good, would be too late. They must be right.

She looked at Fitz's hands: they were perfectly steady. The tremor of the other day had vanished.

"Opium?" she asked, although only out of courtesy. She knew he would need the poor man feeling as little as possible. The last resort for tetanus was cauterizing the wound with white-hot iron.

Fitz nodded.

She prepared the opium and gave two doses to the patient.

"Narcotic, camphorated oleaginous lint," Fitz told her. "Enough for his whole body. Mild. We'll calm him."

"Over the wound as well?" she asked, already moving to prepare them.

"Yes." Fitz was concentrating on the man and his distress, the tensions that very nearly possessed him now. The patient's whole body was in agony, muscle spasms seizing him in spite of all Fitz could do. The man tried to stop himself from crying out, but it was more than he could manage.

They spent all afternoon applying every treatment they knew, and gradually the patient seemed to ease enough to give them hope.

Fitz sat down for a short break, a move in position to prevent his own muscles from aching. Exhaustion led to errors. They both knew that.

Crow and Scuff returned, tired and wishing to help, but there was nothing they could do except put away the new supplies the patient's two friends had delivered. Crow had never had to deal with tetanus, so he didn't have the necessary medicines in store.

"If he survives, there'll be plenty to do later," Hester told him. "Rest while you can."

"I thought it was fatal," Crow said as they stood in the kitchen, waiting for the kettle to boil. He looked tired, his skin pale and bruised around his eyes.

"It is," she answered. "Unless you can stop it with cauterizing. That has been known to work."

He glanced at the oven, with its large cooking hobs. The cauterizing irons were balanced close to them, ready to heat, if there was nothing else left to do. He could not imagine it.

Hester could. In fact, just the sight of them brought back the smell of burning flesh, choking her, making her stomach churn. Physically she was in London, the Shadwell Docks, the cold water of the Thames flowing out to the sea. In her memory there was gunfire in the distance and hundreds of wounded men, so many they would not be able to help. Fresh wagonloads arrived filthy, in agony and already weak from loss of blood.

And then there were diseases that were going to kill most of them. Cholera, dysentery, fevers . . . overwhelming exhaustion and pain that bled away all strength. Fellowship was the only light, the only thing they could cling to. It was universal, or almost. But Fitz had been the gentlest, the one who could always raise a smile when it seemed the most difficult, who would make absurd jokes, laughter too close to tears.

His anger was always at the idiocy of the authorities in England who had sent out an army without medical supplies, wagons to carry the wounded off the field, tents to shelter the badly injured while they were operated on, only pensioners as stretcher-bearers. There were far too few of them and they were old men. Hester did not know of even one who had survived the first battle, let alone the war.

It was agonizing, infuriating and shameful; so much so that no one in England wanted to know. Florence Nightingale had exhausted herself into illness trying to bring about reform.

It was painful, and yet like the opening of a wound that needed the air, to recall these things with someone who knew and had felt them as she had. If Fitz's mind took him back to those times, whether he willed it or not, she could not turn away.

How many times had he been her one link with sanity, and home? Did she have to tell him that she had searched the bodies on the battle-field to find him—and had believed him dead and beyond help? Wouldn't he be happier not knowing? And yet what would the lie do between them?

She had wept many times, when she was alone and no one was watching, or needing her. But thousands of men had died of wounds, or disease. Thousands more were crippled. There was too much to do to indulge in mourning; too many women who had lost husbands, brothers and sons. One wept alone, in the night. And in the morning there was always something to do.

Now, years later, she was accustomed to happiness, to the warmth, the laughter, the safety of love.

She must speak to Fitz and tell him the truth, but more urgent than that now, there was a man in the next room whose tetanus might be getting worse, and they needed to be ready to act.

Fitz examined the patient again. No more pus had secreted from the wound and the edges of it were not swollen, even though the wound itself seemed puffy and raw.

Hester looked at Fitz.

Crow was standing by, a slight hope in his eyes.

Fitz gritted his teeth, taking the forceps in his hand.

In a flash of foreknowledge, Hester knew what he was going to do, and dreaded it as if it had already happened. She wanted to look away, but habit and the knowledge that the others, particularly Scuff, were aware of her, prevented it.

Fitz touched the blade of the scalpel to the very edge of the wound.

The patient let out a cry of agony so intense they were all jerked into rigidity, as if they too had been hurt beyond bearing.

The patient gasped and groaned, unable to control himself, but he could not swallow at all. His efforts were dreadful to watch. His head was thrown back so far the bones of his spine seemed to be endangered. His jaws were locked tight as if his teeth must break.

"We must get some fluid into him," Fitz said to Crow. "You have a bottle with a tube in it. We can force that into his mouth."

"His teeth won't unlock." Crow argued.

"Take two of them out," Fitz told him. "We have to get some liquid into him."

Scuff was standing by helplessly. His eyes were wide and dark, his face gray.

"Fetch the pliers," Crow told him.

Scuff stood motionless, as though his feet were fixed to the floorboards.

"Will," Fitz said gently. "Get the water."

Scuff blinked, then moved, slowly at first then rapidly. He came back with the drinking bottle filled with water. He held it for Fitz to take.

The patient saw it, a glass bottle filled with clean water. His body arched off the table, his eyes wild. He began to convulse, his body thrashing against the constraints, his mouth foaming with saliva and cries torn out of him as if in a paroxysm of terror.

Crow was appalled.

Hester turned to Scuff. "Take the water back, Will." She used his name deliberately. "And put the irons on the hob. Please."

He took the water, disappearing as he was told. She hoped he would be quicker to respond when it came to using the irons. They had not long before the man choked to death.

Crow looked from Hester to Fitz.

"No choice," Fitz told him with a turning-down of his lips. "I've seen it work. Just keep hold of him. Now the water's gone he'll be better."

"The water seemed to terrify him . . ." Crow began.

"It does," Fitz agreed. "God knows why." He looked at Hester. "You'd better go and see how Will is doing with the irons. White-hot . . ."

"I know." She hated the thought, but she too knew that it was now the only hope. Would she have had the nerve to do it alone? Probably not.

She found Will in the kitchen with the irons poked right into the heart of the fire.

He looked at her, his face pale, eyes full of questions.

"Tetanus," she told him. "You can get it in wounds, even small ones, especially off iron. If you ever get a wound to deal with, from a piece of iron, make sure it bleeds before you try to stitch it. Enough to clean out all the blood that touched the metal."

He stared at her while she took the oven glove and pulled out one of the irons to look at the tip. It glowed red. She pushed it back in again, then opened up the stove to add more coal. She took the bellows and blew hard till the flame came off the coals blue-white and flickering. Then she closed the door and waited.

Will said nothing, but he hardly took his eyes from her face.

Eventually the iron was white-hot and she took it out, very carefully.

"Go ahead of me and warn them," she told him.

Will nodded, and did as she said.

She went into the room, keeping the iron in the shelter of her body so the patient would not see it, although he was in such a spasm of agony that it was doubtful he would know if she had carried it in front of her.

Fitz took it from her and touched the white end of it to the wound. The scream that tore out of the patient was so terrible it must have been heard in half the neighborhood.

Fitz did it again, and again. Then with the second iron when the first was covered in dried blood and had lost its greatest heat. It took only moments, but to those watching it seemed an age. To the patient it could only have seemed like hell itself. Hester could not imagine what Fitz was feeling, but not once did he hesitate.

Then it was completed.

Will took the irons away and plunged them into a bucket of cold water in the kitchen.

The patient was covered with sweat. It poured off his face, his body, what they could see of his arms and legs. Even his hair was soaked with it.

"Hester." Fitz's voice was half strangled in his throat. "Fetch the nitrated milk of sweet almonds, add sixty drops of laudanum. And a few drops of Hoffman's Anodyne Liquor. In a glass . . ."

She did so as quickly as she could, and returned with the glass a few minutes later. The patient was sitting up quite normally, his jaws at last relaxed. He took the glass from her and drank all the liquid, carefully at first, then with relish.

Fitz requested the camphorated narcotic liniments as before, and they wrapped the man's body in very warm flannel. At first he sweated profusely, but after quite a short while he sank into a deep sleep, and seemed utterly relaxed.

Fitz also was exhausted and, not surprisingly soaked in sweat. Crow was fascinated, but kept moving his shoulder, as if he too had had all his muscles locked in tension and even their relaxation still left him aching.

Will had disappeared into the kitchen, and Hester assumed he was cleaning up, or even making notes. But he reappeared ten minutes later with a tray of tea and several hunks of bread and cheese, and some slices of cold beef.

"Worth your weight in opium," Fitz said cheerfully. "I'm never going back to war again, but if I did, I'd take you with me."

Will glanced at Hester, then smiled widely and thanked Fitz.

CROW AND FITZ TOOK turns during the night checking on the patient, and found him sleeping. Will went home across the river with Hester.

The following day, Hester went back to Crow's clinic with the further supplies she knew he would need. But mainly she had steeled herself to speak to Fitz today. If she continued much longer without telling him the truth, it would be even more difficult, becoming a lie by omission.

The patient was doing well. He was very weak, but free from the terrible spasms of tetanus, and able to eat and drink. Scuff and Crow were out attending patients they could visit in their own homes, and Fitz was at last taking his turn sleeping.

She checked on the patient herself, then started to put away the medicines she had brought, and was still sorting out others, making notes of what was running short, when she heard movement in the room where the beds were. She went to see if Fitz was up and would like a cup of tea.

Knocking, she received no answer, but she could hear movement. She knocked again, then went in. Fitz was half out of the bed, his arms waving and gesticulating angrily. His face was contorted, his mouth open in a silent scream of such terror it froze her just to see it.

She blinked, horrified at her intrusion on such anguish. It should have been utterly private. Should she leave? Had he even seen her?

Then she realized that he was asleep. Whatever he saw in his nightmares, it had nothing to do with the immediate reality of where he was. Was he back on the battlefield, where they had left him with the other corpses for whom there was no time for burial? In his mind, was he suffocating under the dead and the dying?

Or was he in one of those tents where the floor was piled with the broken limbs of men who had been whole only hours before? You could barely take a step without slipping in the gore of clotted blood.

But should she wake him? Doing so was instinctive, but was it best for him? What could the shock do to him? Would he be humiliated that she had intruded into this private hell of his, and seen him at his weakest and most terrified?

He had stopped moving. His arms were still. Suddenly he drew in a deep, shuddering breath and his whole body was racked with sobs. He wept as if his heart would break.

She held on to him and did not try to stop him. There was no point in speaking; this was primal, too deep for any words to reach.

When at last he was silent, she still held him, until he stiffened a little and tried to move away. Then she let him go.

He turned his head, not looking at her. He was exhausted, and perhaps embarrassed now. What could she say to ease the moment? Silence was no longer enough.

"Do you dream a lot?" she asked.

It was long seconds before he replied.

"Yes. I'm afraid to go to sleep," he said quietly, his voice husky as if his throat ached.

"The battlefield?"

"Mostly. Sometimes it's just noise and darkness. Don't know where I am, except that I can smell blood. It's all over me. I can feel it. At times I'm drowning in it."

She had had those dreams too: an overwhelming feeling of helplessness, as if there were people in pain everywhere and she was doing nothing to help. But not lately; not since she could awaken and find Monk beside her. But that was hardly helpful to Fitz.

She put her hand on his shoulder and tightened her grip a little so he would feel the pressure.

"I can smell death everywhere," he went on quietly. "It's as if there's something I'm not doing, and it's my fault, but I don't know what it is. I wondered once or twice if I was dead and that was hell: the helplessness, and the pain you couldn't reach. Why had nobody found me?"

"Fitz . . ."

It was as if he had not heard her.

"Fitz . . ." she repeated.

Was he so hurt because he thought she had not looked for him?

"Fitz! I . . ." It was so difficult to say. However she worded it, it still sounded like she was making excuses. "I looked for you. I . . . I found you. You were covered in blood and you were cold. I touched your skin, your face. I felt no pulse. I felt as if part of me had died too, but there was nothing I could do. The stretcher-bearers with me were calling out for me to save someone who was still alive, and bleeding. I wanted to take you back . . . I should have." Her throat was tight and the words were difficult to find. "But there was room for only one more on the cart. We took the man who was bleeding. I'm . . . I'm so sorry . . ."

For seconds he said nothing.

She heard movement in the doorway and turned. Will—Scuff—was standing there, his face white, his eyes wide with horror—and blame.

What could she say? Excuses now would make things worse.

"You found him?" Will said shakily. "And you left him there?"

Fitz turned toward him. He too seemed to be looking for words for a moment, then he smiled, and his voice was hoarse, but soft, as if he had found some inner warmth.

"Always save the living, Will. You can mourn the dead afterward. Your own grief doesn't matter . . . not then. She thought I was dead. Hell, even I thought I was dead! She picked up my job to do in my place, and saw to those she might be able to save. The day may come when you'll do that too. Save those you can . . . that's the rule.

"It must have been long after you'd gone when I came to," Fitz went on. "I could hear movement. At first I didn't understand it, then I realized what it was—scavengers!" He let out a little grunt. "The small animals who are forever cleaning up behind us. Black crows, rats, God knows how many things with sharp, slithering feet."

Neither Hester nor Will interrupted him. He must finish what he needed to say.

"I was wet. There was blood all over the place. My arm hurt like hell. There were bones broken, but my legs were all right. I could get to my feet and stand. Most of the blood on me wasn't mine."

He was silent for a little while. Hester knew he was back in those minutes, feeling it again: the guilt for being alive when he was surrounded, as far as the eye could see, by violent death. She had seen it in others, the search for reason, the proof.

He went on in a monotone, describing how he found clothes that were better than his, an almost clean shirt, another to tear up and bandage himself. One of the dead had a canteen of water and whisky.

He had found a barn to shelter in, although it contained little of worth to eat. As the days went by he moved farther away, found help. Then he became feverish, and stayed at a farm where they looked after him. He had no idea for how long.

He moved westward. Much of it was a blur in his mind. He was often cold and hungry, but he found assistance. By the time he got as far as Hungary, he was healed, and finding odd jobs here and there, mainly caring for farm animals.

"Not so different from men," he said wryly. "At least some of them aren't. I never learned much about chickens."

He was silent again, this time for so long that she thought he was not going to say any more. But then he started with more fragments about the Hungarians, and how they took him in, looked after him. Gradually he learned to speak more and more of their language. The nightmares receded, but they never stopped.

He moved westward always. Some places he stayed for a few months, others for years. After leaving Hungary he had gone through Austria, then France. Finally he had reached England, but he was now a stranger here, just as he had been everywhere else.

"I landed in Hull, on the east coast. At first it seemed very odd, but I got used to it. I have no family here, and I thought those people I knew would have presumed me dead. I considered contacting them, but I thought I would rather be a dead hero than a live wreck, uncertain of too much, haunted by nightmares, afraid of the darkness inside myself. I thought of looking for you. I did, and I learned about your life now. I hadn't intended to get to know you—far more than that, for you to know me. Memory can be kinder, and a lot easier to live with."

Injury and disease were always the same, so he was useful everywhere. The dreams grew less, until recently. Now, among people who spoke his own, familiar language, they were back.

He was hunched over as he said it, the words almost muffled as he put his hands up to his face. "Sometimes when I wake up, I have no idea where I am. But I can always smell death."

"Do you remember afterward where you've been, and how you got there?"

Again the moments passed and the silence became tense. Hester was afraid of the answer. She knew now what it was.

"You don't." She said it for him.

"No."

"Fitz, you have to turn back and face whatever it is that hurts you so badly—what you keep looking away from. When you see it, it will lose its power to rob you of your inner self."

Finally his eyes met hers. "Perhaps I don't look at it for a very good reason. I know men who've lost limbs and yet years afterward they still think they can feel them. They still get up out of bed to stand on a leg that isn't there. Sometimes we just aren't strong enough to face it. We lie down to sleep, and we can forget."

"You don't forget, Fitz. You're there in your nightmares. I don't know where, but either the battlefield or the hospital. Or maybe on one of those terrible roads with horses, exhausted themselves, pulling wagon-loads of wounded, every jolt a new pain." She could remember them herself. When she rode in a carriage after a long evening out, every rough stone in the street reminded her.

But there was a happiness inside her, new responsibilities that filled her mind. Maybe once a year she was back again, but it passed with the daylight. She was not alone, in the deepest possible sense.

"Fitz . . . you must face what you can only half remember. It won't be worse than the dreams. You lost patients. Everyone did. And you were out in the field. You tried your hardest. Let the dream play out, and see what it is. If you don't, it will get bigger and bigger."

"Face it?" he said, looking straight at her now. "Look at it all and see where I failed, as if it still matters?"

"I suppose so," she agreed.

"And you?" he said with the shadow of a smile in his eyes. "Have you done that too?" His look was very direct, even probing. Suddenly their roles had become reversed. This was the old Fitz that she remembered. The strength was there, momentarily, the relentless honesty that dealt with life, pain, loss that seemed overwhelming.

"I don't dream anymore," she answered. It was very nearly true. The nightmares had not been banished just by love, or even the happiness of having a purpose. It was that Monk had his own nightmares, and so he understood, if not the details, at least the fact that some things from the past never entirely leave.

"Don't you?" Now his voice was very gentle. "Not even about your father, and then your mother? Not about James; though that wasn't your fault. God knows how many people lost brothers or sons in that bloody war. But Charles? Your brother who stayed at home, the one who wasn't the hero, where his brother and his sister were. The one who had to deal with the bereavement of the family's favorite son being killed, then the swindle and financial loss, the shame, your father's suicide and your mother's death from grief, all without you being there to help? Don't you ever dream about that?"

She stared at him in disbelief. In a few words, a matter of two minutes, he had stripped her naked of all wrappings and defenses that had kept her secrets hidden from others, but most of all from herself.

He gave a sad little smile. "I know you, Hester. We've too much shared past, terrible things endured together. Did you not think you would be the first person I would look for when I got back home?"

She could not find anything to say.

"I went to find Charles. He told me everything that you found when you returned, all the loss and grief. He also told me he hadn't seen you for years. He might have been able to find you, if he'd tried. But what for? There was nothing to say anymore. Old wounds can still be raw. They'd still bleed if you ripped the bandages off."

It was true. All of it. She found her eyes filling with tears and an ache in her throat so tight she could barely swallow.

She felt his hand on her arm, gentle, but too strong for her to shake off.

"Fight your demons too, Hester. 'Physician, heal thyself!' And of course I'll try. You know I never break my promises—not to you anyway."

She did not answer him. Could she do it? It was so easy to tell him to face the worst within himself.

She put out her hand and clasped his. She felt him shaking still, still fighting to keep control. She moved a step closer and very softly put her arms around him.

"I will," she promised.

He relaxed at last, leaning even closer, his head resting against hers, and drew in a deep, shuddering breath.

HESTER LEFT AFTER CROW had returned. Their patient who had suffered so appallingly with tetanus was continuing to thrive, and gave no cause for further anxiety. Another day or two and he would be able to return to his home.

Hester walked the short distance to the riverbank and the nearest stairs, where she would be able to catch a ferry home. It was late afternoon and the sun was already low over the city skyline to the west. She walked across the stone of the dock, toward the steps that led down to the water.

There was a boat coming toward her, but it was still far away.

It was an ebb tide, but still far too high to expose the mud-banks. It would be a hard pull for the ferryman across the tide, and the river was busy.

It was not the thought of Charles or her own half-smothered guilt that troubled her, although it was awoken again, and far from easy. Before she turned to that, she must help Fitz. If she set aside that task, even for an hour, she might be too late.

Perhaps she was too late already?

She didn't worry most about the nightmares, or the pain that was like a raw nerve in his mind; she feared that the times he could not remember, here in Shadwell, might hold the worst yet: a reality he could never escape. Scuff—Will—had told her about finding Fitz wandering in the streets at night, covered in blood, and that Dobokai and his allies had accused him of murder.

This must have been out of fear and prejudice. Fitz was different. Even though he spoke Hungarian, in their minds he was only half one of them. Will had found that Fitz's story was true. He had assisted in a difficult birth.

But the darkest fear in Fitz's own mind lay in the times he had not had Scuff to find him, to check on where he had been. Fitz himself did not know. He had no way to defend himself. In his memory he had been back in the Crimean battlefields, the wretched, filthy and disease-ridden hospitals, or out on the freezing hillsides alone with dying men he could not help.

Or a fugitive, alone and still wounded himself, somewhere in Europe between the Crimea, on the Black Sea, and the English Channel, which bounded Britain's southernmost shore.

If they accused him again, he could not prove his innocence because he did not know it. He had told her openly that there were times he could not remember. She must prove his innocence for him. She must find out where he had been during the murders, if she could possibly do it.

But would there be witnesses who would stand up and swear to his innocence, and be believed, even if their own people blamed him for these terrible murders, and ostracized those defending him, calling them traitors?

Better to prove who really was to blame. It was the only thing everyone would have to believe.

But was Fitz innocent? Even asking herself the question made her feel riddled with guilt. Was it possible that in some nightmare delirium he had done these things?

Why these men? Why the candles?

But then, why would anyone do that? Fitz had spent time, perhaps years, in Hungary. The proof of that lay in his familiarity with the language, so unlike not only English but all the other European languages an educated man might know. It seemed to bear no resemblance to German, French, Spanish, Italian, not even to the Latin every well-educated Englishman learned at school.

What had happened when he was there? Or, more importantly, what did he believe had happened?

She had to prove his innocence to the police, to the public, but most of all to Fitz himself.

No, that was not quite true: most of all to herself.

But she had to do it. For all the days and nights they had spent in the same desperate struggle to save lives, to ease the dying, to keep up hope and heart a thousand miles from home, in a hell that had tested them to the last degree. And because she had found him on the battle-field and accepted his death too easily. If she had insisted on recovering his body, maybe all this would have been different.

CHAPTER

9

It had been a long day, and one in which very little progress was apparent. Monk left the police station at Wapping and walked along the open dock toward the stairs, where the ferry would pick him up to take him across the river and home.

He and Hooper had spent most of their time inquiring into the purchase of large numbers of candles, and especially of varied colors. They were a very usual form of lighting, and everyone bought them pretty regularly. At one point Monk and Hooper discovered a shipment of purple-violet candles, but they had gone to many different hardware shops and chandlers, and no one could recall to whom they had been sold. They were not a different price from the usual yellowish color, so receipts were of no help.

Monk himself spent some time in the library looking up all the rituals he could find. They were many and varied, but none of the books had any reference to the number seventeen. He even consulted the regular police regarding graffiti, unusual symbols and religious sects.

Of course, the newspapers only made it worse. But about the only thing more damaging than gossip and unreasonable speculation was a press censored by a panicking government, no better informed than the public, and no better in its moral intentions.

There were one or two cases of violence, brawls that escalated into knife fights, but although they were attributed to the general terror, there was no proof that they were a result of the murders.

It was another mild late-summer evening. It should have been a peaceful end to a long day. The sound of the rising tide lapping against the piles that held up the wharf was so soft it could have lulled a tired man to sleep. The sharp smell of the incoming flood from the estuary was not pleasant to everyone, with its salt, mud and occasional refuse, but Monk had grown used to it, and there is an element of pleasure in what is familiar.

To his irritation, he heard footsteps behind him. He would have liked to spend the journey home alone. Then he turned and saw that it was Will, whose new, smarter boots had a louder sound than he was used to. Monk had thought it was a man coming. He looked at Will's height, and his fast-broadening shoulders. Perhaps he was not wrong?

"Going home?" he asked, hoping now that he was.

Will smiled. "Don't need me tonight. I can have a real sleep. The man with tetanus—that was awful." He winced as he said it. "Just the smell of it . . ."

"Tetanus smells?" Monk was surprised.

Will gave a brief laugh. "Not the tetanus, the flesh of the wound when you put the white-hot iron on to cauterize it."

Monk let go of his own day, and his frustration at its futility. Will's eyes held a very definite satisfaction, and not only at the fact that the man had survived the ordeal; he was also obviously pleased at the look on Monk's face.

"I'll imagine it, thank you," Monk said tartly. "I suppose he is now alive and well?"

"He's well enough to go home," Will replied, relaxing into a smile.

"Well done."

Will took another breath, then looked over across the water.

"I don't think a doctor should be called Scuff," he said quietly. "It's not . . . it doesn't make you think he knows what he's doing. I . . ." He took another deep breath. "I need people to trust me. They won't get better if—"

"I understand," Monk interrupted. "What would you prefer? You never told us what your real name was."

"I don't know," Will said awkwardly. "Nobody called me . . . anything."

"Then you'd better choose a name."

"I did. When I was in church, with Hester, a long time ago." He glanced at Monk, then away again. "They asked me what my name was." There was a flush of color in his face now. "She said William. So I told Crow and Fitz to call me Will." Now at last he looked at Monk. "Is that all right?"

Monk felt a ridiculous rush of pleasure. He looked at the river, in case Scuff read him too easily. "I think it's very appropriate," he said calmly. "It's a good name for a doctor. Easy to say, easy to remember and strong enough to know that he's serious."

"Oh . . ." Will did not want his emotions to show quite so clearly as they did. "Good," he said, then a moment later, "thank you."

The ferry came and they were rowed across the water in comfortable silence. The wind had dropped and the tide had reached its height. The sun was low and there was a softness in the air, almost a patina of gold, as if the city were not real but an old master painting whose varnish mellowed everything.

They stopped at the Greenwich Stairs. Monk paid the ferryman, but before they had even begun to walk up the hill to Paradise Place, Will began to talk again, quickly, as if he needed to have it said before they turned into their own short street.

"Fitz is sick," he began. "Not in his body, although maybe that too. It's his mind." He kept looking straight ahead as he spoke, and he dragged his feet intentionally, giving himself time. "He has terrible nightmares. I mean really bad." He struggled to find the words, seeming to have some battle inside himself.

Monk stopped, waiting. He could see that whatever Will was going to say, it was of great importance to him.

Will looked at him. "Like I used to have after you got me out of the bilges in Jericho Phillips's boat. The kind that makes you shake and sweat all over, and weep and . . . and you can't really tell anybody, 'cos if they don't know, there isn't any way . . . You don't know the words. I mean . . . words are for saying things when you both know what the words mean . . ."

"I understand. Fitz has been to places we haven't and seen and known things that words can't describe."

Will looked relieved. "That's right. And he couldn't fix it." He hunched his shoulders quickly, and then forced them straight again. "Any doctor knows there are people he can't save. But hundreds of them! And they're all people you know! Screaming out for you to help, and you can't. It's enough to drive anyone . . . mad."

"Is that what you're afraid of, that he's losing his mind?"

Will nodded, not willing to say it aloud. "But, more than us, he's afraid of it too." He looked down at the pavement again. "I was out late a few nights ago, and I saw him in the street. He was walking slowly, as if he was lost. And . . . and he was covered in blood . . . dark gore, like . . . I don't know."

"Why didn't—" Monk started, then bit off the rest of his question. "What did you do?"

"I took him back to his house. I had to calm down Dobokai and a few of his friends. They were all ready to take him by force."

Monk felt both fear and anger well up inside him. He struggled not to let them show.

"Good," he said as calmly as he could. He must not let the pictures form in his mind: Dobokai's smug face with his blazing blue eyes. He could control a crowd better than any other man Monk had seen. He forced his voice to be level. "What had happened? Where had the blood come from?"

"Fitz helped at a difficult birth. It was the afterbirth come away, and he hardly noticed it. I checked. I saw the baby the next day." Suddenly he smiled and all the pain vanished from his face. "A little girl. She was so tiny, so beautiful. The father told me how Fitz helped them. Right that minute he was the happiest man in the world. He looked at that tiny little girl and his face shone . . ." For a moment Will was lost in his own memory.

Monk had never seen a baby not yet a day old. He had never even thought about it. Now, suddenly, he was filled with envy. To have helped in such an event was uniquely beautiful.

Will's voice brought him back to the moment.

"He knew where he'd been that time," he went on. "But he isn't all right, he really isn't. If you'd seen his face after one of those nightmares—his skin is gray, his clothes are soaked in sweat and his whole body shakes all over, like a convulsion. He can't help it. He . . . he hardly knows where he is . . . or where he's been."

Will's eyes were wide and frightened.

"You're afraid he could have killed Fodor and Gazda, and not know it himself?"

Will wanted to deny it instantly, but he guessed the truth was in his eyes. He nodded, only a fraction, but it was enough.

Fitz had a past with Hester, terrible suffering, heroic endurance, courage and pain, victories and losses that stretched every sinew of the mind and even of the soul, shared and understood. Monk knew little of that except what the history books said, and the occasional references she had made, the flares of temper at injustice and her impatience with blind authority.

He had seen some hideous things himself, but all he could remember was here in London, and he knew that in the clinic in Portpool Lane she had seen many of them also. War, day after day, year after year, sights he could not imagine, she had shared with Fitz. How did she remain whole, still gentle at heart? He would like to think he had helped in that, at least a little, but he could not ask, not ever.

Now Fitz was afraid he might have committed these frightful crimes that were turning the neighborhood people one against another. That was something Monk could understand more profoundly than Fitz would believe. When he first woke up in the hospital, remembering nothing, not even the familiarity of his own face in the looking glass, all the evidence pointed to him as having been the one who had beaten Joscelyn Gray to death. Monk had no idea if it was true or not, but the more he investigated it, the more he could believe it was. The evidence suggested it, his own flashes of memory confirmed it and, God knew, Gray had more than deserved it.

Only Hester—when at the time he barely knew her and liked her even less—only she had believed he could be innocent.

Did she now believe Fitz was innocent too?

"Does Hester know?" he asked.

Scuff turned away from him. "Yes."

They were walking slowly now, as if the hill were very steep.

"She's going to try to save him," he added.

Monk was hardly surprised. In fact, if Scuff had said she was not going to, he would not have believed it. Hester had risked her own safety trying to save Monk, when she barely knew him. She had believed in his innocence when he did not believe in it himself. Surely she would do at least the same for Fitz, with whom she had shared and achieved so much.

He was ashamed when he realized how greatly he had resented Fitz and the extraordinary past he shared with Hester, while he himself had so little past of any sort. It was small and ugly to hold back the compassion now.

"Of course she is," he said to Scuff. "She would never walk away."

Scuff matched him step for step. He was easily tall enough to do that now. "But you're going to help, aren't you? I mean . . . he might have done it! Not even knowing what he was doing! Thinking he was fighting Russians, or something . . ."

"Of course I will," Monk replied. He had no idea how he was going to do it; he would just start wherever he could. One thing was certain: there was no point in arguing with Hester.

———

THEY HAD A QUIET supper, and Scuff excused himself to go to bed early, and study his books. Crow had given him a lot to learn, or so he said.

As soon as the door was closed and they heard his muffled footsteps going up the stairs, Monk turned to Hester. She looked very composed, sitting in her favorite chair. He was opposite her, the other side of the fireplace, with his back to the French window that faced their small garden. He had taken that seat because he knew how she loved to look at the sky, and the wind in the leaves of the poplars.

Anyone who knew her less well would suppose that she was at ease, but he noticed the tension of her shoulders, how tight the muscles of her neck were. Her hands were perfectly still, as if she were deliberately keeping them from fidgeting.

"Scuff told me that when he is working he would like to be known as Will from now on," he began.

She smiled. "I hope you don't mind? I was asked—"

"I know. At the church. It is the greatest compliment." He did not say that to assure her; he meant it. "I think he is learning remarkably well."

She frowned slightly, not knowing what else he was thinking, but aware that something further bothered him.

"Hester, he knows that Fitz is ill in his mind. He's seen the fear, the nightmares, the delusions . . ."

"He doesn't have delusions . . ." She stopped, even before he interrupted her.

"Yes, he does," he said simply. "Scuff found him wandering the streets, alone, at night, covered in blood." He saw from her face that she knew something of this but it was far less than the full story he was telling her now. "I'm sorry," he went on, more gently. "Before Scuff could learn much more, they were stopped by Dobokai and a couple of his supporters. Scuff managed to talk their way out of it, but it wasn't easy. Fitz eventually told him that the blood all over him was from a difficult birth, and that turned out to be true, when Scuff investigated the next day."

"Were they all right?" Hester asked. "The mother, the baby?"

He had thought at first she meant Scuff and Fitz. "Oh . . . yes. The blood was afterbirth. It probably looked like more than it was. It doesn't take much blood to look terrible. The point is that Fitz didn't at first know where he was, or what had happened. Scuff told me that he has chills, delusions, nightmares he can't come out of."

He put his hands over hers, holding them. "How much do you know about him, really? Not who he was sixteen years ago but who he is now?"

She looked down at their hands, clasped together in front of them.

"I don't," she answered. "And I know very well that he is ill. He was so badly injured he appeared dead, and he was left on the battlefield with the rest of the casualties they had no time to bury. He made his own way back from the Crimea to England, on foot. He stopped in a lot of places, but mostly Hungary. At first because he was too ill to go on, then later because they were good to him, and he had nothing to return to here."

Monk tried to imagine it: homeless, in pain, belonging nowhere, looking only for survival, a roof, food. He had thought his own total loss of his past, his identity, was hard. After he had healed from the coach crash that had knocked him senseless and broken a couple of ribs, he had no further illness and no lasting injury. Everybody was a stranger to him, even himself, and that was the worst of all, because of the demons that lurked in flashes of violence, and in the eyes of those who did know him, and remembered very clearly the man he had been. He knew what it was to wake in the night covered with a sweat of fear as to what might lie within himself, what horror might have given rise to the memories of violence. If Fitz felt the same, and had no way to find the truth, then Monk understood him far better than Fitz would ever know.

Monk had learned the truth of the murder of Joscelyn Gray, but the understanding of fear had never left him. He was wiser and a lot slower to judge because of it. But Fitz would never know what lay behind him, and within him. Those who could have told him were mostly dead, and those living were scattered everywhere and probably only too willing to forget.

That did not mean he was innocent of the Shadwell murders.

"Why didn't you tell me?" Monk asked. His voice came out more sharply than he had intended. He was hurt that Hester did not trust him with something so sensitive, and so important. Had she thought his jealousy over Fitz's friendship with her would taint his view? That thought was more painful than he wished her to know.

Now she looked up and met his gaze, steadily. "Because it is your job to find out who killed Fodor, and now Gazda, and to prevent anyone else from dying. It is not for me to tell you, to . . . to compromise you in your job. I have to find out if Fitz is innocent, and prove it. You can't do it . . . you mustn't. And he can't do it himself."

Immediately Monk's mind was crowded with all the ways in which she could be hurt. The first that he saw was how deeply it would wound her if in fact Fitz was guilty.

Next was the physical danger to her from Fitz himself, if he was guilty, and she was forced to recognize it. If they were close together when some circumstance made it impossible for him to avoid the truth anymore, would he finally turn against her? Would he allow them to make him see what he had done? Or would he consider it the last betrayal by a woman with whom he had shared the horrors of war, and fight against her?

If that happened, would she fight her way out, and save herself? Or would she still go on trying to save him from the people who were descending into panic, and the violence that panic so often brings? If she sided with Fitz, would his enemies tear her apart also? Would they even see any distinction between them? Panic was a type of madness. He had seen that before. Scalding shame would come after the fear passed, but it would be too late to save Hester!

And what of her own guilt, at her misjudgment if he was guilty? And perhaps even worse, at not saving him if he was innocent!

"Hester—" he began.

"I know," she said, cutting him off. She was facing him now, looking straight into his eyes, and he saw her fear. "He could be guilty. But I have to try. William, there is no way I can sacrifice him to my own peace of mind, just because he might be guilty. I don't believe he is, I really don't. But if I'm wrong, then something has happened to him that is not his fault. Would you have me prejudge him and walk away to preserve my own comfort?"

"Take Scuff with you, when you do—I mean Will! Please?"

She nodded, too filled with emotion to speak. Then she leaned forward and kissed him.

MONK WOKE UP THE next morning to the sound of knocking on the front door. Beside him, Hester was still asleep. It was warm and the sunlight lay in bright patterns on the floor.

The knocking continued.

Monk slipped out of bed and grasped his robe, then went down the stairs as quickly as he could without slipping. He opened the front door and saw Hooper standing on the step, his face white, his shirt buttoned crookedly and his hair askew.

He did not wait for Monk to ask.

"There's been another. A man called Viktor Rosza. Early fifties. Widower. In banking. Just like the others, skewered through the chest, more candles saturated in blood. It's even more violent than the others."

For a moment Monk froze. Why should he have thought it was over? Hooper's shoulders and the grief in his face spoke the reality.

"Who found him?" Monk asked. "Has the police surgeon got there yet? Is there anything new?"

"Police surgeon's probably there by now," Hooper replied. "He wasn't yet when I left. I doubt he'll be much use. He wasn't before. He'll give us a guess at the time of death, but since it was almost certainly before dawn . . ."

"What time were you called?"

"Half-past four. Just coming dawn," Hooper answered bleakly.

Monk glanced at the clock in the hallway. It read almost quarter to six. "I'll get dressed and come. Make yourself a cup of tea—and one for me." He pointed toward the kitchen. Hooper was familiar with it. Once, when he had been badly injured, he had made his way here, and Hester had dressed his injuries and kept him here until he was well enough to care for himself.

Fifteen minutes later Monk was washed and shaved, and both had hastily eaten two pieces of toast Hooper had made and drunk a cup of tea, although it was still rather too hot.

When they were outside in the street, loping down the hill toward the dockside and the ferry, Monk asked for details.

"You didn't say who found him," he prompted. "Don't tell me it was Dobokai again."

"Not this time. It was the constable on patrol," Hooper said grimly. "The door to Rosza's house in Sheridan Street was partly open, so he knew there was something wrong. He knocked, and when there was no answer, he pushed it completely open, and flashed his lantern around. Poor devil. Saw the body skewered to the floor, blood everywhere and candles set all around the room, seventeen of them again, all smeared with blood. Even an icon of the Virgin Mary still hanging on the wall, but with blood on that too. Whoever this damned lunatic is, he's getting worse. I don't know why they make a god out of the Virgin Mary, but what if they do? It's their business. It's not like she wasn't one of the best people who ever lived. You could do a lot worse." He shook his head. "If God trusted her to raise Jesus, you can't place more on a person than that!"

Monk had not given the matter any thought, but when put that way, he was obliged to agree.

"None of my business anyway," he replied. "As long as they don't try to make the Pope more important to obey than the government of our own country, I don't care what they believe."

Hooper gave him a quick, startled glance.

"History," Monk said briefly. "Can't have a Catholic on the throne, because his first loyalty would be to Rome, not to England. So I learned at school . . ."

"Remember that, do you?" Hooper asked with sudden interest. He knew of Monk's amnesia.

"Actually, I do," he replied, as casually as he could. "So much terror and hatred seemed idiotic, until you read about the fires and blood it brought, the threatened invasion of the Spanish Armada, the trials and betrayals, and the fear."

Hooper's reply was lost in the sound of the waves on the steps going down to the water, and Monk's shout as he hailed the ferry about twenty yards away.

They did not speak again until they were on top of the dock at Wapping. It was quicker to walk to Shadwell than to the High Street and look for a hansom. On the way, Monk told Hooper what he had learned from Scuff about Fitz. It felt like a betrayal, yet he could not keep it to himself if there was the slightest suspicion that Fitz was involved in the murders. And maybe, he hoped, if Hooper knew, he could help to prove Fitz's innocence.

Even before they reached Sheridan Street they saw the gathering crowd of angry, frightened people. Carts were stopped, blocking the road, men in work clothes shouted in protest, arms waving, some with fists in the air. Women carrying laundry, others with brooms and buckets, come from scrubbing down doorsteps, joined them. Fear was turning to anger against those who should have protected them from this horror.

Monk saw Antal Dobokai almost immediately. It was not that he was taller than those surrounding him, it was something about his stance, and perhaps the feeling that those near him were turned to watch him.

Fifty yards away there was another knot of people around a different man. He stood with his arms raised, fists tight. He stopped shouting only as he realized that Dobokai had halted and was facing Monk and Hooper. The scene was ugly. Anger was on the surface, because it was less painful than fear, less debilitating, and there was no shame attached to it.

"Gaspar Halmi," Hooper said, indicating the man who was now slowly lowering his fists. "Aspirations to lead the community, hence the confrontation with Dobokai, who seems to have the same goal in mind."

Monk was about to dismiss this as local town politics; then he realized that even if it was not the principal cause of the unrest, it would still be wound through the people's actions and reactions afterward. Passions as deep as these were never static.

Dobokai ignored Monk as if he were just one more member of the crowd. They were close enough now to hear what he was saying, and they got a bystander to translate what they could not understand.

"Keep calm, my friends!" Dobokai's voice carried extraordinarily well. "Can't you see that dividing us and scattering us in all directions is exactly what our enemies want?"

"Passive is what our enemies want!" Halmi shouted back, his tone less clear, far less penetrating. "They would be delighted if we all go home quietly and huddle in corners. They can pick us off one by one!"

There was a cry of agreement from several listeners. An old man brandished a walking stick in the air. Somewhere out of sight, a woman was weeping.

Dobokai responded immediately. "We have to find who it is that is doing these terrible things. We are intelligent, civilized people. We are not barbarians, or panicky schoolgirls. We must use our brains, our knowledge. We must help the police. We are in England now: we live within a law and order where crime is punished." He glanced at Monk, then back at the crowd.

"But the law cannot punish people if they don't catch them. Think! Use your knowledge and your intelligence. Who is doing this terrible thing to us, and why? What are they frightened of?" He swung his arm wide. "Do we have more money than they? Are we bigger, stronger, better armed? Of course not! Are we cleverer? Perhaps . . ." He stopped to allow a few smiles and the odd shout of approval. "Are we landowners?"

There was a burst of laughter.

Dobokai shrugged. "Well, some of us may be. I'm not. Are we funnier, more charming? Of course! Are we introducing new food that tastes better?"

That was greeted with shouts and applause, even a few ribald remarks.

"Then let us show them how to cook! Sell them your cakes and pastries, your soups and stews. Make friends. Make profits. Don't listen to the men like Mr. Haldane, who say we are trying to change their ways. He is jealous. I don't know why. We eat their food— occasionally . . ."

Again he was greeted by laughter, but Monk could hear the raw edge of fear behind it. They laughed only because they wanted a release of the tension crackling in the air.

Perhaps Dobokai knew that.

"We must help the police," Dobokai repeated. "Think of all you know that could assist them in finding who is doing this. It is up to us. They don't know us as we do. Prove to them it is not one of the community, by helping to find who it is."

Halmi tried to cut across him, but no one was paying attention to him now.

"Come on," Monk said to Hooper. "Where's the house?"

Hooper led the way, silently. They passed the crowd, but they could still hear the voices a hundred yards away. They turned one more corner onto Sheridan Street and saw immediately where the mortuary wagon was waiting. The front door of the house was open.

Monk increased his pace. He did not want the police surgeon to leave before he'd had a chance to speak to him. He hated having to go to the morgue. And he wanted to see the body where it had been found. Being told about it, even accurately and vividly, was still not the same as seeing it for himself, seeing the peripheral things as well, things that might seem irrelevant to someone else, or even to him, until later when something jogged his memory.

He strode up the path, Hooper at his heels now, and went in through the front door. This house was nicer than those of the two earlier victims; the furnishings were expensive, the wallpaper pristine, as if it had only just been hung.

He was met immediately by a constable, who started to tell him he could not come in, then realized who he was.

"This way, sir. Poor Mr. Rosza is in the back kitchen."

"Did you know him?" Monk asked.

The constable was pale and he looked wretched, but the crime itself could account for that. It was the ease with which he had pronounced the man's name that caught Monk's attention.

"Yes, sir. He was a good man." The constable's voice wavered a little with the stress of his emotion. "He used to . . ." He stopped, coloring uncomfortably.

"What's your name?" Monk asked more gently.

"Holloway, sir."

"What did Mr. Rosza do, Holloway?"

"Give us a cup of hot soup on a winter's morning, sir. Always had it ready, if there was ice on the street."

"Tell me about him. Did he do this for everybody?"

Holloway hesitated.

"I don't care if you had a hot breakfast here every morning," Monk said impatiently. "All I care about right now is finding who did this to him. Do you understand me?"

"Yes, sir." Holloway straightened up a little. "No, sir, he just did it for some of us younger ones. Said we reminded him of his own son. He said he was killed in Vienna when they had a revolution, way back in 'forty-eight, or about then. Said his wife never really got over it. That was part of why they were here. But she died a few years ago. He used to like to show us some of the things that were hers. Teapots and dishes and the like."

Monk felt a sharp stab of pity. If Hester died, would he keep her small possessions, things she had handled every day, take them out and show them to other people, as if they could see some essence of her in them? Perhaps.

He forced his mind back to the present, and what he had to find out now.

"He didn't remarry?"

"Oh, no, sir. Kept his house like it were still hers. Put new wallpaper up like she would have done. I've been trying to think who would do this to him, and I can't. It has to be because he's Hungarian. He did tell me once that some children had been throwing things, broke a few windows, like, and wrote rotten words on the walls. If I'd have caught them I'd have made them clean it up—and pay for new glass."

Monk imagined he would indeed. Holloway might have cleaned it up himself, but he would not tell Monk that. He just stared back very steadily.

"And did you ever find out who did it?" Monk asked almost casually.

The constable stood very straight. "Yes, sir, but the locals wouldn't swear to it, even though they knew." He hesitated only a moment, then added with a slight smile. "Mind, they did help us clean it up, and put toward getting the glass all replaced, sir."

Before Monk could find an answer, Hyde appeared in the doorway. He looked tired and harassed. His thinning hair stood up in spikes as if he had run his hands through it over and over. His face was almost as pale as one of the corpses.

"You took your time!" he snapped at Monk. "Where the devil have you been?"

"Watching the crowds in the streets, hoping they weren't going to turn into a riot," Monk answered. "And then listening to young Holloway here, who apparently knew the victim quite well. You look as if you've been down a rat-hole backward."

"I didn't find the bloody rat!" Hyde said waspishly. "And neither have you, apparently. What the hell are you doing, Monk? This is the worst damn mess I've seen in years. You've got a lunatic here. For God's sake, catch him, man! He must be raving, slavering at the mouth. If you don't believe me, come into the kitchen and see what he's done. Don't just stand there waiting for me to conduct you." He swung around on his heel and strode back down the passage and into the kitchen, leaving the door swinging behind him.

Monk followed. He did not bother retaliating. It was, in an odd way, quite comforting that at last Hyde's composure was shaken. It made him human, and for the first time Monk wondered what he was like away from his profession. Did he have a family? He had never mentioned anyone. Perhaps he preferred to keep them separate from his work. Did he have pastimes he loved? Music, his garden, long walks alone, the sea in all its moods? Did he take time for himself?

"Don't just stand there!" Hyde snapped at him again.

Monk concentrated on the scene. Now he understood why Hyde was so close to the point where he could no longer keep his professional control. Rosza lay on his back on the kitchen floor. He must have fought for his life. Not only was his chest pierced by the blade of an old and badly rusted sword but his hands were gashed as well, and his right arm, which had bled profusely. The artery must have been torn open. There was blood everywhere. Even his face had been slashed, taking his nose off and slicing open his cheek.

As before, the room was crowded with candles dipped and pooled in blood, but this time they were carelessly placed, several together and many lying on their sides. Still, there were seventeen. Monk counted them. Two were purple.

"He was in a hurry," he said. His voice sounded hard, and absurdly irrelevant in the silence.

Hyde turned to stare at him, then slowly the anger drained out of him, replaced by intense weariness.

"You're right," he agreed. "Maybe it was getting light and he was afraid of being seen. I'm not sure how that helps much."

"We'll question everyone around here and ask if anybody was up early and saw something, even if they didn't understand what it was," Monk began.

"What would that be? You mean someone they didn't expect to see, or it didn't make any impression, because it was the same as usual?"

"It's possible . . ." Monk agreed.

"Do you think it's one of the Hungarians?" Hyde said with disbelief.

"I don't know. But if we find anyone who was around, then we can ask them what they saw. At least account for one of them."

"Glad it's your job, not mine," Hyde responded. "These people have had more than enough already. They're terrified and on the edge of losing control."

"I know that." Monk thought for a moment before speaking again. "Are you sure they were all killed by the same person?"

Hyde was incredulous. "God in heaven, man! Do you think there are two people on the loose in Shadwell doing this kind of thing?"

"Are there any differences at all?" Monk insisted.

"No. Down to the smallest detail, things not reported in the papers or known by the public, or even most of the police. They are identical."

"Damn."

"Why?"

"Then Dobokai can't be guilty."

"Dobokai? Why him?"

"Because everywhere I turn I'm falling over him."

"Then fall over someone else," Hyde said tartly. "Try some new thinking. Get your own prejudices out of the way. You're stuck, man! Get over it and do your job!"

Monk did not reply. Hyde was right, but he did not need to tell him so.

10

MONK AND HOOPER EXAMINED the body more closely, then the rest of the room, and finally the house itself. They found nothing they had not foreseen. Rosza was, outwardly at least, a quiet and unassuming man, who had built for himself a new life in England, succeeded in his banking career and made friends, not only within the Hungarian community but also with a number of native landowners.

Monk felt a sadness at his loss. Small things about his house showed individual taste: a painting of flowers under the shade of a tree, woodland flowers such as violets and, in a splash of sunlight, a bank of primroses. Monk had no idea if such flowers grew in Hungary. Certainly it could have been England. There was also a very good personal drawing of a dog: a pet, judging from the eagerness in the animal's face.

The kitchen was also interesting. There were racks full of spices Monk had never even heard of. Perhaps they had contributed to the soup Rosza had given to the young constables on cold mornings.

Monk's body ached with a sudden twinge when he moved, and he realized that he was rigid with anger at this new, further bestial crime.

"What do they have in common, Hooper?" he said. "Why these men? Why not others? They're all in Shadwell, but otherwise well apart. They're all comfortable, successful but not rich. They're all from Hungary, but different towns. They've been here different lengths of time. They knew each other, but only slightly. They were not close. Most of the Hungarians here know each other—so why these three?"

Hooper shook his head. "I don't know, sir. I've been thinking of that myself. I haven't been able to check Rosza, but the other two didn't do any business together. They're not related. No common investments that I can find. Didn't belong to any club or society that anyone knows of. Never courted the same woman even. All Roman Catholic, but then so is the whole community."

"Then what links these people?" Monk could hear the note of desperation in his voice. "There has to be something. And what precipitated the murders now? They've all been here at least ten years. Why now? What happened?"

"I don't know." Hooper was as exasperated as Monk. This latest death seemed to have affected him more deeply also. Or perhaps it was just the feeling of hopelessness. They were no further along in their investigation than they'd been after the death of Fodor. There was a mass of information, and if it had any meaning, they had not found it.

"Let's go back to Fodor again," Monk said. "There's nothing else here. We may as well walk to the station." He opened the kitchen door and led the way out. He gave brief instructions to the men now waiting in the hall, and he and Hooper made their way into the street. They ignored the crowd gathered there, frightened and angry.

Unconsciously they matched stride, moving rapidly along the footpath toward the river.

"We've examined everything we know about the week before Fodor was killed, sir," Hooper said as they came to the High Street. "No one had a quarrel with him. No one owed him money and he didn't owe anyone. He wasn't having an affair with anyone's wife or daughter—or anyone at all! No threats of any sort."

"Then we're missing something," Monk insisted. "I'm going to check Haldane's story for this one. I'll ask him obliquely."

Hooper frowned. "Why Haldane? His wife's Hungarian. He's one person who has nothing against them."

"He's also an Englishman who's got a foot in both camps, as it were," Monk pointed out. "And loyalties both ways. I'd like to push him a bit harder about the number seventeen. The candles mean something. He may know without realizing its importance."

"Sir . . ."

Monk stopped and turned to face Hooper. "What is it?"

Hooper looked deeply unhappy. "Aren't you forgetting Fitzherbert?" He did not add the rest of the implication, but it was in the air between them, unspoken, all but suffocating.

"No, I'm not forgetting him. He's been in London at least as long as the murders have been happening, and he's, at the kindest, unstable. You don't need to remind me of that, Hooper. I know."

Hooper's face was bleak. "Yes, sir. I don't want it to be him either, but we might have to face it."

Monk did not reply.

THAT EVENING MONK WENT to see Roger Haldane at his home. He expected to interrupt the Haldanes at dinner, and he succeeded.

Haldane himself was clearly disturbed by seeing him, caught off balance. But he did not make any attempt to have Monk leave. In fact, he behaved as if this was a visit he welcomed, despite the unforeseen timing.

Adel Haldane greeted him with evident pleasure.

"We are eating, Mr. Monk. Will you join us? There is plenty. Please? Come in and sit down." As if certain that he would follow her, she turned and led the way.

The dining room was warm, full of cheerful colors. He noticed several hand-embroidered cushions in unusual designs, and a painted dish hanging on the wall.

He realized that Adel was watching his face. He smiled at her.

"Thank you."

"Sir . . ." Haldane invited him to sit, pulling up another chair before Adel asked him to. "My wife will bring you a dish." Having given the instruction, he sat again and resumed eating.

Monk sat down also, thanking him.

Haldane took another mouthful and ate it with relish before he spoke.

"I hope you are moving forward with your investigations," he said. "This . . . this is causing us all a lot of distress. There is no peace in the community. Everyone is frightened, quarreling in ways we never used to before. We are all suspected and we know it, and yet we are the victims." He looked across at Monk, anger in his face, but also confusion.

"I am aware of that, Mr. Haldane," Monk said gravely. "We are looking for two things, and I believe, with your standing among the people, you might be able to help."

"Me?" Haldane looked surprised. "I don't even speak the language well. But my wife does, of course." He took another spoonful of the stew and the fragrance of it wafted across toward Monk. He was delighted when Adel came back in with a large dish and placed it in front of him. The steam from it made him realize that he was really very hungry.

But he must not allow himself to be distracted.

"As I'm sure you know, there has been a third murder," he began. "Again there were seventeen candles." He saw Haldane stiffen, and momentarily stop eating. "Are you sure you haven't heard the number seventeen mentioned anywhere, Mr. Haldane? It is clearly of intense significance to someone."

"Seventeen," Haldane repeated. "I . . . I don't know. You say all the dead men had seventeen candles around them?"

"Yes. In each case two were dark-colored, sort of purplish."

Haldane looked not only puzzled but afraid. He stared at Monk intently, reading his eyes. "I have no idea. It's . . . not natural. If it's some ritual, I have not heard of it." He turned slowly to Adel. "Do you know?" It was almost an accusation.

"No, of course I don't!" she protested quickly. "If I knew, I'd say. If it's some secret society then they wouldn't allow women. None I've ever heard of does." She looked at Monk. "You asked me before, and I've tried to think of anything, but I can't."

Monk changed the subject. He glanced around and a picture of the same young man caught his eye. He was handsome, with high cheekbones like Adel, and her fair coloring.

"How are your son's studies going?" he asked politely.

"Well," she answered. "He is very clever." Then she blushed. "I'm sorry. That sounds . . . too proud . . ."

Monk smiled back at her. "It is natural to be proud of him." He looked at Haldane, to include him, but Haldane's expression was unreadable.

Monk began his meal. He knew Adel was watching him and he looked up at her and nodded, his mouth full. "Excellent," he said, as soon as he had swallowed.

She was satisfied, and resumed her own meal.

It was Haldane who broke the silence.

"The fear is growing. We are beginning to suspect each other, and we are on the verge of violence. There have already been fights in the street. People are watching each other and gossip is growing. Everyone is suspicious of everyone else, even people they have known for years. They are saying it is some Englishman, and I am English, so they blame me. Me! My wife is Hungarian. I am now neither part of one people nor part of the other . . ." There was fear in his voice and on his face.

Adel drew in her breath as if to speak, perhaps to argue, but she said nothing. She also must be torn between the two communities.

It was the perfect opening.

"Well, then you can tell me exactly where you were when poor Rosza was killed, and that will put an end to any suspicion of you," he suggested.

"Of me?" Haldane was startled.

"It is true for everyone," Monk told him, although he was interested that Haldane thought of himself so quickly.

"Will you say so?" Haldane asked immediately.

"Yes, if you wish."

Haldane blinked, and his long, heavy face filled with relief.

"I'm lucky, very lucky. I intended to go to meet a man I do business with this morning. He lives the other side of the river, and I would have had to go quite a long way north, and then cross. No one would be likely to have remembered me."

"The man you were due to meet?" Monk suggested.

"We haven't met before. He wouldn't know if it was me or not. Just letters—and they were to his staff. But he canceled our meeting yesterday. Would have looked as if I had lied. Poor Rosza was killed very early, they say?"

"Yes."

"I could have done it, and then gone on to the ferry."

"Then where were you?"

"I didn't get up until almost seven, as Adel and my servants will attest. And I went to the café on the corner of Cable Street and Love Lane. It's quite a walk, but it's a really good place to sit and talk. Good coffee and spiced sausage and bread."

"Who did you meet there?"

"Matyas Andrassy. You can check. And there were other people there as well. Matyas's wife, Greta, for one. I wasn't anywhere near where poor Rosza was killed." This time he met Monk's eyes with a faint smile.

"Thank you, Mr. Haldane." Monk managed to make his voice sound civil, even as if he were pleased. He would check Haldane's account very carefully, but he believed it.

He glanced at Adel, intending to give her reassurance, but he was intrigued by the look on her face. It was both surprise and relief. Had she not known him to be innocent, or, at the very least, intensely believed it?

Monk finished the meal, too little aware of its taste to appreciate it as it deserved. He found it interesting that Haldane had evidence of his having been at home at the time of Rosza's death. There had been in Monk's mind a growing suspicion that Adel Haldane had had a greater affection for Fodor than was acceptable to suit her husband. He had seen the flash of it the first time they met. It was only a warmth, a skirting around the subject, a shadow across Haldane's face, but he realized now that it had been real, at least to Monk.

And if Adel had had an affair, it might have ended in violence— a fight, or even, accidentally, a death. But there was nothing accidental about the murder of Fodor. It was violent, bloody and premeditated. And the others were exactly like it.

Haldane could not have committed this one, or Lorand Gazda's murder. Antal Dobokai could not have committed the first. The victims all knew each other, but only casually. Monk and Hooper had both tried to find any deeper connection, relationships, and failed.

Was it really a ruthless madman killing Hungarian newcomers to the area, because they were different and, in his mind, dangerous? Threatening what? English businesses, their religion, their freedom or prosperity, their safety in the streets? Nothing, that he could see.

He finished the meal and thanked Adel for it, and Haldane for his hospitality.

"You are welcome," Haldane assured him, shaking his hand with fervor. "Come again."

MONK CONTINUED, WITH HOOPER, to inquire into groups or organizations that might be anti-Catholic, people who had expressed nationalistic or anti-religious views, any secret societies at all. He had to use the four men from his squad, leaving the station short-handed for tackling the other crimes that beset the river. There were no men left to investigate a matter of petty thefts of timber from Regent's Canal Dock. There was a knife fight above Prince's Stairs on the south bank—unpleasant, but no one badly injured—but he had no one to spare for it. Only one man could be sent to investigate smuggling on the East India Docks.

Three days went by and Monk could see no appreciable progress in the murder inquiry. The tension mounted. Tempers were short, the slightest irregularity in anything sparked fear, suspicion, blame. Stories were exaggerated in the telling. Gossip was like a weed with roots that spread under the foundation of everything, and seeds that blew on the wind. Doubts and suspicions were everywhere. False leads came in suggesting dark rituals, obscene beliefs, all of which had to be looked into, and turned out to be nothing.

Then on the morning of the fifth day after Rosza's murder, Monk was awoken again by a loud, sustained banging on the front door. It was daylight already, but in the summer that only meant it was after five.

He stumbled out of bed, unintentionally wakening Hester also. She had no need to ask him what it was. The power and the urgency of the banging could not be misread.

Monk snatched his robe off its hook on the door and went downstairs barefoot. He threw the door open. As he had expected, it was Hooper on the step, again looking ill-dressed, his coat collar half turned under. His face made the question unnecessary.

"There's been another," he said before Monk could speak. "The worst so far. I've got the ferry waiting. You'd better dress for the day—it's going to be a long time before we're back. A man called Kalman Pataki. Hungarian, been here only a year or so."

Monk stepped back and made room for Hooper to come inside. There was no need for conversation. Monk waved a vague hand toward the kitchen, then went back up the stairs, two at a time.

Hester was up and in her robe, her hair in a loose braid, out of the way. She looked at his face, and did not ask. She moved past him to go downstairs.

"No time for tea," he said, already taking off his robe and reaching for his shirt. "Hooper's probably in the kitchen, but I can't stop to rake out the stove or light it again."

"A glass of water, and something to take with you," she said from the landing. "And for Hooper too."

She was gone before he could reply.

He washed and shaved too hastily, cutting himself slightly on the chin. It was only a nick, but of course it bled. Swearing gently, he put astringent on it, and winced. He had too strong a beard to go unshaven; it made him look as if he were not ready, half-asleep still.

Hooper was in the kitchen eating a sandwich of fresh bread and cold meat that Hester had prepared for him. A glass of water was beside it on the table, and the same for Monk.

"Thank you." Monk lifted the glass, drank the water straight off, kissed Hester quickly, picked up the sandwich and led the way out the door, Hooper on his heels.

This body was on Lower Shadwell Street, only one block from the river itself. Kalman Pataki was in a small room in one of the warehouses with frontage onto the water. The whole space was perhaps twelve feet by fourteen, furnished as the simplest sort of office, with an old desk, badly scarred and stained with ink, and water rings where cups and mugs had stood. There was an inkwell on it now, and a scattering of at least twenty sheets of paper: letters, lists and receipts. There were two hard-backed chairs and a number of filing cases and drawers.

But that was all in Monk's peripheral vision. What held his attention and made his stomach churn was the figure of a middle-aged man sprawled on his back across the floor, arms flung wide. A rusty saber jutted out of his lower chest, just about in his stomach, and there was blood all over the middle of his body, pooling onto the floor.

Monk forced his gaze from it, searching for the now familiar candles dipped in blood. They were there, as he had known they would be. There were seventeen of them, as before. They were of a wider variety, different lengths and circumferences, some wax, some merely cheap tallow, but all dripping blood.

But what appalled him was a small plaster figurine of the Virgin Mary. Its face was smashed, and the whole thing was soaked with blood, as if someone had taken it by the feet and jabbed it into the open wound, face-first.

He let out a sigh. There were no words he could think of that seemed adequate. Words could frame the familiar and create the new, but not of this order of horror.

What mind could contain such things?

He was not surprised that the newspapers, the usual police, everyone, were demanding an answer, a solution, an end to this. They had the right to expect it. Why was he not able to see what must be in front of him? How could any man capable of this not be obvious to anyone, let alone a man who had spent his adult life in the police force, or as a private agent hunting those who killed? What was wrong with him that he floundered like this, helplessly letting it go on?

He had suspected both Haldane and Dobokai, and been proven wrong by their ability to account for themselves at the time of at least one of the killings. But the murders were taking place early in the morning, before daylight. Most people were in their beds. Monk was in his! If he did not share a bed with Hester, he would not be able to prove his own innocence.

Haldane shared his with his wife, but how sound a sleeper was she? Or how prepared to lie for him?

Dobokai was not married.

Monk turned to Hooper and saw how pale he was. Were the same thoughts racing through his mind?

"Where's Hyde?" he asked.

"Not here yet," Hooper replied. "Got another crime a mile away. He'll be in no hurry to get to this."

There was nothing to argue with, nothing even to talk about. Monk felt as if he were standing in a now familiar nightmare. The rest of the day unfolded as if he had lived it before, and try as he might, he could not break the spell of it.

The same people were in the street, their faces distorted with fear and grief. Their voices had the same sharp edge. Even the words in Hungarian were making sense because he had heard them so many times. He could not have pronounced them, but he was learning to recognize the often-repeated words for "incompetence," "lazy," "stupid," "dangerous." He would not have argued back even if they had been said in English.

As always, Dobokai was among the gathered throng, pushing his way to the front.

"They think you don't care, because we're strangers here," he explained. "They are saying that if your own people were being slaughtered like animals, you would have found the killer the first time." His face looked weary and his pale skin was tightly drawn across his bones, his nose sharper. "I keep telling them that is not true. You are doing your best, but they begin to disbelieve me." He stared at Monk, searching his eyes, trying to read them. Was he looking for hope? He had a right to expect something.

"Don't you think I would solve such a crime if I could?" Monk asked. "I don't blame them for being angry, and frightened."

"They're helping as much as they can," Dobokai said a little more edgily. "We've all accounted for where we were at the times of the murders. We've offered names of people who've threatened us. What more do you want? Give me something to tell them, Mr. Monk. What is he like, the person who does this? Why? Why us? What have we done that has let loose this . . . monster?"

Monk searched for something to say that would offer comfort and was not a total lie. These people were angry only because they were terrified, and they were right to be. He looked past Dobokai at the crowd behind him, men and women who looked just like anybody else, except that their language separated them.

A man shouted something in Hungarian. A few words were familiar to Monk. It had to do with impatience, and not caring.

"You don't care!" someone else added loudly.

"Wait until it's your own that are butchered!" another man cried out.

"Yeah! Is that what it will take?" the cry was taken up.

The crowd surged forward, forcing Monk to take several steps back. He tried desperately to find words that did not sound trite. Not only did they deserve honesty, they needed some hope to keep them from violence. This was his job, to keep order.

And they did not deserve lies—except that lies might be the only things that offered any sense. He had no idea what the truth was.

There were more people arriving, in twos and threes, now blocking the street.

He looked into Dobokai's challenging face and his clear eyes, blue as the sky.

If the crowd surged out of control they would attack the ones they blamed—Monk, and Hooper standing beside him. Then they would be guilty of murdering police officers. Someone would be hanged, and it would be worse for all of them. The law would never allow anybody to get away with killing a policeman. They could not do so and survive. It would be the beginning of anarchy.

"Tell them that someone is trying to incite them to violence," he said to Dobokai. "I don't know whether it is the same man who did this, or someone else taking advantage of it, but they will be blamed. People will say the Hungarians brought this terrible, inhuman violence with them, they will deny it is English, or has anything to do with them. They will show that you attacked the police because they couldn't solve the crime. You know what that will mean? At least one of you will be hanged, and serve as scapegoat for all. And there will be no peace for any of you. It would be exactly the excuse some prejudiced people are looking for."

Dobokai stared at him. "That's monstrous! We are the victims!"

"I know that," Monk replied, hearing the ragged edges of his own voice. "But it's natural for people to blame others. The rest of the police will blame you if you don't keep order. If you let these men attack me and my officers, you'll be hanged, and the whole community will find itself blamed. That's not fair, but it's true. We never had crimes like this here before you came."

Dobokai took several long, slow breaths, and understanding came into his face.

"It is vile, but you are right. I tell you this, Mr. Monk, you had better find who is doing this to us, very soon, or words will not work anymore. You hear me?"

"Yes, Mr. Dobokai, and I believe you. And if you believe me, you'll do everything you can to help keep order—for your own sakes."

"I hear you."

Dobokai turned around and faced the crowd, which was growing larger every moment. He held up his hands, and even before the people began to pay attention, he started to speak.

Monk had little idea what Dobokai was saying, but the tone of his voice was almost hypnotic. He repeated himself several times, pleading with them, shouting and then speaking softly, as if to friends, even as if they were his own family, imploring, promising.

Gradually they began to calm down. Here and there people were nodding their heads. A woman called out what sounded like a blessing, and someone else echoed her.

Men and women moved closer to each other. A few stragglers walked away, emotionally exhausted. Then more went, and finally there were only a dozen left.

Dobokai turned to Monk and Hooper, but it was Monk he was looking at.

"You don't have long, Mr. Monk," he said quietly. "Two or three days, maybe, then I can't hold them anymore."

Monk believed him.

"Thank you," he said quietly. "We'll do it."

Dobokai nodded and walked away.

"How?" Hooper asked. "Do you know something?"

"No, I don't," Monk admitted. "But we have to find . . . I don't know what! He's right, this won't hold them more than two or three days."

LATE THE FOLLOWING AFTERNOON, Monk was in the street in Shadwell, half a mile from where Fitz lived, when he heard a harsh shout perhaps a hundred yards away.

He turned to see a man gesticulating, throwing his arms around in the air, pointing, beckoning, jabbing his hand to his left.

There was another shout from somewhere to his right.

Two men appeared from around a corner, saw what the man was pointing at, and picked up their pace to a run.

Monk did not go toward them but to his left, and started to move swiftly to the junction of Castle Street.

Then he saw Fitz, standing paralyzed. His body was covered in huge daubs of blood, scarlet, causing his shirt to stick to his body.

Other men were already running toward him, shouting in Hungarian.

Fitz stood as if he had no understanding of what was going on.

Monk caught hold of his arm. "Run!" he shouted at him.

Fitz turned to stare at him. "What?"

The men were a hundred yards away in two different directions, and closing. Their voices were high-pitched. One of them was a tailor and had fabric-cutting shears in his hand.

"Run!" Monk yelled at Fitz, pulling at his arm. "Come on."

As if catching his fear by touch, Fitz spun around and started to run with surprising speed.

There was a yell of fury behind them. Monk dared not turn to see if the gap was closing. They raced along the footpath, jumping the curb and darting between traffic. Monk only just missed being hit by a horse and cart. He scrambled up the slight incline at the other side and saw Fitz appear from behind a wagon of wood.

He gestured along Cable Street where it was level, then saw men ahead of them, waving arms and listening to the shouts behind.

To the right was the turn into King David Lane. Monk knew the area. At least it was not a dead end. If they were cornered, there would be no escape.

There was a police station on the corner. Damn! That was a mistake. Monk had forgotten about that. But too late to turn now. There were more shouts from those behind them.

Fitz started to go right, but Monk knew that it was a narrow street and that Carriage Way, at the junction, was a blind alley to the right. If there were men to the left, they were cornered. He knew how a hunted animal felt.

Should he turn to face them, try to hold them and give Fitz a chance to get away? Where to?

Did they even know who Monk was now? He was not in any uniform.

Where were they? There was Juniper Row: it ended in Glamis Road, then the High Street.

How far could Fitz run? Whose blood was it? If they caught up with him, they'd kill him, even if they did not mean to.

Monk could hear the beating of his own heart and the thumping of his feet on the pavement. Fitz was still a couple of paces ahead of him. Would he fight if they were cornered?

It would not do them any good. There were more men joining in behind them, a dozen. Someone hurled a loose stone and it smashed into the wall a yard from Monk and broke into pieces. One of the chips struck his cheek with startling pain. The mob no longer cared about law or police. They were hunting the lunatic who had slaughtered their people, and had broken the icon of the Virgin Mary and daubed it with blood.

End of Glamis Road: Fitz hesitated. Monk grabbed his arm, almost pulling him off his feet. He waved a hand, indicating Market Hill immediately opposite. He knew where he was now. At the end of that was a narrow alley whose name stayed in his mind—Labour in Vain. They were almost at the waterfront. There were warehouses there, one or two empty. It would give them a chance to hide, and catch their breath.

If he could get Fitz as far as the water, they would have a chance. Monk could not outrun them, there were too many. But on the water he could outrow them, if he could get a boat. He was far more used to the oars than he guessed any of them would be. A few years on the river had broadened his back and given him a strength in his shoulders he had never had before.

But he was not used to sprinting for over a mile. He was breathing hard.

He looked at Fitz, now leaning against the wall and bending forward. He too was breathing hard and his face was flushed.

"Why are you doing this?" he asked. "They'll kill you too."

"They won't kill either of us," Monk replied between breaths.

"Don't be so damn silly! Of course they will. They think I murdered four of their people. And, so help me God, I don't know for sure that I didn't. Get out before they reach us. They'll find us in a few minutes. There are close to a score of them."

"Oh, yes," Monk said sarcastically. "I'll go home and tell Hester that I left you in the street for the mob to tear to pieces. I'm sure she'll understand."

Fitz stared at him. "She wouldn't want you to be torn apart as well . . . and believe me, they will!"

"I know that." Monk straightened again. "Shut up and follow me. It's my job to save your neck . . ."

"So they can hang me afterward?"

"Right. But after a trial, not before. Now save your breath to run!" He started out slowly, down the wall of Labour in Vain Street, keeping close to the side and moving as quickly as possible.

For long minutes there were no shouts close to them.

They turned into Lower Shadwell Street and the row of warehouses backing onto the river. Monk knew which were empty, if they could just get in through a door before the Hungarians saw them. He hoped they would expect him to go toward the stairs. They would be cornered there. It would be hideously easy to throw them into the water and see that they drowned—both of them. Blood would be too high to think of the consequences of murdering a policeman.

But he could not turn Fitz over to them to be beaten to death in the street for crimes he might have committed—and might not!

He was out of breath and his feet hurt badly. He and Fitz now stood outside the locked door of one of the empty warehouses. Monk must keep his hands steady and pick the lock. Quickly! He could hear shouting. They were closing in. There were minutes left at the most!

The lock felt stiff in his hands. He was clumsy. If they were caught here, it would be the end. Was Fitz prepared to fight, or would he give up, and hope they'd leave Monk alone?

Monk glanced sideways at him and could read nothing in his face, not even the panic he felt inside himself.

"I think you'd better be quick," Fitz said with an odd finality in his voice. "There, at the end of the street. I can't see them round the curve, but I can hear them."

Monk felt the lock give.

"I can see them now," Fitz added. "Which, unfortunately, means that they can see us."

Monk felt Fitz's hand on his arm.

"Let them take me," Fitz said quietly. "I might have done it. I haven't any memory of it, and I can't think why I would. The Hungarians were—"

Monk threw his weight against the door. It stuck for an instant, then yielded. He all but fell through, dragging Fitz behind him.

"Be quiet!" he said sharply. "And help me shut this and find something to block it with."

"There are twenty of them, man! They'll have it down in minutes!" Fitz argued.

Monk ignored him and looked for a crate, a box, anything to drag across and block the door. They had only seconds. The inside of the warehouse was lit by a couple of high windows, but there was nothing movable, no crates or boxes of any sort.

Monk swore under his breath. "Come on. Run. They won't be able to see while they're in here any better than we can." He snatched Fitz's arm and half dragged him across the dim floor toward the corner, where there should be stairs. It looked as if the place had not been used in months, or even years.

They moved as quickly and quietly as they could. Monk's mind was racing. They would have their backs to the river, but there were three flights of steps down to the water along this stretch. They were all places where ferries came in. Monk knew most of the ferrymen. All he needed was one, close enough in to get to them before the men chasing them did.

If they chose a narrow place, with their backs to the water, they could not be surrounded. If anyone fell into the water they would be finished, unless someone dragged them out. The tide was coming in; the current was swift, cold and dirty.

And Fitz might be guilty! Was Monk really willing to die for this?

They were scrambling up the stairs to the upper floor, Fitz first, Monk on his heels. He didn't trust Fitz not to go back down again. He might not fight for his life. He did not know if he was innocent.

Monk had just reached the top when he heard the street door crash down and the light burst in, visible even from where he was.

He threw Fitz to the ground and lay half on top of him.

He could hear them shouting below, but it was all in Hungarian. All he understood was the anger. Anyone would have understood that.

"Keep still," he whispered to Fitz.

"What for?" Fitz replied almost under his breath. "This is the end . . ."

"Be quiet!"

Seconds slipped by as no one moved or spoke.

Fitz drew in his breath and stirred.

Monk put his hand across Fitz's mouth and held him as hard as he could with the other hand.

Then he heard the men below starting to shuffle rubbish around, calling to each other.

Monk used their noise to mask the sound as he got to his knees and half dragged Fitz along with him, toward the landing bay and the open front onto the river. He could smell the salt in the air and hear the lapping of the tide. He tried one door, which opened onto a room with a table, chairs and a desk, refuse on the floor.

He tried the next, and it was the same.

The men were coming up the stairs now, the boards creaking under their heavy footsteps.

He forced open the door to the third room and instantly felt the cold breath of the water.

The footsteps were loud outside, voices high with triumph at last.

"Come on!" Monk said urgently. "Hurry!"

"What for?" Fitz looked at him with despair. "There's nothing left to fight for. Perhaps they're right and I deserve this. Stop trying so hard, Monk. If I go with them, they'll leave you alone."

"You're not going with anybody," Monk snapped. "Come here."

Fitz walked over toward him, hands loose at his sides.

For an instant Monk wondered if he was going to attack him with those delicate surgeon's hands. Were they strong enough to break his neck? Crush his windpipe?

They were at the edge of the open bay, the river below them. Monk glanced behind him. There was a ferry twenty yards away. He turned to the water and waved his hands, shouting.

The door burst in and half a dozen men stopped abruptly, their quarry cornered at last, backs to the water and nowhere to go.

Fitz stood motionless, his shoulders bowed.

"Thank you," he said quietly to Monk. "You did all you could—for Hester, I imagine. You owe me nothing."

"I owe you a fair trial and the benefit of the doubt," Monk said tartly. Then he looked beyond Fitz at the men now crowding the doorway. Several of them carried staves and picks. There was the one brandishing a pair of tailor's shears. The light gleamed on the blades, which were sharp enough to cut good cloth without pulling a thread.

The first man moved forward a couple of steps. "You aren't getting away this time," he said clearly in English. Then he glanced from Fitz to Monk. "Don't give us any trouble and we won't hurt you."

Monk knew exactly what the man was going to do. He had seen the ferry coming toward the landing bay in answer to Monk's signal.

"You won't hurt me anyway," Monk said to the man who had spoken. "If you attack me you will have to kill me. And murdering a policeman, when you know he is police, carrying out his duty, will get you hanged, all of you that have a part in it. Is that what you want for your community? Your families? Half a dozen of you tried and hanged, for the murder of the Commander of the River Police? You think you struggle to feed your families now? Wait until your widows and children find out what real hardship is."

"You're protecting the man who murdered four of our men, killed them like a wild beast, but worse!"

The others growled agreement, stepping forward.

"I'm only protecting all of you from a crime you can't ever go back on, you fool!" Monk said furiously. "I'm arresting him and taking him for trial. If you want him convicted, you'll put your weapons down and start behaving like the good citizens you pretend you are."

There was a silence so intense he could hear the water lapping against the piles below, and the bump of the ferry against the steps.

"Do as you're told," he said quietly to Fitz, "if you want either of us to get out of here alive. If the Hungarians were good to you, get into the ferry and save the wives of these men from poverty and disgrace."

Fitz obeyed, his shoulders bowed as if he were too broken to straighten up.

Monk turned his back on the men and climbed with Fitz out of the landing bay, onto the platform, then down the steps to the water, without looking back.

"Thames River Police Station," he told the ferryman. "Just beyond the Wapping New Stairs."

"I know where it is, Mr. Monk," the ferryman said. "You all right, sir?"

"Yes, thank you, I'm fine," Monk replied. "Sit still, Fitz. We've got a way to go."

CHAPTER

11

HESTER LOOKED AT MONK'S pale face and the state of his clothes. He was clearly exhausted and had been in some kind of struggle. Whether his clothes were rescuable or not was of no importance at all, but the smears of blood, the dust all over them and the look in his eyes frightened her.

He came in through the doorway and walked straight to the kitchen. She had gone to the hallway to meet him. Now she followed on his heels, slid the kettle onto the hob, then turned to face him.

"I'm sorry, I had to arrest Fitz," he said quietly. "It was the only thing I could do to save him."

She wanted to put her arms around him and hold him tight, tell him that as long as he was all right, whatever else had happened she could live with it; they both would.

She swallowed hard, choking the instinct to offer a momentary comfort that he would find condescending. "What happened?"

He stood still. He might have thought he had the words ready, but now they were awkward, incomplete. "Fitz," he answered quietly. "He's alive . . ."

"Sit down," she told him. "Did he do it, after all?"

His eyes widened slightly, but he obeyed her and sat down.

"I don't know. I don't think so, but I saw him in the street, covered in blood again. He seemed almost in a daze." He put his elbows on the table and leaned forward, running his fingers through his hair.

She waited, her heart pounding. She felt a welling up of grief she should have been prepared for, but it took her by surprise how much it hurt. Fitz had been part of the wildest, bravest and most dangerous part of her life. The horror was bearable only because of the comradeship that had sustained her, the knowledge that she was never alone in it.

She turned away. She did not want Monk to see the tears on her face. He would blame himself for not having been able to save Fitz, as he had promised. As an excuse to conceal her emotion, she fetched the teapot, scalded it out, and put in fresh leaves and then boiling water.

She brought it to the table, along with milk and clean cups.

Monk looked up at her. "I never did find out where the blood came from, only that it wasn't his. A group of men, more than a dozen, demanded that I hand Fitz over to them. I couldn't. They'd have torn him apart."

She could believe that hideously easily.

"They chased us for over a mile. I went toward the water. I thought if I could get into one of the warehouses we could elude them and find a boat. That would delay them and reduce their numbers. Can't fit more than six or seven men in one boat. And they couldn't be as used to rowing as I am."

She shook her head, just a tiny movement. "But . . . ?"

"They caught up with us in the warehouse. I had to arrest Fitz for the murders. It was the only way to satisfy them. Some of them were armed. I'd have made a fight of it, whether Fitz did or not. I think he would have gone with them, to save me. Hester . . . can you imagine what they'd have done to him? And to me? What would have happened to them for the murder of a policeman? They'd have all been hanged!" He shuddered.

She looked at him steadily. He was weary to the bone, and had been badly frightened, even if he refused to admit it. He had been forced to arrest Fitz for a crime he was not at all certain he had committed. He was physically exhausted but, far more clearly, he felt emotionally beaten.

"If you are waiting for me to be sorry for them, you'll wait in vain," she said evenly. "That is not the way any decent person behaves."

He looked up, smiling for the first time. "Decent people go to war, Hester. You know that. Desperate women sell their bodies in the streets, and all of us do something when we're terrified enough, even if it's only to get drunk. It's never stopped you from helping when you could. It's not like you to be judgmental."

"They weren't threatening you," she said simply. "Not like that," she added, remembering how many other times he had been threatened with exposure of his past, blamed for things he could not remember, simply because he was too close to catching someone and proving their guilt. It still was not quite the same as this.

She smiled back at him, ruefully, frightened and on the verge of losing her composure again. "I didn't say I was right!"

He stood up slowly, the ache deep in his joints. Then he put his arms around her and hugged her as tightly as he dared.

"Don't ask me if Fitz is guilty," he said gently, his face against her hair. "I don't know, and neither does he. And don't blame him for letting me rescue him; I didn't give him the choice. He would have gone with them if I'd let him. But he's safe at the Limehouse Police Station, for the time being."

She said nothing. That much of Fitz, at least, had not changed.

ONE OF HESTER'S FIRST thoughts the following morning was to wonder how Scuff would react to Fitz's arrest. He would understand that Monk had done it out of necessity, to save Fitz from what had nearly become peremptory justice via murder in the streets. Would he blame Monk for not having solved the crime before it came to that?

It would be unjust, even though she knew Monk blamed himself. Some crimes were never solved, no matter how hard anyone tried. But Scuff had become used to Monk's success.

Of course, there had been failures—there always were. But did Scuff appreciate that? The only people whose lives held only success were the ones who never attempted anything difficult, anything that was new or might cost them some part of their inner selves, part of their comfort or belief. That surely was the greatest failure of all.

But that would not stop Fitz's arrest from hurting Scuff.

Scuff wanted to be a doctor. He had to become used to accepting that he would not cure all his patients, and certainly not save every life, unless he never treated a patient with anything worse than a headache or a common cold.

She would make sure he knew the truth of what had happened.

First she would go and see Fitz in prison. She needed to know from him all that he could recall. And he must be assured again that there were people who still cared, whatever the truth turned out to be, even if they never found it. He had been a good man, a good friend. He needed to know that that was still true, even if he was in the middle of a black night.

She told no one where she was going. She could explain herself afterward, or not. She dressed in a soft blue day gown, with crisp white cuffs and a white fichu at the neck. She had learned where Fitz was from Monk, as casually as possible, and it took her something over three-quarters of an hour to get there, most of that time consumed by the ferry journey.

She told those in charge at Limehouse that she was the wife of the Commander of the River Police and had brought Fitz some clean clothes and fresh linen.

She was granted half an hour with the prisoner.

The holding cells were grim, as she knew from previous visits, including one hard and bitter time seeing Monk. She was conducted to a room with a wooden table and two chairs. Her time would be judged to the minute. The clothes for Fitz were taken from her, to be thoroughly searched before they were given to him. This she had expected.

When Fitz came in, he was still wearing the garments in which he had been arrested. He looked far worse than Monk had. He was filthy, caked in dust and dried blood. Seeing him like this, a jury would have convicted him without needing to deliberate.

When he saw her, his face flushed with embarrassment, and then, in spite of it, a certain light of relief.

She knew better than to go to him, or touch him at all. The prison guard was standing by the door. Any infringement of the rules and this privilege would be terminated.

She hoped the look in her eyes would convey the emotion she felt. There was no time for words of comfort now. He would have to understand.

"Sit down," she suggested. "I have brought you clean clothes. They are William's, since I had no time to go and fetch your own. They'll fit well enough."

"Thank you . . ." he started, sitting as she had asked.

She sat opposite him. "We must plan."

"For what?" A flash of the old dry humor was in his eyes for a moment, then disappeared. "A little dignity is about all I can hope for . . ."

"Rubbish," she snapped, although she felt like weeping herself. "The patient isn't dead yet, Fitz. We don't give up—"

"Oh, Hester, please! Even I don't believe in my innocence. I honestly don't know if I did those murders, and I certainly don't know why. When I was in Hungary they were very good to me. That's at least in part why I stayed so long. They're good people."

"Then why would you kill them? And so horribly?"

"I don't know! For God's sake, I don't know anything! Perhaps I'm insane. Whoever did that to another human being has to be, don't you think?"

"If you'd been lost enough, in pain deep enough, I could believe, reluctantly, that you would kill yourself—but not someone else, and then go and do it again, and again. No, I don't believe you did it."

He reached across the table to her. His hands were cold, strong, and his face showed a pain so deep it seemed bottomless.

"I don't know if I did or not. I have nightmares as terrible as anything we ever saw. Worse, because in them I'm not helping. Everything goes to pieces as I touch it. Nobody's helped or healed. Sometimes everybody dies, and it all goes dark, as if I'm dead too." He shook his head minutely. "Leave it alone, Hester. You can't help."

"You have nightmares—I know that. But when you are awake, you function pretty much as you always have. You must know when you came to Shadwell, at least roughly?"

"What does that matter?"

"I need all the information you can give me." She had a notebook and a pencil and was evidently prepared to write down his answers. "Please just tell me. We haven't time to waste arguing, Fitz. Answer me. When did you get to Shadwell?"

"About six months ago. Around February 1870."

"Why did you come here? Why not go any other place in London?"

"I like the Hungarians," he said with bleak humor. "I like their stories, the way they see the land. I like their joy in things, the care they take with simple jobs."

"How long did you live in Hungary?"

"In one place or another, about eleven years."

"In one place, or several?"

"Several. At least a year in Budapest. It's a marvelous city. You'd love it."

"I'm happy in London; I've too many friends here to leave it. Where else were you?"

"Other cities. More often small villages." He gave her a list of a dozen or more, spelling out their names for her. "What help is that?"

"I don't know. Did you practice medicine there?"

"Of course. Sometimes on animals. I like healing things, and I had to earn my keep."

"Why didn't you come home? People are bound to ask."

"I did. I am home."

"Fitz! I'm trying to help."

"I'm sorry. It really isn't any good, Hester. I don't have a complete memory of anything. I can remember the land, how lovely some of it was. I remember how poor some of the people were. And how magnificent the homes of the wealthy were. But that's probably true of every country. I don't remember anyone treating me badly, but the nightmares came and went; they were always in the back of my mind, waiting to surprise me again."

"Did you know any of the people here when you were in Hungary?"

"Not that I can recall." He smiled. "Do you think they all know something terrible about me that I can't remember, and I killed them to ensure their silence? You're wasting your time, Hester. You never did know when to give up. You're going to lose some patients. That's medicine. And it's life. I'm one you can't save. If I killed those people, then you shouldn't even try!"

"And if you didn't?" she said furiously. "Then I should just let you hang, and whoever did it carry on killing? Or perhaps he'll stop, and just get away with it?" Her voice was shaking she was so angry . . . so terribly afraid that he could be right.

"Hester." He reached forward and took her hand again. She was surprised by how strong he was. "I can't plead innocence; all I can say is I don't know. I can't think of any reason why I would do such a terrible thing—but maybe I'm mad. It's possible. Don't break your heart over the ones you can't save. It's a waste of a good heart—in your case, a great one. Keep it whole for all the people you can help. And encourage that boy, Scuff—turned into Will. He'll make a damn good doctor one day. That's a patient really worth saving."

"Tell me how you were wounded and how long it took to heal," she demanded.

"It's not important. It doesn't prove I killed those people, or that I didn't. I wasn't hit in the head, I wasn't beaten or tortured. Nobody did anything but help. The worst things that ever happened were just the cold, the pain and the loneliness. Things that happen to half the people in the world, and are not the fault of anyone in particular."

She opened her mouth to argue, but the guard stepped forward. She had forgotten him, and was startled.

"Time's up, ma'am," he said firmly. "You've 'ad your turn."

Hester touched Fitz's hand lightly. Then she stood up, thanked the guard and left.

SHE WENT STRAIGHT TO Oliver Rathbone's chambers in Lincoln's Inn. Her friendship with Rathbone had been long and deep, and quite varied. At one time he had asked her to marry him.

She had declined, because whether he loved her or not, she knew that Monk was the only man to whom she would give all her heart and a lifelong commitment.

She and Rathbone had remained friends, the first awkwardness passing quickly. They had fought many cases together, both accusing and defending, each with the deepest care and loyalty. And quite apart from that, there was no better lawyer in England.

Another thing about Rathbone, perhaps even more important this time, was that he had made some very bad mistakes himself, and had fought back from them. He was gentler now, far slower to judge anyone. Pain makes some people bitter, others it refines. Rathbone was definitely among the latter.

But to engage his services she would have to be able to tell him as much as possible about Fitz—at the very least, if he himself knew whether or not he was guilty.

She told Rathbone's clerk, whom she knew well after their years of working together, that she urgently needed to speak to his employer.

Not a shadow of surprise touched his face. "Yes, ma'am," he said immediately. "I'm sure Sir Oliver will see you as soon as he has finished with his current client. Would you care for a pot of tea while you are waiting? It may well be a quarter of an hour or so."

Hester realized that she would like it very much, and told him so.

"And perhaps a biscuit or two?" he offered. He was accustomed to crises in the office. Few people came to see a barrister of Rathbone's brilliance in court unless they had some trouble of great seriousness.

"Yes, please," she said, accepting.

He must have assessed her demeanor and assumed she had a five-biscuit problem, because he returned with a fresh pot of tea and a plate of five crisp biscuits from McVitie's, in his opinion the best maker of such things in Britain, therefore anywhere.

She thanked him and tried to order her thoughts so she could persuade Rathbone that there really was a case to fight. Even if Fitz was guilty, there must be some way to help.

However, if he was guilty, then would he want to survive? Would it not be more merciful to allow the law to take its course? Would it not even be what he would want? A trial, three weeks' further imprisonment, and then the oblivion brought by the gallows?

She realized as she thought of it, in such blunt words, that she had not emotionally accepted the possibility that Fitz was guilty. Intellectually, she knew it. She could even say the words. But all the time every other part of her was refusing to believe it.

The door opened and Rathbone came in. It had been two or three months since she last saw him, and he looked almost as she remembered him from when they had first met about fourteen years ago, when she was newly back from the Crimean War, and Monk was desperate to defend the man who had actually killed Joscelyn Gray.

Of course Rathbone was older, but the years of his brilliant career, which had their share of difficulties, now sat lightly. He had recently married again after the tragedy of his first marriage. He was truly happy. There was nothing superficial about it. Pain had hollowed out of him a depth that professional success had not.

He was still slender, elegant, immaculately dressed. He would always be that, but it seemed out of habit now, rather than a defense against the world.

"No doubt there's a disaster somewhere, but it's still nice to see you," he said with a smile.

"I'm afraid there is," Hester admitted. "You look well. How is Beata?"

"Very well, thank you. You look exhausted. Pushing yourself to the edge of despair as you always have, but I would guess"—he studied her face—"it's wearing a little thin. I assume this fearful case in Shadwell has fallen to Monk?"

"Yes. Yesterday he had to arrest Fitz, as the only way of saving his life from the mob chasing him in the streets."

"Fitz? That would be Herbert Fitzherbert? An army doctor I am guessing you knew from the Crimean War?"

"You always did keep your ear to the ground, Oliver. Yes. We worked together quite a lot. Actually, there were not so many of us. We all knew each other . . ."

"And you believe he is innocent?"

"I don't know. Oliver, he's . . . he's terribly damaged. He has nightmares, even when he's awake. He sometimes forgets where he is. Sudden noises terrify him. He loses his temper over nothing, weeps uncontrollably . . . He . . . he can't forget the horror he saw, the piles of bodies, limbs torn off, ground so soaked with blood you slipped on it . . . it squelched. Sometimes the smell of human waste sends him into shock, as . . . as if he were back in the hospital with men dying all around him, and he can't even help their pain, never mind actually heal them. More men died of cholera and dysentery than all those killed by enemy fire put together. Oliver . . . you can't see all that and stay the same as you were. Nobody should have to bear the weight of needing to help . . . and keep on failing so often."

"You did, Hester."

"No, I didn't . . . not like Fitz. He was on the battlefield far more than I was. There were piles of bodies, some dead, some dying, and there was little anyone could do. But he never gave up trying. He was left on the field for dead. He woke up when everyone else was gone, terribly wounded, but with enough knowledge and strength left to save himself."

Rathbone's face was pale as he imagined it, or tried to.

"We left him because we thought he was dead—I did. I saw him in the pile of bodies. He was cold to the touch. And I left him there . . ."

Would Rathbone understand why she had done that? How terrible that mistake was, and how easy to make? Scuff had not—until Fitz himself had told him.

"He had to try to survive alone," she went on. "It took him ages to heal, but when he did he made his way slowly westward until he ended up in Hungary. He stayed there because he liked it, and they were good to him. He was still weak and he had a lot of healing left to do. He only got back home to England half a year ago."

She searched Rathbone's face, and saw no condemnation in it. What did he think? It did not matter now. Only his help was important.

"He told you this?" he asked.

"Yes . . ."

"I will have to verify it, but it shouldn't be too difficult." He was making notes as they spoke. "Did he know these people who were killed? Or perhaps I should be asking whether they knew him?"

"He didn't know them; that we can trace. But he could still be guilty. I don't know, and he doesn't either. But he knows of no reason why he would hurt anyone. He is still a great doctor. He worked with Crow and Scuff, and I helped. He hasn't changed much, not in medicine. The years have been very hard. I've seen him having nightmares. He's . . . he's back there in the Crimea, seeing men die all around him. I don't know if he sees the Hungarians in Shadwell as Russian soldiers on the battlefield—I don't know anything. But I knew Fitz when he was one of the best and bravest doctors in the whole British Army, when he would stay up operating on shattered men all day and all night, and all the next day, trying desperately to save lives, mend bodies, save limbs."

She took a deep breath. "It wasn't only the soldiers who were close to starvation sometimes, it was us too. He'd give me the last piece of bread, having to pretend it wasn't. We laughed at nothing, at terrible jokes, and wept in each other's arms when we lost man after man, friends who were whole the day before, and now just . . . just . . ." She could see the bodies in her mind, torn apart, almost robbed of dignity, even of humanity, left nothing but a sea of pain.

"Don't!" Rathbone said abruptly. "Hester, stop it! You don't need to persuade me. I'll do everything I can."

She let out a long, slow breath. "Thank you . . ."

He hesitated, on the verge of telling her something, then changed his mind.

"I don't know what I can pay you, much less what he can . . ."

"Stop. I don't need money. I can well afford to defend a man because he needs it. And from what you say, he has already given his country—my country—more than most men give in a lifetime. He deserves everything we can do to save him from injustice, if that's the case, and from far crueler punishment than he deserves, if he did indeed kill these unfortunate men. What I do need is everything you can tell me about him: his success in the army, his medical character now. That you can do. You may be the only person involved in the case, on either side, who was there, and saw, most intimately, what he endured. If I cannot prove him innocent, then his suffering may be our only resort. Either way, I will need you to create the setting for us."

"Of course."

"I know it will be painful, but we have to see it. The prosecutor, whoever he is, will make everything he can of the horror of the murders. Fitzherbert's experience in the Crimea must be equally wrenching."

"Of course." She said it automatically, but she knew already that it would be bitterly painful, the dragging up of things she had long ago buried in the necessity of forgetting. She had not realized until she saw Fitz again that forgetting was a blessing not everyone had. And Rathbone would spare her nothing, however much he hated doing it. She knew that from long experience. His loyalty would be toward Fitz, as it should be. One of the things dearest to her in his character was his utter commitment.

"And I shall need all Monk can tell me," he added.

"He'll do that. He . . . he tried to save Fitz, very nearly at the cost of his own life." What sounded like disgust permeated her voice, but it was actually a cold burst of terror at how close it had been. Admiration and fear did not always sound as such.

Rathbone smiled bleakly. He also knew Monk well. They had shared most of their best and worst cases.

"Thank you for trusting me with this," he said quietly. "I can only imagine how much it matters to you. Now, please tell Monk, and have him get ready for me all he can. I will go and meet Fitzherbert."

She nodded, then impulsively reached forward and kissed him on the cheek.

EVEN BEFORE THE INITIAL exhaustion had worn off, and while his body was still stiff from the chase, Monk redoubled his efforts to solve the crimes. On the assumption that Fitz was not guilty, he sent Hooper to trace everything he could about the doctor: his arrival in Shadwell, the people he had treated and all the movements he could verify and collate. It was just possible that a pattern would emerge, even something that would prove his innocence.

He had one of his other men check the saber that had been used in the fourth murder. It was a military weapon. Did anyone have a collection of such things? Was someone missing a saber and had been afraid to report it? Question harder. Who had access to such a thing? When was it last seen? Was anything else missing, from anywhere?

Monk had a third man check for any connection at all between the victims. Did they have more than a passing acquaintance? Were there family connections that had been overlooked? Business between them? Did they belong to the same clubs, the same church? Had they courted the same woman or wanted the same job?

And what about the rare purple candles? They had all been fine beeswax. Were they bought, or stolen? Candles had been stolen from a chandler—was there any way of knowing if the ones used in the murders came from that box? Even asking might turn up something.

He considered the facts. Sickening as they were, they were the same in all the cases, essentially identical. The newspapers had not released all of the details. That was only common sense.

Surely the murders were too much alike, even in the most trivial aspect, to be the work of more than one person? The symbolism was not common enough for multiple people to have used it. He had thought deeply about what the various signs might mean to whoever had done this.

Candles dipped in blood? Religious? Sacrifice in payment of some sort? Something more personal? And why always seventeen?

The smashing and desecration of icons such as the statue of the Virgin Mary—was that specifically against Roman Catholicism? Or incidental, and nothing to do with religion?

Piercing through the chest, leaving the weapon in the wound?

Broken fingers, a hand disabled?

Was there some common thread he was missing? He had talked it over with Hooper, and learned nothing.

There was hatred in it, violent and bestial. It was hard to imagine that any man could have such hatred within him, yet outwardly look just like anyone else. Surely he must appear different in some way to the intelligent eye, at least enough to make him uncomfortable.

It was a deeply frightening thought that there was nothing at all to distinguish such a man from the friends you knew, the colleagues you worked with every day, even your own family.

The murderer could not be Antal Dobokai. Monk had been over his account of where he had been at the time of Fodor's death. He had walked the route Dobokai had taken, checked every fact he had given. He could find no fault in it anywhere, and he had dearly wanted to. He did not admire himself for that, but there was something in Dobokai that made him uneasy.

He must go back to the crimes to check each one individually. He had been concentrating on what they had in common, but this had not got him far. Perhaps he should consider what they did *not* have in common?

He knew the crime scenes far too well. They were, as far as he or anyone else could see, absolutely the same. What was the meaning of each feature that the killer had to repeat it so absolutely the same, over and over, with such outwardly different victims?

The key was not in the victims, it was in him!

Candles? Drury had said purple was for power, but he thought, from what Monk told him, that any kind of ritual with the candles showed signs of being hurried and incomplete. Perhaps it had nothing to do with religion at all.

Was it merely a number? Seventeen. No one had been able to find any group in Britain or in Hungary—religious, cultural or anything else—to whom the number seventeen had any particular significance.

Was it of meaning to the killer only? Seventeen people? Seventeen things of value? Something done seventeen times?

Time—seventeen years ago?

Where had Fodor been seventeen years ago? Here in Shadwell. Who else had been here then?

It took Monk half an hour of rereading to know that none of the other victims had been here seventeen years ago. But Roger and Adel Haldane had been here, two years married. Dobokai had been in England, but not in Shadwell. According to all Monk could find, he had been in Leeds, in Yorkshire—miles away, as he himself had said.

It was late afternoon, but he called Hooper anyway, and together they went to Fodor's house. The streets were hot and dusty, filled with the traffic of people on their way home.

"What are we looking for?" Hooper asked, keeping step with Monk. Until now he had been silent.

"I'm not certain," Monk replied. "History. I'm looking for something that happened seventeen years ago."

"And has just come to the surface now?" Hooper kept the disbelief from his voice with obvious difficulty. "An old hatred so violent, and it waited this long?"

"The injury was seventeen years ago," Monk corrected him, thinking it through as he spoke.

"And we're going to look for some record of it still in Fodor's house?"

"Can you think of anywhere better to look for it?" Monk snapped. "If it were generally known, don't you think somebody would have mentioned it by now?"

Hooper did not answer. They reached Fodor's house, and Monk produced the keys. Though Fodor had died at his office on the docks, the house still bore the mark of tragedy. No one had been in or out since the police had originally searched it, and found nothing of help.

Monk closed the door behind them. The air was stale. There was a fine layer of dust on the hall table. A fly had been trapped inside, and lay on the once polished floor.

"Where shall we begin?" Hooper said quietly. His voice held regret, as if he felt he were trespassing on the dead.

Monk understood. He felt the same sense of intrusion. They were not here about the crime itself; they were here to dig into the past, to uncover what Fodor had intended to be kept secret.

"Bedroom," Monk answered. "Least likely to find much there. We'll get the simple ones done first. Finish with wherever he kept books, mementoes, personal things. I don't know what we're looking for. Either of us might recognize it—or not."

They looked in near silence for over an hour, learning nothing unexpected. They ended in the sitting room, where the desk and the bookshelves were. They took out the books one by one, holding them open so anything between the leaves would fall out.

Hooper had said nothing, just worked methodically. His extreme forbearance irritated Monk, because he was feeling increasingly that they were on a fool's errand. Either they had seen it, and not known its meaning, or there was nothing to find.

"Sir?" Hooper interrupted Monk's thoughts.

"Yes?"

Hooper had a book in one hand, and held up an old photograph in the other. He turned it toward Monk.

"Who is it?" Monk held out his hand.

Hooper passed it to him, watching his reaction.

Monk looked at it. It was a fair-haired young man of possibly twenty, good-looking, eager-faced, staring at the camera. He looked familiar. Monk tried to recall where he had seen him before.

Then he remembered. "It's Haldane's son," he said. "Odd that Fodor should keep it, and inside a book rather than an album." He looked at Hooper questioningly.

"No, it isn't," Hooper said. "Looks like him—a lot like him. But see the background, sir. The writing on the glass behind him is Hungarian. And the clothes. That's in Hungary, sir, and a good while ago."

Monk looked at the picture again, then up at Hooper. An idea was beginning to take shape in his mind. "It's Fodor, isn't it?"

"Yes, sir, I'm pretty sure it is. And from what you said, sir, Haldane's son was born about seventeen years ago."

"And Haldane just discovered that? How?"

"Well, if he somehow saw that picture, or one like it, it doesn't take much putting together," Hooper replied. "That would be why Mrs. Haldane was so keen to get the boy off to university somewhere."

Monk thought of Adel's pride in her son, and now he could recall very vividly that Haldane had not had the same light in his face. In fact, there had been an anger in him that Monk had attributed to the murder, but perhaps it was more to do with the fact that he already knew the boy he had once been so desperately proud of was not his at all.

"It'd be enough for some men to kill," Hooper said, breaking into his thoughts. "You can't wrong a man much more than that—especially when you've raised the boy yourself, not knowing, being happy, proud, maybe boasting a little. Mrs. Haldane's lucky he didn't go for her too."

"The reason would be too obvious," Monk answered. "He wouldn't want anyone to know. Her punishment is that she has to live with it."

"Can we prove it?" Hooper asked. "This photograph would pretty well prove the fact, but it wouldn't prove that Haldane knew. And it has nothing to do with all the others."

"Haldane didn't do the others," Monk said quietly. "At least I don't think so. Certainly he didn't do the second one. Or the third."

"Who did? And in God's name, why?"

"I don't know. I'll start with Haldane. We need to prove it."

"I doubt he'll argue, sir. I think the fact itself is what hurts more than anything else. Does Mrs. Haldane know, do you think?" Hooper asked.

"Yes." Monk remembered Adel's face, the ashen, bloodless skin when she realized what the seventeen candles meant in the crime.

"Yes," he said aloud. "She knows, even if she won't admit it to herself. This is going to be . . . hard."

Hooper did not answer.

THERE WAS NO WAY the confrontation could have gone well. Monk hated it, but there was no alternative, and now that he knew, he would be responsible for anything that happened, to Adel or to anyone else, if he didn't act tonight.

He and Hooper arrived at the Haldanes' home, knowing that at this hour, Haldane himself would be there, having dinner.

Haldane answered the door. He saw Monk and was about to speak, but seeing Hooper behind him, his face froze.

"Mr. Haldane, I am arresting you for the murder of Imrus Fodor— only that crime, nothing else."

Haldane froze.

Monk knew that at any moment he could lash out, attempt to run.

Adel appeared at the entrance of the dining room, likely concerned as to who was at the front door.

Monk did not take his eyes from Haldane.

For an instant Haldane thought of resistance, perhaps even flight. It was there in his eyes. Then it died.

"My wife knew nothing about it," he said. "She has no fault."

Monk felt a moment of sharp pity for him. He saw the tears on Adel's face, but dimly, only over Haldane's shoulder.

Haldane held out his hands.

Monk slipped the manacles over them, in front of him, not behind. He might regret it later, but this was a humiliation that was unnecessary now. He hoped he would not be mistaken.

12

"Isn't there something we can do to help Fitz?" Will asked Hester when she stopped by Crow's clinic with a few supplies she knew they would need: cinchona bark, quinine, surgical spirit, camphorated wine, more bandages of all sorts. She put them down on the table. She felt the deep ache of helplessness at not being able to heal Fitz's type of pain; he was lost in an abyss while the rest of them stood by, unable to reach him.

Scuff took the bottles and packages to put them into the right cupboards, but made no move to begin.

"We've got to be able to do something!" he protested.

Monk had told him about Adel Haldane, and the strong probability that Fodor had been her son's father. Monk had felt very little sense of victory in Haldane's arrest, even though the man had, with a sudden dignity and unselfishness, submitted quietly. It was a solution to only the first murder, none of the others, and in spite of its ferocity, Monk had felt an intense pity for all of them. For a few terrible moments, Haldane had found the very worst in himself, and he would pay for it for what remained of his life.

Hester thought briefly of telling Scuff that there was a chance the authorities would understand Fitz's injuries, and his behavior. She looked at his face and remembered vividly, as if it had been only days ago, the boy he had been. How slight he had been, narrow-shouldered, slender-necked from years of foraging for food along the riverbank. Now he was taller than she, hard-muscled, already almost the man he would become.

Crow had taught him well. He had seen pain and death, and dealt with them as a doctor should. He did not deserve to be told comfortable lies that would disappear in days. How could he trust her again if she did that? It would break something very valuable in their relationship. It would be as if she refused to let him grow up. He deserved better than that.

"Do you believe it was Fitz?" he asked.

She met his eyes squarely. "I don't know. If it was, then something happened to him that was more terrible than I can imagine. But that's possible . . ." She was about to add his name, Scuff. She changed it to say, ". . . Will."

He smiled very slightly, then blinked hard. "That tells me you think it could be true." His voice was husky, too close to tears.

"It could be," she admitted. "But I'm going to choose not to believe it unless I have to. I don't know who else it could be, or how to prove that either."

"Mrs. Haldane?" he suggested.

"She wouldn't be strong enough to do it alone. And why would she?"

"Because she loved Fodor?" he suggested. "And when her husband killed him, she killed the others to make us think he killed all of them?"

She did not answer.

"I don't know," he said miserably. "But why would Fitz murder for Haldane? He didn't hate any of those people. He doesn't hate anyone at all. It's a stitch-up, because they've got to get somebody. Monk only arrested him to save him from the mob."

"I know that. But what other answer is there?" The moment the words were out of her mouth, she regretted them. She had as good as admitted to Will that she thought Fitz was guilty.

Did she?

Perhaps.

What did people do in nightmares, the sort that are even worse when you wake up? They go on, and on. Reality disappears.

And yet it was Fitz who had helped her keep sane during the terrible days in Scutari when every day, every night, more men were dying. Cholera raged through the hospitals. The smell of vomit and diarrhea choked the throat, and there was nothing they could do to save the men. Young men, healthy and beautiful, brought in with cannon and saber wounds, dead within days.

Fitz had been steady then. Even when nurses started dying as well, he had never lost faith. Or at least he had never let them see it.

Surely she could do as much for him now? She had given him her word. That, at least, she could keep.

She straightened her shoulders a little. "I have no idea how we're going to win," she said firmly. "I don't even know what else to do. And only Sir Oliver can visit him. But we aren't going to stop fighting. I promised Fitz that if he faced his demons, I would face mine. I haven't done that yet. How can he believe me if I don't go and do it now?"

Will looked at her, frowning. "You have nightmares too? I'm sorry. I didn't think of that . . ."

"No, not very often. My dreams are different." This was difficult to do. What would he think of her for letting her family down so badly? If she would abandon her own parents and her surviving brother, why should Will not think she would abandon him, if he became inconvenient, or needed more from her than she was willing to give? She would nurse strangers, but not her own who had loved and trusted her.

He was watching her, waiting. If she lied, or evaded the answer now, he would know it was something she was ashamed of, which it was, but he would also know that she did not trust him, and that was far worse. No apology afterward would wash it away.

"While I was away, in the Crimea, my father was cheated out of a great deal of money. But what was far worse for him was that many of his friends trusted his advice and invested with the same cheating man. They lost too, far more than they could afford." She was rushing through it, but it hurt just as much as it always did.

Fitz had been right. She must face it, and do what she could to repair what was left.

"My eldest brother was a soldier," she went on. "He was killed in the Crimea, at Balaclava. There was only my second brother, Charles, at home. My father felt that the only honorable thing to do was to take his own life, which he did."

She saw the horror in Will's eyes.

"And my mother died shortly afterward. She . . . she couldn't bear it. I didn't know until I arrived back in England, and it was too late to do anything then. I don't think Charles ever forgave me for that."

"But you didn't know!" he protested.

"I didn't have to go to the Crimea," she tried to explain. "I could have married the decent man they had chosen for me, and then I would have been there to help. I was close to my father. I might have been able to support him enough that he would have realized it was not his fault! He was . . . he was taken in by a very clever man, a Crimean army officer who said he had been with my brother the night before the battle, and had paid his debts, or lent him money, or something like that. He used that deceit on several people. My father never lied, and he never suspected other people of lying—not an officer and a gentleman, which Gray was. His father was an earl, or something of the sort. I can't remember now. I try to forget all of it." She swallowed the ache in her throat. "I'm trying to . . . and it works most of the time. It all seems so long ago. And there's nothing anyone can do to help."

"What about your brother Charles? The one who's still alive?" His face was very grave. He held out one hand toward her, tentatively, as if he wanted physically to bridge the gap that was emotionally opening between them.

She moved a step closer and took his hand. She was startled by how strong he was now. His fingers clasped hers.

"That's what Fitz wanted me to do—see Charles," she answered.

"When are you leaving? Do you need me to go with you?"

His offer, the speed with which he made it, and the warmth in him, was the catalyst that brought the tears. She ignored them.

"No . . . no, thank you. I must go alone. You are needed here. Fitz can't help Crow now, and you can. I'll go and find Charles. I know where he lives. I don't know what he'll say, but at least I will try. That was my promise to Fitz. I wouldn't blame Charles if he didn't want to see me. He lives here in London. I'll be back this evening." She looked down a moment, then back up at him. "Thank you . . . Will."

He blushed, knowing what she meant by the use of his new name. He could not find any words that were right. He just smiled, and tightened his fingers for a moment before he let go.

IT WAS TWO OMNIBUS rides back to the neighborhood where Hester had grown up and where Charles had bought a house. After the financial distress of his father's loss, Charles had sold the family house toward paying the debts. He'd kept his own house for his mother to live in, for the short while she had left. His wife was from the neighborhood also, and preferred to remain close to her friends.

It was only now that Hester wondered if this had been Charles's own wish or if he would have much preferred moving away from all the memory of pain. Had he stayed for his wife's sake? It was a big price to pay.

As she walked along the street, she was surprised to find how familiar it was. It was very pleasant. The late-summer trees were in full leaf, and many of the small front gardens had roses in bloom. It seemed unchanged over the many years since she had been here. Far too many years. The guilt was already deep in her. She had been the one who was always moving around, living in lodgings, or even staying in the home of a patient she was nursing for a period of time. It had been appropriate that she be available at all hours. She should have gone to Charles.

She came to the right number, and it looked so unchanged that it seemed like only months since she had called. But it had been over a decade, very well over.

She would not falter now. She had no idea what she was going to say. There were no decent excuses, and, actually, she was not looking for any. Only an apology would be of any purpose.

She pulled the doorbell rope and waited.

After several moments the door opened and a nice-looking parlor maid asked her politely if she could be of help. Since it was a Saturday, there was a good chance that at this hour of the morning Charles would be in.

"Good morning," Hester answered with as much of a smile as she could manage. "Is Mr. Latterly at home? I am his sister, and I regret to say that I have not been in touch for far too long."

The maid looked puzzled. "Mr. Latterly, ma'am?"

"I believe I have the right house? Number twenty-six?"

"If you'd like to come inside, ma'am, I'll ask Mrs. Wynter if she can be of help. I'm afraid I don't know a Mr. Latterly, but I've only been here three months." She held the door wider for Hester to go in.

Hester glanced at the door. It had "26" written on it in large brass numbers. Had her memory played a trick on her?

"Thank you," she said. Perhaps Mrs. Wynter could redirect her if she had made a mistake. How stupid of her! She had trusted her memory.

She followed the maid into the morning room and waited while she informed her mistress.

Hester looked around. There was a laurel bush outside, close to the house. It was bigger than she remembered, but its dark-green shape seemed to belong in her recollections. The fireplace was the same; she could remember the carved scrolls on it. It was oak, which was less usual than mahogany. She had liked it because of the difference.

The bookcases looked the same, but the books were completely different. Had Charles suddenly taken an interest in stamp collecting, and ancient coins?

The door opened and Mrs. Wynter came in. She was a handsome

woman, dark-haired with a dramatic, beautiful streak of white sweeping back from her brow.

"Hester Monk," Hester said, introducing herself. "Charles Latterly is my brother. I am so sorry to have troubled you. I must have misremembered his address. It is . . . far too long since I have seen him. I apologize."

Mrs. Wynter's face reflected only sadness, no irritation or sense of having been disturbed.

"I'm so sorry, Mrs. Monk, but Mrs. Latterly passed away over two years ago. Mr. Latterly closed his business and sold this house. He moved away, outside London. But I do have his address. Naturally there was much to forward, at first." She gave a slight smile, her eyes not moving from Hester's. "He seemed a nice man. Even in his grief he was so pleasant to deal with. I hope he is doing well."

Hester was stunned, her mind whirling. Charles had lost his wife, and closed his business. She had been so distant she had not even known! He had not wanted to tell her—or had he not known where to find her? A deep, cold feeling told her that it was the former. Surely he would have found her if he had really wanted to? He didn't have the easy charm that James had had, the warmth or the grace. He was very much the second son, always somewhat in the shadow. But he was certainly clever enough, even if he didn't believe that himself.

Poor Charles. No one left in his family but Hester, and he had not felt close enough to her to reach out. Her guilt dug deeper, far deeper.

"Thank you," she said to Mrs. Wynter. "I would be most grateful if you have any note of his address." She would have liked to explain to this woman, but there was no explanation. Any attempt would only make the situation more awkward. She had simply become so involved in her own life, and Monk's, that she had not thought of Charles. He had never needed her love, or approval. It was James's acceptance he had wanted, and his father's.

No, that was a cheap excuse. She had offered him nothing. She had seen how he adored James. James himself had not. Had she been just as blind?

Mrs. Wynter rose and excused herself. She came back a few minutes later with an address written on a piece of paper, and an envelope to put it in.

"I hope you find him," she said gently. "If you do, please give him my best wishes."

Hester could feel the heat burn up her face.

"Thank you." She accepted the paper, glanced at it, then put it in the envelope. "You are very kind."

Mrs. Wynter offered her a cup of tea, but Hester declined it. She had the address. Please heaven Charles was still there. She wanted to go as quickly as possible. In fact she would walk to the nearest main road and catch a hansom. She would not take the cheaper, and slower, omnibus.

The address was in Primrose Hill, north of Regent's Park. She found a hansom quickly, and it was not so very far, less than four miles as a bird might fly, yet following the lines of the road, and occasionally slowed by traffic, it seemed to take hours.

When finally she reached the street Mrs. Wynter had written down, she stared at the houses in fascination. It was not as she would have imagined any place Charles would have chosen, or been able to afford. It was not an especially wealthy neighborhood, at least on the surface, but there was a quality of elegance about it, as if its residents had lived here for generations. Hedges were thick and well clipped; flowers climbed high over arches and pergolas, years' worth of growth. Lawns were thick and green, even if the houses they surrounded were not of great size.

She asked the driver to wait until she told him to leave, in case she had made a mistake. She felt foolish, but she would feel a lot more so if this was a total error. Was Mrs. Wynter wrong? Or had Charles given her a misleading address on purpose? Had he sold his business, or lost it?

She walked quickly up the path to the front door. If something difficult had to be done, better to do it quickly. She rang the brass bellpull.

In minutes the door was answered by a competent-looking woman of middle age. She was dressed in a plain dark skirt and a white blouse. There were keys on a large ring carried at her waist, the only clue that she must be the housekeeper.

Hester took a deep breath. "Is this the residence of Mr. Charles Latterly? I have been directed here from his previous home, and I am not sure if I am correct."

"Indeed it is, ma'am. May I tell Mr. Latterly who is calling?"

"Yes. Yes, I am his sister."

The woman looked slightly surprised, no more than a servant should.

"Indeed, ma'am. I'm sorry, but Mr. Latterly did not give me your name."

Of course not. Why should he? For him she had ceased to exist.

"I was Hester Latterly. I am now Hester Monk."

"Then please to come in, Mrs. Monk. If you would care to wait in the sitting room, I shall tell Mr. Latterly that you are here."

"Thank you."

Hester was too tense to sit down. How would Charles have changed? Would he even speak to her? Had he remarried, that he now lived in such a charming place? It was not a house for a man alone. Even looking around this room, there were touches of warmth and imagination, things that were feminine. There were pictures of beautiful scenery, paintings of an older woman, perhaps in her seventies, her face still lovely, eyes full of life.

The door opened and Charles came in. He looked much as she remembered him, except that there was considerable gray at his temples. It suited him. The hard angles of his face had softened, the tension she associated with him had also gone. He looked happy.

"Hello, Hester," he said in some surprise. "What are you here for?" He stopped at least six feet away from her.

"Mrs. Wynter gave me your address . . ."

"Then you must have asked her for it."

"I did. I . . . didn't know you had moved."

"Why would you?" He raised his eyebrows slightly. "To where should I have sent a letter to inform you?" There was a sudden sharpness in his eyes. She thought it was anger, then realized it could have been pain. She had come to apologize, not to make matters even worse.

"I'm sorry, Charles. I didn't even know your wife had died, or . . . or that you had changed your business. I should have. If I had been in touch you would have told me, and perhaps I could have been some use."

"What could you have done?" he said reasonably. "It's all in the past now. I left the country for a little while . . ."

He was interrupted by the door to the garden opening, and a young woman came into the room. She was slender, at least Hester's height, and her long fair hair was tied very loosely. She had a face of extraordinary intelligence.

"I'm sorry, Uncle Charles. I didn't know you had company." Without the slightest lack of ease, she moved forward and offered her hand to Hester. "I'm Candace Finbar. How do you do?"

"How do you do, Miss Finbar?" Hester replied, totally bemused. Now that she looked more closely at the girl, she could see that she was about fifteen, or possibly sixteen at the most. And Charles had no nieces or nephews. His wife had been an only child.

It was Charles who interrupted. He was smiling, all the apprehension gone from his face, so that not even a trace of his anger was left.

"Candace, this is my sister, Hester. I think I mentioned her to you."

Candace gave him a wry smile, affectionate, amused, patient.

"Once or twice," she agreed, then turned to Hester. "He speaks of you very often. I'm so glad you've come to visit us. I think you were the person he most wished to be like."

Hester was completely lost. She looked at Charles and saw the blush rise up his face.

Candace looked at Hester, as one woman to another. "He rescued us all from a volcano erupting on Stromboli," she explained. "And solved a murder, and fought the person who committed the murder, and killed him, even though he nearly lost and was almost killed himself. He's being modest," she added, as if the explanation were necessary.

"That's an exaggeration, Candace," he said awkwardly. "We all saved ourselves.

"Why are you here, Hester?" Charles changed the subject, but there was no anger in his voice. Clearly he was embarrassed, and yet the girl's admiration was of the utmost sweetness to him, and he could not hide it.

Hester decided to seize the moment. She would never have a better chance. He could explain the girl's presence later.

"I came to tell you how sorry I am for having been out of touch for so long." She released the words in a rush. "And for being in the Crimea when I was so badly needed at home."

Charles's face lost the very last trace of its reserve.

"There was nothing you could have done," he said gently. "You were of more use where you were. I missed you. But you couldn't have changed anything." He looked toward Candace. "Her uncle and guardian died on Stromboli. It was all very dramatic and dangerous. When he knew he would not live very much longer, Finbar asked me to be her guardian. I felt very inadequate to the task, but I couldn't refuse."

Hester bit back her amazement. This was a man she did not know at all. She had never seen such a possibility in him.

"Would you like . . . I don't know . . . elevenses?" Candace offered. "We could have lemonade? Are you hungry?"

Nothing was further from Hester's mind, but to refuse would be churlish. "Thank you. Lemonade would be excellent, if it is no trouble."

"None at all," Candace assured her, and with a quick look at Charles, she excused herself to fetch it.

"There was nothing else I could do!" Charles said as soon as the door was closed behind her.

Hester found herself smiling so widely that she must have looked absurd.

"Of course not," she agreed. "And why would you? She seems delightful."

"She is the best thing that ever happened to me in my life," he said simply.

"I understand. I sort of adopted a mudlark . . . a child who—"

"I know what a mudlark is, Hester!" But his pleasure and interest robbed the words of any sting.

"And he's eighteen now, and learning to be a doctor," she added.

"Why have you come now?" he asked, the lightness vanished. "You look troubled."

"I am." Very briefly she told him about the murders in Shadwell, and about Fitz. She had barely finished when Candace reappeared carrying a tray with a jug of lemonade, three glasses, and several very generous slices of fruitcake.

Charles took it from her before it overbalanced and set it on the small table. Cake and lemonade were shared among them. Hester took the refreshment out of courtesy, and found that the cake was delicious. She could not remember when she had last eaten any so good.

"What can you do about this poor man?" Charles asked, not critically, but with obvious concern.

"I don't know," she admitted. "I . . ." She was unwilling to say it.

"You don't know if he's guilty or not," he said for her.

"And even if he's guilty, you'll still fight for him, won't you?" Candace said urgently. "Friends do, don't they? What mistake is big enough to make you stop being friends?"

Hester could see layers stretching far beneath the simple words of the question. She had no idea what griefs or judgments lay in the child's past, or who had abandoned her, whether by force or by choice. Clearly Charles had not, and that mattered to her intensely. Would she judge Charles by what Hester did? It would be a natural thing to do—she was the only person in Charles's past, his family, that she could know.

Hester must be careful what she said.

"No," she said simply. "But I can't ignore the possibility that he did kill those people, even while I'm trying to prove that he didn't. If he did, then he believed he had a reason."

"Whoever did it, they believed they had a reason," Charles pointed out. "Have you any idea what it is? What do the victims have in common, apart from living in Shadwell and being Hungarian, originally?"

"Nothing we can find," she replied. "They don't even come from the same part of Hungary."

"Neither did we, in Stromboli, come from the same place," Candace said quickly. "But we were all there at the same time. Maybe it's something they all did, or saw? Or something they all knew?"

"Even though they didn't know each other before coming to England?" Hester asked.

Candace thought for a few moments. "Maybe there's someone they all knew, even if not at the same time?"

"Why would that be a motive to kill them?" Hester was puzzled.

"I don't know," Candace admitted ruefully. "But there has to be something, doesn't there?"

"Yes." She looked at the girl's face, soft with youth, skin glowing with the warmth of the late-summer sun, and yet she could see the anxiety in her eyes, the need to hear Hester's answer that she would never abandon the friend who so desperately needed her. "I won't stop looking. But we haven't got very long."

"Well, why would Fitz kill all these people? Don't they have to prove he had a reason?" Candace argued.

"I wish they did," Hester agreed. "But the way people feel at the moment, all they want is to blame someone, and hang them. They don't care why."

Candace was clearly horrified.

A look of surprise hit Charles's face, and then sudden amusement.

Hester was about to demand an explanation, but Candace got there before her.

"That isn't funny, Uncle Charles," she said with grave disapproval. "No matter how scared you are, it's still wrong to judge people without looking at everything."

"I'm two years older than Hester," he told her. "I can remember her when she was your age."

Candace was taken aback. She looked at him, then at Hester.

Hester was taken aback also. It seemed so long ago, and both of them had changed so much. Or was that an illusion? They had been friends then.

Charles was still looking at Candace. "You remind me so much of her. That is exactly what she would have said, which is probably why she is not arguing with you now. That and perhaps her good manners, but once she knows you, you will get the truth, defiantly, unvarnished."

Candace turned to Hester. "Will we get to know each other?" There was a flash of hope in her eyes; then, aware of it, she looked down.

All sorts of answers, prevarications, came to Hester's mind. She ignored them and gave an honest answer. "I hope so. But you will have to take Charles's advice on that. I do a lot of things he may not care for . . . at least, he may not wish you to have much to do with them, for a while."

"Solving murders, and protecting people? That's not wrong."

"I also run a clinic for . . . women who . . ." She did not know how to put it delicately. Judging from her confidence and her precise grammar and diction, Candace clearly came from an excellent family.

"You mean prostitutes," the girl finished for her.

It was Charles's turn to be taken aback.

Candace smiled at him. "You told me Hester was different. I think my aunt Lucy would have approved of her." She looked back at Hester, her face filled with pride. "My aunt Lucy was called an adventuress by people who were envious of her. She did all sorts of marvelous things, and was more alive than anyone else. We are going to help you as much as we can . . ." She turned back to Charles. "Aren't we!" It was a challenge, not a question.

"We are going to try," he agreed. He looked at Hester. "There must be a reason these particular people were victims. If it is not something in their past, as I suspect it may be, then it must be in their present. Were they particularly vulnerable? Lived alone? Needed help of some sort?"

Hester could see the sense of what he said, but she had no answer.

"They didn't come from the same town. They weren't the same age. Some were successful, others ordinary. They didn't seem to know each other more than slightly. They had different occupations and were not rivals in anything."

"But they were all Hungarians, now living in Shadwell?" he asked.

"Yes. That's all. There is nothing to say they ever met before they came here."

"There has to be something in common," he insisted.

"And Fitz," Candace added. "You said you were afraid he might have done it, and not even know it now . . . I'm sorry . . . I hate saying that. But if he did it, then he knew something about all of them. Even if he can't remember it now when he's . . . all right."

Charles leaned forward a little, his face very earnest. "That's true, Hester. Fitz may hold the answer, even if he doesn't understand it. You said he came here from the Crimea by traveling across Europe, and he spent a good while in Hungary. It's a very difficult language, not like any of the other European Romance languages, or the German or Scandinavian ones. How well does he speak it? He wouldn't become fluent in a few months."

"He lived there for years," she replied. But that didn't mean he couldn't be the key to the murders, even if he didn't know it.

"Did any of them fight back when they were attacked?" Charles asked.

"Not very much from what I've heard," she said, thinking about it as she spoke. "So they were not expecting it? Is that what you are saying? They had a terrible enemy that they did not even know was there? I hadn't thought of that."

"No wonder everyone's afraid." Candace shivered. "And I suppose they can't have known who it was, or they would have done something about it. Told the police, at least!"

"Can you have such an enemy and not know it?" Charles was thinking ahead. "If they had a secret, they would at least know it themselves, even if they did not know who else shared it. I don't see any sense in it."

"Then we've got to try harder," Candace said immediately. She looked at Hester. "What else could it be?"

"They don't realize it . . ." Hester was thinking aloud. "They knew something terrible, but they didn't connect it with the murders."

"That would make sense." Charles did not look as if this gave him any hope. "But what sort of thing? And when the second and third and fourth murders were committed, and still nobody realized it, doesn't that make them unbelievably stupid?"

"Yes," Hester said miserably.

The lemonade was finished and the cake was all gone but the crumbs, and not many of those.

"We won't give up," Candace declared, facing Charles, then Hester. "You will stay for luncheon, won't you? There are so many things I would like to talk about with you."

"Of course I will," Hester said, accepting, then turned to Charles. Candace had invited her without consulting him. Clearly she was very comfortable with him. There was a degree of trust that seemed completely natural. They were quite obviously friends: a young woman who had lost all her family, and a lonely man who had gained a young, proud and intelligent ward who would test his patience, his character and his intelligence . . . and perhaps bring him happiness such as he had never known before.

It was nearly three when Charles drove Hester, in the small gig he kept for Candace and himself, from his home to the nearest omnibus stop. He would have taken her farther, but she was hoping to have time to herself on the ride, in order to attempt to give some form to the ideas now filling her mind.

"When does the trial begin?" Charles asked as they rode through the quiet streets, passing only a few people out walking, either to visit friends or for the sheer pleasure of the day.

"I don't know, but very soon," Hester answered.

"Tell me, please, Hester. I have no idea what, but is there anything I can do to help?"

She was bitterly aware of how generous an offer that was, and how it contrasted with her own absence when she was needed, even if there had been little she could have done. She searched for hurt or anger in his face, now that Candace was not with them, but she saw nothing but concern.

"Thank you," she said. "I owe Fitz a great deal," she added suddenly.

"Do you? More than friendship?" he asked. "Did you not help him as much as he helped you?"

"In the war, perhaps. But it was he who persuaded me to come and see you, even though I . . . I put it off so long I made it hard for myself." She did not look at him as she said it. She was not sure if she was laying too much weight on so new and fragile a reconciliation.

"Then I owe Fitz a great deal as well," he replied. "But mostly I want to give Candace a family, more than just me." Now he was looking at the road ahead, keeping his face turned forward. "She reminds me of you. You used to be like that. Not quite as graceful, perhaps, but just as clever, and as stubborn . . . and as brave. She doesn't have as sharp a tongue as you, but I suppose if I'm not careful she could develop one. She needs another woman to trust, and I have no intention of marrying again." That was the first note of bitterness she had heard in his voice. She had not thought his marriage was sweet, but he had never admitted the loneliness that she sensed now.

"Of course," she said instantly. "You don't think I'm going to put myself through this twice, do you?"

"Was it so hard?"

"Yes." Then she made herself smile. "But if I had to, I'd live through it again to see you now."

Charles smiled as well. "I'm coming to the trial, and I'm quite sure Candace—"

"You can't bring her! Charles, the murders were very savage, very terrible. It's not the place for a young—"

"She's sixteen, Hester. She's already seen a murder, and a volcanic eruption where she fled for her life before the lava flow. In three or four years she could be old enough to go and nurse soldiers in a war!"

"I was in my twenties!" she protested.

"And if you'd been nineteen, would that have stopped you?"

"That's not the point!"

"It's exactly the point. Don't end this visit by fighting with me."

She smiled with startling sweetness. "You are right, of course."

CHAPTER

13

Hᴇsᴛᴇʀ ᴛʜᴏᴜɢʜᴛ ᴏꜰ ᴡʜᴀᴛ Charles had said about the four victims all knowing something that had happened in Hungary. They were of different ages, had grown up in different cities, had no associations in common, and yet someone had murdered them all with extraordinary ritual violence.

Was it something to do with them, or with the murderer? Did the victims even know why they had been singled out? If they hadn't, why not? And if they had, why had they done nothing to avoid their own deaths?

The only answer was that they had not known. Or else that it was so secret, so shameful, they preferred to remain silent and risk being the next victim rather than take any visible steps to defend themselves.

What could be so appalling?

And why now?

In heaven's name, what could it be?

Then the answer became obvious. Fitz was the only one who had arrived here recently. And if she could see that, certainly the prosecution would. Even if they didn't know the exact reason, it hardly mattered; the jury would grasp the suggestion of Fitz's involvement quickly enough. And sometimes the horror you could not name was worse, more terrifying, than the one you could.

And if Fitz was not guilty—and that was the only possibility she was willing to accept—then something had happened around the time he arrived in Shadwell, something no one else had noticed, or understood. Perhaps if she could find out what it was it would explain itself—and the killer.

She told this to Monk as they sat with the French windows open to the summer night. It was still balmy enough to be pleasant, and the rustle of the poplar leaves in the twilight breeze was a kind of music.

She had told him of Charles and Candace over supper. It was something good in all this tragedy, and for a short while they both rejoiced in it. Then it was time to face reality. Fitz was due to stand trial for the second, third, and fourth murders in the middle of the next week, only four days away.

"I need to see Fitz again," she told Monk.

"He's not doing well . . ." he began.

"Something happened, William, something . . ."

"He doesn't remember! He's . . . he can't help, Hester. He's quite willing to believe he did it. He's too tired, too frightened and too beaten to fight anymore. I think the nightmares, waking and sleeping, are too much for him." He looked at her with an aching gentleness. "I'm seeing . . ."

"I have an idea," she said tentatively. "It may not work . . ."

"Hester . . . it—"

"I have to try!" She was close to tears now. She knew that it was perfectly possible that Fitz was guilty. Some purgatory in his own mind had driven him into retaliation against ghosts.

"What? There's nothing left that we haven't already done. And no one has got into Fitz's mind, because it's changing from one day to the next."

"I'm not going to try to make him remember. Something triggered this. Whoever killed all these people, something made him begin . . ."

"We all know that."

"But we don't know what it was." She leaned forward. "Just listen to me, William. I know Fitz won't remember it, or if he does it won't sound like anything sensible to the jury, but if there was something, maybe it will be in the local newspapers."

"We've looked at them."

"The Hungarian ones? The local ones the community puts out that keeps people up to date with personal things? And news from Hungary itself?"

"If there was anything personal, we can't read them or understand what might—"

"No, of course we can't! But Fitz could!" She put her hand over his and clasped it hard. "It's just a matter of getting copies of the papers for the month or so before the first murder, and having him read them—just tell us what they say. It's worth trying, isn't it? Do you have a better idea? Someone will give us copies. People keep things like that. Their love of the old country, the old ways, is strong. And they'll all have family and friends over there."

"Who are you going to ask for them?" he inquired, but there was a lift in his voice.

"I'm sure they'll keep them in one of the shops, if not several. But I'll see what the man in the café says. He likes Fitz. He'll do what he can to help."

"Be quick. We have only a few days. Fitz must be . . ." He stopped.

"Terrified," she filled in. "I know. I think the very worst thing is that he has to wonder if they are going to prove that he did it. How do you live with that?"

"I don't know," he answered. "I thought I might have to, after Joscelyn Gray, and I didn't know then. I still don't."

"If they do convict him, they'll hang him, won't they?" The words came out hoarsely, choked with tears.

He put his arms around her and held her, allowing her to weep.

IN THE MORNING SHE ate a slice of toast, forcing it down, and drank a cup of tea, although it was too hot to be pleasant. Then she set out to see Crow, hoping he would be at his clinic. If he was not, then she would have to ask for Scuff's help.

The trip across the river seemed to take ages, and she could smell the first touch of chill warning that summer was ending. In a month there might be fog shrouding the water like a veil. Sunsets would carry a blaze of color, washed over in moments.

It was a short walk from the ferry steps to Crow's clinic. She was fortunate. Scuff had been on duty all night with a sick patient, and was asleep now. Crow was wide-awake and making himself breakfast in the kitchen, his black hair overlong, as it so often was, and falling half across his face.

He looked up at her.

"What is it?" he said immediately. "Something happened?" He moved a chair for her to sit down. He took the opposite one and sat astride it, facing her over its back.

Very briefly she told him her idea about the local newspapers, some of which were just a leaflet, and the thought that something must have happened that started off the series of murders. "If Fitz read them, he might see things we could look into. The trial should last a few days . . . at least . . ."

"I'll get you the papers," Crow said immediately. "I know people who keep all the back copies for years. And they are certainly patients who owe me more than a few favors. But will the police let you see Fitz?"

"I don't know. But if they won't, I'll ask Oliver to give them to him, and really force him to read them."

"Would Fitz know what it would be? What is it you think they might say?"

"Something that changed and stirred up a memory, a danger, some reason those four people were killed, and so terribly. Something happened! Nobody, even a lunatic, just gets up one morning and takes a sword or a bayonet and impales someone with it. And all the candles, always seventeen, and the broken fingers, and . . . and the icons defaced. Something started it . . ."

Crow stood up. "I'll start now. I don't think Scuff will wake up for a while, but if the patient has any trouble, call him. The patient's in there." He waved his hand toward the room where they kept the beds. "I'll be back when I've got the papers for the last three months or so. Have some tea."

Time seemed to crawl as Hester sat down, then stood up again, paced back and forth across the room, and checked on the patient, who seemed to be sleeping without any distress. She listened to his breathing, even took his pulse without waking him.

Finally Crow returned with a sheaf of papers, all editions of the local bulletins.

"Sorry it took so long," he said. "But no one had all of them. Had to pick and choose, and chase down a couple. They might have been the ones that had something. Here, I'll put them in a bag so they don't blow about." He fished in a cupboard and brought out a cloth bag. He pushed the papers in and handed the bag to her.

She thanked him profusely, then without another word left and strode as fast as she could to the main road, where she could get a hansom to Rathbone's chambers. If he was not in, she would wait for him as long as was necessary.

"I'M SORRY," HE SAID after she had waited a mere ten minutes to see him. "They are forbidding any visitors at all, and I daren't jeopardize my own chance of speaking to him. Not that it is doing any good."

She passed him the papers. "Get him to read them," she pleaded.

He frowned. "I'll try, but he's given up, Hester."

"I know. But I haven't. Sometimes we need someone else to believe in us, even when we don't believe in ourselves. Something happened that started this cycle of murders. We've looked and we can't find it. This is another place to look."

Rathbone bit his lip, a mark of unusual indecision for him. "Do you really believe he's innocent? He is the only one who has no account of his whereabouts for any of the murders, and they began not *that* long after he arrived here. Apart from the probability that Fodor was the father of Haldane's son, and Haldane had just learned that, no one seems to have a motive, and there's nothing we know of to connect the victims . . ."

"There's something," Hester argued. "They have all been killed in exactly the same way. Or are you suggesting we've got four murderous lunatics loose in Shadwell, all with exactly the same kind of madness that requires impaling the chest, breaking the fingers and extinguishing candles in blood? I don't think any jury is going to accept that, Oliver."

He looked at her gravely for several seconds, his face filled with a gentle exasperation.

"You are quite right. There is something connecting them, of course there is. But it may be recognizable only to a madman—or should I say a man driven mad by pain, isolation and the loneliness of the terrible things he has seen, and could not help. But yes, I will ask him to read them, for you. I will tell him that you believe in him, and that whoever killed these men—Fitz or anyone else—in their own mind had a reason. Something started it."

"Thank you."

IN THE DAYS BEFORE the trial began, Hester received no answer from Rathbone, except that he had given the papers to Fitz, who had said he would read them.

The day before the trial was due to begin, Hester, Monk and Rathbone sat late into the evening making final plans. They were in the house in Paradise Place, not sitting in the armchairs but in the dining room at the front of the house, with the panorama of the evening sky and the last light on the river. Sunset came earlier each night as midsummer had passed. Now all they could see were a few yellow gleams of riding lights on the water and the black tangle of masts moving very gently as the tide rocked the boats at anchor.

"I've no defense except madness," Rathbone said with a flat note of defeat in his voice. "We have no other believable suspects."

"Except that Haldane has been arrested for killing Fodor and is awaiting trial, and someone else killed all the others," Hester argued, but her tone was desperate, and she could hear in her own voice that she did not believe it. Neither would anyone else.

"And the prosecution will point out whatever Haldane felt about Fodor, and Haldane will probably deny that he knew anything about his son being Fodor's. We can't expect Adel Haldane to admit it either. We will just look desperate, and vicious. Then we have to convince the jury that someone else, we don't know who, killed all the others in an identical fashion—and I don't mean similar, I do mean identical, down to the last detail. And we don't know why! Or how they knew the tiny details, like the colors of the candles, and always seventeen!"

"Were they really all identical?" Hester asked.

"Yes," Monk told her. "And we never allowed that to be in any of the newspapers, nor, as far as I know, did anyone know that apart from Hooper and Dr. Hyde. And me. Hester, it isn't believable. We have to face it now. It's too late to be undecided. The trial starts"—he glanced at the clock on the mantelshelf—"in eleven hours."

"We need more time!" she said, her voice climbing in desperation.

"There isn't any," Monk said gently. "We have no legal reason to delay it, and honestly, I don't think they will." He looked at Rathbone.

Rathbone shook his head. "Public feeling is very high, and you can hardly blame them. We have no reason . . ."

"Then plead 'not guilty,'" she urged. "Make the prosecution prove everything!"

"Just dragging out the—"

"Make them!" she insisted. "If they say Fitz changed everything in his life, in his nature, and killed all these people he didn't even know, then they have to prove it, beyond doubt!"

"Beyond all reasonable doubt," Rathbone corrected her. "And I'm not sure your idea of reasonable is going to be the same as the judge's."

"Make them prove it anyway," she insisted.

Rathbone looked across at Monk.

Monk nodded. "We might as well play it to the last card," he answered.

————

THE FOLLOWING DAY THE trial began. As always, it was held with all the due circumstance of the law. It opened in the Old Bailey, the central criminal court of London, next to Newgate Prison, where public hangings had taken place up to two years previously.

The presiding judge was Justice Aldridge, arrayed in gown and full-bottomed wig. The twelve jurors were all men, of course, most of them middle-aged and prosperous-looking. One or two were younger. All were very serious indeed; in fact, one kept clenching and unclenching his hands on the railing in front of him.

The usual formal opening seemed to take ages. To Hester it had the rigidity of a church service, the same age-old words repeated without variation. Did anybody listen to them?

Fitz, white-faced and thinner than he'd been just a few weeks ago, sat in the dock, a space raised above head height, like a small room in the side wall, reached by another door and a flight of steps. There were guards on either side of him and his wrists were manacled.

Hester should be used to this now, but it always seemed new, like a nightmare she had had many times, but which could still veer off in some different, terrible way, and end in tragedy.

That was ridiculous! It was already a tragedy. Four people were horribly dead, and Fitz had changed from one of the bravest and most generous people she knew into a man who had lost himself, lost his balance, his judgment and his belief; possibly he was even guilty of these murders.

Had he read the Hungarian newspapers? Was it an idea that mattered at all, or just the last delusion she clung to?

The formalities were complete. The judge asked Rathbone how the accused pleaded to the charge.

"Not guilty, my lord," Rathbone replied.

The prosecutor, Mr. Elijah Burnside, turned an astonished gaze toward him, as if he could scarcely believe what he had heard. He was a big man, broad-shouldered, barrel-chested, and he had a mane of thick white hair and a full beard to match. However, his chief weapon was a

magnificent voice. He could have found success as a singer, had he chosen to.

Justice Aldridge, a small, neat, meticulous man, with a dry sense of
humor, made no comment at all.

Burnside called his first witness.

In this silent room, no one was even fidgeting, so tight was the tension. Antal Dobokai took the stand and swore to his name and his place
of residence. He did so calmly, in a voice that sounded perfectly English,
except for a slight hesitation before certain words. He looked completely
composed. Even from where Hester sat, the light caught his remarkable
eyes, like pale blue glass, clear as the sky.

Under Burnside's guidance Dobokai told the story of his visit to
Fodor's workshop, and of finding the terrible scene in the office.

"I had never seen anything so . . . so horrifying," he said gravely. He
swallowed hard. "It is almost impossible to describe."

"I am sorry to distress you, sir," Burnside said with evident regret.
"But the jury has no knowledge of what you saw, unless they have read
reports in the newspapers, which may or may not be accurate. Will you
please tell us what you recall."

Dobokai straightened himself a little, although he was not leaning
against anything.

"Yes, sir. I hardly recall the room. But as soon as I was in the door, I
saw the body of Imrus Fodor splayed across the floor. He was lying on his
back and there was an old bayonet sticking out of his chest, still attached to a rifle. It was . . . at an angle, about . . . so." He described a
diagonal with his arm. "There was blood everywhere. I had never before
seen so much. It seemed to be . . ." He hesitated, swallowed, closed his
eyes and then opened them again. ". . . on candles all around the room,
and on the floor."

"Candles?" Burnside interrupted. "There is no gas in the workshop
for light?"

"I . . . I have no idea," Dobokai said. "I didn't notice. The candles
were on many different surfaces, all capped with blood, as normal candles might be with melted wax."

"I see. Do you remember anything else?"

"No, I'm afraid not."

"And Mr. Fodor was unquestionably dead?" Burnside's magnificent eyebrows rose.

"Yes, I kneeled and touched his hand. It was cold."

"Then what did you do?"

"I was deeply upset, as you may imagine. I asked one of the employees to send for the police. Then I stepped back and closed the door. I waited there, knowing they would wish to speak with me."

"Thank you, Mr. Dobokai." Burnside waved his hand toward Dobokai, then turned to Rathbone.

Rathbone rose slowly to his feet. Hester, watching him, wondered if anyone in the jury knew how little he had to work with. He looked calm, elegant as always. The light caught more silver in his fair hair than she had noticed before. It suited him.

"Your English is excellent, Mr. Dobokai," he said courteously.

"Thank you," Dobokai acknowledged. Clearly it pleased him. "I try to speak it well. It is a beautiful and very flexible language."

"Indeed. And you are obviously a keen student. You hear and you remember . . ."

Burnside rose to his feet. "My lord," he complained, "I am very conscious, as I am sure your lordship must be, of the poverty of Sir Oliver's case for the defense, but we are wasting time complimenting Mr. Dobokai on his mastery of English. The court must already be as aware of it as we are."

"My lord," Rathbone responded, "my learned friend is wasting time objecting. I have reason to believe that Mr. Dobokai is an intelligent man who has adapted unusually well to a change in his circumstances, and has thus become something of a leader in the Hungarian community in Shadwell. It is his standing in that role that I believe may be of help to us."

"Proceed, Sir Oliver," Aldridge directed. "But I would like to see you make this relevant as soon as possible."

"Yes, my lord." Rathbone turned to Dobokai again. The witness stand was a small tower in the open area of the court, and the person in it, having climbed a small staircase up to it, was able to look down on the arena of the court.

"Mr. Dobokai," Rathbone resumed. "Clearly these appalling events have greatly disturbed the lives of those in your community. There must be fear, dismay among people. I am led to believe that you have done a great deal to prevent panic in the streets, and even civil violence. Am I correct in that judgment?"

Dobokai hesitated only a moment.

Hester wondered what Rathbone was doing, other than playing for time.

"I hope my efforts have helped," Dobokai said.

Rathbone smiled. "I am certain they have. Modesty is very becoming, Mr. Dobokai, but we are here very desperately searching for the truth. Please put such feelings aside for the moment. You are a natural leader. You have helped the police both in guarding the community from panic, and in doing all you can to find out who is responsible for these crimes."

Burnside shifted his position, as if he was uncomfortable.

"Yes, sir," Dobokai replied.

"You found the first body, that of Mr. Fodor," Rathbone continued. "I imagine the police made a very thorough examination of your whereabouts at the time Fodor was killed? It would be usual, and cast no suspicion upon you, simply a routine procedure to rule you out."

"Yes, sir." Dobokai sounded perfectly comfortable.

Hester knew that Monk had done everything he could to challenge Dobokai's statement, and had failed.

"Did you know Dr. Fitzherbert?" Rathbone asked.

"No, sir. I have excellent health, but should I require a doctor, I would use the Hungarian in our community."

"You did not, for example, encounter him in Hungary? Before you left?"

Dobokai shifted his weight a little. Inner discomfort? Or simply that he had stood in exactly that position long enough?

"No, sir."

"That is what I thought you would say." Rathbone smiled. "Thank you. I may have questions for you later, but you have been very clear." He walked back to his place and sat down.

Burnside called Dr. Hyde to the stand.

Hyde looked well scrubbed and barbered. His fair hair was thinning a little, but he was still a vigorous man, and clearly not in a good temper. Perhaps he knew Burnside and did not like him.

Hester wondered if Rathbone had noticed this, and would use it. Above all, she wished passionately to know if Rathbone actually believed Fitz could be innocent. It would be enough if he believed the possibility, even if not the actual likelihood.

Hyde was describing the scene of Fodor's death as he had found it. He spared no details.

Watching the jurors' faces, Hester could sense their distress, and now and then one of them glanced up at Fitz in the dock. She did not want to look up herself. She had missed her chance earlier, and if she did so now, he would think she was seeing him with the same horror that was on other people's faces.

Would they be more moved by emotion than by reason? The horror had to be paid for. If the police had charged Fitz, then they must have thought that he was guilty. No sane man could let him go.

She felt panic and despair rise inside her.

Hyde was still describing the scene, and the bayonet sticking out of Fodor's chest.

Burnside went on to ask him about the second victim, and his answers were equally vivid and shocking, and delivered with the same curt words.

They adjourned for lunch, and resumed in the early afternoon. Burnside asked Hyde to describe the third victim, and the fourth.

"And they all died in agony, drenched in their own blood?" Burnside finished dramatically. "Their fingers smashed just to create pain. Fingers are intensely sensitive, are they not, Dr. Hyde?"

"Lots of parts of the body are sensitive, sir," Hyde said tartly. "And I did not say they died in agony. Please do not embroider my words for your own purposes."

Burnside spread his arms wide, as if to appeal to the gallery, the judge, the jury, against Hyde's unreasonable charge. "It was not agony?" he said incredulously.

"To be speared through the heart is a very quick death," Hyde replied. "Lots of blood, but I doubt they knew that. Over almost instantaneously."

"And the fingers? Was that painless too?" Burnside's sarcasm was scalding, as if Hyde were less than human in his lack of pity.

"There were no bruises, sir," Hyde told him. "Almost no blood."

"Oh! Dear me! No bruises? Just broken bones—is that all? And hardly any blood. Was it really worth mentioning?"

"It had meaning," Hyde explained with elaborate patience, as if to a slow child. "They were broken after death. As far as we can tell, the dead feel no pain, or anything else."

The color flooded up Burnside's face, but it might have been anger as much as embarrassment.

"You are quite sure of that, Dr. Hyde?"

"Of course not! I've never been dead! Although no doubt my turn will come."

"That they were broken after death, you . . ." Burnside restrained himself with difficulty.

"The lack of blood, either in bruising or where the flesh was torn, indicates that the heart had already stopped," Hyde answered.

"In all cases?"

"Yes."

"In your medical opinion, Dr. Hyde, were all these poor men killed and their fingers broken by the same person?"

"I have no idea. I'm a police surgeon, not a detective. I can only tell you that there was no discernible difference, except that the weapons were all different, obviously. But then since they were left in the wounds, that was a matter of necessity."

"Are you saying that there might be four different criminal lunatics running around Shadwell?" Burnside's hands were in the air again.

"Please don't credit me with your imagination, sir." Hyde was equally acerbic. "You asked me for medical evidence. I gave it to you. What you deduce from it is entirely up to you."

Burnside controlled himself with difficulty, and invited Rathbone to make something of Hyde, if he so chose.

Rathbone rose to his feet. He had no illusion that Hyde would be any gentler with him than he had been with Burnside.

"Did whoever killed these men require any particular strength to do so? Beyond what an average man might possess?"

"No, sir."

"Or specific medical knowledge? Assuming that we all know roughly where the heart is," he added quickly.

"Assuming that, none at all," Hyde agreed.

Rathbone decided to leave it while he was on a positive note.

"Thank you, Dr. Hyde. You have been most helpful."

Hester let her breath out slowly. Perhaps they had regained a little ground, but she feared it was mostly because Burnside's temper was frayed. Had he not expected any fight from Rathbone? Surely he knew Rathbone better than that, if only by reputation. Rathbone had had a major setback in his career. She felt a twinge of pain even at the thought of it. He had actually been in prison, until his trial. He was only just back practicing law after his disgrace. But thinking of the last few months, and looking at him now, defending a case without payment, one that no one thought he could win, he had an inner peace about him. It would be easy to mistake the feeling for professional confidence—but actually she thought it was happiness—in the knowledge that he did not have to prove himself every time he faced a courtroom.

He was gentler also, and perhaps wiser. Was that what disconcerted Burnside?

Burnside rose to call his next witness.

Hooper was dressed neatly, and looked very different from the way Hester usually saw him. He was a big man, loose-limbed. It was natural for him to look casual, slightly untidy. He could easily have passed for a dockworker or, even more likely, a sailor, which he had been.

Today he was tidy, his hair pushed back, collar fastened and neat.

He managed to appear quiet, even subdued. Would Burnside misread that as nervousness?

Hester found herself clenching her hands until her fingernails bit into her palms. She cared far too much about every part of this.

Burnside asked Hooper to identify himself and his role in the Thames River Police, then walked out into the central arena of the court and looked up at the witness box. He knew how to make the most of his resemblance to an Old Testament prophet, at once familiar and awe-inspiring.

"Mr. Hooper," he began, "in all this terrible, tragic, violent business, you have worked closely with Commander Monk. You were there when he visited the scene of the first abominable murder. You were with him in his questioning of witnesses, and you knew his conclusions, and how he reached them. Please help this court to understand it all, and how he came to the inevitable conclusion that Herbert Fitzherbert was guilty, in spite of the fact that he claims to have no knowledge or memory of these acts, and no reason he can think of for committing them." Burnside gave a very slight smile, a concession to courtesy. "Of course, a step at a time," he added.

That sounded to Hester more like condescension. Did he plan to patronize Hooper into losing his temper? Or merely to make him sound inferior, so any agrument he presented could be dismissed? He was dealing with all the different issues through Hooper, rather than Monk, so he could establish all the facts, as far as the jury was concerned, before Monk had a chance to fight back.

Did Rathbone sense that? How could he combat it?

"To begin with . . ." Burnside said clearly. He had no need to raise his voice, there was not a sound in the room. No one rustled or fidgeted. Every juror was looking at him.

Hester could see a slight stiffness in Hooper's body, but only because she knew him. No one else, except Monk, would see it. And Monk was not in the room, because he was a later witness.

". . . you were with Commander Monk when he was called to the scene of the first murder?" Burnside asked.

"That of Mr. Fodor? Yes, sir." Hooper was not going to go a step ahead of Burnside and offer anything further.

"The court has already heard from Dr. Hyde how terrible the scene was. We will not need to hear it from you. But did you learn anything from what you saw that led you to a line of investigation? It was surely extraordinary enough to give you much to consider?"

"Yes, sir," Hooper agreed.

"Such as what, man? Don't play this for melodrama! It is a very terrible death, and we need to convict the man who committed these four murders and, if left loose in the community, would commit God knows how many more." He was careful not to name anyone, which might allow Rathbone room to create an objection.

"There was nothing taken, that we could see," Hooper answered him levelly. "It appeared to be a crime of unusual hatred, with possible religious overtones."

"Possible?" Burnside raised one of his arms wide. "What would it take for you to be certain, man?"

Rathbone half rose to his feet.

"What?" Burnside thundered. "Are you going to quibble over every little detail, when we all know that in every murder there were vile religious defacements, smearing of blood, damage, smashed glass? Or are you just allowing me to make more of it because you plan to say your client is utterly insane? Religious hatred is not a defense."

Justice Aldridge leaned forward. "Mr. Burnside, please allow Sir Oliver to make his own mistakes. Do not make them for him. And do not blame Mr. Hooper, in either event."

Hester wanted to laugh. Nothing was funny; it was just a momentary release of the tension.

"I beg your pardon, Sir Oliver," Burnside said sarcastically. Then he looked back at Hooper. "What did your investigations lead to, Mr. Hooper, apart from three more murders, increasingly hideous?"

"Do you wish for it step by step, Mr. Burnside, or conclusion by conclusion?" Hooper asked politely, but there was an edge of insolence to his voice, just a slight lift in tone, no more.

"Perhaps a conclusion, and your reasons for it, if that is not too difficult?" Burnside responded.

"Yes, sir. Between Dr. Hyde's evidence of the state of the body indicating that he had been dead a couple of hours at least, and the testimonies of the workers who had blocked the only way into the offices by their presence outside the workshop below, we worked it out that the men were together all the time, so none of them could have done it, and Mr. Dobokai arrived far too late to have done it then. We traced all Mr. Dobokai's movements during the time before the workers arrived, back before that. We couldn't find any doubts or contradictions."

Burnside looked surprised. "Did you suspect Mr. Dobokai?"

"We suspect anyone, sir. It's just a matter of seeing what's possible and what isn't, before you go any further."

"Then what? Please tell us only what is relevant."

"We questioned the community, sir. We heard quite a lot about possible racial or religious dislikes. There did seem to be a good deal of hatred in the crime. Various members of the Hungarian community were very helpful."

"But not helpful enough for you to recognize any suspects of this . . . abomination?"

"No, sir."

"Did you look outside the Hungarian community? Surely this appears far more like an attack against them rather than by someone among them? Is it not openly anti–Roman Catholic? Surely that occurred to Mr. Monk, even if not to you?"

"It had that appearance, sir," Hooper agreed. "And there were certainly people in the area who did not like the Hungarian immigrants. Enough of them that no one stood out in particular."

"So you discovered nothing? What happened to make you finally realize that the accused was . . . different?" Burnside's tone was one of exasperation, as if he were dealing with someone who was not only slow but intentionally obstructive.

"We were able to rule out many people," Hooper replied. "And to learn a lot about Mr. Fodor's relationships."

"And the other victims?" Burnside asked. "You cannot have forgotten Lorand Gazda? Or Viktor Rosza? Even more violently and terribly killed. Or Kalman Pataki, the most violent of all? Surely in all that time you discovered something relevant? Something of use?"

Hester knew perfectly well that Burnside was doing his utmost to make Hooper lose his temper. He wanted drama, conflict, so he could lose his own temper and accuse the police of incompetence, ratchet up the fear and anger of the gallery, and, far more importantly, of the jurors themselves. Horror and a feeling of impotence would make them bring in a conviction even more surely than the slow drip of evidentiary detail.

It seemed as if Hooper knew it too. If Hester had not known the man's warmth, his occasional dry humor, looking at him now she would have thought him stolid, devoid of empathy or imagination.

Burnside was waiting.

Hooper looked down at him, his face calm. He appeared to be thinking of a useful answer.

"Well, sir, we did suspect Mr. Roger Haldane, at one point, and so we checked on his whereabouts at all the relevant times—for all the deaths, that is . . ."

"Roger Haldane?" Burnside affected amazement. "For heaven's sake, why? Had he ever shown signs of disliking Hungarians? Or of being anti–Roman Catholic? Good God, his wife of twenty years is both Hungarian and Catholic."

"No, sir . . ."

"Then why? It makes no sense at all. What is the matter with you, man? I know you were desperate, but this . . . this incompetence is absurd."

Rathbone said nothing.

Justice Aldridge looked at him inquiringly, but Rathbone did not respond.

Burnside's contempt for him was scalding. He could not resist the gibe.

"I see that Sir Oliver is not about to come to your rescue. Perhaps you can find some way to defend yourself?"

Hooper breathed in deeply.

The entire room was silent.

"Yes, sir. We seriously suspect Mr. Haldane of having committed the murder of Imrus Fodor, and we charged him when we discovered that Mrs. Adel Haldane, who is, as you say, Hungarian, is the mother of the son Mr. Haldane is so proud of, but Mr. Haldane was unable to give her a child. The father was actually Imrus Fodor . . ."

The rest of what he was about to say was drowned out by the uproar in the courtroom. People rose to their feet, shouting. There was a scramble as reporters rushed to get out and break the news.

Justice Aldridge called for order, but it was several moments before it was restored, with everyone in their seats again.

Hooper remained impassive.

Hester realized with a blaze of fear and excitement that this was exactly what Hooper and Rathbone had intended from the time Hooper took the stand. Without realizing it, she sat forward, urgently, listening to every word.

"Mr. Burnside?" the judge asked coldly. "I daresay that was not the answer you foresaw. Nevertheless, it is the answer you received. If you do not wish to pursue the line of questioning, of course, you do not have to. I am sure Sir Oliver will do so regardless."

"Thank you, my lord," Burnside replied. "But I shall do so myself." He turned to Hooper, his face red, his voice like ice. "Mr. Hooper, perhaps you would like to enlighten the court as to why, and exactly how, you arrived at your extraordinary conclusion regarding the reputation and honor of Mrs. Haldane, which in your mind gave her husband, assuming he believed your version of . . . events . . . motive, despite your charging of Dr. Fitzherbert with the murders of three other men, who so far appear to have nothing whatever to do with the fathering of Mrs. Haldane's son. I admit, I am at a loss to see any sense in it at all." He gave an elaborate shrug of his large shoulders. "I am correct in assuming that you charged Dr. Fitzherbert, am I not?"

Surely Hooper must have been expecting this?

Hester was staring at him, and she knew that everyone else in the courtroom was as well, including every member of the jury. If nothing else, he had their total attention.

"Mr. Haldane could account for his whereabouts, without any question whatever, during the time of one of the other deaths," Hooper said slowly and clearly. "Since the details of each seemed to be identical, and not known to the general public, and, more than that, because of the violence of the crimes and the unusual things that were unrelated to the actual deaths, we believed they were all committed by the same person. In the case of the second and the third one, it could not be Mr. Haldane."

"But it could be the accused!" Burnside interrupted him. "Indeed! I see your point, Mr. Hooper. Murder for hire! By a criminal lunatic? Do we know this? Or is it purely a very practical guess? Because you lack any other answer?"

A sad smile touched Hooper's mouth for a moment, then vanished. "Actually, sir, I think Dr. Fitzherbert's arrest was principally to save his life—and the lives of the citizens whose terror had driven them crazy enough to try to murder him themselves, out of fear that he might be the man we are looking for. I have no idea whether he is guilty of anything at all, except the terrible nightmares he has from his experiences in the Crimean War, and of being left injured and presumed dead on the battlefield. Can you imagine waking up in physical agony, half buried beneath the blood-soaked corpses of your friends?"

A woman's sobs were the only sounds to break the silence.

Even Burnside had no immediate reaction.

It was Hooper who spoke first. He seemed to consider speaking to Burnside, then changed his mind and turned to the judge.

"My lord, we don't know who killed these men, but we believe that Roger Haldane killed Fodor, in a rage when he discovered that his wife had betrayed him, and the son he had loved and raised as his own was actually Fodor's. Who killed the other three, we don't know, nor can we yet prove why—"

Burnside found his voice at last.

"My lord! This is speculation of the grossest sort. They have offered no evidence at all—"

Now Rathbone was on his feet. "My lord, Mr. Hooper answered the questions that my learned friend put to him, openly and honestly. My learned friend has no grounds to complain if it was not the answer he wished."

"Indeed," Justice Aldridge agreed. "Nevertheless it has created something of a difficulty. If the police do not believe the accused to be guilty of the first crime, then why is Dr. Fitzherbert charged with it?"

Hester guessed the answer to that immediately: in order to be able to raise the question of whether or not all the crimes were committed by the same person, and to extend the trial for as long as possible while they continued their search for the real perpetrator. And also for it to be as confusing and complicated as they could make it.

The judge looked back at Burnside, who was by now bristling with righteous indignation.

"No doubt you will have opportunity to ask them," he continued. "Possibly you would like a day's adjournment to consider this?"

"This is absurd!" Burnside exploded. "The police charged him with all four murders! Now they are saying they think the murders were not committed by the same person! They are identical in every respect, except that since the killer left the weapons behind them in the corpses, they had, of necessity, to find a new one each time. This is deliberate obstruction, my lord!"

"Possibly," Aldridge agreed drily. "But not of Sir Oliver's creation, Mr. Burnside. Do you wish to adjourn for a day in order to sort yourself out?"

"It is not my—" Burnside looked at the judge's face, and changed his mind. "Thank you, but I believe I will not require to so inconvenience your lordship, or the court. I shall amend the charge to murder for hire. It seems that Mr. Haldane may indeed have had excellent reason to hate Mr. Fodor. And since the crimes were clearly committed by the same hand, Dr. Fitzherbert went on to repeat the crime over and over for no apparent reason, other than that the victims were Hungarian men who had settled in Shadwell. He is clearly insane." He shot a look of triumph at Rathbone, then bowed to the judge and resumed his seat.

Hester looked across at Rathbone and saw his face pale, features suddenly drawn.

"Perhaps, Sir Oliver, you would like to resume your cross-examination of Mr. Hooper tomorrow?" the judge suggested.

Rathbone rose to his feet. "Thank you, my lord, I would."

Burnside smiled with rich satisfaction. He looked across at Rathbone and nodded.

14

"Did you know he was going to do that?" Hester asked Rathbone as she laid the plate of sliced cold meat on the table in her sitting room. The curtains were still wide open, but it was early dusk and the front windows were closed. They had gathered here as soon as they could after the court adjourned, but it was some distance and a river crossing from the Old Bailey.

Rathbone sat with his legs crossed, comfortable in surroundings he had long known. Monk had been home longer and Hester had already told him, at least in general, what had happened. Since Monk might well be called as a witness and couldn't attend court, he was making profitable use of his time by searching for anything at all that might help Fitz. Nothing could make it worse. There was still too much they did not know.

Rathbone smiled bleakly; it was self-mockery rather than real amusement. "Mr. Hooper has depths I was unaware of. At least he has given us quite a bit more time. Please God, we can use it to some effect!"

"He certainly knocked Burnside off his pedestal of superiority," Hester said with some pleasure. "He gets up there with his flowing hair and beard, and looks like Moses descended from the Mount, making everything he says sound infallible."

"I would like to have seen that," Monk said with feeling. "It's going to take a call on divine intervention to save Fitz." He looked at Rathbone. "I'm sorry. I can't tell you that I believe he's innocent, in the legal sense. I really don't know."

"In the moral sense?" Rathbone raised his eyebrows.

"Yes, whatever that means. If he did it, he has no memory of it, and he must have been in a nightmare at the time."

"What nightmare?" Rathbone asked, taking more meat and a pickle and putting it on his bread. "What nightmare could possibly make it justifiable to break into a man's house or office, drive a metal shaft of some sort into his chest, and then dip the candles you happen to have brought with you in his blood? And why always seventeen? They come in dozens. I would plead insanity, if I could, but I'm still looking for some sort of delirium that makes any sense at all."

They both looked at Hester.

"If I knew of anything, I would have told you," she said unhappily.

"But you've witnessed his nightmares," Monk insisted. "Please . . . at least tell us what you think he sees. Where is he? What is he struggling against? Who does he blame? Anything!"

She looked from Monk to Rathbone, and back again. What they were asking was reasonable. How could they continue, either Rathbone to make a credible defense or Monk to go on searching amid the chaos of evidence, if they did not even know what they were looking for? Please heaven, Fitz would find something in the old newspapers. Time was so desperately short. Burnside could be tricked or manipulated only so far. The truth was that they had no defense. No weakness they could name, or invent, would account for the deliberate and planned ritual murders of four people who had nothing in common except their Hungarian origins.

She answered the first question while searching her mind for something that made sense.

"He seems to be dreaming of the battlefield station where they brought the wounded. Some he could help, many were beyond anything, thus he could only be there so they wouldn't die alone and untended. It was . . ." She tried to find words without drowning in her own memories. "It was hard to cling to your sanity there. You were surrounded by appalling pain, dismemberment, blood everywhere and people you could not help. It could have driven many men out of their wits. You saw it in people's exhaustion, when they simply became too ill to continue. And of course the hospitals were, in a way, worse. Men came in only slightly wounded, in comparison, then died of gangrene or lockjaw, or most of them of dysentery. I would rather be shot or blown to death than die like that."

Rathbone's face was pale, bleached with exhaustion and lack of hope. "I don't doubt you, but even saying all that, even if I could, these murders were planned. Whoever did them found the weapons and the candles first and took them along. It wasn't done in a brief bout of insanity, without memory afterward. Burnside can call witnesses to prove that—chiefly Monk himself. Or get Hooper back—or Hyde, even."

He spoke gently, but his words were harsh. "If he's insane, Hester, it's far deeper than a simple breakdown because of what he's seen and endured."

"It's not simple!" she said, her voice rising in desperation and confusion. She was searching for meaning, even detached from reason, but could not find any. She had no idea what Fitz could have thought that would make him act as the killer had. What did he imagine? What was he fighting against? Who?

She looked down at her white, clenched hands. "I don't know. We know nothing about what happens to people who have seen too much, who are pressured by horror until they break. We ought to! If we think ourselves a civilized society, and we send our best and bravest people out into hell's chaos and pain, then we should care passionately what happens to them if they survive and come home. But once a war is over we don't want to know about it anymore, and we resent people who make us go back and think of it again. If we knew what our soldiers, doctors, rescuers face, we couldn't live with it. We couldn't send those we love next time. We can only do it in ignorance, and when we are terrified of what will happen to us if we don't fight, and win. But as soon as it's over, we want to forget. Caring for the casualties reminds us of the cost. And it isn't ever finished for them. We feel guilty, and we don't like it. It's worse if we can't even see the point." She stopped abruptly and looked down, avoiding their eyes.

"You're right," Rathbone said softly. He turned to Monk. "Burnside is going to call evidence about the weapons tomorrow, but he may be brief. He senses that I want to string it out as long as possible, so he'll do the opposite. He can't prove how Fitz got the weapons, only that he could have. He'll have to do that, but he could get it all over in a few hours. As soon as he's done that, he'll start calling the people who witnessed Fitz's episodes. He'll give Scuff a pretty hard time. He's not above publicly eviscerating a vulnerable witness, if he thinks it will make his case. And you can be certain he knows exactly who Scuff is to you. He'll try to get you to withdraw Scuff from the case somehow, to save him."

"There's nothing I can do to protect him—" Monk began.

"Except moderate your own testimony on the case," Rathbone said.

Monk was silent.

Hester waited.

"And you," Rathbone told her. "He must know all the other times you've testified, and exactly where your weaknesses are. I can't protect you—heaven knows, I would if I could. I won't call you, but he'll know why I haven't, and he might still call you himself. He'll expect you to defend Fitz, and be emotional, and therefore vulnerable. Maybe he'll draw attention to the fact that you haven't come forward. In his place, I would."

"I know." Hester's mind went back to the mistakes she had made testifying in the past: the emotions that had driven her to say things she had not meant to, and invalidate the very testimony she had desired to give. He did not need to be specific to bring it all back to her.

"Burnside will focus on the evidence that seems to damn Fitz,"

Rathbone went on. "If he makes the jurors frightened enough, they'll convict him, because it's the only action they can take that will make them feel as if they are doing something."

Monk interrupted. "Have you asked Fitz to go through all the local papers? You haven't said anything yet. It's the only hope we have of finding out what started this off. We know why Fodor was killed, but not the others."

Rathbone's face was tight, his eyes bleak. "Fitz is looking at them, but I fear halfheartedly. I'll press him to keep reading, for any use it will be. Burnside will say Haldane had Fitz kill Fodor for him, out of jealousy, which is easy enough to understand but hard to prove. The son was the pride of his life, and to discover he was not the father would be enough to tip the balance of his mind. Then when Fitz got away with it, he just went berserk. He got a taste for blood, and went on killing. He didn't need to have a reason."

"Even people who are insane have a reason in their own minds," Monk argued.

"Whose idea was the candles?" Hester asked. "Birthday candles. Why seventeen?" She was thinking aloud. "If the son is seventeen, isn't that young to go to university?"

"Not if he is very clever," Rathbone said slowly. "And we have only Mrs. Haldane's word that that's where he went. In her place, I would have sent him anywhere away from here. Wouldn't you?"

"So whoever killed Fodor, the seventeen candles, anniversary candles of the betrayal, were Haldane's idea?" Hester said quickly.

Rathbone smiled. "Looks like it. But Burnside can still say Fitz just kept on doing it, because he copied everything. It doesn't have to make sense beyond the first time." He rose to his feet. "I'll go back to Fitz and see if he's looked at the papers. I don't care if he sits up all night, it's about his only chance left."

"He believes he could be guilty," Monk said gravely. "I don't think he's fighting anymore . . . or hoping."

Hester stood up also. "Even if he did do it, he will want to know why," she insisted. "I'm coming with you."

"I don't think they'll let you in." Rathbone put his hand on her arm gently, pushing her back a little.

She took his hand away. "He's entitled to a lawyer, and to a degree of medical attention. I'm coming."

"What medicine?" Rathbone asked her. "You'll need to have something."

"Peppermint water. It can't do any harm. Even Burnside will want him to look alive and fit enough."

HESTER FOLLOWED RATHBONE OBEDIENTLY, and for the most part without speaking at all. She was bitterly aware that her trip might be futile, but this was not a time for grief or even pity. There was a job to be done—or, at the least, attempted.

Fitz had been moved to Newgate Prison, next to the courthouse of the Old Bailey, as were all prisoners who were currently on trial. The guards were reluctant to allow Hester in with Rathbone, but he insisted that her aid was necessary to ensure that Fitz was well enough to answer questions. They all knew that in a few days, when the trial came to an end, there would be no chance for anything further. A condemned man had three Sundays, and then he faced the gallows.

They found Fitz sitting on his bunk, still dressed, looking as if he was in a daze. Hester knew immediately that he had given up. The papers that Rathbone had brought him were in a pile on the floor.

He barely looked at Rathbone as the heavy iron door was closed and the lock fastened with a leaden sound. Only when Hester spoke did he register that she was there.

At first he was embarrassed.

She felt the pain of it for him, but better that than the apathy of not caring at all.

She pointed to the papers. "Did you read them?"

"Some," he replied. "It's just local gossip from various places in Hungary, different towns that people came from."

She forced herself to sound as if there were a point to this.

"All of them?"

The ghost of a smile touched his mouth for a moment. He looked terrible. His skin appeared as if it would tear as easily as paper.

"Then please look at the ones you didn't . . ."

"There's no point, Hester. What is it going to tell me? That so-and-so's cousin in Budapest passed his exams and qualified as a doctor? That the performance in the conservatory was brilliant? None of it matters now."

"Something happened to start these tragedies. It might be there. Please, Fitz? There's no one else to read them that we can trust. I can't do it. I don't know a word of Hungarian."

"There's no point," he repeated. "Let me at least go with a little dignity, please? Hope is a torture I don't . . . I can't cope with. Don't go on believing in me. I can't bear it . . ."

"Just read a couple . . ."

"You sound like a nurse trying to make a patient who's dying drink a last teaspoon of medicine."

"I can't help that. I am a nurse. One teaspoonful . . . please?"

"And another . . . and another."

"Yes, of course. As long as you can."

Rathbone passed her the sheaf of papers and she chose one near the bottom and handed it to Fitz.

He read it aloud, translating as he moved from line to line. As he had said, it was notices of births, deaths and marriages, graduations, the opening of a new school, the appointment of a new mayor to a town. He passed it back to her without comment.

She passed him the next one and he hesitated a moment, then took it obediently. He started to translate it, then stopped.

"What is it?" she asked.

"A scandal," he replied with harsh, dry humor. "A schoolteacher has committed suicide. He was in his late sixties; he slashed his wrists."

"What's his name?" Rathbone said quickly.

"Donat Kelemen," Fitz replied. "He was a mathematics teacher in a boarding school just outside Budapest."

"And the scandal?" Rathbone pressed.

Fitz looked up at him. "He had sexually abused boys of twelve or thirteen, in exchange for higher marks on their exams. If someone had killed him, there would be a valid excuse for it, but there is no question that it was suicide. It hardly helps me. The abuse was from twenty or thirty years ago until recently. And there is no question whatever that he killed himself."

"For higher marks?" Hester said.

"Yes. Rather obvious, when you think about it. Great power, a schoolmaster in the right place. He could fail you if you refused him, or if you told anyone. Each boy might well have thought he was the only one. It's a vile thing to do." There was emotion back in Fitz's voice, anger and pity. There was even a tinge of color in his face. "If someone had killed him, they would be worth defending."

But there was an idea faintly forming in Hester's mind, like a wisp of fog, slender, but definitely there.

Rathbone saw it. "What is it?" he said urgently.

"His victims will have hated him. But they took the high marks, and probably prospered because of it."

"That doesn't mitigate it at all!" Fitz was angry now. "It was still an appalling abuse!"

"I know that, Fitz, but how would they feel if they were exposed now? That they were abused was hideous, embarrassing to a degree almost unbearable, which he no doubt relied on at the time, but . . ."

"But what? You can't hide it, and you can't ever prosecute him now! He's escaped that."

"But . . ." She guessed the idea, forcing it into words. "But they didn't speak then, which we all understand. Now he is exposed, so once they—"

"It wasn't their fault!" Fitz was angry, deeply outraged.

"I know that. But their marks were still false."

"Does it—" Fitz began.

"I see!" Rathbone was suddenly, vitally alive. "Some of those boys could be here in London, in Shadwell! They didn't know each other, because they may all have been there at different times, but the school is named. If that is where they passed their exams, then any high marks in mathematics would be suspect, rightly or not!"

Fitz stared at him, suddenly beginning to realize what he was saying.

It was Hester who put it into words. "Someone here in Shadwell saw this news article, and they were one of the boys involved. This person had some way of knowing who else was there—he could have found their records, or even known them. He was protecting himself from anyone else knowing his marks were not earned . . . except in the most hideous way . . ."

"There's your hatred," Rathbone said very quietly. "But we have a very short time in which to prove it."

"You can't do it in time to save me." Fitz looked from one to the other of them. "But my God, I'm glad to know it wasn't me. That's better than freedom . . . it's a freedom of the soul. I don't care so much about dying, now I know that. I'll be free of the nightmares, of being afraid of what else I might do."

Hester felt the tears welling up in her eyes. It was a totally improper thing to do, and perhaps not what he wanted, but she did not care. She went over to Fitz, bent down and threw her arms around him, hugging him as tightly as she could, feeling the gauntness of his body beneath the cotton shirt.

She said nothing, and made no promises. They all knew it was late now, and hard work was before them.

MONK HAD HEARD EVERYTHING Hester and Rathbone had learned and began the day with feverish activity, putting all the men he could spare into learning everything about the four victims and their education and qualifications, most specifically where they had been to school. Obviously it was too late to get written records of anything. Memories of other people, remarks made, proof of education in order to get employment would have to do.

He could not use Hooper, since he might be recalled to the stand, either by Burnside or by Rathbone. Monk knew now that Burnside would call him, and he had only a day or two before that happened. He trusted that Burnside would prove all he could without facing him on the stand. And of course Rathbone would stretch everything out as far as he could.

On the way into the courtroom Hester noticed a young woman of perhaps no more than sixteen, but with unusual grace. She felt a sudden lift of pleasure so intense it robbed her of a moment's breath. It was Candace Finbar. Beside her was Charles.

As if sensing her gaze, Candace turned, and immediately Hester caught Charles's attention. They moved toward her.

Charles looked concerned, but before he could speak, Hester did.

"We know what it was all about! Last night, late, Fitz translated a collection of local papers. I don't know if we can prove it, but at least we know that Fitz did not kill anyone." She found the tears thick in her throat and was furious with herself for such a display of emotion. "And he knows! Thank you, Charles . . ."

Charles's face lit with a sweet smile, but he was at a loss for the appropriate words.

Candace threw her arms around Hester and hugged her, then stepped back, blushing. "I'm so glad!" She did not bother to look at Charles. "We shall be here. If there is anything we can do . . ."

The crowd was pushing them to get through the door of the courtroom and find seats before they were all taken. There was no time to say anything more.

Burnside began the day by recalling Hooper. He looked confident, even slightly amused, as if yesterday had been part of his plan, and he hadn't been caught off balance, as it had appeared.

"Good morning, Mr. Hooper," he began smoothly, standing out in the area beneath the witness stand.

"Good morning, sir," Hooper replied.

Hester had had no chance to speak to Hooper and tell him of their visit with Fitz, or what the paper had revealed. She hoped Hooper felt better than most men might have in his situation.

"Mr. Hooper, you said under oath yesterday that you could not believe the accused to be guilty, in spite of the fact that you yourself, and your superior, Mr. Monk, arrested him and charged him with these crimes. Is that correct?"

"Yes."

"Because you feared for his life? Do I remember correctly?"

"Yes."

"Perhaps you can explain that for the court." Burnside made it sound like an invitation, but everyone knew that Hooper had no choice.

"Certainly," Hooper replied. "People are horrified by the brutality of these crimes, and frightened that they will continue—"

"Because you were unable to prevent them, and keep the commitment safe?" Burnside interrupted.

Hester was aware that he was trying to knock Hooper off balance. Hooper must have known it too.

"Yes, sir," Hooper admitted. He had no choice. The answer was clear to everyone.

"So you arrested him in spite of the fact that you did not believe him to be guilty?" Burnside said with apparent incredulity.

"If he had been cornered in the streets and murdered by a mob, that would not have helped anyone," Hooper said patiently. "If you are asking me if I believe Dr. Fitzherbert to be guilty now, no, I don't."

"I did not ask!" Burnside snapped. "I was going to ask you only if the people in Shadwell believe Dr. Fitzherbert is a lunatic. Surely your investigation discovered at least that much? Then perhaps you would explain to us why they believed him to be guilty, for a dozen different reasons, and yet you still do not?" A smile of incredulity lifted his voice almost to a squeak.

"You'll have to ask them, sir," Hooper answered with studied politeness only just short of offense.

"Oh, I will ask several people," Burnside snapped. He gave the slightest of bows toward Rathbone, and resumed his seat.

Rathbone rose. He walked elegantly over to the center of the open space—the arena, as it were.

"Mr. Hooper, you have made it clear that you do not believe Dr.

Fitzherbert to be guilty of these crimes. You must have some reason for that belief. Would you be good enough to share it with us"—he glanced at Burnside, already rising to his feet again—"briefly. It might aid us in understanding what my learned friend has made sound very . . . odd."

"Yes, sir," Hooper replied. "Before they became frightened out of their wits, the people in the community thought very well of Dr. Fitzherbert. He treated a lot of their sick, especially those who didn't have much command of English. Spoke to them in their own language, very well, and they would talk to him about Hungary, and he'd listen. He spent some time there, and said they were very good to him when he was sick and on hard times. Repayment, he said. That's what a good man does. You could find any number who'd testify to that. I'll find them for you, if you like?"

"Thank you, Mr. Hooper. If it comes to that, I'll ask you. I have no further questions for you now."

Burnside called Scuff. Hester had been afraid that he would. He could easily have called Crow for exactly the same evidence, or at least much of it, but Scuff was far more vulnerable. She felt helpless, forced to watch and take no part. He would feel bitterly alone. He would defend Fitz, out of loyalty to Hester, and because he believed him to be innocent. Burnside would attack him mercilessly, as Scuff would be the most overwhelmed by the formality of the court, the most susceptible to being made to look foolish.

Scuff walked across the open space and climbed up the steps to the stand. He swore to tell the truth, and nothing but, then faced Burnside.

Hester noticed how young he looked. He was almost as tall as Monk, but slender, his skin fair, more a boy's than a man's.

Burnside regarded him thoughtfully. "Will Monk, you said. But that is not the name you were born with, is it? It is one you—borrowed, shall we say?"

Hester felt her chest tighten, as if she could not draw in breath.

Rathbone half rose in his seat, then changed his mind and sat back down.

"Is that a question, sir?" Scuff asked, clearing his throat a little.

"Have you an answer?" Burnside raised his magnificent eyebrows.

"Yes, sir. I don't know what my name was when Commander Monk took me in. They called me Scuff, but that's only a nickname. When I had to have a proper name they gave me that, and I'm proud of it, sir. It's not borrowed, it was given to me."

There was a murmur of approval around the gallery.

Hester let her breath out in relief, although she did not imagine Burnside would take kindly to the charged atmosphere. In fact, he might well resent it and try to manipulate the crowd back to the show of contempt he wanted. Scuff had not made a friend. But she was proud of him all the same, even though her every instinct was to go in there herself and tear Burnside apart.

Burnside began again. "Took you in? A nice phrase. You were homeless, I believe. You lived on the riverbank, scavenging small odds and ends from the mud when the tide went out and selling them where you could. As do many unwanted children. A mixture of salvage and theft. Not a fortunate start in life for one who wishes to testify in the highest court in the land as to the good character of a man accused of murder."

Scuff's face was pale, except for the two spots of color high on his cheeks.

"You called me, sir. Maybe because I watched Fitz treating people, helping them, and I know some of the wrong reasons why some thought he might have killed people, just 'cos they jumped to conclusions. Folks do that when they're scared out of their senses. Blame everyone, because they want it to end."

"Have you seen a lot of that in your . . . eighteen years of life?" Burnside asked with a very slightly sarcastic edge to his voice. "Oh, I beg your pardon. You don't know how old you are, do you?"

"No, I don't, sir. But eighteen's close enough, and yes, I've seen a lot of people blaming anyone else but themselves, if they think there's a chance of getting away with it. Not many people take the blame for anything if they think they don't have to. I'm surprised you don't know that, being a lawyer an' all."

There was a ripple of laughter around the gallery.

Rathbone smiled.

Burnside kept his temper. "You want to be a doctor one day, I believe. So you have been taking lessons from Dr. Fitzherbert? You admire his skill?"

"Yes, sir, I do."

"And would you know a good doctor from a bad one, Scuff? I mean, Mr. Monk?"

"Yes, sir. A simple man might say a doctor who could save a dying man and set him back on his feet again is good. But if you'd like me to describe an operation for you, I can. I've seen him do a few. And I can give you the names of the people he saved. I've seen him treat an infection in a man who was half dead, and several days later the man walked out the door on his way home. Another man had lockjaw. His back was arched off the table and his jaw locked like steel. I saw Dr. Fitz cauterize the wound he had with white-hot irons, one after another. I handed them to him myself. And the man's alive and getting better. That's a good doctor, sir."

A couple of people in the gallery applauded and were instantly silenced.

"That's a clever doctor." Burnside made the difference sound subtle and important. "Good is another matter. You admire Dr. Fitzherbert, don't you, Scuff? Your friends call you Scuff, don't they?"

"Those I regard as friends call me Will, sir. And yes, I do admire Dr. Fitzherbert's skill. It is extraordinary. I also admire his willingness to treat people without money, if they don't have it, and to teach people like me, who want to become doctors."

"Tell me . . . Will . . ."

Rathbone rose to his feet. "My lord, my learned friend is uncommonly condescending toward this witness. He is suggesting to the jury that he is a child. Mr. Monk is a young man learning and practicing medicine, and should be addressed as such by the court."

Justice Aldridge nodded, then looked at Burnside. "Mr. Burnside, will you please treat your witness with the same courtesy you would others. I don't wish to have to remind you of this again."

Burnside acknowledged him with a mumbled word, and looked back at Scuff.

"Did you have at least one occasion to search the streets for Dr.

Fitzherbert, and find him wandering, dazed, half insensible and covered with blood?"

"Yes. He had been up for nearly twenty-four hours and he was exhausted. The blood came from a difficult delivery of a baby."

"Were you there?" Burnside affected surprise.

"Yes, sir."

"Really? You are under oath, Mr. . . . Monk. You do understand the idea that you are obliged to tell the truth, don't you?"

"Of course I do."

"I put it to you again, were you there?"

"Yes, sir. I also doubted Dr. Fitzherbert's word and went back to the area where the baby had been born, and I asked around to make sure they were well. They were."

"You are evasive, sir! You were not there at the time of the birth!"

"You did not say at the time of the birth," Scuff said innocently. "I checked that Fitz's story was true . . ."

"So you doubted it!" Burnside said triumphantly.

"No, sir, but I knew that you, or someone like you, would."

"Ah! So you foresaw the likelihood of Dr. Fitzherbert being charged with murder, and brought to trial for it! Why was that . . . Mr. . . . Monk? I put it to you that it was because you yourself suspected him of exactly that!"

Scuff stood absolutely still, his face pale.

Hester ached to be able to help him, but there was nothing she could do. He was completely alone.

"I could see the probability, sir," Scuff agreed. "I didn't want it to be him, but I could see that it might be. If it was, best we stop him as soon as we could. But it wasn't him. Surgeons get blood on themselves sometimes. Surgery can be messy."

"I don't doubt it," Burnside said with distaste. "But the sight of blood doesn't bother you. I daresay you see plenty of it."

"A doctor's not much use if he's busy thinking about how he feels, not the patient," Scuff said calmly.

"Ah! I'm glad you mentioned that. Did you have occasion to see Dr. Fitzherbert having nightmares, delusions, hysterics, whatever you like to call it? You are under oath! I am still not satisfied that you understand that. Please do not play word games with the court. This is a deadly matter. Did you see the accused in a state of divorce from reality? Imagining that he was somewhere else, and generally behaving without any restraint whatever in his . . . delusions?"

"I saw him in extreme distress from a nightmare, sir," Scuff answered.

"Ah! And how did you know that? Did he say so? Did he make some explanation of what he saw, or believed he saw? Describe him, please, for the jury."

Scuff turned a little in the box and looked at the jurors, who stared back at him solemnly.

"He was covered in sweat, his clothes were soaked, and he was trembling as if he were freezing. His eyes were wide open, but he did not seem to see the men around him, or me. I have no way of knowing what he did see, except that he told me afterward he thought he was back in the war in the Crimea."

"And you believed this? You accepted that this was real? Why? Because you admired his surgery? Because you liked him; he was kind to you? Offered to teach you surgery? Why did you believe him, Will?" He said the last word with exaggerated care, bordering on sarcasm.

Scuff's voice dropped a little, but he turned back to face Burnside.

"Because I was trapped once, in the bilges of a boat, boarded in. It was a man who trafficked in ways for . . . for prostitution. I thought I would never be found. I dreamed about it for ages afterward. It wasn't as bad as what happened to Fitz, but it made me understand a bit."

It was not the answer Burnside had expected, and it knocked him off balance. Scuff had the immediate sympathy of the courtroom, and Burnside knew it. He was obliged to back away and change tactics.

"So you understood his . . . his nightmares," he said more gently. "You had sympathy for him. Is it possible that he misled you, playing upon your fellow feeling?"

"No. He didn't know anything about it. It's . . . it's not something I like to talk about. I only told him afterward."

"I see." Burnside was having to rethink his attack altogether. He walked away, turned and then looked up at Scuff again. "You are a very loyal young man," he said gravely. "I'm sure the court respects you for it. But tell us, when Dr. Fitzherbert was in the state of nightmare, waking nightmare, did he know where he was? Did he recognize you, for example?"

"I don't know. I don't think so."

"Did he ever tell you about his long journey home, on foot, across the whole of Europe?"

"Not much."

"Could he have killed people there, in his delirium, his tension to be free from the suffocating corpses of the battlefield, when his supposed comrades left him to die?" Burnside spoke in a voice laden with disgust.

"I've no idea. He didn't say much about it, except that the Hungarians were kind to him. It's Hungarians that are dead, sir, not British soldiers. Not that the British left him behind on purpose. They thought he was dead, like so many hundreds of others."

"It sounds like the sort of nightmare that would drive any man insane," Burnside said quietly. "Thank you . . . Mr. Monk." He turned to Rathbone. "Your witness, Sir Oliver."

Rathbone rose to his feet. "Thank you, but I believe Mr. Monk has told us all he can."

Burnside looked disappointed. "In that case, if it please your lordship, I would like to adjourn for the day, and tomorrow call Commander Monk of the Thames River Police."

THAT EVENING HESTER, MONK and Rathbone sat together again, preparing for what might well be the last day of Burnside's case. They still had far too little to be able to prove that there was reasonable doubt as to Fitz's guilt, except for the first crime, and there was still nothing to disprove Burnside's contention that Fitz had actually committed that one as well, even if at Haldane's bidding and with possible payment, although that was unprovable too, since there had been none.

"He'll ask you about your investigations, in detail," Rathbone warned Monk. "He'll go over the weapons with you, where they were traced to and the fact that anyone could have got hold of them. He'll show that Fitz was familiar with the use of a bayonet in a way that no one else was—for example, Haldane. That Fitz knew anatomy well enough to strike with one blow to the heart. That he had no witnesses to his whereabouts for any of the murders, and that he was so used to death, he was callous to it, perfectly capable of such brutality—that being with death day after day, month after month, had made him capable of such things without showing any more aftereffects of shock than the nightmares we all know he had. He will suggest they were caused by guilt, and it will be easy for anyone to believe."

Rathbone leaned forward over the dinner table.

"And what is possibly far more important, they will want to believe it, because it is much better to think that a man was driven mad by war than that it was an ordinary citizen who did these things. We all want to believe it was something alien, preventable, a once-only happening, because it means we will be safe from now on. It's very difficult indeed to dissuade anyone from believing what he needs to in order to feel safe."

"Then we must contain it," Hester said immediately. "If we can't win with logic, then we must win with emotion."

Monk smiled at her, a little bleakly, but there was an extraordinary gentleness in his eyes. "What emotion?" he asked.

She bit her lip. "I don't know yet . . . Do we have any idea who really did it? Haldane probably killed Fodor, but who killed the others? Was it because of Professor Kelemen and the abuse, the exam marks?"

"But how did they get it exactly the same as for Fodor's death?" Rathbone asked. "Even to the candles and the blood, and the smashed Catholic relics and things? Who else even knew?

"I don't know," Monk admitted. "But I believe it was Antal Dobokai—"

"You've always wanted to blame him," Hester said sadly. "Why? I know he's ambitious and self-serving, but that's a long way from murder."

"And why the savagery?" Rathbone added. "If the three other men all suffered abuse from Kelemen and kept silent about it, to get them higher marks, wouldn't it be far wiser to agree to act together and keep it a secret? Or did one of them try to blackmail the others? If that is so, then as soon as the second one was killed, wouldn't they get together and defend themselves? It doesn't make sense, Monk."

"They were there at different times," Monk replied. "And they had no idea that that was the motive for the murders. One man got high enough marks to make him a suspected victim of terrible abuse, consistently. He would kill to keep that secret. He would destroy his own records, and only other students would care about it."

"But the savagery!" Rathbone exclaimed. "Why? It wasn't their fault. If he'd done that to Kelemen, I would understand. I'd even defend him."

"Because it obscured the motive," Monk replied. "It tied it irrevocably to the murder of Fodor, who had nothing to do with it at all."

"How? The four murders were identical," Rathbone argued. "And you never released the details of the first, not the number of candles or that the fingers were broken. It was all Haldane's hatred of the man who had slept with his wife, and fathered the son he was so proud of! The other three had nothing to do with that!"

"Dobokai found Fodor's body," Monk replied. "That was pure chance. But he took advantage of it. He had a memory like taking a photograph in his head. He could see every detail of the murder scene. The crimes weren't similar, they were identical, to the number of candles and where they were placed, the fingers broken, everything. It wasn't a man repeating himself; it was a man copying what he had seen."

"How can we prove that?"

"I don't know. It's all circumstantial, things we know are tied together, but he could still say it was Fitz who did them all, and we can't prove it wasn't."

They talked far into the night, planning and then realizing the flaws, the points Burnside could tear apart, and beginning again. It was always the same conclusion: Monk was vulnerable, and Burnside would know it, intellectually probably, instinctively always, as a dog smells fear. Rathbone could not protect him.

Why was Burnside not calling Hester, who knew Fitz far better?

Rathbone smiled, with a slight downward turning of the lips, rueful. "Because you have leave to speak of him in the Crimea. It is a natural part of your testimony. If he didn't ask you, I would. Even if you told only of your own experiences, you could show the horrors of the war as only someone who had lived through them could. No one could challenge you, either for what you said or why you said it. And he has probably looked at your testimony in previous cases and seen that you are now far too experienced, too careful of your feelings, to be tricked. He is very carefully skirting around you, and getting from others all the testimony you could give. That way, I have no reason to call you. It would become obvious that I was doing it for sympathy, not relevance. He has a hot temper, and he's something of a poseur, with the hair and the beard. But he is very far from a fool."

No one argued with him. Rathbone stood up and suddenly held out his hand, clasping Monk's and gripping it firmly. It was an odd gesture of trust, and unmistakable.

THE TESTIMONY IN THE morning began with Burnside calling Monk to the stand. The very first question made his tone apparent.

"Why were you called to this crime, Commander Monk? Did it have anything to do with the river, which is your . . . beat, is it not?"

"The warehouse in whose offices it occurred faces onto the water," Monk replied.

"I see. The victim, Imrus Fodor, had business on the river?"

"Yes."

"Did you therefore assume that the crime could be connected with trade and travel on the Thames?"

"I didn't assume anything."

"Indeed. You don't, in fact, appear to have arrived at many conclusions at all, other than the obvious one, that the crimes had so many extraordinary characteristics, not made public, that the only reasonable deduction was that they were committed by the same person. Is that not so?"

"Yes. They were identical." Monk could not leave the reluctance to agree out of his voice.

Burnside nodded. "And of course you and your men investigated each crime, all of the circumstances, the weapons used, where they were obtained, the strength and skill required to use them? We will not bore the court with having you repeat all these things. It is sufficient to say that from all of that, you deduced nothing of use. Is that fair, Commander Monk?"

It would serve no purpose except to magnify his own failure were he to argue. "That is fair," he agreed. "But we would have been derelict in duty had we not done so."

"Of course. I do not suggest for a moment that you were derelict, Commander. You were merely totally unsuccessful. Is that not so? Even after four hideous deaths, of identical nature, you had no more idea who was guilty than you had at the beginning . . ."

Rathbone rose to his feet, but reluctantly. That was clear from his hesitation. "My lord, my learned friend is belaboring the obvious. Commander Monk is his witness. Surely he called him for some purpose beyond insulting him?"

Burnside bristled. "My lord, I am merely setting the background against which the arrest finally occurred. It is germane to its validity. Commander Monk has personal connections to the accused. I need to show the jury why he was so slow, even reluctant, to arrest him. Otherwise they may doubt that the police really believe him to be guilty. Indeed, the extraordinary Mr. Hooper has already admitted as much."

"Your point is taken, Mr. Burnside," Justice Aldridge agreed. "Sir Oliver, your objection is overruled."

Burnside smiled.

In her seat in the gallery, Hester felt her stomach knot with tension. Rathbone could not have meant to, but he had just shown his own weakness.

Burnside looked up at Monk. "You must have ruled out many people as suspects, Mr. Monk, by the sheer weight of your work. Among those you excluded were Mr. Dobokai and Mr. Haldane. Is that correct?"

"Yes."

"And yet you have arrested Roger Haldane, so one has to assume you believe he was indeed guilty of the first crime, and that one only. Someone else copied him—to the most minute and ghastly detail? Is that also correct?"

Monk could not argue. "Yes . . ."

"In your long experience of crime, have you ever come across a series of identical—your word, I believe—identical crimes like this, where two people carried out exactly the same execution of a murder, in grotesque detail, and with no connection with each other, except place, method, time of day, choice of weapon, and such gruesome acts as bringing with them an identical number of candles and dipping them in the victims' blood? And ritually breaking their fingers, after death? And smashing Roman Catholic religious objects, such as icons of the Virgin Mary and so on?" His voice was now laden with sarcasm. No one could have missed it.

Monk did not answer immediately.

The courtroom was absolutely silent.

"Mr. Monk? Or should I address you more formally, Commander Monk?"

"No," Monk said simply. "The copy is exact. There is no difference at all, as if someone was working from a photograph."

Burnside's eyebrows shot up. "Are you suggesting that someone took a photograph of the first scene and then committed the other murders in ghastly mimic? How could you permit such a thing to happen?"

Rathbone rose again. "My lord, Commander Monk said that was the degree of likeness, not that it had happened. Please instruct Mr. Burnside not to draw unjustified conclusions and then state them as if they were fact."

"I think Mr. Burnside meant to throw doubt upon such a possibility, Sir Oliver, but I shall ask him to be clearer. Mr. Burnside, is the court to take it that you are using this . . . dramatic rhetoric to say that you be-lieve it impossible that there was more than one perpetrator of these crimes?"

"Yes, my lord. I thought Sir Oliver would have found that clear enough, but if he needs it in the simplest of words—yes! There could have been only one murderer of such . . . such precise and hideous in-sanity. Regardless of Commander Monk's peculiar beliefs to the con-trary."

"Please continue."

"Thank you, my lord. Mr. Monk, at what point in your investigation were you when you encountered the accused in the street, covered with fresh blood, dripping blood; when you rescued him, fled with him from the crowd of furious and terrified men?"

Monk gave a bleak, almost wolfish smile. "Looking for a motive," he replied. "Something that would be a way to find what the victims had in common, and apart from everyone else. We have found it now."

There was a gasp of breath around the room.

Burnside was confused. His expression went from disdain, to sur-prise, to uncertainty, then to a deliberately expression of disbelief.

"And yet you have, oddly enough, chosen not to inform us of it? Why is that, now?"

"That is the job of the defense to draw out, Mr. Burnside," Monk said with satisfaction. "I have told you all I can."

Burnside threw both his arms up into the air, like an Old Testament prophet summoning thunder and lightning.

"Please! Sir Oliver! We are waiting with our breath indrawn, and our patience stretched thin as a coat of paint. Please!"

"If you are finished, Mr. Burnside, I would be delighted to begin the defense," Rathbone replied. "I would prefer, if it pleases your lordship, to start by recalling Mr. Antal Dobokai, the man who not only found the body of the first victim but who has become something of a leader of the Hungarian community in Shadwell. I believe I can draw from him a picture of these events that will make the sense of it all that we are searching for. I would beg the court's permission to begin that tomorrow morning. If your lordship wishes, I can call another witness to Dr. Fitzherbert's professional skill . . . ?"

Burnside had not yet sat down. He swiveled to face the judge.

"The Crown agrees that Dr. Fitzherbert is an excellent surgeon, even brilliant at times, and that he served with courage and honor in the Crimea. We see no reason the jury, and indeed the court, should be subjected to further distress by hearing even more of the details of suffering. Many of them will have friends, or even family members, who died in that conflict. We are already drenched in the horror of these crimes. We need and deserve no more."

"I quite agree," Rathbone said with remarkable confidence. "I am quite willing to begin tomorrow."

Burnside was unwilling to concede anything. "It is a waste of the court's time," he pointed out. "And of your lordship's. We should proceed after the luncheon adjournment."

Hester was now far too tense to eat a meal. She found a place to serve her a hot cup of tea, and a couple of slices of toast, then was back in almost the same seat as before when Rathbone called Antal Dobokai to the witness stand.

Burnside looked smug, as if he knew he had already won. He seemed set to savor his victory, his first over Rathbone in twenty years.

Dobokai stood on the witness stand, his thick dark hair combed back off of his brow, his blue eyes luminous.

Rathbone was cautious, even respectful.

"Mr. Dobokai, you were the person unfortunate enough to discover the appalling scene where Imrus Fodor had been murdered. You already described it for Mr. Burnside. Just to remind anyone who might have forgotten it in the horror, and the details, of what they have learned since then, would you please tell us about that day again."

"Yes, sir," Dobokai said calmly. "I rose early, I always do. I am a pharmacist and I went to deliver some medicine to two people I know are up early. Then I had a very good cup of coffee at my favorite café and spoke with the proprietor. I had a foot potion to deliver to Mr. Fodor. I did not go to his warehouse until eight o'clock, because I knew that was when his workers arrived, and even if he was not there, I could leave the package in his office."

Rathbone nodded.

Burnside did not interrupt. Dobokai had established the impossibility of his having committed the crime, and Rathbone had had him repeat it, without any challenge. Burnside was smiling now.

"And the scene in his office?" Rathbone prompted.

"Very . . . terrible," Dobokai said gravely, his voice quiet, as if he were recalling it with awe, the wave of emotion engulfing him again.

No one objected. The entire courtroom was silent.

Dobokai described the corpse, the bayonet sticking out of his chest, the candles around the room, dipped in blood.

Rathbone stopped him to go into greater detail—the exact number, the paintings, the dripping blood.

Burnside's smile grew brighter in his satisfaction.

Justice Aldridge appeared displeased, but he did not interrupt.

"Did you see the scenes of the other murders?" Rathbone asked politely.

"No, sir."

"Would it surprise you to know that they were exactly the same?"

"No . . ." Dobokai cleared his throat, his face expressionless. "He appears to be driven by some compulsion . . . to have to repeat. I don't understand it."

"I asked Commander Monk, who saw them all," Rathbone said almost conversationally. "He cannot remember any of them as clearly as you do."

Burnside looked uncomfortable. Perhaps it was because he did not understand the purpose of the question.

Dobokai said nothing.

"Your memory is remarkable," Rathbone commented. "I have made inquiries of others who know you, and have worked with you. They say you are possessed of an extraordinary gift of exact recall. Do they exaggerate?"

Dobokai hesitated only an instant. "No, sir. I have a . . . a gift."

"It is amazing." Rathbone moved a little across the open space, as if considering what next to address.

"You know this community well," he observed. "Indeed, you are more or less the leader of it. You have kept its residents from panicking in this harsh and very frightening time . . ."

"Thank you, sir. I have tried."

"Do you know of any motive anyone might have had for killing the victims?"

Burnside rose to his feet. "My lord, Sir Oliver is clearly completely lost in his efforts to raise any reasonable doubt and is now merely delaying the inevitable verdict. Herbert Fitzherbert is guilty of these crimes. Rather than waste the court's time, perhaps Sir Oliver could accept defeat, and allow us to render a verdict now."

The judge looked at Rathbone. "Sir Oliver, is there a purpose to this?"

"Oh, yes, my lord. There certainly is," Rathbone said vehemently. "I believe Mr. Dobokai knows very well what the motive is for these crimes."

Burnside made a gesture of exasperation, and then of futility. It was not lost on the jury. He pulled his gold watch out of his pocket and glanced at it.

"I think you should stay," Rathbone said with a slight nod. "I do not want the court to say afterward that I had an unfair advantage."

Burnside glared at him. "You have no advantage at all, sir! Fair or unfair!" he snapped.

Rathbone ignored him. "Mr. Dobokai, do you read the small news sheet that the Hungarian community puts out every week in Shadwell?"

Dobokai looked puzzled, and perhaps a little concerned. "Of course."

"Forgive me." Rathbone inclined his head. "It was a rhetorical question. I know that you often give a hand at editing it, and have contributed some most interesting articles . . ."

Burnside rolled his eyes, half rose from his seat, then subsided again.

"The point, Sir Oliver," Justice Aldridge prompted him.

"Yes, my lord." He looked back at Dobokai. "About a week after

Fodor's death there was a very tragic piece of news from Budapest. An elderly mathematics professor, by the name of Donat Kelemen, had committed suicide. The letter he left explained that it was because the scandal was about to break that he had given the boys he taught extra high marks on their exams in return for sexual favors of a very explicit and intimate kind . . ."

He was prevented from continuing by the wave of shock that passed through the courtroom. People gasped, shouted, moved around.

"Order!" called Justice Aldridge. "I will have order. Sir Oliver, is this . . . regrettable piece of news really germane to four murders here in Shadwell?"

"Yes, my lord. Each one of the victims was taught by this wretched man. It is the one thing they have in common. They were of different ages, they grew up in different towns and villages in Hungary, but at one time or another they all attended this school, and studied mathematics with this . . . man."

"So what does that have to do with their deaths?" Burnside shouted. "The scandal is broken! If they were going to testify, then for God's sake they would have done so by now. Kelemen, or whatever his name is, is dead! They should rejoice. My lord, this is the basest and most disgusting attempt to draw our attention away from these terrible murders, and to a tragedy, albeit revolting, that happened years ago. It is irrelevant. And certainly it has nothing whatever to do with Herbert Fitzherbert. Or are you going to say that he was hired by the wretched man, Kelemen, to kill his victims before they could give their accounts of his . . . abominations?"

"No, sir, not at all," Rathbone replied equally sharply, and over the noise of the courtroom. "Dr. Fitzherbert is an English army officer who happened to pass through Hungary, and speaks the language. He has nothing to do with this at all. He is no more than a convenient scapegoat, because of the experiences he endured in the Crimean War."

"Silence!" Aldridge said angrily to the body of the court. "You had better prove the relevance of all this, Sir Oliver. I abhor grandstand performances, except in the theater. Do I make myself plain enough?"

"Yes, my lord. Mr. Dobokai, I have asked those who knew them well, and each of the victims attended the school at one time, during the tenure of Professor Kelemen, and were taught by him . . ."

Dobokai was ashen.

"As did you yourself," Rathbone continued. "You obtained the highest marks in mathematics, which enabled you to win a place at the university in Vienna. The tragedy is that your marks were probably well-earned, even if you had to . . . perform certain acts in order to be granted them. It is a high crime Kelemen committed against you, and if you had killed him at the time, you might have been justified, even in law. But you didn't. Possibly shame, and your doubt that you would be believed, prevented you, as it did all the other boys. You took the marks and left, remaining silent, like everyone else. When the scandal came to light now, by chance you saw the murder of Imrus Fodor, and you remembered it, exactly. You copied it to get rid of all the other men who could have found out your secret, or deduced it.

"When these others read of Kelemen's death, and where he had taught, your secret could easily have come out. Then what respect would you have had? They knew the humiliation and the pain that you had endured, the indignity, the disgusting intrusion into your body. Maybe their marks were earned by favors? The worst for you was that they would assume yours had been too, and you could not live with that. So you made it look as if an innocent man . . ."

Dobokai's face was parchment white, and he grasped the railing as if he would fall were he to let go of it. Then very slowly his hands went up to his cravat and slipped one end loose, and he bent forward.

It was Monk who realized what he was going to do and lunged forward up the steps of the witness stand. He reached the top just as Dobokai threw himself forward over the rail. The knot held on the railing, the whole stand listed with his weight. The drop was not enough, but the cravat still jerked his head hard sideways, so sharply that it broke his neck.

The judge was frozen for a moment.

A woman screamed.

Burnside looked oddly shrunken. He had foreseen none of this.

Rathbone himself was at a loss for words. His anger of a few seconds before had evaporated. There was only pity left.

Some order was restored. Everyone waited while ushers carried Dobokai out, carefully, as if he were ill rather than dead.

"My lord," Rathbone said as soon as they were gone. "I request that the charges against Herbert Fitzherbert be withdrawn, and he be released."

"Into whose care, Sir Oliver?" the judge asked.

"I . . ." Rathbone had no idea what he could say.

It was at that moment that Charles Latterly rose to his feet. "With your leave, my lord? My name is Charles Latterly. The Crimean War nurse who served with Dr. Fitzherbert, and whom Mr. Burnside did not call, in case her testimony as to his experiences earned too much sympathy, is my sister. I have a large house and staff. I will be happy to look after Captain Fitzherbert until he is recovered, for however long that may take. I believe the Latterlys have a debt to him in particular, as have all of us in general. It would be my honor."

"Thank you, Mr. Latterly," Justice Aldridge said quietly. He looked up at the dock. "Dr. Fitzherbert, the charges against you are withdrawn. You are free to go. I suggest you accept Mr. Latterly's offer. We owe you, sir, for all those you have unsparingly helped. Allow us now to do what we can to help you."

"Thank you, Charles," Hester said through sudden tears. "Thank you, Oliver. And thank you, William."

ABOUT THE AUTHOR

ANNE PERRY is the bestselling author of two acclaimed series set in Victorian England: the William Monk novels, including *An Echo of Murder* and *Revenge in a Cold River*, and the Charlotte and Thomas Pitt novels, including *Murder on the Serpentine* and *Treachery at Lancaster Gate*. She is also the author of a series of five World War I novels, as well as fifteen holiday novels, most recently *A Christmas Return*, and a historical novel, *The Sheen on the Silk*, set in the Ottoman Empire. Anne Perry lives in Los Angeles and Scotland.

anneperry.co.uk

To inquire about booking Anne Perry for a speaking engagement, please contact the Penguin Random House Speakers Bureau at speakers@penguinrandomhouse.com.

ABOUT THE TYPE

This book was set in Goudy Old Style, a typeface designed by Frederic William Goudy (1865–1947). Goudy began his career as a bookkeeper, but devoted the rest of his life to the pursuit of "recognized quality" in a printing type.

Goudy Old Style was produced in 1914 and was an instant bestseller for the foundry. It has generous curves and smooth, even color. It is regarded as one of Goudy's finest achievements.